"Les Cowan is daring
controversial and comp
rooted in the familiar a
makes his stories not ju
engaging. The chaotic
surround David Hidalg
ridiculous insistence on doing the right thing, give
us *pause for thought, if not his accidental hero."*
G.J. Martin, author of *The Orcadian Trilogy*

"*A powerful exploration of how ordinary people
can get caught up in extremism.* Blood Brothers *is
a truly thrilling novel with a profound insight into
family love and religious hate."*
**Fiona Veitch Smith, author of the *Poppy Denby
Investigates* series**

Praise for the David Hidalgo series:

"*Exciting and thoughtful... and also gentle probing
of how faith and conscience work in the face of
obsession. Runcie's* Grantchester *has a rival in
Edinburgh with a hero unlike our friend Rebus."*
***Press and Journal* Saturday magazine**

"*Another cracker from Cowan... pacey and
relentless... The author has found a rich seam
of crime fiction."*
Scots Magazine* review of *Sins of the Fathers

"*Cowan spins an engrossing, suspenseful yarn
in which spiritual themes are noticeably more
prominent than in a regular thriller."*
The Herald

The David Hidalgo series:

Book 1: *Benefit of the Doubt*
Book 2: *All that Glitters*
Book 3: *Sins of the Fathers*
Book 4: *Blood Brothers*

Short stories:

"David Hidalgo and the Badvent Calendar"
"David Hidalgo and a Case of Forgetfulness"

Non-fiction titles:

Loose Talk Collected
Orkney by Bike

Blood Brothers

Les Cowan

A David Hidalgo Novel

LION FICTION

Published by
Lion Hudson Limited
Wilkinson House, Jordan Hill Business Park
Banbury Road, Oxford OX2 8DR, England
www.lionhudson.com

ISBN 978 1 78264 313 5
e-ISBN 978 1 78264 314 2

First edition 2020

Image credits: background © JoseIgnacioSoto/iStock;
figures left and right © FotoDuets/iStock

A catalogue record for this book is available from the British
Library

Printed and bound in the UK, July 2020, LH26

For Andrew and Donald

Acknowledgments

Grateful thanks once again to those who have helped in one way or another in the evolution of David Hidalgo, even just by reading a book and posting a review.

Specifically, I am grateful to those who took the time to read and comment on early drafts, and in particular, Fiona Cowan, Angus Mackay, and Mija Regoord.

Also Jessica Gladwell, Mike Belcher, Fiona Veitch Smith, Julie Frederick, and the team at Lion for continuing to support the Hidalgo series. I would also like to express particular appreciation to Phoebe Swinburn from Midas PR for the amazing feat of getting reviews and exposure where I thought none was possible. Also thanks to Ron Ferguson for continued encouragement and reassurance that David Hidalgo had indeed something worthwhile to say.

Finally, thanks to many wonderful friends in Madrid, Galicia, and all over Spain for their kindness and generosity in sharing their culture with me, which has enabled David to go where he goes and do what he does.

Prologue

La Mezquita

"So here we are, ladies and gentlemen." The guide gestured around, smiling with the air of someone who had just pulled a very large, impressive rabbit out of a deep top hat. "A UNESCO World Heritage site, one of the most visited locations in Europe, and the jewel in the crown of Al-Andalus: the Great Mosque of Córdoba. La Mezquita."

She had probably delivered that opening speech several thousand times before but still tried to make it sound impressive, and mostly succeeded. However, the dozen or so Americans, Australians, and a few Brits gathered around weren't really listening. They knew what they had come to see and were ready to be overwhelmed, even without the hard sell. They slowly spread out like snooker balls given a gentle tap, passing awestruck through a forest of delicate rose marble pillars, which supported arches of alternating pink and white blocks, more like sugar icing than stone. Above the arches, a fairy woodland canopy of ancient beams completed the Hansel and Gretel effect. iPhones and selfie sticks were out in force but conversation was in whispers. They tiptoed up and down the avenues of pillars, craning to see the exquisite carving of the capitals, glancing into side chapels, and wondering about the mysterious, exotic Abd al-Rahman I, founder of the Umayyad dynasty and architectural mastermind.

Eventually, the guide called them together and began her description. In comparison with the visual – even spiritual – impact of the mosque, the facts seemed almost commonplace. Started by Abd al-Rahman I, Emir of the Caliphate of Córdoba in 784, the

Mezquita had been variously enlarged by his successors until it was finally lost to the Christian *Reconquista* of 1236. Thereafter the central square was summarily flattened to make way for a cathedral. Holy Roman Emperor Carlos V, visiting years later, commented, "They have taken something unique in all the world, and destroyed it for something commonplace."

The tour continued through the prayer hall towards the cathedral, the guide commenting on interesting features along the way.

Two young South Asian-looking men in their late teens or twenties brought up the rear. "So what do you think?" the taller, skinny one whispered, looking around.

"It's incredible!" the shorter, stocky one replied, looking back into the maze of pillars and arches.

"Of course it's incredible. It's Islamic. That's not what I mean. You remember – what we spoke about. What do you think?"

"I don't know. It's been here so long. It's not doing anyone any harm. Can't we just leave it as it is?"

His companion was dismissive. He gave a snort and shook his head.

"You don't get it, Little Brother, do you?" he said. "It's perfect. Symbolic. It's an image. The heart of Islam defiled by the infidels. They knocked down the greatest art in the world to put an imposter in its place. Now it's time to reclaim it. To take back what's rightfully ours. It'll mark the beginning of the new age when everything is put right. Our turn to knock something down. The new empire from the ashes of the old. It's exactly what the Prophet told us to look for."

His younger brother kept looking around nervously and accidentally caught the eye of a security guard.

"Keep your voice down, for goodness sake," he hissed. "They can hear you in Edinburgh."

"I don't care." The older brother laughed. "Let them. We'll be unstoppable."

Then, abruptly, an idea occurred to him. "We should pray," he said. "Take your shoes off."

"What?"

"You heard me. Take your shoes off. Down on your knees!"

The guard was now watching them closely. As soon as the trainers came off he was on his radio mic. Burly uniforms rapidly appeared from all directions.

"*No es permitido,*" a swarthy man with the build of a boxer said in a tone that didn't invite negotiation. He grabbed the upper arm of the older boy and heaved him to his feet.

"Not permitted," another repeated.

"Get your hands off me! You've no right."

The tour group twenty yards ahead looked around at the scuffle but a couple of teenage tourists were no match for a half-dozen ex-cops and amateur weightlifters, so it didn't last long. Seconds later they were out on the street. The taller one tried a kick at one of the guards and ended up on his backside as a result.

"You'll see! You don't know what's coming!" he shouted at the retreating team, who were already back slapping and joking, enjoying a little action for a change.

"You idiot," his brother muttered. "It's you that doesn't know what's coming. You'll get us all killed."

Chapter 1

Marchmont

Dr Gillian Lockhart yawned, stretched like a contented cat, smiled, and reached out towards the other side of the bed. Finding only a warm, empty space, she hooked a strand of dark hair behind one ear, pushed herself up on an elbow, and opened a sleepy eye.

"David? Where are you?"

"Just coming! One toast or two?"

She smiled again, luxuriously, arranged the pillows, and sat right up, the downie pulled tight around her.

"Usually two. Depends what they're with."

Just then the door nudged open and a figure appeared. Sandy hair, a bit dishevelled, gold-rimmed glasses slightly squint, mid-fifties, a navy blue dressing gown barely holding together, and a tray.

"Ta-da!" he announced, placing the tray across her knees. She laughed.

"Wow. To what do I owe the privilege?"

"Sunday morning. First Sunday back, Mrs Hidalgo. This is the new normal. Get used to it."

The tray held two plates, each with smoked salmon flutes stuffed with cream cheese next to piles of creamy, slightly runny scrambled eggs and two rashers of bacon. A wire rack held toast triangles. A jar of marmalade was fighting for space on the tray with a coffee pot, a small milk jug, one large mug, and a cup of tea.

"Colombian Arabica for you, Earl Grey for me. I'll go and stick another toast in."

"Don't worry," she laughed, grabbing the tray. "This is more than enough. How long have you been up?"

David Hidalgo walked around the bottom of the bed, dumped the dressing gown, and peeked through the curtains before climbing back in.

"Oh, since midnight more or less. It took a few attempts to get it all right."

"Liar. I know what you were doing at midnight and it didn't involve scrambled eggs."

"Tut tut," he said sternly. "Birdsong in the morning."

Gillian leaned back as if needing a run at it to tackle the trayful in front of her and sighed again.

"So is the new normal just for today or do you do this every morning?"

"When I can get the ingredients. It's a mercy to be able to find real marmalade again. The idea that apricot jam is a reasonable alternative defies description. Despite the fact it's made from Seville oranges, it apparently hasn't made the crossing to Mallorca yet."

Gillian took a bite of toast and a forkful of egg.

"But you've got to admit the rest of it was pretty ok," she said, munching. "The hotel, the weather, the beaches, the dinners. The sleeping arrangements."

"Only because I choose my travelling companion very carefully."

They settled back into a companionable silence, working their way through the spread.

"I suppose there's going to be lots of this," Gillian finally remarked.

"Breakfast? Daily, I hope."

"No, stupid. Be serious. Getting used to new things. I don't think a honeymoon really prepares you for actually being together – I mean in the normal way. I know almost nothing about you – at least the sort of things wives are supposed to know about their husbands anyway. When do you go to bed? Do you read before you sleep? What's your morning routine? What newspaper do you read? Do you hang shirts up or put them in a drawer? What's your favourite cheese? A million things. And you don't know that about me, I suppose. And we're in my flat. Your choice but that might be a challenge for us both."

David took another sip of tea and put the cup on his bedside table. He scooped up the last mouthful of egg.

"I know enough to know I made the right choice," he said quietly. "And I know we're meant to be together. You made me whole again. I've no idea what state I'd be in now if we hadn't met. You're the answer to a prayer I wasn't even able to make."

Gillian moved the tray to one side, snuggled down, and put her head on his chest.

"A marriage made in heaven then?" she said dreamily.

"It's inexplicable any other way. If I hadn't come back from Spain, if you hadn't decided to brush up on your Spanish, if one of my students hadn't needed help and we hadn't gone to Hacienda to talk about it, if Jen MacInnes hadn't gone missing, if her grandmother hadn't asked me to help, if you hadn't had an idea of where to start looking, if we hadn't been attacked and you ended up in hospital… That number of links in the chain strains credibility if there wasn't another hand at work."

"I'm glad. And if I hadn't met you I'd be another sad divorcee in her forties looking for something slightly better than being alone with no direction, no self-confidence, and no faith. You put me back together again too."

"You rescue me, I rescue you."

"*Pretty Woman*, in fact."

"You certainly are. I love you."

"Ok then," Gillian said, suddenly brisk and businesslike, bouncing out of bed. "What am I going to wear for our first Sunday back?"

"Well, you're looking pretty good right now…"

She made a face.

"Don't be cheeky." She pulled the wardrobe door back with aplomb. "Now, Señor Hidalgo. Choose!"

They wandered down Middle Meadow Walk towards the University in no particular hurry. The cherry trees were in leaf. It was late summer so the students weren't around, which made the Meadows seem deserted. No American football practice, no tai chi in the park, no couples lying on a rug on the grass – or on top of each other – and only a couple of joggers. The Festival was over and term hadn't yet begun, which made it seem like Edinburgh was drawing breath after one bout of exertion and getting ready for the next one.

"Nice that they organized someone else to speak this morning," Gillian remarked.

"Very humane," David replied. "Sermon prep really hasn't been uppermost in my mind the last two weeks."

"Who is it?"

"I'm not entirely sure. An American pastor, I think. Somebody new in town who wants to do the rounds of the city-centre churches and get to know us. More than that I'm not sure. Juan seemed enthusiastic so I let him get on with it."

"I'm surprised he has the energy with a new baby."

"From what Mrs MacInnes tells me he's still walking on air. Even if half asleep."

They continued hand in hand to the far side of the Meadows, around the back of the University Library, and along Buccleuch Place towards South Clerk Street. Southside Fellowship's upstairs premises above a charity shop and a Chinese restaurant were getting busy these days. The general hubbub of conversation was clearly audible even from out on the street, and by the time they got to the top of the stairs sounded like a speed-dating event in full swing. They pushed through the double doors. It took a few seconds for recognition to dawn before they were greeted by a general cheer, spontaneous applause, and a few wolf whistles. Irene MacInnes – treasurer, property convener, and general bulldog in the interests of the pastor – came bustling over from duty at the tea urn.

"Señor David! And Señorita – or is it Mrs Señor? I'm never sure. Welcome home!" she beamed.

"Just Gillian is fine," the señora replied, smiling. "Thanks."

"Thanks, Mrs MacInnes. Nice to be back." David waved modestly around. As the cheering died down they tried to slip into the back row but stood no chance. The few dozen people milling around in the aisles had suddenly turned into a queue as everyone wanted to say hello, welcome them back, ask about the honeymoon, and in a few cases tell them the latest news: more babies on the way, an engagement, wedding plans, etc. And also a departure or two. Robin had got work with an IT company in Toronto, and he and Jodie would be leaving in two weeks' time. And the elderly Mr Grant, initially a very reluctant convert to the Hidalgo way of doing things, had passed away right in the middle of singing the previous Sunday morning.

"I like to think he didn't miss a beat between 'In Christ Alone' and the heavenly choir," Mrs MacInnes whispered as the queue began to ease. Last in the line, Juan and Alicia appeared carrying baby Félix. Juan embraced David, gave Gillian *dos besos* – the customary Spanish two kisses – then took the baby to let Alicia do the same.

"How are you coping, *amigo*?" David asked.

Juan tried to shrug and look cool.

"*Bueno*. It's a change," he said, noncommittal.

"He's very good," Alicia said firmly.

"Félix or Juan?" Gillian asked, all innocence.

"Oh, by the way, I introduce you," Juan suddenly remembered and half-turned to a tall, blond guy behind him – maybe late forties or well-preserved early fifties. "Mike. Our pastor, David Hidalgo. David, this is Mike MacGregor. From Charleston, South Carolina. You remember. I mention him."

They shook hands.

"Pleased to meet you, Mike. I gather I've you to thank for the day off."

"No problem, sir. Happy to help."

Mike was wearing a lavender V-neck over a primrose yellow polo shirt and nicely pressed cream flannels. David thought he looked like a golf professional on his day off but said nothing.

"Just visiting Edinburgh, Mike?" Gillian asked. "Sounds like there might be some Scottish heritage in there somewhere."

"Indeed there is, ma'am. That's part of it but actually I'm a missionary from my church. We feel we owe a debt of gratitude to the Scottish people and want to help. We hear things are really hard here for the gospel, that many have turned away and lost the faith. So I'm sent over to see how we can help. The first step is just to get to know the locals, then our Foundation would like to invest in Scotland. I contacted Juan here and he was good enough to invite me. I have to say it's my first time preaching in a Scottish church and it's a privilege, sir, it surely is."

Gillian's eyebrows had been rising gradually through this speech but she bit her tongue. First impressions can be mistaken, and she had often found an excess of enthusiasm a very American trait. But on the other hand, maybe it wasn't the worst failing in the world...

"Well, Mike, I hope we don't disappoint."

"No fears of that, ma'am. I'm sure."

"Ok, Mike," David took over. "I'm very grateful anyway. Welcome to Scotland." He noticed the look on Gillian's face but ignored it.

"Anyway," he pressed on, "better let you go. Looks like we're about to get started."

The data projector switched from announcements to songs, the worship band started up, and David took a seat, breathed out slowly, and glanced around. He didn't often get the chance to sit at the back and survey the congregation. What a change in his three years here. From an ageing company of Edinburgh pensioners and a few grandkids, they now had a healthy mix of ages – even during the holidays. Young graduates got jobs in the city and had chosen to stay. Entire families seemed to find the informality and sense of community to their taste and at last they even had something you could reasonably call a youth group, not just three uncomfortable teens trying to disappear into the plasterwork. There even seemed to be a few backs of heads he wasn't sure he could reliably connect to a face. Long, glossy dark hair that might be South Asian. A middle-aged man with a bald spot just about to take over. A new family with squirming twins. That was healthy. New people coming he didn't recognize was a sign of growth. In fact, he knew he'd been putting off the tricky question of whether they'd need to look for bigger premises to let the growth continue. Maybe next leadership meeting.

Finally the music got going, and nowadays even that wasn't embarrassingly bad. And neither was Mike once he got started either. He spoke from Paul in Athens in Acts 17 about the importance of understanding a culture to communicate effectively. *Not bad*, thought David. *More or less as I'd have put it myself. At least he seems to understand that speaking English doesn't automatically make you a native in another English-speaking country.* Soon enough it was over, and David managed a few appreciative words with Mike, then let him take his place shaking hands at the door. He had his own queue to deal with of those who hadn't managed to grab a few words before things had got started. Glancing around, he finally noticed the owner of the bald spot face on.

"Excuse me, do you mind if I just catch someone else over there? Stuart! This is a bit of a surprise! I didn't think you were 'the darkening the church door' type. Everything ok?"

Detective Inspector Stuart McIntosh smiled grimly.

"Not really. Kirsty and I had another blazing row last night. She was gone this morning and so was her suitcase. I just needed to get out of the house and out of my own company. Hope you don't mind."

"Absolutely not. I'm really sorry. Look, you don't need to tell me anything you don't want to, but if you want to talk I'll listen. No well-meaning advice, ok?"

McIntosh nodded. "That's great. Thanks."

David nodded, then a thought seemed to strike him.

"Just a minute," he said and set off in search of Gillian, who had her own eddy of chatters washing around. He whispered in her ear. She gave a quick glance in Stuart's direction, then nodded. David fought his way back through the melee.

"Any lunch plans, Stuart?" he asked. "If not, come and eat with us. Nothing fancy; it's just standard Sunday chicken, but there should be enough."

McIntosh hesitated for a few seconds and looked about to decline.

"Actually, if you don't mind that would be really good," he finally said, giving a long sigh. She's not answering her mobile and I really don't fancy going back home just yet. That would be great."

"Ok. A bit more meeting and greeting, then we'll go."

"I've got the car. I can meet you there."

The hall began to clear as people drifted off and finally only the stalwarts and a few stragglers were left. It was then David noticed the other newcomer he couldn't place. The long, lustrous, dark hair, the dark skin and almond eyes, the nervous smile. Maybe Pakistani or Bangladeshi background? Maybe early twenties? She did look somehow familiar but he couldn't find a name. He walked over.

"Hi, I'm David Hidalgo. I don't think we've met. First time at Southside?"

"Hi. Yes. We have met, but a few years ago now. I used to live in Bruntsfield. Just downstairs from your flat."

"Oh? Anything we can help you with?"

The nervous smile began to look distinctly shaky. Whatever it was, it had clearly cost her a lot to show up.

"I want to ask your advice. And your help," she said in barely a whisper.

"Of course. Whatever I can do."

"Well," she began slowly. "I'm Muslim. Obvious, I suppose…" A nervous laugh. "But with everything that's been going on, I'm not sure I want to stay Muslim any more. I'm thinking of converting. I'd like to discuss it with someone."

David raised an eyebrow. This didn't happen every day. He replied very slowly.

"Ok. That's a huge step. You need to be sure. I can certainly help you think it through."

"And there's something else," she pressed on in a rush, as if any

19

hesitation would make it impossible to get started again. "If I do – I mean, if I convert. I wonder… could you speak to my parents? Help them understand? They'd listen to you."

Now he was completely flummoxed.

"Well, I can see it might be helpful to have someone to help explain things, but I'm not sure I'd be the right person. I mean, we've just met. I have no idea who your parents are. I'm really not sure that's going to be useful."

"No, it would be," the girl insisted. "They'd listen to you; I know it. You're a friend."

"Really? Who are your parents?"

"Ali and Ayeesha Khan. They have the shop downstairs from your flat. I'm Samira."

"Ali and Ayeesha! Incredible. I bet they didn't see that one coming," Gillian said as they walked back across the Meadows. The sky had clouded over since the morning and the wind picked up. One or two spits of rain were beginning to fall. "Get out of that one, Mr Hidalgo."

David sighed loudly and shook his head.

"Well, our first Sunday back didn't lack drama anyway."

"You do seem to attract it, you know."

"I've noticed. The lack of a quiet life isn't for lack of trying. You were there. I didn't do a thing. Honestly. Anyway, what do I do now? Let down an inquirer or incur the wrath of friends? I can't see a third alternative."

"Well, I think to begin with you just have to keep quiet and listen. Let her tell her story, then see what you're dealing with. Juan might want to gobble her up and get her to sign on the dotted line, but I think you've got to take it easy."

"And who's to say he's wrong? On the other hand, there were those Jesus more or less sent away to think it over and count the cost. It's all so complicated, isn't it? You try to do what's right and sometimes it just works out all wrong. Or people do the entirely wrong thing and get away with it. And you can't guess in advance which way it'll go!"

He groaned and Gillian squeezed his arm.

"Well, you did the right thing inviting Stuart for lunch at least. We don't need to help him decide his future, I suppose. Whatever's wrong with you, Sunday lunch usually improves things. Where is he now, by the way?"

"He had the car so he's making his own way. Via an off-licence, I imagine."

"And what do we make of Mr Mike the American?" Gillian asked as they waited at the lights to cross Melville Drive. "For real, do you think?"

"No complaints on what he said. I've always thought one of the biggest mistakes in missions has been to ignore the culture. So sometimes the message seems to be that you have to be Dutch or English or German to be a Christian. Not Malay or Pashto or Lakota Sioux. I think things are improving but we still need to keep it in mind. Even the culture of different sides of town like Muirhouse and Morningside, I suppose."

"And his table of wares?"

"Yes. That I wasn't so keen on. I'd have done something about it if we'd been a bit earlier."

"He looked like half his luggage from the Land of the Free must have been books and CDs."

"And bookmarks, and inspirational wall hangings, and candles, and brooches. I hate that stuff. It's just tat. No different from other tat except it has a Bible verse slapped on."

"Tempted to overturn the table then?"

"Definitely. And drive him out with a whip. A pity because he seemed a friendly enough guy. Maybe it's just culture again – evangelical culture this time. Anyway, who is that lonely figure clutching a bottle I see outside your front door?"

"Correction, Mr Hidalgo. *Our* front door!"

DI McIntosh was indeed clutching a well-wrapped bottle of something and waiting on the pavement.

"You said chicken so I got an Albariño. Hope that's all right. And thanks again for the invite."

"Perfect." Gillian smiled, hunting for keys. "I'm sorry to hear about things. You're very welcome."

By mutual agreement Gillian raced around sorting vegetables and putting another few potatoes in while David and Stuart went into the living room.

"Lovely place you have here," Stuart began. "Very tasteful."

"All Gillian's doing. Up to me and I'd have woodchip everywhere and bookcases from B&Q."

David had opened the bottle and poured a generous couple of glasses.

"I imagine that'll have worn off by the time you're driving again."

Stuart nodded, took a sip, and sat looking around in silence.

"It's not the first time," he said after a bit, "but then things get said and you can't unsay them. On both sides. However much you want to. She's not been there in the morning before but the suitcase has never been missing. So it's not looking good, I suppose."

"Well, as I said, I'm not going to offer any advice," David said. "But if it helps to have somewhere else to hang out, come when you like."

Gillian popped her head around the door.

"Any hungry hippos?" she asked.

Prawns in Marie Rose sauce with avocados preceded roast chicken with parsnips, carrots, slightly caramelized onions, broccoli, and roast potatoes, followed by an apple strudel bar out of the freezer and Orkney ice cream.

"Fantastic," the off-duty detective pronounced, leaning back and finishing the last swirl of wine. "I appreciate this. I wasn't looking forward to beans on toast."

"No problem," David repeated. "These things can come out of the blue and you just need a hidey-hole for a bit."

"Yeah, well. This isn't really coming out of the blue. It's been boiling for a while. The job doesn't make it easier of course. Things can be unpredictable. An emergency blows up, then you're late home or disappear for the weekend. Worse than that if leave gets cancelled and two weeks in Orlando goes up in smoke. That was the trigger this time. It wasn't a happy conversation."

"I can imagine," Gillian sympathized.

"And what about the wonderful world of policing when there's not an emergency on?" David pressed on, aiming for more neutral territory. "Is the policeman's lot still not a happy one?"

"Oh, comes and goes, like anything, I suppose."

"What's the big ticket right now then? Still drugs?"

"Yes, there's always that. And terrorism. Now we don't have the IRA, INLA, UVF, Tartan Army, and whatever else, it's all about preventing people nipping off to Syria or promoting hate online. Regular job creation scheme."

"Which gives the 99 per cent a bad name, I guess. What contacts I've had with the Edinburgh Mosque have always been very reasonable."

"Likewise," McIntosh agreed. "In fact, the one hothead they did have – called himself 'the Prophet' – was chucked out pretty quickly."

"I thought you couldn't do that in Islam," Gillian said, "that Mohammed was the final prophet and there weren't supposed to be any more."

"Exactly," Stuart confirmed. "Which is why he got his marching orders. Persona non grata, apostate, un-Islamic, and out on his ear. We were briefly involved but they sorted it out themselves."

"Is he still around?' David asked.

"Still around, yes. But exactly where, nobody knows. It's actually quite a funny thing. I'm still in European Liaison so I wasn't directly involved but I heard from the counterterrorism guys that up to the point they kicked him out he was basically just a loud-mouthed troublemaker with very few followers and next to no impact. But then, soon afterwards, he started turning up on social media with lots of likes. Now apparently there's even a website on the dark web and weekly broadcasts. He's getting lots of publicity and causing some sleepless nights. We have all of his contact details and know his name and so on but none of that is helping. Just vanished off the face of the earth, then turned up bouncing with energy in cyberspace."

"Well, at least if he's not in Edinburgh – that's something, I suppose," Gillian remarked.

"We have no idea where he is except for online. He could be next door for all we know. But that's not my problem, I'm glad to say."

"Nothing else we know that gives him an identity you can trace?" David asked, interested.

"Yes. Strangely there is one thing that might be a lead. Again I'm only repeating what the specialists are saying but it might be of interest to you. When he was preaching in the mosque it was all the usual stuff: America, the great Satan; Britain, the little Satan; freedom for the Palestinians and death to Israel. But online he's taking a whole different tack. Suddenly it's Spain."

"Really?" Gillian asked, surprised. "What on earth has that to do with modern Islam? They're not oppressing anyone as far as we know."

"Ahh, I think I can see where this is going," David came in just as Stuart was about to reply. "It's the Caliphate, isn't it? I've heard some whispers about this. The Moors ruled Spain for over 700 years until they finally got pushed out by Ferdinand and Isabella. I can see that would be an attractive argument to get European Muslims on board. You don't have to go to Syria and get your head blown off. You can just get on a flight to Madrid and start a jihad nearer home. Anywhere near the mark?"

"Spot on, I'm afraid," Stuart agreed. "Terrorism isn't my area in Scotland of course, but I'm in touch with the Spanish police and it does come up from time to time. There are rumblings and they step on things pretty hard if they get wind of anything. Anyway, academic interest to us at this point, I hope… But how about you two?" He changed tack in an effort to lighten things up. "How's married life treating you?"

"Fantastic," said Gillian and "Tolerable, so far," said David simultaneously.

"Let me correct that," David added, quickly getting an energetic dig in the ribs. "Wonderful. Marvellous, etc, etc."

"Close thing there, Pastor David." Gillian looked at him threateningly. "See me after class."

The rest of the afternoon dawdled on in small talk. Coffee appeared then disappeared. The rain began to put in more of an effort and large drops swam like transparent tadpoles down the windowpane. David turned the heating on, and in typical Sunday afternoon fashion Stuart McIntosh first fell silent, then closed his eyes, then began to breathe more deeply before beginning to sound like a series of small boulders rolling down a hillside.

"I imagine that didn't help the marital bed," Gillian remarked. "Come on. Let's do the dishes and let him sleep. He's probably exhausted. Oh, and by the way, while I remember: I want to learn all I need to know about the restoration of the Córdoba Caliphate from the papers, not from you just lending a hand. Understood?"

"Perfectly," said David, picking up a tea towel. "Nothing would interest me less."

Chapter 2

Hacienda

Samira was wearing a Parisian-style beige trench coat and red beret to match her lipstick over smart black trousers and court shoes, not a hijab or a burka, as she trudged up the Bridges heading south. The glacial gouge that was Princes Street Gardens was like a wind tunnel channelling an already stiff breeze into near gale force, bombarding the bridge with bullets of rain. She pulled up her collar and tried to walk almost crab-like half turned away from the volley. *This is madness*, she thought grimly. *Number one: I should be at my business studies degree placement. Phoning in sick does not show the superior level of keenness required. Number two: if not that, then I should be at home studying the pros and cons of matrix management over traditional hierarchy for the next assignment, not meeting a Christian pastor to talk about converting. Number three: if that had to be, then it should be someone totally anonymous that nobody knows from the Archbishop of Canterbury, not a family friend who used to live upstairs.*

It was wrong, wrong, wrong at every level – disloyal, deceitful, and possibly dangerous. She knew that whatever happened her parents would never try to harm her but there were those who might. Probably nobody she actually knew; more like someone who heard what had happened through the grapevine and decided that she had disrespected her patrimony and the Prophet (peace be upon him) and didn't deserve to live. These things happened. A grocer in Glasgow had been stabbed to death outside his shop for sending his Christian customers a Happy Easter message. She pulled out the address David had given her and checked the street number, though she knew it by heart already. She pushed it carefully back into her pocket, aware that she was losing touch with her fingers.

Finally she reached the shelter of the shops and hotels heading up towards the Royal Mile and relaxed a fraction. Although a total stranger might have been safer there was something indefinable about David Hidalgo that seemed to invite confidence. When she had still been helping at her parents' shop on Saturday mornings he often used to come in for some obscure spices or a bag of her mum's home-made naans. He was nice and would ask about her progress at school and university plans or compliment how she looked – just enough to make her feel like he was treating her as an equal, not just the girl behind the till. In fact, she'd come to look forward to these micro interactions so was disappointed he hadn't recognized her at church. But it had been a while and she was two years older now. At any rate, he'd invited her to talk without any strings attached. Maybe that was better than a stranger after all.

David Hidalgo was also feeling the cold that morning. He had accompanied Gillian across the Meadows towards her office in David Hume Tower – generally acknowledged as the ugliest, most out-of-place building in Edinburgh. A quick peck on the cheek, then she went off to work on her new lecture series – "Modern Urban Scots in Movies and Media with Particular Attention to *Trainspotting*" – then he kept on, shivering in the bitter wind, towards Hacienda in South Clerk Street.

When his life had so suddenly fallen apart in Spain it was Juan Hernandez – brother of the woman he suddenly had to start calling his *late* wife – who had saved the day. Juan and the lovely Alicia had invited him back to his childhood home of Edinburgh, where they had set up a Spanish restaurant. They undertook to look after him when it became clear that after Rocío had been murdered he was no longer fit to look after himself. The deal was that they'd feed him in exchange for him doing some part-time preaching at Southside

27

Fellowship, the church they'd connected with, who couldn't afford a paid minister. That was to give him something to do to make him get out of bed in the morning; if he was due to speak the next Sunday morning, then he couldn't jump off the Forth Road Bridge at least until Monday. And the people at church, led by the redoubtable Mrs Irene MacInnes, were so warm and grateful that he usually decided to give it another week, and then another. As for nourishment, he was supposed to eat as often as he wanted at Hacienda – *gratis*. Actually, food, even tasty familiar Spanish food, was the least of it. They nurtured him and coaxed him back to life.

Then he managed to pick up some Spanish language tutoring for the University and happened to meet a very cute, very intelligent, and finally altogether bewitching lady called Gillian. Together they had plotted how to rescue a teenager in despair, about to drop out of her Spanish degree, and starting off from that had ended up rescuing someone in altogether more serious straits. Jen MacInnes, Irene MacInnes's granddaughter, had been dazzled by the glitz and apparent glamour of a bunch of Colombian drug dealers who had set up in town. Once in, it wasn't so easy getting out.

After that, rescuing people seemed to have become something of a theme in David's CV, which was not a completely unnatural activity for a Christian pastor. Unfortunately, this seemed to involve interactions with some that his younger congregation might describe as total bampots and nutters. They weren't far off. But in all the rescuing, slowly, imperceptibly, almost stealthily, he'd suddenly found himself *rescuee* as much as *rescuer*. Be it Gillian, God, the universe, some unidentified providence – some days he still wasn't altogether sure – but whoever or whatever, it had done a good job.

Now married and home from the honeymoon, he found he was waking up without a clue where he was: Spain, Scotland, single in a freezing flat, or what. Then, slowly swimming up to the surface, it would come back. Loved and in love. No longer lonely. Scotland, Spain, or the moon – it didn't matter. There was a warm breathing body next to him. He tended to wake up first and had come to cherish these moments of total tranquillity before the day began. She was with him. They were together. Properly, legally. Even spiritually. Her habits were different from his and it was taking some adjusting, with her in her forties and he in his fifties, but she could have started each morning by painting herself blue and he wouldn't have cared.

Love, the apostle had said, covers a multitude of sins. The commentators usually took that to mean that when there was love people could forgive each other unmeant offences, but he had found something else. Love had also mended the deliberate and utterly unrepented-of evil that had robbed him of Rocío and in a moment blown him clean off the highway and into the scrapyard. The nightmares had stopped. He could think back now and remember happy times. Memories of that other life were once again precious, not just like a limb that had been suddenly chopped off but still seemed to ache even in its absence.

The wind was rising. Trees around the Meadows were bending and large drops were beginning to whip across his path. He buttoned up, crossed George Square, and headed east, the rising gale now thankfully behind him. Juan was polishing cups and glasses behind the bar when he arrived at Hacienda. The idea of opening in the morning for coffee and churros had been Alicia's and it seemed to be working well. Not only did they get the business lunchers and evening diners but also the morning laptop brigade who needed somewhere warm to get a decent cup of coffee and free Wi-Fi. Nobody in this morning yet, though.

"*Buenos días, caballero*," David announced, pushing through the swing door.

"Good morning, my friend." Juan looked up smiling. "*¿Café con leche?*"

"*Si. Gracias. Grande.* How are you? Sleeping?"

"Sometimes. It's an interesting experience. But we prayed so long for a child I can't complain."

"I know. I think you'll be wonderful parents."

"Well, Alicia at least. I get a bit – how do you say? – 'grampy' in the middle of the night."

"Grumpy. Yes. I can imagine."

"So, you have a Muslim that wants to follow *El Señor*? *¡Estupendo!*"

"Well, I don't exactly know. *Vamos a ver.* We're meeting just to talk. Let's see what she says."

"But a Muslim! It's very rare. There are many obstacles. We need to encourage her."

"Yes, because there are many obstacles I want to know what's in her mind and why. It's a serious decision."

"Well, there is rejoicing in heaven over every sinner, whatever the case. May God bless you in your talk."

"I'm sure he will. But in the meantime, *¡café con leche, por favor!*"

David took his coffee to a corner table, opened a week-old copy of *El País,* and waited. She arrived at 10.30 – exactly on time. She looked wet and windswept but also somehow determined. Like a seagull aloft in a gale, balancing against the gusts. She ordered a green tea.

"I'm really sorry I didn't immediately remember you," David began. "It's been a few years. You used to work in the shop, didn't you? What have you been doing?"

Samira sipped her tea and nibbled the tiny biscuit that came with it.

"Business admin at the University. About to start final year. Mum has this idea of making us a global power in peshwari naan and butter chicken so they encouraged me to study business. The workload's crazy but I enjoy it. I had to stop working in the shop though to keep up. Then I found it was getting hard to study at home so I moved into a flat. It's more expensive but I can get more done. Nothing against Mum and Dad, but when you're the only person trying to study – well, y'know... so that's why I've not been around. I have a placement on the Royal Bank campus out at Gogarburn so there's been a lot of travelling too. Actually, I should be there today."

She sounded confident but her hands were shaking as she lifted the cup.

Juan came over with some fresh, hot churros dowsed in sugar, then diplomatically retreated to the kitchen.

"Have you tried these before?" David asked, offering the plate.

Samira took a bite.

"Mmm. Delicious. I'll have to get Mum to try making them."

"It's just a batter mix piped into hot oil. Dead easy."

They sat in silence, pots and pans clattering in the kitchen and traffic rumbling outside. David had hoped a bit of small talk, a relaxed venue, and something sweet would put her at ease and get her talking without him asking the question outright but it wasn't working. She looked like she knew what had to be said but simply couldn't get it out, as if she were about to confess to running over next door's dog. Finally David broke the silence.

"So, do you want to tell me what's been going on? It's a big step."

"I know," she nodded. "I think it's been building for a while. You know what Mum and Dad are like. Dad loves Edinburgh. He's Muslim but he doesn't really have much connection to the Muslim world. They go to the mosque from time to time, but really they're both Scottish. We grew up with that. We've all got Islamic names – Rasheed, Karim, Samira – but we might as well be Ian, Andy, and Fiona."

She gave a faint smile for the first time. David nodded and tried to bounce it back.

"I know," he said. "Your dad and I have spoken about that a few times."

"I'll bet. But anyway, I remember things started changing when I went to high school. I'd never felt any different from my friends, but then suddenly people started talking about jihad and terrorism and I just started feeling different. Like some kind of barrier had come up. Then Syria happened. That changed everything. I stopped getting invited for sleepovers at the weekend. People would look at me differently in the street. You don't have the chance to say, 'I'm not like that; it wasn't my fault.' You know they think you're part of it too, just by the colour of your skin. I don't have an Asian accent, I dress exactly the same as my friends, I don't drink alcohol – but neither do some of them – so what's the difference?"

Now Samira had got started it felt like years of pent-up frustration and a sense of injustice were bubbling up like overflow from a storm drain. David was trying to keep completely neutral, just nodding when it seemed appropriate.

"I tried to talk to Mum about it but she'd grown up at a time when everyone was welcome and nobody thought you were dangerous just for what religion you were. And Dad thinks Scotland is the promised land anyway so he didn't understand. Then at university there seem to be two different kinds of Muslims: those that are always arguing about Palestine and Iraq and telling us to be more religious, and those that go drinking at the weekends like everybody else. I didn't want to be either. So I ended up with friends who weren't Muslim at all but were serious about studying and learning and thinking about the world. They accepted me. It wasn't like I came from another planet. Some of them were Christians so we talked about that too. Then, I remember waking up one Saturday morning and thinking I just don't want to be Muslim any more. It's too much effort and I'm fed up with all the contradictions. They talk about equality but women aren't equal. They talk about peace but there's so much violence. They talk about unity but then there's Sunnis and Shias and all the other sects. I just thought, why do I need to keep defending it or even trying to understand it? Can't I be just what I want to be? Why not?"

In the end it had all come out in a bit of a rush. David got the feeling that she'd never been able to say just exactly how she felt and that he was the catalyst that made it possible.

"So it's more about rejecting your identity as a Muslim than becoming a Christian as such, Samira? Would that be fair?"

"Yes, I suppose so. I want to be me. Not somebody else's idea of who I should be. But everyone needs some sort of identity. I have no idea about Hinduism or anything else, but the Christians I've met have been nice. They never try to push it. And I remembered you. I don't know what you're supposed to do to be a Christian but I'm willing to learn."

David took a sip of his coffee and a bite of the *churro* that wasn't so hot any more. Things weren't indeed always how they seemed to be. A young woman in distress looking for a way out was different from someone who felt God was at work in their lives calling them in another direction. But they both needed listening to.

"Let me get you another tea," he said, stalling for time.

"Forgive me for asking," he added when the tea and another *café con leche* had arrived, Juan delivering them under watchful brows, "but what's been your experience of Christian faith so far? I suppose you had assemblies at school?"

"Muslims didn't have to go to the Christian assemblies. We just got this old imam who kept telling us about the duties of a Muslim wife." She laughed. "I could write a book about how to cook pilau rice and bring your husband his slippers!"

David smiled.

"You didn't miss much. It maybe would have been more useful if we'd learned how to cook rice. By the way, what did you think of our Sunday morning?"

"It's the hardest thing I've ever done," she said quietly, not laughing any more. "Crossing the door of the church. I thought I'd go straight to hell. Or you'd throw me out. Or you'd all be dancing around like lunatics. Sorry."

"Yes. Not much dancing at Southside," David admitted. "And the content. The songs? The talk?"

"A bit weird, but ok. I actually quite liked the talk – about understanding cultures to communicate. One of the problems some Muslims have is that they want to live in Britain and get all the benefits but they really want it to be just like Pakistan: the food, the dress, the customs, the language. There are women who've been here fifty years and hardly speak a word of English. It's ridiculous."

"I've heard. Anyway, I'm glad you weren't too offended. A visiting speaker can be a bit unpredictable."

"Actually, I did have some idea what to expect."

"Really?" This conversation was already so full of the unexpected David thought nothing would surprise him further. He was wrong.

"I've got a boyfriend."

"It's normal."

"He's a Christian."

"Maybe not so normal."

"He comes to your church."

Samira was attractive, intelligent, well dressed, from a good family, and doing well at university, but her particular talent seemed to be the unexpected, like a conjurer producing a live dove from a handkerchief.

"He's Turkish. He came here to study engineering but stayed for his PhD. He's almost finished. We want to marry. He converted and he doesn't want to become Muslim again. So... I think I need to be Christian."

David tried to think.

"Enver?" he asked.

Samira seemed to blush though it was hard to be sure. She looked down and nodded.

"Well, congratulations! I don't know him very well but he seems a really nice, serious guy."

"He is. We met at the charity ball. He comes from a Muslim family in Istanbul but he met some Scottish aid workers who were Christians and got interested. He converted a year before he came here. His family totally disowned him, of course, so he spent a year sleeping on sofas and working in cafés to pay for his studies. It was hard. He's worried that might happen to me."

Neither of them spoke. The coffee was getting cold and the churros no longer looked inviting. Finally Samira just leaned forward, put her head in her hands, and wept.

"I love my family," she sobbed. "I don't want to leave them."

David wasn't sure of the etiquette of an older man who was not a family member touching an unmarried Muslim girl but felt he couldn't avoid some gesture of support. He put his hand on her arm and hoped that wasn't offensive.

"It might not come to that," he said. "Dry your eyes. Let's talk some more. I'll get you another tea."

He went to the bar and caught Juan's attention.

"So, how's it going, brother?" Juan asked, all smiles. "Do we have a new sister yet?"

"Not yet," David said quietly. "It's really not that simple. Anything nice we can nibble? I'd stay off the pork chorizo."

By the time he'd got back to the table Samira had recovered herself somewhat. David put down a dish of roasted almonds and another one of dates.

"These are very Moorish," he explained. "And moreish. You probably know Spain was a Muslim country for hundreds of years. They introduced a lot of new foods and fashions. Apparently the three-course meal was a Muslim invention!"

Samira managed a smile and took some almonds.

"So, can I summarize what I think you've told me?" David began. "You love your family and you have no problems at home. Your dad doesn't force you to dress in a particular way and I don't suppose there's an arranged marriage on the cards."

Samira nodded, then shook her head, not sure which was right.

"No, not at all. Dad and Mum fell in love and defied their families too. They've never suggested a boy."

"Ok. So you're doing the same, except a bit more extreme."

She nodded again and gave a rueful smile.

"I guess."

"Fine. And you're also not delighted with some of what's been happening in the name of Islam. I think lots of Muslims would agree with you there."

"My parents hate it too," she said. "My dad doesn't get angry much but every time there's another attack on TV he goes ballistic. You should hear him swearing in Urdu."

"And you're in love with a Christian boy, from a Muslim background. So in some people's eyes he's apostate already."

Another nod.

"And you think if you go ahead your family might disown you."

"Yes."

"Tell me, Samira," David asked with a change of tone, "how much do you know about Christianity? About Jesus, for example?"

"Not much," she admitted with a shrug. "Jesus is in Islam. We call him *Isa ibn Maryam* – Jesus the son of Mary. But he didn't die on the cross. Allah took him straight to heaven. I know Christians believe he rose again. That's about all I know. I've asked Enver but he doesn't want it to come between us. I had to just about break up with him to get him to let me come to church and promise that he wouldn't be there!"

"Sounds like he doesn't want to make things more difficult for you."

"Definitely. He's really nice. So this is not about doing it to please him – this is for me."

"Hmm."

David took a couple of dates and popped them in for thinking time.

"I don't think this is something we're going to solve today," he announced finally. "And I'm not sure converting is the answer to your problems. I think it is important that you know what Enver believes so I do think we should talk about it. But becoming a Christian isn't just about ticking the box in the opposite column. It usually happens when there's something we want to grow closer to, not just something we want to get away from."

Now she actually looked relieved.

"So what should I do now?"

"That's for you to decide. But let me say I think you've been incredibly brave coming to church. That's for starters. And the fact that you're so upset is actually another positive. It's absolutely clear to me that the last thing you want to do is hurt your family. I can tell them that without any problem. On the other hand, it is important that a couple planning their future together should understand each other and as much as possible share the same outlook. So that might be a hurdle you have to overcome one way or the other. But converting just like that – well, I don't think that really solves anything, and even if you insisted I wouldn't be a party to it right now. It may come to that but you definitely need to find out more and think through what you want and why. Then we can meet again – with Enver this time. If you want to come back to church – together – you can, but I don't want you to go much further without telling your parents what's going on. How does that sound?"

For the first time she looked reassured rather than terrified.

"Ok," she said, and carefully dabbed around her eyeliner.

Gillian got home late and kicked the door shut behind her, balancing a brown paper bag of groceries and an enormous black leather messenger bag full of her laptop and papers. She went to the kitchen to dump the paper bag. There was a radio playing but nobody was there.

"Hi! Anyone home?" she shouted, going back along the hall.

"In here."

The living room was gloomy in the fading light. David was sat in the window with an empty cup balanced on one knee, staring out of the window.

"Honey," she said, coming over, "you ok? Didn't it go well?"

"No, it went fine. Better than I'd expected. I'm just mulling it over."

"For how long?"

David glanced at his watch.

"A couple of hours."

Gillian arched an eyebrow.

"Not healthy," she said. "No mulled wine to aid the mulling but would a Martini help? I got a cheap copy at Tesco."

David breathed slowly in and out.

"I think so. Thanks."

Gillian came back with two glasses with ice, handed one to David, and sat opposite him.

"So if it all went well – what?"

"I don't know. Rubbish really."

"Want to tell me what sort of rubbish?"

"I've just been wondering what sort of pastor it is who's supposed to be pointing people to God and meets with a girl who wants to convert and stops her."

"Is that what you did?"

"More or less. It's complicated. Turns out it's more about not wanting to be Muslim any more than wanting to be anything else. And partly to be like her Christian boyfriend – who turns out to be Enver from church."

"You've been mulling that over for a couple of hours?"

David grunted.

"Not just that. It's the whole thing about religion. I'm used to people who either don't believe anything or are just cultural Christians. It's the first time for a while I've had a serious conversation with someone who has a definite religious identity but wants to change it. And of course it's a lot more than just identity. We always say 'relationship not religion', don't we? I'm asking myself what exactly the implications would be. I mean, if she's really determined it could be akin to a death sentence, as well as ripping a family apart. And if something serious did happen, what would be the responsibility of whoever helped in the process? Juan would say we are saving a soul from hell – he might be right – but are we sufficiently sure of that to endanger a life here and now? I've just been wondering what exactly I'd do if she is really determined – I mean, once she gets things clear in her head."

"I can see the dilemma."

"And what I'd say to Ali if his daughter ended up dead because the pastor who used to live downstairs – who he thought was a friend

– helped her betray her own faith to the point that some nutcase with a machete decides to give her what's coming to her."

"Can we go back to the question 'What sort of pastor'?" Gillian spoke gently but firmly. "I would say a sensible, reasonable, compassionate pastor who is not a fanatic who only cares about numbers but wants to listen to someone in distress and help them chart their own way forward. If she's determined, that's her decision, not yours. As far as the fires of hell are concerned, I've never bought into that. And as far as Ali and Ayeesha are concerned, I think you need to speak to them as soon as Samira agrees. With her. And maybe with Enver too."

David nodded but didn't look any happier.

"And another thing: have I ever told you you think too much?"

"Many times."

"Well, this is another time. You don't need to carry the weight of the world, Muslim or Christian. If God is involved at all, and having been through something similar myself recently I wouldn't be surprised, then it's not all up to you. Understood?"

"I guess so."

"In the meantime I'm not going to have my new husband sitting in the dark being gloomy for hours. Drink your drink." So saying she got up, took him by the hand, and pulled him up too.

"I've an idea that might distract you."

As she led him into the hall the radio in the kitchen started Patti Smith's "Because the night". That seemed appropriate for lovers.

Chapter 3

Córdoba

"How about this one?" the shorter, younger brother asked, pointing to a listing on Trip Advisor on the laptop open in front of them. "Pensión El Moro. '*Moro*' means Moorish, doesn't it? From the Caliphate."

His older brother leaned over. They were in a café near the bus station in Córdoba.

"Pensión El Moro," he read, as if his younger brother might not have got it right. "Three stars. Twelve Euros a night each or ten in a twin room. Breakfast included and a weekly laundry service. On the bus routes, near the centre of town. Looks ok."

"And '*Moro*'. Maybe it's a sign…"

"Maybe it is, Little Brother. Well spotted."

Seven years between them but it might have been a hundred. Older Brother, Little Brother. Older Brother is always right. Older Brother says what he wants, does what he wants, can be what he wants. Little Brother has to fight just to keep up. If they lived to be old men that would never change. But that didn't make it easier to swallow. *One day*, Little Brother often thought, *one day*... So now, finding something first – however trivial – was something. He was pleased. They checked the routes and found a bus that would be leaving in ten minutes. They drained their black tea, paid, and crossed the road to the stop.

Flushed with success, Little Brother thought he would push his luck once they were seated in the bus.

"Why was it so important that we need to live here?" he asked.

"What we need to do could be done in a day, with a week of preparation. Why do we need to live here?"

"The Prophet instructed it," Older Brother replied knowingly. "And I can see why. We are to familiarize ourselves with every aspect of the Caliphate – the architecture, the art, the science, the history. The Prophet needs those who understand these things so that when the Caliphate is re-established he can have wise rulers who will know how things should be. Don't you want to be Caliph? Or at least the brother of the Caliph? And there are the other cities: Seville, Granada, Toledo – they're all important too. We need to travel there. And Medina Azahara of course. We'll rebuild it. It will be more beautiful and more glorious than ever."

"What's Medina Azahara? It can't be very big. I've never heard of it."

"It's not a town, Little Brother. It's the remains of the palace complex built by Abd Al Rahman III in 940, destroyed in 1010, and only rediscovered in 1911. It's about five miles away. Nobody knows about it. The ignorant tourists all just go to the cities but Medina Azahara was the real jewel. And it will be again."

Older Brother's eyes had taken on the glow of a devotee but then he laughed.

"I've been doing my homework. You should too. The Prophet says we need to know the glories of the past and the promise of the future to sustain us in the present. Look; here's the stop. Ring the bell."

Pensión El Moro was small and cramped, squatting between two other grander buildings like a child between two grown-ups, but seemed clean and freshly painted in ochre and orange. The sign outside had a pair of crossed black scimitars with a red turban on top – actually more Turkish than Moorish but no doubt tourists got the general idea. The girl at the desk could also have been Turkish or Moorish. She looked as if she might have just got off the boat from North Africa with the invading Berbers. In reality she was 100 per cent *andaluza*, which meant definitely nearer to Moorish than

Spanish. Jet black shoulder-length hair. Eyes like cinders and huge gold hoop earrings that almost touched her bare neck. The exotic effect was somewhat undermined, however, by a Marilyn Monroe T-shirt in a Warhol pop-art style with the slogan "More lovers than hot tortilla". Still, she spoke English, and that was something. They booked for a week to begin with, paid in advance, dumped their stuff, and went out to explore.

The centre of Córdoba was more like a city-wide open air museum than a modern metropolis. Of course it had its ugly high-rise suburbs like everywhere else, but the old town was "*Patrimonio de la Humanidad*" and you just about needed UNESCO permission to clean your windows. Narrow streets with upper-floor iron balconies almost touching led to tiny squares with fountains. Houses were only two or three storeys and painted in brilliant white, yellowish cream the colour of *natillas*, the Spanish custard dessert, or deeper shades through mustard to a full vibrant orange. Sometimes a line of houses and small shops would give way to a high wall hiding a courtyard with huge iron double doors, stone lintels parallel up to head height then blossoming around into an elegant pointed arch like the bud of a flower. Every flat surface seemed decorated with geometric figures, crests, and shields. Through the crack in the gates, green spaces were just visible, again with the sound of fountains and a hint of wide, gracious courtyards. Sometimes a narrow street would unexpectedly open out into gardens of willows, oak, and orange trees and yet more fountains. The Moors who had built the city seemed to be saying, after a lifetime in the desert, *we never want to be far from the sound of running water again*. If the aim had been to build the nearest thing to an earthly paradise, they seemed to have come quite close. Although it was summer and the sun a blazing fireball, the shade of narrow streets, overhanging branches, and the sound of running water seemed to make the whole *casco viejo* feel like an oasis. Camels and spice traders would not have been surprising. In fact, the whole mood seemed to suggest that the Moors and their tenth-century Jewish and even Christian neighbours

42

had just popped out to attend to a few things and would be back any minute. Rubbish containers in the street, crude adverts, and shops catering to tacky tourist mementos would all be swept away in a wave of purification and life would return to normal. As it had been before. As it was meant to be.

Older Brother certainly thought so and gave a running commentary on what he would do as Caliph. This would be preserved. That would be plucked out like a thorn in the flesh. This would be restored to its former glory and the great and grand houses that were only hinted at behind high walls and locked gates would all be inhabited by Muslims. As in the Caliphate, those of other faiths would be tolerated in a gesture of peace and goodwill – if they paid the requisite taxes – but decision-making, prestige, power, well, that would be where it should be. Girls and women would be treated with respect and shielded from prying eyes. The filthy Western trade in naked skin would be outlawed and punished without mercy, but those who accepted the new order would be welcomed and promoted. After all, many Jews and even Christians had served the Caliph well and reaped their due rewards. Quite the opposite of what had happened when, through a mixture of indolence and treachery, the city had been lost. Then the new rulers – "their most Catholic majesties" – had relentlessly turned the screw, gradually reducing those of other faiths to poverty, then exile or the fire. Older Brother wondered if it would be appropriate to take some revenge for that even though the Prophet had reminded him that Allah was merciful and they should be too.

Little Brother wandered through the streets also wondering but he was wondering about the girl at Pensión El Moro. Such dark hair and eyes could almost have passed for South Asian but the T-shirt was far from Islamic. The mullahs would condemn it – and her – without hesitation. Wanton, lustful, immoral. But she had just seemed friendly, confident, independent, assured. That was all. He assumed the T-shirt slogan was a joke, not a personal history. So maybe she was just laughing at all excesses he'd been taught to hate and fear. *Curious*. Then he wondered more about the train of events that had brought him here. Older Brother's monotonous stream of approbations and condemnations, depending on what drew his attention, had ceased to register as he took things in for himself. The Islamic-influenced art and architecture was of course impressive, but the people didn't look like they needed a religious revolution. A couple of old men were sitting on a bench leaning on their walking sticks and talking. Maybe not about the weather like they did in Edinburgh, since it didn't change much here. Maybe about their children who never phoned, their wives who spend scandalous amounts in the hairdresser's, or the disgusting amount of rubbish in the streets that nobody ever cleaned up. Normal talk. It wasn't the earthly paradise Abd Al Rahman had planned but equally it wasn't the cesspool of iniquity the Prophet said it was. It was just ordinary people getting on with ordinary life, trying to get by. One of the old men must have said something funny, as his companion suddenly roared with laughter, beat his stick on the ground, and took out a handkerchief to wipe his eyes.

The Prophet didn't have much of a sense of humour. The West was a corpse still walking but riddled with corruption, he said. The Middle East was a banquet that had descended into a cannibal feast as a dozen different factions all claiming to be the true Islam ripped each other apart in the hope that the last mullah standing would enjoy the remains. It was time for a new front in the battle, he said. Time to give the worm-infested West the final push that knocked it over then true Islam would step into the void and return the glories of the Caliphate. There would be universities doing real research and pushing back the boundaries of knowledge as the scientists of Al-Andalus had done a thousand years before; algebra was, after all, an Arabic word and the number system the world now depended on had been invented by Muslims. There would be communes of artists painting, sculpting, writing, drawing – not debased filth but beautiful harmonic pieces infused with the beauty of the Koran and mathematics. Politics – the endless struggle of one partisan mob against another – would be finished. The holy texts interpreted by the best and wisest of scholars would govern every aspect of life. But before any of that could happen, the Prophet said with a degree of weary sadness in his voice, there needed to be a clearing of the ground. No one could build a temple on a rubbish heap. The rubbish would have to go. It would be like lancing a boil, purifying with fire, or expelling the intruder.

Younger Brother wondered a lot about this. Could it be that the Prophet used such violent language because he was, underneath it all, a violent man? Was the talk of warfare only a necessary prelude to peace? Or would the revolution end up always having to be extended for one more season, as so often was the case, until violence and repression became the norm? He wondered about this, because the Prophet had begun his endeavour to unite all Islam and bring about the new age by being thrown out of the Edinburgh Mosque as a heretic and troublemaker who had taken himself outside the bounds of Islam and was now considered apostate. Older Brother always insisted that the Prophet had chosen to withdraw because his words were twisted and wilfully misunderstood but that was simply parroting what the Prophet himself said. Younger Brother still had friends in the mosque and they said the opposite. And if the Prophet was leading a worldwide movement that had Allah on its side and was growing daily with thousands of fighters and influential thinkers, why was it that he and Older Brother were here – a 19- and 26-year-old – not a hundred skilled and experienced, battle-hardened warriors? Older Brother said the Prophet had his reasons but Younger Brother couldn't shake these troublesome thoughts. Doubts came in the night. He honestly could not imagine his headstrong, impulsive brother as the Emir of Al-Andalus, far less himself as Minister for Home and Foreign Affairs as he'd been promised. In the daytime he tried to talk the talk but in the dark hours before dawn when nightmares came it seemed about as likely as, well, as likely as getting to know the girl at reception. And he'd already given up his job at the carpet warehouse in Glasgow, rudely abandoned all his friends, and told the only girl he had been friendly with that she was unworthy of Islam. Not a train of events he could easily unravel. So between a rock and a hard place.

"Look at that!" Older Brother spat out. "Look at it. Disgusting. I'll light the fire myself once we're in charge."

Younger Brother looked. It was a poster for this week's offers in Lidl: sports bras and joggers. He didn't find it disgusting at all. The model was beautiful. He thought again about the dark-haired girl. In a sports bra and joggers. Nineteen virgins in paradise might be nice in theory, but right now he wasn't getting any nearer to flesh and blood than signing his name in the register opposite the nice-looking receptionist.

David Hidalgo put on a clean shirt, gathered his papers, and screwed on his blue felt fedora.

"That's me off," he called into the bedroom.

"Ok," Gillian replied over her shoulder, bending into the dressing table mirror and applying a quick repair job of lip gloss.

"You remember I'm at aikido tonight so I'll be late."

"Ok. Have fun. Tell Sensei Sam I'm asking for him. Don't break a leg – yours or anyone else's."

This would be the first Leadership Team ("LT" among those who always preferred abbreviations) of the new post-summer year of activities. Although the financial year was the same as everybody else's and the calendar year was pretty fixed, the real year for a pastor began in early September after the summer break. Sunday School got cranked up again, youth groups, ladies' groups, house groups, play groups; all got restarted and often a new sermon series began to take shape. But it all needed organization. So an LT in late August was called for.

"Ok. Welcome everyone. Maybe we should get started?" David said in an effort to get the buzz of conversation to ease up and focus on why they were here. A beautiful summer's evening could only be enjoyed once the business was over.

"Before we start we should do some quick introductions. We all know each other, but there's a few new people looking after some new activities so it might be good to hear what's planned for the year."

There was no objection to this, so they went around hearing from Lesley about Sunday School, Juan about upgrading the AV desk, Julian about the preaching team who covered when David was away, Mrs MacInnes about finances – healthy in the meantime but some challenges to come – Sophie about the youth group she ran with her husband George, Gavin about the small groups network that seemed to be flourishing, and Sandy Benedetti about outreach events particularly centred on Christmas, Easter, and the Edinburgh Festival. All very interesting and positive, but David was only half-listening until finally Enver Durak started speaking about the student and young adult work. To be fair, he did a reasonable job of being both brief and comprehensive, a difficult balancing act since they both knew that wasn't the main event. It was one of these I know and you know and you know that I know and I know that you know moments. Enver looked gloomy and spoke clearly in very good English but was clearly nervous and stumbled a couple of times over simple expressions. To anyone paying attention he looked as if this might be his final summing up in an appeal against deportation. Mrs MacInnes was watching him closely.

"Are you all right, Enver?" she asked when he had finished. "Let me get you a glass of water."

"Thank you, Mrs MacInnes. That would be nice," he replied, not daring to raise his eyes from his notes.

David could have been very mean and questioned some of his plans but that wasn't his nature. He was remembering his first meeting with Gillian's dad; despite being in his fifties and married before, it still felt like an encounter with the Grand Inquisitor. So he did the decent thing.

"Thank you, Enver," he said. "That was fascinating. I think you've really got a handle on that – I mean it's under control – and I think we can look forward to an excellent year. Remember, the aim is to be an oasis in the city for young people far from home who may be struggling with growing up, with the workload, with a new culture, maybe even with the new freedoms they might have. What they bring us is vitality and energy but it's more about them than us. If we get a few like you who choose to stay and contribute – fantastic – but we want to help them through their time in Edinburgh and make it something they'll look back on positively for the rest of their lives. Thanks, Enver. That was great."

After that they ploughed relentlessly though the remaining internal agenda. With no meetings over the summer there was a lot to catch up on. Then finally it was almost over and they hit "Any Other Business".

"Normally," David began, "I try to avoid any unexploded devices in AOB – and I think we've all had about enough tonight – but there are two things I'd like to raise here that I think are appropriate." Enver cast a nervous glance in David's direction.

"One is the church flat in Bruntsfield. As you all know, Gillian and I decided to move to her place in Marchmont – at least initially – which leaves Bruntsfield empty. That's not an ideal situation both in terms of upkeep and that fact that the church is paying a mortgage on it and we could maybe be getting some income."

"Thank you, Pastor David; I was going to raise that myself," Mrs MacInnes agreed. "My neighbour's daughter works in a property letting company. I was thinking of asking her opinion."

"Perfect," David continued. "However, I may have a shorter-term solution while we investigate that for the new academic year. A friend of mine, Stuart McIntosh – some of you may know Stuart from some of our little, how can I put it, 'escapades'; he's a Detective Inspector with Police Scotland, as thoroughly respectable as you can get. He's in need of some short-term accommodation. I'll not go into the details if you don't mind. He's quite prepared to pay commercial rates but would prefer not to have to trail around the property agencies or answer adverts. I said I would put it to the meeting. What do you think?"

David wasn't sure exactly what was meant by "short term" – maybe a few months. Yes, he would pay Council Tax and all utilities. No, he didn't have any furniture to move in, just personal items. Yes, he would be there on his own. Maybe kids for the odd overnight but no one else.

"Well, I can't see any objections," Mrs MacInnes summed up. "I had a quick word with the gentleman on Sunday morning and he seemed perfectly pleasant. I just hope whatever his situation things work out and I'd be happy for us to help in the meantime."

"Ok. All happy? So finally then – really finally – I think we're going to need to look at the question of premises. We're filling up quite rapidly, I think, and the first week someone comes and can't get a seat or a family come and can't sit together could well be the last time they come. So at some point soon we need to discuss property, ok?"

Nods around the table and that wrapped things up.

"Enver, can I just have a very quick word?" David asked as they wandered out of the back committee room and through the main hall. Enver nodded morosely, knowing his time had come. They grabbed a couple of chairs in the corner.

"Samira said you might want to talk to me," he said, studying the floor as if hoping it might take pity and dump him in the Chinese restaurant below.

"Yes. But nothing bad. It's not an easy situation; I expect you know that."

Enver gave a bit of a grunt. "The thought had occurred."

"But since Samira got me involved – and you are part of Southside – my job is to help if I can."

Enver relaxed a little as it became clear that he wasn't going to be subject to a personal Bible study on not being unequally joined with unbelievers but still didn't look very cheerful.

"I think her dad will want to kill me," he mumbled. "And her brothers. I suppose she's got uncles and cousins as well."

"Maybe," David didn't disagree. "But she seems a lovely girl. I think she's brave and resourceful. She wants to explore Christian faith – maybe not exactly for the right reasons yet but it's a start. People can change and they can survive. You did, for example."

"I did," Enver agreed, "but I would never want anyone to go through what I had to go through. You know in Turkey to be Turkish is to be Muslim and to be Muslim is to be Turkish. Change one and people think you're changing the other as well. Converting is the most unpatriotic thing you can possibly do. I had death threats. I was attacked more than once. My tyres were slashed repeatedly. I lost three jobs. Of course my parents threw me out right away and none of the rest of my family would talk to me. I was eating out of what the kebab shops chucked out. It was horrible. The last thing I would want is for Samira to have to go through that. Do you know I was offered a job at MIT last week and I almost decided to take it? But I couldn't. We love each other and I just couldn't leave her. We thought we might have a quiet wedding then emigrate. Maybe Canada or Australia."

David wasn't sure if Turkish men were more emotional than the Scots but Enver looked on the verge of tears. However, he wasn't about to hug him.

"Ok, Enver," he said in as kindly a way as he could. "It may come to that but I don't think we're quite there yet. I've said to Samira that we should talk together – all of us. And I'd like to involve Gillian, if you don't mind. She's forgotten more about people skills than I ever knew. And I think we need to speak to Samira's mum and dad sooner rather than later. The thought that we've been plotting behind their back is only going to make things worse. How does that sound?"

Enver nodded, looking slightly happier, but didn't seem to trust himself to say anything.

The Blind Poet pub was quiet. Students weren't back in town yet and a lovely summer's evening encouraged people to walk, not sit in a drinking den. Stuart McIntosh was perfectly happy to sit in any sort of den that got him out of the house. Kirsty had laid down the law. This was it. *"You're married to the police, not to me, so go and sleep in St Leonard's police station if you like. It won't make much difference. You're there more than you're here anyway."* On the basis of the bare facts, he couldn't disagree. But this was not how he had wanted it to end. He knew he couldn't chuck it all in and work for a security firm in Sighthill, and he knew he was better than collaring shoplifters in Boots. *And* he was still eight years off retirement. So what was the alternative? Simply try to be as civil as he could about it for the kids' sake, find somewhere else short term, and longer term aim to try to do what so many people of his generation seemed to be doing: kick start the whole thing all over again and find someone else. In the meantime the immediate problem was the "find somewhere else short term". So he had phoned David Hidalgo. Actually he hadn't even remembered about the Bruntsfield flat and was just putting out feelers, but David immediately suggested he put the idea to his leadership team at their meeting that evening, then chat afterwards and see where they were up to.

"David! Over here!" McIntosh shouted through the bar-room buzz till David located him and sailed over. "Hail fellow. Well met, I hope," the detective said, pulling out a chair. "What'll you have?"

"Eh, let me see…" David gave the matter some serious thought, dumping his briefcase and fedora. "Do they do *tinto de verano*, do you think?"

"I have no idea. What's that when it's at home?"

"Means summer red wine. It's a mix of red wine – probably not very good – with lemonade, bit of fruit, sometimes a shot of brandy if you're lucky."

McIntosh shrugged.

"I can but ask," he said. "And if not?"

"Oh, pint of Guinness I suppose. Extra cold."

A few minutes later McIntosh was back at the table with a pint for himself and a large wine glass clinking with ice, a half slice of orange balancing on the rim, and a couple of sad chunks of apple floating on top of what was certainly the colour of red wine.

"Apparently they do," he said, surprised. "Never heard of it, but Sylvia says the Spaniards are always asking for it and since they now make up about a third of the clientele they added it to the list. So – Bob's your uncle. Cheers."

"Cheers," David said, chinking glasses. "I'm afraid to ask you how things are."

"You should be," McIntosh replied. "Not very good. If this were a case I'd say police are continuing their inquiries but there are no leads and no immediate hope of a breakthrough."

"Hmm. That's what I was afraid of."

"Well, life goes on I suppose. Where there's beer there's hope."

He took a big slurp and put his glass down next to the two other empty ones.

"So what's the story? Are the Christians going to be happy with a cop?"

"Very. No problems. They put a bid in for no parking or speeding tickets during the tenancy but are willing to negotiate. Basically, yes. No problem."

"Good. I'm pleased. I'll set up a standing order if you give me the details. Would it be unreasonable to move in tonight?"

David raised an eyebrow.

"Well, I don't see why not. I still have a key on my ring. There's a bed and bedding but no food or anything."

"Let me tell you, a bed and bedding is better than what I've got waiting for me at home. If you've no objections I'd be really grateful."

"Fair enough."

David was a bit dubious about Stuart driving – friends don't let friends drive – but Stuart insisted and declared he knew where all the speed traps were and could claim he was following a dangerous criminal, which might be true whichever route he took. At any rate they got to Bruntsfield without mishap and David pushed open the flat door, ushering the detective in. Stuart had been there before so basic orientation didn't take long.

"I really appreciate this, David," Stuart said as David was on the point of leaving. "Please pass on my thanks."

"Of course. I'm sorry it's come to this. Gillian and I will have you round for a meal some night."

"Great. Thanks."

David let the common close door slam behind him and was just about to head off across Bruntsfield Links towards Marchmont pondering the complicated nature of human relationships when he heard a shout behind him.

"Hey! You there. Think my naan breads aren't good enough for you now? You can make better curry than my wife? You found a better place to buy your garam masala?"

David was taken aback for a second, froze just about to cross the road, and then turned to see an Asian shopkeeper midway through moving all his display boxes of fruit back into the shop prior to closing up for the night.

"Ali!" he called back and changed direction, smiling. "Of course not. I apologize. How are you?"

"Ahh. Business is bad," Ali Khan intoned in gloomy tones. "I've lost my best customer. I'm thinking of moving back to Pakistan. But I can't get good Scottish whisky there for some reason. So, you know. Gloomy on all fronts." He managed to hold the hopeless expression for a few seconds before bursting into furious laughter.

"I got you, I got you," he shouted. "For two seconds you believed me. Ha!"

"You miserable sinner!" David shot back. "Not a hope. Any more and I'll organize a boycott. So how are you really doing?"

"Ah, ok. Ayeesha's cake business is really taking off. I think we've got the contract to do every wedding in Southside for the next five years."

"I wouldn't be surprised. The cake you made for ours looked fantastic. And tasted great too."

"I know," Ali agreed. "I came back for extras. So, married life? How's the little love nest in the city?"

"Nice. Really nice. I'm a happy man, Ali. However, I'm sorry you're now a bit off the beaten track. I promise I'll make a special trip to see you soon."

"In that case, you're forgiven. Ayeesha is desperate to speak to Gillian and hear all about the honeymoon."

"Well, why don't you come for dinner then?"

"We'd love to but it's our turn to have you, surely. Remember you did that Indian, Spanish, Italian, Greek thing?"

David laughed.

"It wasn't meant to be Indian, Spanish, Italian, Greek but I can see it made an impression. No, we must have you in the new Hidalgo residence. I'll speak to Gillian and have you round sometime soon."

"Meter la pata" is the expression in Spanish that means "put the paw", quite close to "put your foot in it" in English. David had truly just meant to say, "See you sometime" and then head off, but for some unaccountable reason heard himself asking how the kids were doing and instantly wanted to bite his tongue off.

"Ah, that's another story, my friend," Ali intoned, now genuinely gloomy. "It seems like our happy family is suddenly just a happy couple – and not even so happy. I'll tell you when I see you. I promise to bring some of Ayeesha's home-made naans – if you're good!"

Chapter 4

Firth of Forth

It turned out that the dark-haired, dark-eyed girl with the Marilyn Monroe T-shirt – whom Older Brother had already designated as immoral and dangerous – made excellent coffee, as they discovered at breakfast the next morning. When she found out they were from Scotland and both native speakers of English despite their Indian appearance, she was even more friendly and told them all about her sister, who was working in a hotel in Musselburgh just outside Edinburgh.

"I need really to get out of Spain," she said slowly and carefully. "I've a *carrera* in the studies of film and my master's and all I can get is to working in my parents' hostel. But I need improve my English first. Is terrible."

"No it's not!" Younger Brother replied before Older Brother could stop him. "You speak really well. I know exactly what you're saying."

"You think so?" she asked, surprised and pleased. "Enough to work in a bar maybe?"

"Of course. Sure."

"I think we're in a hurry today," Older Brother interrupted. "Can we get some toast and more coffee?"

The girl shrugged and headed back to the kitchen.

"That was really rude! She was just being nice," Younger Brother protested.

"We are not here for girls – especially not that sort. I have an important programme for the day. Drink up."

55

The "important programme" turned out to be more or less exactly the same as the day before – wandering around taking notes and getting familiar with where the important buildings were; not just the tourist sites but the hospitals and health centres, the government buildings, the schools. And for Younger Brother another day of listening to an unceasing tirade against moral laxity, the public display of the half-naked female form, the long hair of men, girls in jeans, bars on every corner, and the advertising of matters that are so personal they should not be displayed where children and unaccompanied women could see them. In other words – at least from Younger Brother's point of view – it was a dismal, repetitive day. All he could think of was the girl who wanted to improve her English. Her coffee was already perfect.

Finally they were through, Older Brother's notebook stuffed with addresses and locations. There didn't seem any point in arguing about the value of all of this. Everything was "because the Prophet has commanded it". *I wish the Prophet had commanded us to get to know local people and understand their culture*, Younger Brother thought. *That might do some good and would certainly be much more enjoyable.* But right now he felt as much use as an umbrella on a bicycle. Or chicken in a fruit salad. Or anything else totally useless and out of place. Older Brother had dragged him along with promises of future high office and reminders of the Prophet's instructions but it had never felt like his thing. Now less than ever. Still, he tried to believe in the Prophet and kept his doubts to himself.

Since Spanish custom dictated that the main meal be eaten in the early afternoon and only a very late supper, they ate in a cheap restaurant at about 2.00 and took fruit and bread back to the *pensión* for the evening. The girl wasn't at reception this time, which was severely disappointing – at least for one of them. The boy on duty spoke no English and their Spanish was still at the phrase book stage so the conversation was brief. Older Brother was frustrated.

"The Prophet has commanded that we should improve our

Spanish," he announced once they had got back into their room. "I will look for an academy we can enrol in tomorrow."

"I'm no use in a classroom," Younger Brother insisted. "You know that. I'd rather find a personal tutor."

Older Brother shrugged. It was true. He had got five straight As in his Highers, likewise in Advanced Higher Maths, Physics, and Computing, then a first in Computer Studies followed by a plum programming job with Centaur Systems in South Queensferry. Younger Brother had struggled to get three basic passes and was working for their uncle in his carpet warehouse in Shettleston in Glasgow when the Prophet called. Normally Older Brother would have insisted on keeping his eye on the situation but he was under pressure. The Prophet wanted results.

"Ok. If you can find somebody."

Younger Brother had someone in mind already.

"And there's something else I have to organize," Older Brother said solemnly. "It's my duty." For once he didn't look confident and in control.

"What?"

"I can't tell you. The Prophet has commanded it."

Younger Brother shrugged and pulled a couple of oranges out of a bag. Another pointless bit of posing. He was getting fed up with this. But at least he now had an excuse to speak to the dark-eyed girl. He wondered what sort of reception he'd get.

"You said *what*?" Gillian asked, not quite believing her ears.

"I know. Stupid. Unforgivable. It just came out. I've no idea why."

"Well, hardly unforgivable but maybe not the most tactful."

"Anyway, I've said to Ali we'll have them for dinner, at least to thank them for the cake. And see what comes up about family."

"Ok, we'll try to keep it neutral. I can ask Ayeesha about those fantastic marzipan sweets she turns out. It's Dad's birthday in a couple of weeks. I'd like to take him something nice."

"I've a meeting with Samira and Enver tomorrow morning. I bet she knows the recipes as well."

"What time? How long do you think you'll be?"

"Ten thirty, I think. Maybe an hour. Why?"

"Because it's Saturday and I've arranged a treat for tomorrow; it's about time. I think you'll like it."

No further information was forthcoming and David knew better than to try to insist. Gillian made beautiful chicken satay skewers with couscous for supper and they watched *Pretty Woman*. Again.

But before Samira and Enver, David had another meeting that might or might not turn out to be useful. Mike MacGregor turned up in the same general uniform. This time it was a sky blue V-neck, a lemon polo shirt, and beige chinos, but the effect was the same.

"Good morning, sir!" he enthused. "A pleasure once again."

David rose from his place in a booth at Costa and reached for Mike's outstretched paw.

"My pleasure. I'm afraid this isn't really going to be a distinctively Edinburgh experience, but good coffee maybe isn't our speciality."

"Maybe I should have a good strong cup of British tea then?"

David had suggested a quiet, friendly pub that did excellent flat white and home-made scones with raspberry jam from a family producer in Arbroath, but Mike seemed allergic to any alcohol even nearby. So Costa it was.

"So… impressions of Edinburgh so far, Mike, or is it too early to tell?"

Mike took a sip of his Americano and smacked his lips.

"No. Not at all. It's a fantastic city. I'm sure you're used to hearing that from tourists but I really mean it. I'm hoping not to be a tourist for too long. I've already updated my status to resident of Edinburgh!"

"Great. So here for the long term?"

"Well 'long term' is a long time. But we do feel an affinity for Scotland: John Knox, the Covenanters, Dr Livingstone, Robert Reid

Kalley, Mary Slessor, and so on. Such a heritage. Then to see how much things have changed... We want to make a contribution."

"Forgive me," David tried to ask with some delicacy, "but just who exactly is 'we'?"

"Reasonable question, sir. We are a coalition of churches. All the different denominations. The One World Foundation, we call ourselves. The idea is to recover particularly European Christian heritage. We feel that while Europe sent a flood of its missionaries all around the world, the tide has receded now and left things high and dry. We feel an obligation to send something back. I'm here to try to spy out the land, if I can put it that way, from the lands blessed by the Europeans – particularly, I might say, the English; forgive me 'the *British*' – we hope to help in the work. And especially for the Scots who did more than their fair share, I might add. We have lots of trained and experienced candidates just waiting for the word. Does that make sense?"

"Perfectly," David said dryly. "So personnel and expertise then?"

"And money too. We Americans don't think 'money' is a dirty word; maybe that goes without saying. It's the love of money that's at the root of all evil, not the money itself, if you follow. Speculate to accumulate. Invest in the best. Money where your mouth is. Know what I mean? And we want to invest our resources – human and material – in Scotland. New projects and existing churches. So it was definitely a pleasure to visit your place of worship Sunday last and meet some of your wonderful team. We'd just love it if there was something we could do that would help you folks along in the work."

Hmm, free money, thought David. *Wonder what the catch is? Do we really want to get into bed with the One World Foundation?* But all he said was "interesting" and took another sip of coffee.

The rest of the hour was largely taken up with Mike enthusing about the Castle, the Museum, New Town architecture, shortbread, tartan, and the hunt for his ancestors who had lived somewhere near Oban, he thought. David felt he had to clarify that the emphasis is on the *O* not the *ban*. Finally, by the time he had only ten minutes left,

David forced himself to get to the main event. Mike seemed to be a Christian brother bearing gifts, and while he might suffer from an excess of enthusiasm, that wasn't the worst thing in the world. So what was it that made him uneasy? He wasn't sure and pushed it to the back of his mind.

"Anyway, Mike, I'll have to head off shortly. But just supposing that Southside was looking at funding sources – say to move to larger premises – is that the sort of thing your group might be interested in supporting?"

Mike looked as if David had just offered him Scottish citizenship and the Freedom of the Burgh.

"Well, that would be just wonderful," he declared. "Of course we're looking for partnerships but I hadn't expected we might find something so soon. Just from my short visit to your little group I'd say that was exactly the sort of thing we'd love to get behind and help. Yes, sir. I can't promise but I'd love to take a proposal to the board."

David tried again to push down his nagging discomfort. *Little group indeed*, he thought. But it shouldn't be written off just for differences in terminology. They parted with another mighty pumping of the arm from Mike, and David emerged blinking into the morning sunlight with a feeling that he'd just escaped from a hyperbaric chamber.

After that Samira and Enver were a pure pleasure. They sat in David's first choice of watering hole with a pot of tea and a pile of scones and jam in front of them, the young folk looking like they'd been called up to see the headmaster. David tried to put them at ease as best he could.

"So this terrible secret you haven't told your father yet, Samira," he said, "is it that you want to convert from Islam and marry a Christian boy, or is there something else?"

"No, that's it." She almost giggled with a release of tension. Even Enver managed a smile.

"Ok, tell me from the start. What awful train of circumstances has led us to this point?"

So they did. It was a charity ball that had started the rot. She apparently had come in a sapphire-blue sari with silver stars and an almost transparent gauze scarf in gold thread. He was with friends from the Backgammon Society and couldn't take his eyes off her. He plucked up courage and bought her a glass of champagne, after checking that was ok. Then they danced. He claimed two left feet but she guided him around the floor well enough to avoid embarrassment to either of them. They started with an Orcadian Strip the Willow but ended with a cheek-to-cheek waltz and agreed to meet for coffee the next day. Enver got home past three but reckoned he only managed about two hours' sleep and woke up a wreck. Samira slept like a baby with a smile on her face and woke up totally refreshed and with that funny floaty, dreamy feeling you can get after a deep massage, illegal substances, or falling in love. She knew it wasn't either of the first two. They saw each other every day and texted almost on the hour every hour for the first two weeks before Enver finally brought them back to reality. "I'm not sure your dad is going to like this," he had said. "Although I'm Turkish I'm not actually Muslim; I'm Christian."

"So did you have an idea how things were going to work out after that?" David asked.

"I think we just hid our heads in the sand," Enver admitted. "I guess maybe it felt exciting and forbidden. Then, once we really got to know one another and decided it was serious, it kind of hit home. After all I'd been through I didn't think I could ask Samira to go through it as well."

"So he broke up with me!" Samira said, with only half a smile at her boyfriend. "I was totally miserable for a fortnight but I was determined not to call him."

"I gave in first," Enver confessed. "My flatmates told me they couldn't stand it any longer. They stole all my underwear and held it to ransom. No fresh boxers till I called her," he added ruefully.

"And you were still willing to see him in that condition?" David joked.

Samira giggled again, this time relaxed and at ease. She hugged Enver's arm.

"I think he smells nice," she admitted, looking at him sideways.

"Not too much Turkish delight, I hope," David commented, then wondered if that was a bit too relaxed. Still, it didn't seem to cause offence.

"So, what do we do now?" he asked. "I gather you're both determined."

"Yes," Samira said firmly. "I'd rather not run away. I told you; I love my family. I want my parents to accept Enver but if they don't…"

"I suppose your parents aren't a problem, Enver?" David asked.

Enver gave a snort of disgust.

"I'm not in touch with them but if I were they'd be delighted. Maybe they'd think it would bring me back into the fold. But honestly, I've not said anything against Islam or the Prophet – peace be upon him – to Samira, have I?"

"It's true," Samira confirmed. "We talk about things of course but whatever problems I've got with how things are going, they're my problems. Though since we've been together I have been watching the news a lot more and reading the web. It's just a total mess. How can we say to the world we're a religion of peace when there's just one war and bombing after another? And all the factions fighting each other…"

"I can see that," David agreed. "Though I'd say Christianity is a religion of peace, there are plenty of people claiming to be Christians who have slaughtered each other over the years as well. I think it's often just tribal, really. One group who identify themselves in one way – maybe religion, maybe nationality, maybe language, whatever – they feel oppressed or threatened or just want more land or power. Then it's old-fashioned war. Religion's just the peg they hang it on. If more people were like your parents, Samira, we'd not be having this conversation."

She nodded.

"But maybe my dad's not going to be so peace-loving when I introduce him to Enver."

"Maybe, maybe not. We'll have to see. Anyway, we're having them round for a meal quite soon. Your dad says he has a family matter he wants to ask my advice about. I suppose we can guess what that might be."

Samira frowned.

"I don't know how he can possibly know," she said. "We've been extremely discreet."

"Well, who knows how rumours start. In my experience mothers have some kind of killer instinct when it comes to boyfriends."

"Not sure I like the sound of that," Enver muttered.

"Well, anyway, we're going to meet them. I have an idea for how we might play things. See what you think."

By the time David got back to the flat, Gillian had packed a picnic and was ready to go.

"Wear something warm," she told him. "And you won't need the fedora."

They drove west out of the city towards the Forth Road Bridge.

"Here. Stick this behind your ear," she said, crossing the Dean Bridge. "Guaranteed to solve all nature of ills."

"Uh-oh. I think I can see where this is going. And I'm not a happy bunny."

"Well, follow nurse's instructions and you'll be fine."

David peeled a small plaster-sized patch out of its packet and reluctantly did as instructed.

"I'm doing it, but I'm not going to like it," he said.

"Now, if we start with that attitude, where will we be?" Gillian said in her best Morningside schoolmarm voice. "The last time you were sick, but this patch is claimed to be guaranteed to stop that – so what's to worry about?"

David didn't reply, though he had some ideas. He sat in gloomy silence awaiting his fate as they headed out Queensferry Road, past the Cramond Brig Restaurant, and eventually arrived in South Queensferry. Gillian deftly navigated off the main road, under the Bridge, and parked at the Port Edgar Marina. She climbed out, put on her sailing jacket, and got the picnic out of the boot before David had even undone his seatbelt. She swung his door open.

"Come on, scaredy cat. That patch behind your ear protects against seasickness, airsickness, homesickness, and the waltzers. You'll be fine."

He got out with the enthusiasm of a man heading for the firing squad. They walked down the pontoon past rows of dazzling white plastic gin palaces the size of Moby Dick till they stopped at a rather squat light blue and white 26-foot yacht.

"Welcome to *Maiden Voyage*, of which I own one-third," she announced. "I told you the girls and I were going to invest in something a bit bigger and more comfortable than we went out in last time and here it is. Westerly Griffon. 1980. Tried and tested. Sound as a bell. New engine, electrics, instruments, and sails. Every possible convenience: cooker, fresh water, toilet, beds – if you're so inclined. And standing headroom. Dining room table and wet locker. Perfect for the gentleman sailor and his companion. Or the lady sailor and her gentleman companion. Here, let me give you a hand."

Gillian had already hopped over the guard wire and turned to point David in the right direction.

"No. Don't try to step right over in one go. Put your foot on the rail on the pontoon side, then step the other leg right over. Hold onto the shroud."

"Whatever it is, calling it a 'shroud' sounds ominous," he commented as they made their way aft into the roomy cockpit.

"Well, the first thing to learn is that nothing on a boat is called what you think. Everything has a name but generally things don't mean the same as on shore. So the shrouds are simply the cables holding the mast up on either side. The front support is the forestay and the back support the aftstay. And there is no such thing as a piece of rope. There are shore lines and reefing lines, halyards, sheets, and strops. The mast is the mast but the horizontal beam that attaches at the back of it is called the boom, so called because that's what it sounds like if you don't get your head out of the way."

"It's giving me a headache already," David complained.

"This is the companionway," Gillian pressed on regardless, unlocking the main cabin. "These are the washboards" – she deftly pulled out the two wooden boards that slid into the bulkhead leading in – "this is the hatch, and this is how you go below. That's downstairs to you."

At that she hopped nimbly onto a square surface in the cabin but still at cockpit level, turned around, and stepped lightly down about a metre onto the cabin floor.

"Voila. Now you."

David's entrance could not have been called light, deft, or nimble, but he made it without injury.

"So, like I said, every mod con."

David surveyed the space. It was indeed both roomy for the size of the vessel and cosy at the same time. Berths upholstered in dark blue and gold were on either side; to his right was a cooker and sink, instruments of diverse kinds – none of which he understood – on the left. Shelves above and behind the berths were stuffed: cups, plates, plastic glasses, a few bottles of wine, and a medicine chest on the cooker side; maps, charts, pilot guides, and reference texts on the engine; instruments and electrics on the other side. A brass clock and barometer were fixed to the wooden bulkhead straight ahead along with what looked like a folded-up ironing board.

"Dining-room table," Gillian announced, pulling back a couple of catches and magically unfolding a table surface in beautiful dark hardwood.

"Wow. Impressive," David admitted, "if I had a clue what I was looking at."

"And for'ard – that means towards the bows – we have a toilet, called 'the head', a hanging locker, and two more berths."

David poked his nose "for'ard" as indicated and found a tiny toilet compartment, and further forward yet a double bunk in a V-shaped arrangement tapering towards the bows. Not an inch of space seemed wasted and everything just seemed to fit. While firmly tied to the pontoon, it did indeed seem to be a thing of beauty and a joy to behold.

"So which third is yours?" he asked. "I think I'm hoping it's the third that keeps us afloat."

"That and the wine," Gillian clarified. "You remember I told you I met Trish and Angie on a girls-only sailing course in the Med? Trish is from Port Seton and Angie's from Stirling. We keep in touch and get together for a pub lunch every few months. The idea of buying something together just seemed to materialize without anyone specifically proposing it. We got a tiny trailer sailer first of all, then last year this. Along with you it's my pride and joy. Sometimes we sail together but each of us can also book sole use for up to fifty days or eight weekends in the season. I booked for today. Now we're married it's time you learned to sail. You'll love it – promise. Anyway, just a minute till I turn the gas on then I'll make coffee and explain a bit more."

David thought he'd already had the entire explanation and probably more than he could absorb at one sitting but wisely kept quiet while Gillian jumped back up to cockpit level, fiddled with something, then back down again like a circus performer. The kettle was soon boiling and over two coffees – "only instant, sorry" – she went on to slowly and methodically work her way around the cabin, explaining instruments and safety features including lifting the engine lid, which was what they had been using as a step down, and fitting David out with waterproofs and a life jacket.

"Whose is the jacket?" he asked. "I don't suppose Trish or Angie fit into this."

"It's yours. Bought it to fit you last time I was down."

"Blimey. You do think of everything," David said. "It's going to be pretty difficult to tell you I don't like sailing after that."

"Impossible – and messy. We don't like blood on the deck. So you slip the life jacket on just like a waistcoat. Now this line goes from the back between your legs…"

"Careful…"

"You should be so lucky. Then we clip the waistband together and the crotch strap goes in here."

David thought the safest thing was to stand with his arms up and let her get on with it – whether it was needed, which he severely doubted – or not.

"And in the unlikely event of landing in water, what am I supposed to do to get it to work?"

"You've flown enough to know, surely. Pull the red toggle sharply downwards."

"And if the life jacket should fail to inflate?"

"Sorry, there's no mouthpiece. If the red toggle doesn't work you can cash in your chips. No toggle, no workey – so don't lose it, break it, cut it off, or swallow it. Clear?"

"As a bell," he said, pulling the jacket down and trying to make it feel comfortable. "I'll resist the temptation to eat it."

"Ok, so now you're kitted out, back upstairs and we'll talk about lines and sails."

If David had thought the below decks briefing was confusing, then this was in another league. Gillian had been right when she had said that everything has a name and none is what you think it should be.

"Don't bother trying to remember everything," Gillian said, as reassuringly as she could. "It'll all become clear in due course. I'll be doing everything complicated. I may just ask you to pull something now and again."

"I thought I'd pulled adequately already," David muttered darkly, but Gillian wasn't listening. She was already on top of the cabin roof, unzipping the sail cover and attaching a line of some sort to the top corner.

"Ok," she said, all businesslike. "I'll open the seacock, get the engine going, and the instruments on. You undo these fenders and stow them in this locker. Then drop the bow lines onto the pontoon and we'll be just about ready. I've looked at the forecast. Force 2–3, northerly. So we motor out and reach back and forth for a bit then run back in, followed by dinner at the Cramond Brig. The picnic is just for nibbling. Ok?"

In a way it felt a bit like a medical procedure. David had no idea what was going on but the staff seemed sufficiently relaxed and capable that he didn't really need to. In fact, asking too many questions and fussing was only going to delay things and get in the way. The important thing was to undo your shirt, roll your sleeve up, take off your shoes, and lie on the bed without complaining. He tried to do the marine equivalent and found it was ok. Gillian was being a complete model of unruffled competence. She poked things in, pulled them out, loosened, attached, wound up, released, hung up, and folded back as if she could do it in her sleep. The truth was that she did – quite often. The engine hardly even coughed before it was running like a sewing machine. A wooden panel attached to the side of the companionway was swung out with a depth sounder and chart plotter on. Another instrument claimed to show wind speed and direction and yet another one speed. David earnestly hoped they all stayed as low as possible. In fact, zero might be good.

Next she swung a long dark wood tiller down that David hadn't even noticed up to that point, dropped off the last lines, pulled the throttle lever back about thirty degrees, and suddenly they were backing out of the berth. The tiller was pushed across, they described a wide quarter circle till they were now pointing out into the river Forth, the throttle went forwards, and they were off. A bit of close manoeuvring out of the marina, past the breakwater, then suddenly they were free. The depth sounder quickly registered four metres, six, eight, ten. The wind was showing ten knots and they were making five. Remarkably, David was not yet throwing up, terrified, confessing his sins, or gripping anything with white knuckles.

"Nice, isn't it?" Gillian remarked as *Maiden Voyage* began bobbing lightly over the wavelets.

"Still reserving judgment but not yet as bad as I expected," David grudgingly conceded.

"Now my favourite bit," Gillian said. "Take this line and pull when I say."

She eased the throttle back slightly till they were only marginally moving forward, constantly glancing up to the top of the mast for some reason. Then when she was satisfied, she said "Now!" and David pulled. Magically, metres and metres of glistening white canvas appeared out of the sail cover snaking up the mast. It took only a few seconds for the larvae to shed its skin and the butterfly to emerge. Once the sail was up, Gillian stepped forward, took the line from David's hand, slipped a couple of loops over a metal drum, and started tightening with a lever. The leading edge of the sail grew taut. Next she grabbed the tiller again, pushed it over to the right, and the bow swung left.

"Now this one," she said, handing David another line, this time leading forward towards the bow.

Pulling this produced a second miracle. The front sail, which yet again David simply hadn't noticed, had been tightly wound around a tube running from the top of the mast to the point of the bows. Now it unrolled smoothly, forming a huge triangle with the line in his hand pulling the bottom corner. Once out Gillian took it with a free hand, draped it over another drum, and pulled in the slack.

"And finally," she announced, "push in that button, then turn the key to vertical." The engine came to a halt. And suddenly they were sailing. Unlike driving, where you have to constantly watch for buses, cyclists, and taxis, here there was just the wide-open water in front of them. Instead of traffic noise and the dinging of approaching trams or even the reassuring chug of the engine, now there was just wind and lapping water. David looked over the stern. The rudder was a blade slicing down into the water and their wake was bubbling and foaming behind them. The boat heeled slightly to the wind like a lover to gentle attention. The bows rose and fell gently as if eager to get ahead. The sail above David's head was a cloud taut to the breeze against a plane of blue above.

"Told you you'd like it," Gillian grinned.

"You did," David agreed, sighing and stretching out on the windward side next to Gillian, who was in the aft corner gently teasing the tiller with tiny adjustments. "I think I can see a fragment of why you like it."

"This has been my dream, d'you know?' she continued. "The two things I love the most. If I can call you a *thing*. Both together. Getting acquainted. So I might not have to implement plan B after all."

"Can I ask what that was?'

"I was going to seduce you in the cabin before we cast off to force a happy association then wake you up when we were in the middle of the Forth, then keep doing it till you admitted you liked sailing."

"Oh," David sounded disappointed. "Missed my chance. Have I told you how much I'm hating this?"

The rest of the afternoon unfolded exactly as Gillian had predicted. They tacked gently back and forth until David had got the hang of the various tasks required and was merrily singing "ready about", "lee-ho", and "standby to gybe" as if he actually knew what he was talking about. Gillian kept a steady hand on the tiller – they joked about that – and subtly took over whenever required.

Then it was over. The sky had clouded and the wind grown chilly. Gillian eased out the line connecting the end of the boom to the stern of the boat – "mainsheet", she explained – till the mainsail was stretched out almost at right angles and they coasted home with the wind behind them.

"I feel like a Viking," David announced. Gillian stifled a laugh.

"And what does a Viking feel like? Not ready for rape and pillage I hope?"

"No. I just feel like I've sailed over the North Sea in the teeth of a gale and I'm about to hit land and claim a corner of Scotland."

"So not like a sailor from the Spanish Armada?'

"That too. And Columbus. And Magellan. And Ellen MacArthur. Anything you like. Why didn't you tell me it was like this?"

"Because they've only just invented that seasickness patch behind your ear. But for that it would probably have been a different story."

"Well, three cheers for the drugs; that's all I can say."

Gillian guided them smoothly into the berth, tied up, made everything shipshape, and helped David off with his life jacket. Ten minutes later they were in the car heading back towards the city.

"Mummy? Can we do it again?" David joked.

"Only if you're good and eat all your greens. Speaking of which, we're booked for seven. We're a bit early. Glass of bubbly to celebrate your maiden voyage?"

It was late by the time they got home. David was in a dreamy haze – the result of sea air, the high of a fear faced and overcome, and a few glasses of rioja reserva. It had been a perfect day. The meeting with Mike the Missionary had been a bit strained but might prove useful. Samira and Enver were lovebirds and he was determined to help them if he could while keeping the family together, and the sailing had been a surprising delight.

The telephone answering machine light was blinking red as they came in. Gillian went to hang up her sailing jacket while David pressed play. It was hard to recognize the voice through the sobs.

"Mr Hidalgo. It's Samira. I don't know who else to call. Enver was attacked tonight. He's in casualty. Can you come?"

Chapter 5

Edinburgh Royal

Samira was huddled into a ball in a corner of the waiting room of the Edinburgh Royal Infirmary. The confident, bright, self-assured young woman of the morning before seemed to have taken a vacation and been replaced by a shivering ghost. Her eyes were red, her hair a mess, make-up running, and her face blotchy. When David and Gillian came through the double doors she immediately jumped up, then froze. Just behind them were her mother and father. The wheels could almost be seen turning as she adjusted to the new reality. Then she launched herself towards her mother, almost knocking her over, and clung on sobbing. Ayeesha held her daughter, smoothing her hair while Ali looked on.

"I'm sorry," she kept repeating through the sobs. "It's all my fault."

Ayeesha shushed and rocked her.

David's former neighbour stood apart, no longer the jovial grocer. Eventually Ayeesha managed to peel Samira off. It was obvious that she wanted to hug her father but wasn't sure how. They regarded each other warily for some seconds before Ali put his arms out and enfolded her. He whispered something in her ear and rubbed her back. Eventually they parted and everyone drifted towards the rows of hard orange plastic chairs.

"I'm sorry, Samira," David began. "I just thought your parents needed to be involved. Sorry for not asking your permission. I was hoping we might have introduced Enver a bit less dramatically."

Ali cast him a not entirely friendly glance.

72

Samira nodded, dabbing her eyes.

"Are you mad at me, Babu?" she asked.

Ali looked like a man who had just found a snake under the bed put there for a joke but managed to shake his head.

"Getting mad isn't going to help," he said quietly.

David guessed that getting mad was exactly what Ali thought was an entirely appropriate response but that gentler counsels had prevailed. He could imagine the conversation in the car.

"What happened?" Ali asked, just managing to keep his tone under control while Ayeesha looked nervously on.

Samira gathered herself and spoke in a whisper.

"Enver and I had been at the cinema. He was walking me home over the Meadows. Four men came at us. One of them grabbed me. The others set about Enver with clubs. They were going for his legs, body, and his head. I couldn't help him. I was screaming but nobody came. There was nothing I could do. I think I maybe managed to scratch the guy's face who was holding me but I couldn't help Enver. When he fell down they started kicking him. It was horrible. Then they just left. A white van pulled up and they jumped in. I was left with Enver on the ground. I didn't know if he was alive or not. I jumped in front of a taxi. I got them to phone the police and an ambulance. When we got here I phoned David."

"Why did you not phone *me*, Sami?" Ali asked pointedly.

When she didn't answer he tried another tack.

"Do you love this boy?"

"Yes, Babu. I do."

"And does he love you? Will he be good to you?"

"I think so, Babu. Yes."

"Well then, we have to get through this. You must know this isn't my first choice. I think I could have given you good advice if you'd asked me."

Ayeesha put her hand on Ali's arm as if to say that's enough – this can wait.

"But this is where we are," he continued. "And if you're going to be together we need to protect you. That's what families are for. Muslim, Christian, whatever. So we need to find out who did this and stop them."

"You're not mad at me?"

"I told you. It's not my choice but here we are. I hope you know we just want the best for you." Ali looked at Ayeesha, who finally managed half a smile.

"So can we meet the Christian boyfriend?"

Samira shook her head.

"I don't think so. The doctors allowed me in to see him but just for a minute or so. He's a bit of a mess."

Just then a doctor who looked about sixteen despite the white coat came up to them.

"Miss Khan?" he asked

"Yes, that's me," said Samira.

"My name's Ewan Ross. I'm the A&E house officer on tonight. Can you come with me?"

"This is my family and friends. Can they come?"

Dr Ross didn't look enthusiastic but nodded and led the way. They crowded into a tiny room with a desk and monitors.

"You are Mr Durak's girlfriend?"

"Fiancée," Samira corrected him, with a nervous glance at her dad.

Ali looked away.

"And your mum and dad?"

"Ali Khan, Doctor." Ali held out a hand.

"I'm Ayeesha."

Hands were shaken all round.

"Forgive the formalities," the doctor continued, "but you are...?" He raised his eyebrows in David's direction.

"Enver's pastor," he said. "This is my wife, Gillian."

"Ok then. Well, the good news is that we don't think there's any risk to life, but he's taken quite a beating – broken ribs, concussion, left knee's a bit of a mess. Gashes to the scalp. Broken nose, collarbone. Lots of bruising around the abdomen. Thankfully none of the ribs pierced a lung. Loss of blood. But believe me, it could have been a lot worse. So he's poorly but stable. You can see him through the glass but I think it would be best not to disturb him at least overnight. I'll be doing a report for the police in the morning. You're welcome to come back whenever you want. Anything more I can tell you?"

"Do you think he'll be able to identify who attacked him?" Ali asked.

"I've no idea. Both eyes are swollen and closed right now. Depends what he saw before that happened."

"They were wearing balaclavas," Samira put in.

"So I doubt it. But you never know. Police are going to come sometime tomorrow to try to get a statement. I think we have your phone number, Mr and Mrs Khan, don't we? Someone'll call you when we know when they're going to be here. Nothing much more I can tell you, I'm afraid. I'm on from 8 a.m. tomorrow morning so I guess I'll see you sometime during the day."

"Thank you very much," Ayeesha said as they got up. "We appreciate it."

"How are you feeling, Ayeesha?" Gillian asked as they went back out into the night. Ali, Samira, and David were walking ahead. Ali had his arm around his daughter.

"Shaky. I suppose that's to be expected. We were just heading for bed."

"David and I feel terrible that we knew something about your daughter that she didn't feel ready to tell you. She asked David to try to smooth things over. You know, try to explain a bit before you spoke to Samira herself or met Enver. I'm afraid this has made all of that a bit redundant. We weren't trying to deceive you – just find the right way to help Samira tell you. She was very nervous about it."

Ayeesha let out a long sigh.

"We're not mad – just disappointed I suppose. We've always

encouraged the kids to talk to us. Normally Samira was actually better at it than the boys. This is the first time I can think of she's ever kept anything back. Ali is disappointed she didn't trust us enough to tell us herself. I don't blame you at all. It's a difficult situation. I've had it from other members of the family. When someone says, 'I want to tell you something but don't tell my parents,' what are you supposed to do?"

"That's good of you to see it that way. But I still feel terrible."

"Well don't. Why don't you come back for a coffee if it's not too late? I think Ali would like to talk to David as well."

So they did. It was past midnight by the time all five of them got back to Bruntsfield and climbed the stairs above the A&A MiniMart. It was agreed without any real discussion that Samira would spend the night at home. Ayeesha made her a cup of hot chocolate and saw her to bed. Then she made decaf coffee for the remaining four. For some minutes they sat in silence, simply taking in the night's events. Finally Ali spoke up.

"David, you're a Christian pastor," he began. "You know that has never come between us. I'm sorry Samira put you in a difficult position. But since we're here I need to ask you a few things to get this straight in my head."

"Go ahead."

"Ok, so can I ask you…" And thereafter he hardly stopped for what felt like hours. What about Christian attitudes to Islam? How would a mixed marriage work? Would Samira have to convert?

David explained that they had already begun this conversation and that Samira would have to make her own choices, but at this stage he was encouraging her to think very carefully about what she wanted and why. Was it just a matter of identity or did she really want to know what made someone a Christian inwardly?

"That sounds remarkably liberal for a Christian pastor," Ali mused. "I appreciate that."

In turn Ali also explained how Islam viewed conversion. It wasn't very positive.

"So I'm afraid so-called 'honour' attacks do take place. And sometimes they end up being killings. Mostly in Pakistan but sometimes here in the UK as well. It's a part of my culture I'm not exactly proud of but you have to understand where people are coming from. I don't condone it and I don't excuse it, but traditional Muslims – what the papers call 'hardliners'…" Ali gave a grim smile, "all they've ever known is the Koran and Mohammed – peace be upon him. Some of them feel Islam is under attack from every side. And I don't mean just politically or militarily. It's maybe even more so in terms of culture and customs. Attitudes to sexuality, marriage, equality, media – anything you like. You know we're not like that but some people feel the only way to maintain our customs is to turn Islam into an armed camp and repel outsiders. As I think we've seen tonight."

"So do you think this was an honour attack?" Gillian asked.

Ayeesha nodded.

"It all fits," she said. "A gang appears out of nowhere. There's no warning. They use clubs not firearms. Samira isn't touched. Nothing was taken. The aim wasn't to kill but to give a serious warning. I love my daughter, Gillian, and I want to help her do what she wants to do. But she's putting herself in harm's way for this boy. I don't think there are any guarantees that they'll be happy or they'll be safe. Can you see our dilemma?"

Gillian nodded.

"I'm sure I'd feel exactly the same if it were me," she said.

It was past three by the time they left, and although everyone was exhausted there seemed to be a feeling that the air had been cleared. Gillian and Ayeesha hugged and David and Ali shook hands.

"That is a remarkable man," David commented as they walked to the car. "He has every reason to be bitter and angry at me, at Christianity in general, at his daughter, and at the boyfriend, but he seems determined to simply understand as best he can and work with it. Amazing. I very much doubt if there'd be such a positive attitude in many Christian homes if the boot were on the other foot."

Gillian nodded in the darkness, holding onto his arm.

"They're great. I must say I don't really think of them as Muslim and us as Christian. We're just people. Friends. We all have to do what we have to do. However, I don't envy what they're going through."

"Agreed. But you're a remarkable woman too, you know."

"I doubt that," Gillian laughed.

"No. It's true. You've had to shift your worldview quite a bit as well. And you've done it with grace and style. No tantrums, no sulks. You've taken your time and got on with it. That isn't very common either."

She said nothing but held his arm more tightly.

"Not to mention brilliant academic, expert navigator, all-round smooth operator."

"Well I think you managed tonight's choppy waters pretty well. Ali seemed a happier man when we left."

"I hope so. Anyway, there's the car. Take me home, Dr Lockhart, and put me to bed."

"That I can manage," she said, opened the door, and slid in.

David made it through Sunday morning on autopilot, hoping nobody noticed, choosing not to broadcast the situation "just for prayer". His hopes were soon dashed.

"Trouble at mill?" Mrs MacInnes asked *sotto voce* with one raised eyebrow as he came for his cup of tea afterwards.

"How did you guess?" David sat down heavily. "Enver's in hospital. Did you know he was going out with a Muslim girl? He was set on in the park last night. What's left of him is in the Edinburgh Royal. Not life-threatening, we're told, but they seem to have done a good job. It looks like what they call an 'honour attack'. Supposedly defending the honour of a Muslim girl against an unbeliever."

"Hmm. Not very honourable if you ask me," Mrs MacInnes commented dryly, pouring another cup.

"Anyway, it's all getting a bit complicated. The girl's mum and dad are actually friends of ours. Do you remember at the wedding – Ayeesha, who made the cake? And the girl, Samira, came to me for advice before telling her dad. So I think relations are a bit strained right now."

"I can imagine. But surely they can't think it's your fault."

"No, but I think a father feels he should know before people outside the family. I can understand that. I'm involved in any case because of Enver. We're going back to the hospital this afternoon."

"Tender emotions then as well as bumps and bruises."

David had to smile.

"Mrs MacInnes," he said, "you have a way of putting your finger on things."

She drew herself up to full height, which didn't actually make much difference.

"Morningside isn't Madrid, but it's not as sheltered as you might think. Hope all goes well. I'll send an email around my praying ladies and ask them to remember Enver. And the pastor…"

David and Gillian and Ali and Ayeesha met in the waiting room of the Edinburgh Royal Infirmary that afternoon. Samira was already there. She got up and kissed her mum and dad.

"How is he?" Ayeesha asked.

"Better. He's speaking and the police took a statement this morning. But the gang were all wearing balaclavas so I don't think that'll help. The guy holding me was smelling of garlic but that probably doesn't narrow it down much. How are you, Babu?"

"I'll survive," Ali commented dryly. "Coming to terms with it. I want to meet this guy and make sure he'll be good to my daughter – or I'll beat him up some more."

Samira managed a weak smile.

"I think they're doing something with Enver just now so I had to come out. We can try again later. Do you want a coffee? I've found out where the café is."

"Great," David nodded. "That means we're safe from the coffee machine at least."

David queued while Gillian sat with the Khans. The mood seemed to have lightened considerably since the previous evening. Samira was nearer her old self and Ali was manfully trying to be positive. Ayeesha sat with her arm around her daughter and although not saying much seemed to be the silent orchestrator of proceedings.

"Babu, there's something else I need to tell you," Samira began once the coffee had arrived, "since we're getting everything out in the open."

Ali rolled his eyes then studied the ceiling.

"What now?"

"We can leave if it's something personal," Gillian immediately put in.

"No, it's ok," Samira countered. "It might be good if you're here."

David wasn't sure what that meant but hoped it wasn't to act as referee.

"So tell me Sami. What is it this time?"

She paused, then spoke carefully. "It's not about me."

"That's a relief."

"It's the boys."

"What about them?"

"When were they last in contact?"

"I'm not sure."

"Karim sent a card for my birthday," Ayeesha offered. "That was three weeks ago. Rasheed… I'm not sure."

"Did you know they've both given up their jobs?" Samira asked quietly.

Ali looked shocked.

"No! How do you know this?" Then to Ayeesha, "Did you know this?"

She shook her head but said nothing as if she had an inkling of something.

"About a fortnight ago; I saw it on Facebook. They were asking if anyone knew where Rasheed was. Seems he just didn't go in to work one day and nobody's heard from him since."

"And Karim?" Ali continued like a man who has just found out that one bank account had been cleaned out by fraudsters and was asking about the other.

"The same. Left the same day. Rasheed hasn't replied to anything I've sent him but Karim sent a message the first day he didn't go in."

"So what did he say?"

"Just something like 'Off on a bit of a trip. Don't worry about me, big sister.'"

Ali looked around in bewilderment.

"Did you know anything of this?" he demanded of Ayeesha.

"I knew something was going on – mother's instinct," she said, "but no; I didn't know they'd both left. To be honest I've been worried about Rasheed for a while. Ever since that preacher got thrown out of the mosque."

"And does nobody think a father should be told these things?" Ali demanded again, looking around. "It seems I'm the last one to find out about everything." The hostile look took in David and Gillian as well.

"I think we should leave you for a bit," David said, getting up. "This is family business."

"No. Can you stay?" Samira asked quickly. "There's something else you can maybe help with."

He shrugged and sat down again. Gillian had reached across and was gripping Ayeesha's hand. Right now she seemed the one more in trouble.

"So what's this 'more'?" Ali demanded, on the very verge of blowing up.

"Well. It is connected with the guy that calls himself 'the Prophet'. Rasheed tried to get me interested before he stopped talking to me. I think they've gone abroad."

"IS?" Ali asked, as if every new revelation was more and more unbelievable. "Are they in Syria?"

"No, not IS, I don't think. But the Prophet only speaks to his followers. There's some kind of secure website. You have to answer all sorts of questions to get in. You know, to prove your devotion or something. Somebody on my course was interested for a bit, then managed to get himself out."

"So if it's not Syria, where is it? Yemen? Iraq? Egypt?"

"No. None of these. I think it's Spain."

Chapter 6

Pensión El Moro

"I can't believe what you're telling me, Rasheed." Karim was sitting on the bed of their tiny shared room looking at his older brother in disbelief. The early morning sun slanted in through the window. They had just finished breakfast and gone upstairs to collect their things for the day. Older Brother was going to his Spanish class in the centre of town and Younger Brother had a language exchange with the girl from reception, whom he now knew to be Beatriz – Bea for short.

"It's true, Little Brother," Rasheed confirmed. "There isn't any doubt."

"We always knew Samira wasn't very religious, but a non-Muslim boyfriend? Are you sure?"

"Of course I'm sure. I've been making inquiries." The first thing Rasheed had done when they had gone upstairs was to check his laptop as if he were expecting a message. He had clicked his email client, gone straight to the first message, clicked it open, scanned down, and grunted his satisfaction before closing the lid. Karim had been pulling out some books from under the bed when he'd told him to sit down, that there was some news.

"So do we know anything about the guy? Are you sure he's not Muslim?" Karim asked in disbelief.

"He's Christian, and not just in name only. He goes to church. He's a leader of a student group. He takes it all very seriously."

"Wow." Karim put his books down and let his shoulders drop. "Incredible. I'd never have expected it."

"Do you remember David Hidalgo, the minister that used to live upstairs from the shop?"

"Yeah. Sure. He was a nice guy."

"Well, he's the boyfriend's minister. Dad's still quite friendly with him, even though I told him it wasn't appropriate."

"Do you know anything more about the boyfriend? Is there any way to discourage her?" Karim pressed.

"Yes to both. It's the worst it can be. He's Turkish and ex-Muslim. So he's not only an unbeliever but apostate too. But don't worry about discouraging them. That's already been taken care of."

"What are you saying?" Karim said slowly, astonishment giving way to concern. "I hope you're not going to say something's happened to Samira!"

"Samira, no. Just shaken up a bit, enough to make her think twice. But the boyfriend's been taken care of quite effectively I hear. The Prophet told me it had to be done and put me in touch with good people who would do it. Just enough – no more. He'll get the message."

Karim looked aghast. "I can't believe it," he blurted out.

"I know," Rasheed agreed, "our own sister. You read about these things but you never expect it to happen to you. She's brought shame on the whole family."

"That's not what I mean," Karim explained, shaking his head. "I can't believe that you've been involved in hiring a bunch of thugs to attack your own sister, whoever her boyfriend is. This is too much, Rasheed. Where's it going to end? If she insists on still seeing him, will you have him murdered? And if they manage to get married, will you kill them both? You're insane! You've lost the plot. Following the Prophet to try and restore Islam – that's one thing. Nobody could disagree with that. But your own family? And what if *I* get a Christian girlfriend? Would you do the same to me? This is it, Rasheed; I've had enough. You want to destroy the enemies of Islam – fine. But when it comes to destroying your own family you can do it on your own. I'm out. The first flight back and you're on your own."

Rasheed sat opposite on his own bed, showing no reaction, as if he knew the player opposite had a king and would play it but was keeping the ace in his own hand secret.

"Put out your arm, Karim; I want to show you something," he finally said.

"What for? No more games."

"No, this is the last thing. If you want to fly home after this then you can. I won't object. I won't try to stop you."

Karim let out a long sigh, as if this was stupid and pointless but if it got him out of the situation without any more of a fight then it might be worth it. He stretched out his arm.

"Now roll your sleeve up," Rasheed ordered. Karim did it. "Take your watch off." The watch was dropped back onto the bed and the instant Karim's face was turned, his older brother grabbed something out of an open drawer and snapped a black segmented band much like a chunky watch strap around Karim's wrist. The younger brother was dumbfounded for a second and kept his arm outstretched.

"What's this?" he asked. "I don't want this."

"Too late, Little Brother; you've got it," Rasheed replied. "I didn't want to do this but you've left me no choice. The Prophet saw that this might happen. I told him no, that you were faithful, but he doubted you. And he was right."

"What is it?" Karim repeated, turning his inner wrist uppermost and fiddling with the catch.

"I wouldn't do that if I were you, Little Brother," Rasheed said slowly and clearly.

"Why not?"

"Because if you do, the least that'll happen is that it'll blow your hand off. Or you might blow us both up. Let me explain. This is a small – very small – explosive device. You know the collars that give your dog a little shock if you press the remote? Well, this is the human equivalent. To make people come to heel. There's a special key needed to unlock it. Here it is around my neck. Without the key any tampering just sets it off."

"You…" Karim didn't finish the sentence. "I hate you, Rasheed," he said. "You know, I think I've always hated you. There was always something sick about you, Rasheed. Now you've proved it. You've left true Islam and forced me to as well. They say the Prophet is apostate and now so are we – and much more than just having a Christian partner. Well, it won't wash. I'll take the risk. I'm flying home the first flight I can book. I'll find somebody to get this off. And I'll tell them about you, Rasheed – what you're planning. You and the crazy Prophet."

Rasheed shook his head, almost sadly. "I'm afraid I can't let you do that, you know, Karim. You are the weakest link. You always have been. But I was willing to take you along with me. You could have gone down in Muslim history as one of the two brothers who changed everything, but you don't have the stomach for it – nor the brains, if I might say so. That device on your wrist reeks of Semtex – amazing what you can buy on the dark web. It'll set every alarm bell ringing from Madrid to Heathrow. And every counterterrorism officer for miles will be down on you like a ton of bricks. Do you think they'll believe your story? As far as they're concerned you'll be a suicide bomber trying to board a plane. They'll lock you up and throw away the key. So whether or not you help me, you won't be going back to Edinburgh. And you won't be talking to the police either if that's what you're thinking. If you're not where you should be every moment of the day I'll know. There's a GPS tracker built in as well – a little modification of my own. And I can set it off remotely just from my mobile. So do what you should and go where you should or at least lose your hand. Just like a common thief. And of course you might bleed to death as well. You choose. I told you I wouldn't argue with you if you wanted to leave and I won't. It's your decision."

Then something happened that neither of them had expected. Karim launched himself from the bed, his hands around Rasheed's throat. They fell back together onto the narrow space under the window. Karim was shouting, cursing, swearing, spitting, while Rasheed tore at his hands to get some air.

"Be careful, you idiot!" he was shouting. "You'll set it off and kill us both!"

Karim had landed on top, which gave him an advantage, but Rasheed was bigger and stronger. It wasn't clear which way it was going when Bea's father came in to see what the noise was about. He'd always found a bucket of water effective against cats and was willing to try it on Brits. Then he reached down and hauled Karim up first. Rasheed was coughing and choking and rubbing his neck.

"*Los dos – ¡fuera!*" the owner of the Pensión El Moro said in no uncertain terms. They didn't need to understand Spanish to get the gist. "*Diez minutos,*" he added to make it clear that they didn't have all day. Without a glance at each other they slowly recovered and began packing. Halfway through, Bea came in, not at all happy.

"I ask my father to let you stay. He says ok," she informed them flatly, avoiding Karim's eye. "But it happens another time you go – last chance." She slammed the door.

Karim sat on his bed panting and regarding Rasheed with cold fury.

"You are no longer my brother," he said quietly. "I will tell our father what you have done, sooner or later. He will understand. I've always hated you calling me 'little brother' all the time. Now you aren't my brother any more. You are no longer Muslim and no longer a part of our family. I don't know you and I'll do what I can to stop you. Tell that to the Prophet. Now I've got an appointment with a Christian girl."

Ali and Ayeesha closed the shop the following morning, although Monday was usually a good day as people stocked up after the weekend. Neither of them had the heart for it. Ali pottered about tidying this and moving that. Ayeesha took the chance to sort some of her cake recipes on the computer. She was thinking about a book and wanted to get things into shape before either approaching a publisher or doing it herself online. The atmosphere wasn't hostile but they both just had too much to process to be ready to talk.

"A cup of tea, my love?" Ayeesha asked around eleven.

"Thank you, my sweet. That would be perfect."

They sat down on the sofa close together, touching from shoulder to hip. Ayeesha poured the tea and held up a plate of yellow marzipan fancies. Ali took one, savoured it, and took a sip of tea.

"Where do you think we went wrong?" he said at length.

"Nowhere," Ayeesha replied firmly. "You do your best, then it's up to them. You remember my parents didn't want us to marry?"

"That was different. At least you were Muslim."

"But you weren't Muslim enough for them," she countered. "You hadn't studied the Koran enough, you weren't in the mosque enough, you didn't revere the Prophet – I mean the real Prophet, peace be upon him – enough."

"But that still isn't a *Christian*," Ali insisted. "I'm not trying to blame either of us. I'm just trying to make sense of it. And the boys. Who would have thought it? The only thing in its favour is that Spain might not be as dangerous as Syria. But our boys? Terrorists? It's unbelievable."

They sat in silence, sipping and nibbling. Then the phone rang. Ayeesha went to answer it. Ali could hear her talking in the other room. She came back in.

"David and Gillian have invited us for lunch. Do you want to go?"

Ali sighed and shook his head.

"I haven't the energy," he said.

"I think they'll cheer you up," she replied brightly. "Let's."

"Ok, my sweet. Whatever you think. I'm out of ideas."

They met in a restaurant owned by a family friend of the Khans. David insisted it was their treat but the management gave a generous family and friends discount. Conversation was light and inconsequential on the subject of the reliably non-controversial Scottish standby – the weather. Apparently it had been quite a good August and the long-range forecast was for an Indian summer.

"Don't thank me," Ali remarked.

David apologized yet again and Ali told him to forget it. Gillian tried to get Ayeesha onto the subject of fashion but it didn't lead anywhere. Finally David tried as diplomatically as possible to address the elephant in the room.

"I went in to see Enver this morning," he started. "Apparently Samira hasn't left his side. It looks like he might be over the worst."

"I'm glad to hear that," Ali said, though whether he was or wasn't couldn't really be guessed. Then finally he seemed to take a decision and roused himself.

"David. My friend. I think I owe you an apology," he said.

"How come?"

"Firstly because I was mad at you for knowing something I should have known and didn't. It wasn't your fault Samira came to you. I'm glad she didn't go to someone else. I know you would advise her well even though you're not family." David inclined his head to accept Ali's sentiment.

"And another thing. I feel I should apologize on behalf of the Muslim community for what happened to a young Christian man who is part of your congregation. He isn't to blame for going out with my daughter. In fact, I think it's very understandable. She is a lovely girl. I'm not biased of course. And he's certainly not to blame for being attacked by Muslim thugs. I suppose they are Muslim and they're certainly thugs. I've been so fixed on Samira and now Rasheed and Karim that I haven't been thinking about Enver. He's the one in hospital, not any member of my family. So I apologize."

"You've no need to apologize. Really," Gillian broke in, "I think your reaction has been entirely normal. It's not something you expected or wanted. Honestly, we were going to have you over and somehow explain what Samira told David and try to put it in a way you'd understand."

"We appreciate that," said Ayeesha. "And we're not going to let this come between us, ok?"

"Agreed."

Ali was finishing off a very saucy Balti lamb, shoving a torn-off corner of naan around the rim so as not to leave a trace of gravy in the dish.

"What did the Beatles say about yesterday?" he asked. "Troubles out of sight or something like that?" Gillian resisted the temptation to correct the quotation. "Now everything is upside down. I thought we had a fairly harmonious family. Now look at it!"

"I don't think you should blame yourselves," David put in. "I end up spending quite a lot of time with parents asking the very same questions. I don't think it makes much difference if you're Muslim or Christian. Parents try to do the right thing and it doesn't always work out the way you want. It's just life. Much more important in my experience is how you react to it, how you cope. You can learn something from the experience or not. You know, I've been through some stuff I wouldn't wish on anyone. But I certainly learned a lot about myself in the process. And maybe about life as well."

A waiter came, nodded to Ali, and began to gather things up. It felt like no one was quite ready to leave yet so they opted for simple desserts and coffee and sat back a bit to let it all settle.

"Well there's one thing I'd certainly like to learn," Ali declared. "Where my boys are and what they're up to. And why Spain, for goodness' sake? It's hardly the front line of the battle for Islam!"

"Maybe I can help you a bit there," David suggested, and proceeded to explain about the Córdoba Caliphate and the movement – small and disorganized to date – to restore Muslim influence in Andalucía, known in its heyday as "Al-Andalus".

"According to a police friend of mine – I think you met Stuart McIntosh at a party at my place – the movement is gathering force and young men are being recruited to go to Spain and await orders."

"That's incredible," Ayeesha said. "I mean, incredible that our boys should end up involved. I knew they were keen on the guy they called the Prophet but I never thought it would come to this. Especially for Karim. Rasheed was always a bit inclined to go overboard on things. Whatever he was interested in he always gave it 100 per cent. We always thought that was a good thing; he loved anything connected with computers and did really well at university. Then got a good job. But to throw it all up for some ridiculous idea that'll only result in Muslims being even more hated in Europe..." She gave a heavy sigh. "You can't help but wonder if they never really understood what makes us Scottish *and* Muslim."

Desserts came and went then the coffee arrived. No one had any answer to Ayeesha's question. Finally Ali took up the theme again.

"I suppose the first thing is to try to find out where they are, though I've no idea how we go about it."

David took a sip of his coffee, looking thoughtful.

"I wonder if there's a stage before that, Ali," he said carefully. "You want to find out where they are and what they're involved in, of course. And the idea must be to stop them before they do something stupid. But I wonder if there's another question you need to ask first?'

"What?" Ali asked, unsure what David could be thinking of.

"Well, I wonder if before you find out where they are, maybe you need to find out *who* they are."

Ali frowned. "What do you mean? I know who my boys are. I raised them, didn't I?"

"Of course you did," David began, but Ayeesha interrupted him.

"I think I know what you mean," she said. "I think it's obvious that somehow we've lost touch with them. They're not the boys you played football with on Bruntsfield Links, Ali. They've had their own lives for years now – their own friends, their own interests. We see them once in a while or when they need money – birthdays, holidays. But I, at least, don't think I really know what makes them tick, especially Rasheed. Karim was always the more open. I am disappointed that he's disappeared but his older brother has always had a strong influence on him. I bet it's been Rasheed at the back of it and Karim just went along with him. I think David's right. I'm not saying we shouldn't try to find out where they are, but for any of it to make sense – if we're to stand any chance of getting them back – then we need to find out why they've gone off the rails, like David says."

Ali sat even further back in his chair and thought. He was having a difficult week.

"And how do we do that, can I ask?"

"How about starting at their work?" Gillian suggested. "You said Rasheed loved computers and he had a great job. So maybe his boss or his colleagues know most about him. You could at least ask if there was any hint of things going wrong. They might have some other names of friends who could tell us more."

Ali might have taken his time to follow the idea, but once he got it he made up his mind very quickly. "Ok," he said. "Tomorrow first thing I'm going to be on the phone to Centaur Systems. I think his boss was called Justin. Would you be willing to come along, my friend? You seem to know what you're talking about."

David immediately looked to Gillian. The pact they'd had about a quiet life was still pretty hot off the press. No international crime. No helping police with their inquiries, and absolutely no shootouts – anywhere. But there didn't seem to be a prohibition on helping a friend. She nodded.

"Ok," he said. "My main concern has to be Enver. But getting to the bottom of this can only help him be safer too, I suppose."

"You're not suggesting our boys had anything to do with the attack in the park, are you?" Ali asked, aghast.

"No, absolutely not. I'm just saying that anything that helps us stop one terrorist incident – if that's what's on the cards – that has to be good for everybody. Muslims and Christians in general."

"That's a relief. I'm glad nobody thinks they would go that far against their own family. I'll call in the morning and let you know. Ravi! Can we have the bill please!"

Chapter 7

Rincón de Miguel

Karim spent the morning walking aimlessly around town. The wonders of Al-Andalus no longer held any charm. As usual the city was full of an even mix of tourists and those who made their living off them: Americans, Japanese, and Germans on the one hand; and shopkeepers, delivery truck drivers, waiters, and waitresses on the other. He also took in tour guides with coloured flags for their gaggle of tourists to follow, a few old men sitting chewing the fat, and kids with their rucksacks or armfuls of books heading to or from class. It all looked so peaceful and tranquil, everybody apparently getting on with each other. And they all had one thing in common: they didn't have an explosive wristband on. He could feel it tight on his left wrist. Every moment he tried to think about something else, he'd bump it against his leg or catch it on the flap of a pocket and suddenly remember that if it bumped too hard maybe the latch would detect the force and think it was an attempt at tampering and blow his arm off just to be on the safe side.

But who could he tell? As far as he knew Rasheed hadn't committed any actual crime yet – at least not in Spain. So what would he say to a policeman? And what if he couldn't explain himself properly, which was almost guaranteed? And what if the policeman thought he needed help to pull a jammed Fitbit off his wrist, gave it a yank, and blew them both up? Even if he got his story entirely clear from scraps of phrases in his phrase book, if he went to the police there was always a chance his whereabouts were being tracked and Rasheed would panic and press the button anyway. And what would there be left to trace one dead Muslim suicide bomber and a blackened police station to a young programmer from Scotland on holiday in Spain?

Obviously, actually trying to leave Córdoba was out of the question. His clever older brother seemed to have every angle covered. He quickly corrected himself – the crazy fanatic who used to be his older brother. Rasheed had also confiscated and hidden his mobile so he couldn't easily send a message home, and probably his email account was hacked so that even if he used an internet café it would be intercepted and reveal all. Even if he could send a message home, who would he send it to? He desperately did not want his parents to know what was going on. Samira wasn't likely to be sympathetic, given what she had just been through. Although he'd had nothing to do with the attack, who would believe him? Frankly, at this point he didn't care whether his sister went out with the Grand Mufti, the Chief Rabbi, or Gary Lineker. She was his sister and he had let her down. And his parents. Maybe he should just be done with it, pull the wretched thing off himself, and suffer the consequences. In fact, maybe that wasn't a bad idea. Except he'd wait till he could get as close to Rasheed as possible. He doubted if that would count as martyrdom, so no celestial virgins for them. And he certainly deserved to go to hell for what he'd let himself be talked into.

Looking back it seemed ludicrous that Karim had ever been convinced. But Rasheed was clever and had a way with words and ideas he knew he lacked. At first it had all seemed so exciting, so revolutionary – the chance to hit back against all the prejudice and discrimination, though, to be fair, he couldn't remember ever being discriminated against or suffering prejudice in Edinburgh. He had Muslim friends and Scottish friends (though he considered himself as Scottish as them), and religion just wasn't talked about. Nobody was interested. You do your thing, I'll do mine. Who cares? So the fate of the Palestinians was a tragedy, so America and the West had invaded Muslim lands and manipulated leaders for generations. True, but what was that to do with him? Like his dad was always saying, you don't accept an offer of hospitality, enjoy a nice dinner, then crap on the carpet. He had to admit there was something in that.

Scotland was a free society, more or less. Keep the law and go about your business. His business had been selling carpets and it had been going ok. He'd been given an entire sector of the business to himself – contract carpeting for offices – and it had been going really well. They said he had a talent for getting along with people, gaining their trust then gaining their business. For one so young they seemed to think it was unusual. Now all of that was blown to kingdom come. How could he ever go back and win anyone's confidence, including his own family's?

The only redeeming feature was that he'd finally seen Rasheed as he was – or at least as he had become in the last few years. A singleminded, dyed-in-the-wool, true blue, wide-eyed fanatic who seemed to have lost the most basic sense of right and wrong. Or perhaps he'd come to the conclusion that Allah was on his side, commanding these actions, so what did normal rights and wrongs mean any more? If God is on your side, who cares what the world thinks – who cares who gets hurt? It's just a matter of details in the big picture. He was glad he had come to his senses at last. But then the question was whether it was too late to prevent a tragedy. He knew the "Prophet" wanted them to blow up the cathedral in the middle of the Mezquita, but he had no idea how it was supposed to happen. How on earth were they supposed to get enough explosive into one of the most visited sites in Europe without anyone noticing – and then get out alive?

Then an even worse thought dawned: maybe they weren't even supposed to get out alive. Maybe this was meant to be a suicide bombing from the very beginning. So all Rasheed's talk about being Emir and First Minister was total hogwash from first to last. How could he have been so stupid? Rasheed was so single-minded when he got an idea into his head that nothing would deflect him. Funny how one man's dedicated disciple is another man's ruthless fanatic. And in the space of a couple of hours Rasheed had jumped from category one to category two in Karim's mind. If the plan did succeed, he knew that hundreds of thousands – maybe even millions

– would regard the attack as a holy act of jihad to be celebrated. Rasheed's name would be revered and taught in the radical madrasas. Perhaps that holy act might even be sufficient to cover up for the fact that they weren't even orthodox Muslims any more. So maybe it all came down to this. Somehow or other Karim had to stop what Rasheed and his stupid Prophet were planning – if possible, without losing his hand, his arm, or his nerve. He wasn't ready to die just yet. He had an appointment with a nice girl who seemed friendly and might get more so. At least for the time being, life went on.

Bea did not seem at all friendly when Karim presented himself back at reception at the appointed hour.

"You're late," she said and flicked the hair out of her eyes.

He had been pretty sure he was on time but had neither a watch nor a mobile so couldn't be certain. He decided not to argue.

"Sorry. I got lost in town."

"*Vale*. Then we go to a bar I know. We speak there. Is more quiet and I'm not on duty again till afternoon."

They walked across the street to what was clearly Bea's local bar, sat down on the *terraza*, and ordered. She asked for a *caña* – apparently a small beer – and he ordered a Coke.

"You know you're only still here because I spoke to my father," she said. "I offered to – I looked it up – to 'vouch' for you. Is correct?" Karim nodded. "To guarantee you. So any more problem and my ass is out the window as well. I looked that up too. It works?"

Karim grinned. She seemed to be making a joke of it, which he appreciated.

"Yes, it works. Very good."

"So now I am your boss. What happened?"

Karim shrugged. It didn't seem a very good way to start a friendship by lying but he could hardly tell the truth and say sorry for the upset – *we're actually a couple of terrorists here to blow up your town's most famous monument, which a few thousand jobs depend on. Just a simple misunderstanding on how to go about it. It won't happen again.*

"My older brother…" he said, "he says things that get me upset sometimes. Don't worry about it. It's nothing."

"It don't look like nothing," she remarked, taking a sip of the frothy top of the beer that had just been delivered.

"So what does *rincón* mean?" Karim asked, to change the subject. "Miguel is the owner, right?"

"*Sí.* Miguel is my uncle. *Rincón* means a corner inside a building. *Esquina* is a corner outside."

"Hey. That's really useful," Karim said. "English only has 'corner'. In Scots I could say *neuk* but that's old-fashioned now. Great. Anyway, your English is really good. My Spanish is about zero."

"No, my English is *fatal*," Bea insisted. "I am in the official school of languages four years now and I still am B1. I failed B2 again last year. So this year I have to pass. There are twenty-three of us so you never have the chance to speak. They put you full of *la gramática* but what good is that if you can't tell what you want?"

"I see," Karim agreed. "Well, I'll help if I can. What do you want to do?"

"If you have time I need speaking. And I can help with your Spanish. How about half hour each?"

"Sounds great. You want to start with English?"

"*Vale,*" she said and pulled a large format textbook out of her bag. "I have to prepare a talk on the new technologies. Can you listen and correct me?"

Sitting in a bar, sipping a cold drink, basking in the sunshine, and listening to Bea talk about mobiles and tablets and social media was the sort of simple pleasure Karim hadn't had for a long time it seemed. It took his mind off other things. She spoke well enough and he understood everything she was trying to say but she was hesitant at times, searching for the right word. Sometimes she would lean forward to look at her notes, letting her hair fall around her face. She was wearing quite a loose T-shirt – not the Monroe one this time – and Karim tried not to look. And certainly not to be caught looking.

He was beginning to relax but he guessed he was still on probation, with Bea as well as with her father. Best not to put a foot wrong. He shifted his chair so he wasn't sitting directly in the line of fire.

This was so... he searched for the right word but only found "nice". He remembered Miss Lambert at school always told them when they put "nice" to think of a better word. But he couldn't think of anything better. It was, quite simply, "nice". Not spectacular, not enchanted, not wonderful but also not terrible. It was just "nice". Bea also seemed really nice, but that was a different nice. She seemed simply like a decent human being trying to better herself and willing to help him too in the process. Who Rasheed was trying to help he couldn't entirely say. Supposing he succeeded, what difference would that make to anyone's political rights in the Middle East? But it probably would make a difference to the tourists and guides and staff crushed under falling masonry or with bits of their bodies blown off. Karim shook himself and forced his attention back to this really nice girl talking in a nice way about nice things.

"Can I say the internet is 'taking over' the world? Is correct?"

"It certainly is. And it's true."

"Phrasal verbs just kill me."

"Sorry, what's a phrasal verb?"

"You don't know? It's one of the hardest parts of English!"

"No; I wasn't that good at school."

"But native speakers use them all the time," she insisted, unconvinced. "You know, 'get up', 'get over', 'take apart', 'take over', 'sit up', 'blow up'. They're phrasal because you have a main verb and a particle. Makes a phrase. But it just means one thing. So if you know 'blow' and 'up' it still doesn't help. 'Blow up' is different from 'blow'...", she gestured by blowing a puff of air, "... and 'up'." She tipped her head back and blew upwards. "See?"

"Yes, I do see. I've never thought about it." He found himself hoping it was just a coincidence that she happened to choose "blow up" as an example. Surely she couldn't know why he and his brother were really here. But she seemed completely focused on the problem and not referring to anything else – or she was a very good actress. Anyway, at least he could help her with what the phrases meant, even if he didn't know what they were called.

So they talked about technology for the rest of the half hour. She talked about Facebook accounts, the way everyone seems to have a perfect life online. When you have a degree and a master's and you're working in your father's cheap hotel at the age of twenty-five that doesn't seem so perfect. Karim explained that he didn't have a computer, his mobile was bust, and he didn't use internet cafés. She couldn't believe it.

"You mean not at all?" she asked, incredulous. "Never?"

"Well, I did back in Scotland but I don't have anything here right now. I don't miss it." What he failed to say was that his location and intentions were not things potential terrorists tended to advertise.

"Well, at least you have a fitness band," she said, pointing at his wrist, "so you're not completely – can I say 'technophobic'?"

"That's right but it's not a… I mean it's a… well, it's not working very well right now," he ended lamely.

Then her phone beeped.

"Half an hour," she announced. "Now Spanish. *¿Hablas español?*"

"*No, no hablo. Mi nombre es Karim. Soy de Escocia. Tengo diecinueve años. Soy estudiante.*" He was called Karim, he was from Scotland, and was nineteen; however, saying "student" was simpler than "carpet salesman" and sounded better so he stuck with that. From this shaky start she began by teaching him some more simple phrases, including some vital questions like "Can I have the bill?" and "Where are the toilets?" From that they went on to "can I" and also "I can" and the question words "where", "when", "why", "how", and "how much".

"So now I can say not just 'Where are the toilets?' but also 'When are the toilets?', 'Why are the toilets?', 'How are the toilets?' and even 'How much are the toilets!'"

"*Exactamente!*"

Half an hour of Spanish went all too quickly. She checked the time on her mobile.

"Ok. I have to work now. *¿Mañana?*"

"*Sí, mañana,*" he managed to say, then off she went, leaving a few coins on the table.

Karim sat looking after her. How long had it been since he had sat for a full hour with a nice girl talking about something fun and useful, helping another human being, and getting help himself? Suddenly it struck him. Rasheed was always going on about civilization, how the West was totally uncivilized, that the Prophet was going to restore true Islamic civilization. But that was all so vague and seemed to mainly consist of stopping people doing things or making them do things. There wasn't much room in Rasheed's view of the future for *allowing* people to do things or even *helping* them do things. Maybe this was civilization – simply feeling safe and carefree, sitting in the sunshine with a friend, helping each other. What's not to like?

Then he remembered that he hadn't eaten and that Rasheed had all the money. He still had his bank card, though Rasheed had told him never to use it. There was a branch of Santander across the street. He got up and wandered over, scanning nervously around. Nothing happened. He stuck his card in the machine. Still nothing happened. He withdrew a hundred Euros. Nothing. Then he wandered back, had a look at Miguel's *menú del día*, and ordered macaroni with tuna, grilled ribs, and – why not? – a *caña*. The sun was still shining and the sky had not yet fallen on his head. He ate lunch, had a nice dessert followed by coffee, then went for a walk in the park. So far, so much better than this morning, yesterday, and the day before.

Samira was sitting by Enver's bedside when he woke up on Monday morning. He was young and fit and thirty-six hours had made a big difference.

"Hey, baby," he whispered.

"I'm here," she said, gripping his hand.

"What happened?"

"What do you remember? Do you remember the movie?"

"I think so. Sure. It was an *X-Men*. We went out of the cinema and I was seeing you home. That's all I remember."

"Maybe that's a good thing," she said, smiling at him. "A bunch of guys came out of nowhere and attacked you. I think there were three of them. Another one was holding on to me. There wasn't anything I could do!"

"Ssshhh," Enver quietened her. "What could you have done? If it was just two to one – no problem – but three…" he tried to joke.

"I stopped a car and they phoned for an ambulance. That was Saturday night."

"What day is it today?" he asked.

"Monday."

"Wow. I missed Sunday. It was my turn on the AV desk at church."

"David and Gillian have been in to see you. I don't think they mind."

Enver managed a weak smile. "How are you? Are you ok?"

She nodded. "Shook up. And so angry against my own people!"

"Why?"

"Well, my parents think it's because I was going out with a non-Muslim boy. Somebody decided you needed to be scared off."

Enver turned his head and stared out of the window.

"It'll take more than that," he said at length. "So your parents… they know?"

She nodded again.

"And does your dad want to beat me up even more once I get out?" he said, with the nearest thing to a grin he could manage.

"Not any more, I think," she replied, gripping his hand even more tightly.

"So having a Christian boyfriend is ok then?" he asked.

"I wouldn't say that exactly. And anyway, you're not my boyfriend any longer."

His face fell for a second before he saw the mischief on her face. "I told them all 'fiancé'," she said defiantly.

"Wow," was all he could manage before letting his head sink back into the pillow. He tried to turn slightly and gave a sharp cry.

"Don't move," she said. "Broken ribs."

"Anything else?"

"Yes, but it's quite a list. Better ask the doctor."

"But I can still be a father?" he asked in mock concern.

She gave a laugh. "Well, I haven't exactly asked about that, but as far as I know there are no reports of damage in that department."

"I'm relieved to hear it."

Just then a nurse came in, saw that he was awake, and went for the house officer. Samira was asked to leave while they did whatever they had to do, then she was allowed back in.

"Ms Khan?" she was asked by yet another new doctor she'd never seen before. "You are Mr Durak's partner, I understand."

"No," she corrected. "Fiancée."

"Well, here's the situation. Enver is going to be in hospital for some time. There's quite extensive damage and we need the bones to start knitting before he's fit to move – nothing permanent though. We want to keep an eye on the concussion and there's always the danger of blood clots in the brain so he'll be on meds for that. But it could have been a lot worse. We have pretty flexible visiting hours nowadays so you're welcome to come when you can."

They sat in silence once the doctor had left.

"Are you sure you're up for this?" Samira finally asked.

"What – a couple of weeks in hospital?"

"No, a Muslim girlfriend. With everything that means."

"I don't have a Muslim girlfriend," he said. "If you're referring to Ms Khan, she's my fiancée."

Chapter 8

South Queensferry

Ali and David met outside the A&A MiniMart, which Ayeesha had now reopened and headed out to South Queensferry Business Park in Ali's new black Audi with the leather seats and a Bluetooth sound system that would blow your ears out.

"So business must be booming, Ali?" David asked as they headed down through Tollcross and cut left at the Standard Life building onto the Western Approach Road.

"We've put a lot of effort into the shop and Ayeesha's cake business," Ali said. "It was always my dream to be independent – not to have to rely on a boss and be in by a certain time and out by a certain time. I probably work more hours than anyone else I know, but it's for us. Originally I had meant it to be for the kids too but that seems to have gone up in smoke."

"Maybe not, Ali. I learned once that you can't guess what the end will be just from the beginning. Things develop in surprising ways. Like me going to teach Spanish when all I wanted to do was hide under the covers. Then I met Gillian."

"And the rest is history, my friend, yes?"

"Yes."

"So I'm a bit like you then. Like you don't have a boss either?"

"Well, I think I have a boss, just not one that keeps a time sheet."

"Ah, I get it. Working for God."

"And for the congregation. And trying to help my neighbours. But it's not like selling apples and oranges. It can be hard to see what progress you're making sometimes. Then a family you've put

103

a lot of effort into decide to leave the church and it feels like it's all for nothing."

"But someone else comes and you start again." Ali clicked some buttons on the steering wheel to turn the music down for David's reply.

"Of course. I'm the sort of guy who likes to know where we're going and when we're going to get there, and that often doesn't fit with the job. Being a pastor has lots of details but really it's a big-picture job. You rarely get to see the impact you're having. You have to hope that every day you're helping people get closer to God, not further away."

"And what about those who are going further away, David: what happens to them? I mean, the unbelievers. Like Muslims, for example? Are we all going to hell?"

David laughed. "Well, that's definitely a big-picture question," he admitted. "There are many Christians who would say, 'Yes, you are.' I'm not so sure. What the Bible says about hell is actually not nearly as simple as some people would like it to be. But if you really want to know…"

"I do. I couldn't sleep last night. The radical mullahs say that a suicide bomber who kills himself for the sake of Allah goes straight to paradise. I think they go straight to hell. They certainly deserve to. If there is an afterlife, I want to be with my wife and my children. I think that's a reasonable thing to hope for."

"Very reasonable," David agreed. "So, the short version is that the Old Testament has no clear teaching on heaven or hell. In some verses the place of the dead is just a state where there is no longer any knowing or acting or being. In the New Testament, Jesus talks a lot about hell but one interesting thing is that everything he says about it he says to Jewish people – the people who were supposed to be the believers of the time. When he interacts with outsiders like Romans or non-Hebrews he doesn't mention hell at all. You'd have thought it should be the other way about. And elsewhere in the New Testament the word for 'hell' can also mean total annihilation.

Nothing. Kaput. So it does depend a bit on where you take your evidence from. My opinion, if you want it…" Ali nodded, "is that the one thing I am absolutely sure of is that hell is not a place of conscious eternal agony that God has prepared, planned, and chosen and that both God and believers in heaven will know about it. I'm afraid that doesn't always put me in the mainstream of Christians but I just can't imagine being content knowing that many of my friends and family are in agony downstairs. How could you?"

"What I think exactly," Ali agreed. "In Islam we call Allah 'the merciful'. Mercy seems to be the last thing on some Muslims' minds just now. Beheadings, crucifixions, starvation, lashes, stonings. These are the acts of vicious, wicked men, not a merciful god – whatever we call him. Ah, here's something you'll like," he continued, abruptly changing the subject. "Jazz on Indian instruments. How about that?"

He turned the music up again and they settled into silence as the miles slid by.

Centaur Systems was in a large modern building with a predictable logo above the door. They gave their names at reception and a minute or two later a tall thirty-something with a huge beard and messy hair came bounding down the stairs and greeted first Ali then David.

"Mr Khan," he said. "I'm Justin. Chief Technical Officer. I was Rasheed's boss. We were very sorry to lose him. In fact, it left a lot of projects in deep doo-doo. I was hoping that *you* might know where he'd disappeared to. Coffee?"

The upper floor was a huge open-plan space with cubicles arranged like a task in *The Crystal Maze*. There was a quiet hum from the air conditioning, the low chatter of keyboards, and snatches of conversation. A couple of Justin clones – slightly younger but otherwise pretty similar – stood by the water cooler. Next to that was the biggest fridge David had ever seen.

"Of course you can have a Coke or something else, if you'd like. Only alcohol-free beer in working hours I'm afraid. If you want to stay to lunch the canteen is free. Mainly pizza and veggie stuff I'm afraid but that's what there is."

"Coffee would be fine," Ali assured him. "If I could have decaf?"

"No problem. My desk is up at the end," Justin continued, "but we have a few side rooms for meetings and stuff. We'll use one of them."

He led them into a space that took David's breath away. A huge plate glass picture window looked out over the river and had a fantastic view of the various Forth bridges. The conference table and chairs looked like Ercol or some other high-quality solid oak manufacturer. Sonos speakers were dotted around. Another, slightly smaller, fridge was behind the door next to another coffee maker.

"Sorry. There might be a bit of noise," Justin commented. "I'm afraid we're next door to the fitness suite, so you sometimes get a bit of puffing and panting. Anyway, please have a seat. Let's see if we can get to the bottom of the mystery!"

"I'm Rasheed's father, as you know," Ali reintroduced himself. "This is David Hidalgo, a family friend."

"*The* David Hidalgo?" Justin asked, suddenly interested.

"Well not the David Hidalgo who played guitar for Los Lobos anyway," David conceded.

"No; the other one. There was that thing in the paper. You're a pastor from Spain. It was about people trafficking. And then the priest they shot at the top of the Scott Monument. Was that you then?"

David gave a heavy sigh. This was beginning to happen with alarming regularity. "Well, it was me. I mean, it *is* me," he fumbled for the right response. "But it wasn't nearly as dramatic as the way it was written. Honestly."

"So another David Hidalgo mystery, then?" Justin pressed on, undeterred.

"I certainly hope not," David remarked, trying to close the subject.

"Rasheed," Ali said, bringing them back to the point. "We're not a particularly close family and we don't keep in touch very regularly, so I only found out at the weekend that he had given up his job and disappeared. Nobody seems to know where he is. I was hoping you might be able to shed some light on it."

Justin shook his head. "'Fraid not," he said. "As far as we're concerned he just disappeared. Dropped right off the radar. In here working as usual one Friday. Monday morning nowhere to be seen. As I said, he left a load of projects at various stages. It's been causing a lot of problems."

"No sign of unhappiness, then?" David asked.

"None at all. Maybe a bit less talkative than usual for a few months. Seemed to be going into his shell a bit. But his work wasn't affected. I have to say, Mr Khan, that Rasheed was one of our star players. They say there's a factor of ten between a top coder and the average. Rasheed was well up there. Worked quickly, elegantly, and accurately. He'd come up with beautiful solutions to problems that were stumping the rest of the team. In fact, we formalized that and allowed him to spend up to 10 per cent of his time on consultancy for other staff members. He was already head of his section and could certainly have put in for my job if I move on. Initially we thought he'd been headhunted by someone else but he didn't even come in to collect his things. He left a very nice watch in his desk, and other personal things. He didn't do any damage to other systems and there's absolutely no evidence that he took any trade secrets with him. Nothing. Just vanished."

Ali let out a deep breath. Pummelling sounds came through the wall that could have been from a treadmill or a recalcitrant employee being given corrective advice.

"Justin, this may sound odd, but could you tell me what sort of person Rasheed was? In your experience," Ali said.

Justin's eyebrows lifted a fraction but he shrugged.

"Sure. Very single-minded, I would say. Clear. Logical. Rational. Maybe a bit obsessive. He would work at a problem till he solved it. We had a particularly difficult contract trying to read blood pressure from a fitness band and correlate it with location. So, for example, does your blood pressure go up just for the very fact of entering a hospital? That could be useful to know, because if that's the case then medical examinations will always tend to read high. The client ran out of money and cancelled the project but Rasheed insisted on trying to solve the problem. In the end we had to tell him to stop doing it on company time but he would stay late until he got it sorted. So now it works but we don't have anyone to sell it to. That's a bit extreme, even in our industry, which I have to say does tend to attract some extreme characters."

"Did he have lots of friends? Like going for a drink after work?"

Justin reflected for a few seconds. "No," he replied. "Probably not. He did the usual team-building stuff but I do remember he phoned in sick on our last away day. And he avoided the paintballing. Now you mention it, he did tend to opt out of most of the corporate fun and games. Around the office he was fine though. Didn't spend a lot of time at the water cooler but we tend to see that as a positive actually. What else can I say? Hard worker. Didn't socialize much outside of work. Had his own circle of friends I suppose. That's it. Sorry I can't be more helpful."

"No special friends at work then?" David asked.

Justin shrugged again. "Not really. Hang on… I think he went out with Tam for a bit. Maybe you'd learn more there?"

"Tam?" Ali asked, incredulous. "Tam? Do you mean to tell me my son is gay too?"

Justin held up his hands. "No, not as far as I know. I mean Tam as in Tamsin not as in Tom. She works in marketing. Do you want to speak to her?"

Ali was still reeling from what seemed like the latest in a never-ending stream of surprises. "Yes, if it's no trouble. That would be very enlightening."

"I'll see if she's in."

Justin disappeared and the door swung slowly shut on its spring.

"Rasheed had a girlfriend?" Ali asked no one in particular.

"So it seems."

"He never had a girlfriend – and not a boyfriend either. He never seemed to have the time. Or he used to say he'd never found anyone who liked the things he liked. I don't know why I'm so surprised. I'm just finding out things about my son that a father should know without asking a total stranger."

The two of them sat drinking their coffee for a minute or so more till the door opened and Justin came back in with maybe the last person in the world Ali would have thought would appeal to Rasheed. Tamsin had a pale face, ginger hair tied back in a colourful ribbon, and was wearing loose denim dungarees rolled up to mid-calf over a bright orange T-shirt. A few studs decorated ears, eyebrows, and nose. She was wearing the most vivid red lipstick Ali had ever seen. A badge clipped to one strap of her dungarees declared "free the inner hippo", whatever that might mean.

"Tamsin, this is Rasheed's dad," Justin introduced him. "And David Hidalgo. We're talking about whether there are any clues as to where he might be."

"Sure. No problem," said Tamsin in an accent that would have been completely at home at the Cheltenham Festival.

"Thank you very much for agreeing to see us," Ali began. "I'm afraid it's a bit embarrassing, but I only found out Rasheed had packed his job in and gone missing a few days ago. I thought I might get some information here but I had no idea he'd had a girlfriend – if I can put it like that."

"No problem," Tamsin repeated in a completely open, friendly tone. "Yeah. We went out for about six months last year and over Christmas. Just kind of came to an end in the spring."

"And what sort of person did you find Rasheed to be?" Ali pushed her.

"Well, I liked him of course. I actually asked him out, not the other way around. He's very intelligent; I suppose you know that. Fantastic programmer. Everybody here rated him. Could be a bit obsessive." She paused for a second to get the right word, "... and possessive, I guess. That's how we broke up. He was getting into his religion a lot more and kept going on about the evils of the West. Well, I pretty much agreed about the problem but we disagreed on the solution. He thought people had to be controlled. Strict laws about dress, behaviour, and stuff. Control of advertising, limits on free speech. I didn't see things that way. You can probably guess that on the dress codes." She laughed. "So that was it. No big break-up though. To be honest, I think he would have taken the first step pretty soon if I hadn't."

"I'm really sorry to ask you personal questions, eh… Tam… but I'm guessing you're not Muslim," Ali asked.

She laughed again. "Not at all. I'm Buddhist, if I'm anything. Though that may change. I never went to the mosque with him and he never asked me to."

"And you have no idea where he might be?' David put in.

"Well, I just assumed he had got fed up here and went off to work for another company. In our business that could be anywhere: Melbourne, California, Hong Kong, Moscow. Or just his bedroom. Sorry I can't help you any more."

"That's been really helpful, Tam. Thanks," Ali said and meant it.

"Back to the grindstone then."

"Sorry we're not really getting anywhere," Justin apologized once Tam had left. "We're as mystified as you. Anything else we can help you with?"

"No," Ali said but David interrupted him.

"Could we see Rasheed's desk area if it's not too much trouble?"

"Yeah sure. You're just in time. We interviewed this morning and the new guy takes over tomorrow. We have to get a load of projects going forward again. We haven't cleared the area in the hope he might turn up again."

Justin led the way into the heart of the open-plan metropolis and pointed to an area about two-metres square.

"Welcome to cubicle land," he said. "Actually, I have a phone call I must make. Can I leave you here? You're welcome to take his stuff away. I don't think he's coming back now."

Ali slumped into what had been Rasheed's chair. He shook his head in disbelief. "This is getting weirder and weirder. Rasheed was a star programmer – and he had a girlfriend, who wasn't a Muslim. And he worked on stuff he wasn't even paid for. I remember when he was fourteen he had a stamp collection and he used to work at it incessantly, getting everything in just exactly the right order, so I knew he could be a bit fixated but this is all a revelation. And the girlfriend. I can't get over it. Exactly the opposite sort of person I would have thought Rasheed would have gone with. I knew he was getting more and more religious so I was expecting him to bring back a Muslim girl from a nice respectable family some time. I can't get over it."

"Look at this," David remarked, scanning around the grey fabric dividers that separated one cubicle from the rest. "What do you see?"

Ali looked. "I don't know," he said. "It's all Greek to me. Post-it notes, lists of numbers. Are these flow charts? A company structure chart, I suppose. Stock market prices. Nothing that makes any sense to me."

"How long did Rasheed work here, do you know?"

"Five years, I think. Something like that."

"So in five years, in this cubicle he has no personal objects. There aren't any photos. No mementos. No souvenirs. Nothing. With one exception. Look here."

David pulled out a pin that was holding an A5 leaflet.

"What is it?" Ali asked.

David turned it over and looked at both sides. "It's a guide to the Great Mosque of Córdoba," he said. "With a floor plan."

A trip that afternoon to Glasgow to Ali's brother's carpet warehouse held fewer surprises. The report was that Karim was normally a happy, sociable boy who was a quick learner and had been rewarded with some important accounts of his own. He took part in anything social and was always up for a joke. The most recent was an attempt to smuggle another worker past reception in a rolled-up carpet like

111

in the movies. The plot only failed because Karim couldn't keep a straight face and the entire cavalcade collapsed on the floor in gales of laughter. Karim had been staying with his uncle while he tried to save enough for a deposit on a flat. Ali and David went to Uncle Hakan's home and saw the bedroom. Nothing of note. Some posters of racing cars, a Bollywood singer, a topless model inside the wardrobe door, an Xbox and a big screen TV, clothes all over the place. Exactly like he had nipped out for a burger and would be back any moment.

"It's a total mystery, Ali," Hakan admitted. "I'm sorry I didn't tell you earlier but I didn't want to get the boy into trouble. He's been a really good worker – unlike my own boys, I'm sorry to say. I thought maybe something was troubling him and he just needed some space. I'm afraid I've just been so busy. I was going to call you this week. Honestly."

"Has he changed in any way over the past few months?" David asked.

Hakan shrugged. "I'm sorry. Like I said I've been so busy. Maybe too busy to notice. Mati! Can you come a minute? Maybe she knows better than me. Ali and his friend want to know if we noticed any difference in Karim before he disappeared."

Hakan's wife looked down and nodded.

"Well, what is it then?" her husband demanded with some impatience.

"He made me promise not to tell," she said. "I'm sorry. The last week he was here he hardly spoke. He would come in from work, eat something, then go to his room. I didn't see him till the next morning. The last day I saw him he told me he was going to have to go away. He said he hoped it wouldn't be long but he couldn't tell anyone where or why, but I knew it had something to do with Rasheed. I heard them speaking on the phone sometimes. I'm so sorry. I thought he just meant a couple of days, then he'd be back. When it got longer I didn't want to say I knew. I was hoping he would come back and things would be like normal. Maybe it was something to do with a girl. I don't know."

Hakan's face was drawn tight. "We'll speak about this later," he said heavily.

"What made you think it was something to do with a girl?" Ali asked.

"Well, Karim was always very popular. All the girls liked him. Then suddenly he stopped going out and wouldn't answer phone calls. I had a girl called Sunna calling almost every day wanting to know where he was. I though maybe there was trouble and he was running away from it. That's all I know."

"Do you mind if we look more in his room?" Ali asked. "There might be something."

"Go ahead," Hakan replied. "If you find something tell me. I want to know where he is too. When he comes back I'll welcome him with open arms then kick his arse all around the warehouse!"

David and Ali took the room apart bit by bit while Hakan looked on. There was nothing they might not have expected – except maybe a packet of condoms in the back of a drawer under his socks. There was a tiny bookshelf above the bed. It had one copy of the Koran in Arabic, another in English, a notebook-sized guide to the new Formula One series, and a copy of the *Rubáiyát of Omar Khayyám* inscribed, "To Karim. Thank you for a lovely weekend. With love from Sunna." It looked like it had never been opened.

"Nothing," Ali said when they had finally finished and tidied up.

"It's disappointing," Hakan remarked. "A boy I had high hopes for. Well, at least I'm going to get rid of these," he said, picking up the condoms and dropping them in the bin. "And this." He pulled open the wardrobe door, grabbed one corner of the topless model and ripped it off the woodwork, then crumpled it up. Just as he was closing the door, David, standing at the end of the wardrobe looking into the open angle of the door, put his hand out and stopped Hakan.

"I'm sorry Mr Khan, do you mind?"

He pulled the door fully open again. Under where the topless model had been was another poster. It looked like a tourist brochure opened up. It was the interior of a huge hall decorated with red and white marble pillars. It was the inside of the Great Mosque of Córdoba. The Mezquita.

"I think it's about time we found out a bit more about 'the Prophet'," David said.

Chapter 9

Bruntsfield

Stuart McIntosh arrived on time, bringing yet more booze and, this time, a friend as well.

"This is Gary Morrison," he said. "Detective Inspector in counterterrorism. You said it was ok."

"Absolutely." Gillian took their coats and ushered them into the living room.

"Gary's in – how can I put it? – somewhat similar circumstances to me right now, so I knew he'd appreciate it and I think there's something in Gary's line you wanted to talk about. So, two birds with one stone."

"Perfect, but let's leave the shop talk till later. What can I get you?"

DI Morrison produced a bottle from somewhere as well so they decided to open that one first. Just as Gillian was heading back to the kitchen, David appeared so they re-ran the introductions.

"Nice to meet you, Gary," he said. "From Edinburgh?"

"Niddrie. So I think that counts as yes. Trying to keep the capital safe at least till Stuart and I retire."

Gillian reappeared with four glasses and a corkscrew.

Dinner was a shoulder of lamb pierced with slivers of garlic in a tomato, carrot, and olive sauce and was pronounced delicious all round.

"You're an unusual creature then, David," Gary commented over a succulent mouthful. "A man who actually likes to cook and doesn't do it just to avoid starving."

"Only because I like to eat. And I get to open a bottle of something to keep me company while I'm doing it."

"Maybe if I'd done a bit more of that we wouldn't be where we are now," Morrison commented gloomily. "Anyway, it's great. Thanks again for the invite."

They kept it to small talk through the main and dessert – Gillian's unbeatable pavlova with peach slices – then retired to comfy seats for coffee.

"So, you seem to have been pretty successful in counterterrorism so far," David remarked. "At least as far as what reaches the front page of *The Scotsman*."

"Touch wood," Gary replied. "Glasgow's been a bigger target. And London and Birmingham of course. You'd expect that with bigger Asian populations perhaps, though we always emphasize this is terrorism by people who happen to have an Asian Muslim background – not Asian Muslim terrorism, if you see the difference. Anyway, yes – I think we've been largely ok so far. Of course we've also managed to knock a few on the head before they got to the operational stage. Anyway, Stuart was telling me you have an interest in our 'Prophet'."

"Unfortunately I do. I'd love not to have the least interest but it's come through a family friend. In fact, your neighbour now, Stuart – Ali Khan, just through the wall. He has the MiniMart downstairs. It kind of looks like his two boys have got mixed up in it all. They've both gone AWOL. Nobody has a clue where and they both had stuff to do with the old Moorish Caliphate in Spain lying around. Stuart mentioned the Prophet had an interest in that. We were wondering if there might be a connection."

DI Morrison toyed with his coffee and thought for a bit.

"You're a friend of Stuart's, who he obviously trusts, so I'll speak more freely than I normally would, but maybe we just need to clear terms of reference first, if you don't mind."

David nodded. "Go ahead."

"So, you're a friend of a colleague and a concerned citizen, but I gather also minister of a church in town."

"That's right. And one of our younger folk was beaten up recently – we think in an honour attack on account of his Muslim girlfriend. So that's one thing. I'm concerned when religious tensions impact on our own folk. And there's the Khan kids. I'd like to help a friend if possible."

"I see," Morrison replied slowly. "Well, for the purposes of this discussion you never told me that. I am sharing some information with a concerned community leader, which we do all the time. We would not be giving out information to a private citizen – however much concerned – in order to help out a friend. Understand?"

"Perfectly. I thought that might be the case, so we purposely didn't include Ali and Ayeesha tonight."

"Very wise. So, what can I tell you? The identity and activities of the man calling himself 'the Prophet' are of considerable concern to us. However, it's been extremely difficult to get a handle on it. Your two boys might be the lead we're looking for but that's really after the fact – not the reason I'm telling you this. So what do you know about 'the Prophet'?"

"Only what Stuart has told us," David replied.

Morrison shot a quick glance at his colleague. "Which is…?"

"Nothing at all," Stuart quickly put in with a deadpan expression. David regrouped.

"What I have heard 'on the grapevine' is that he's some radical preacher who got chucked out of the Edinburgh Mosque, partly, I gather, for styling himself as a new prophet, which isn't permitted in Islam. After disappearing from there he's turned up again online in a new improved version. And his new focus seems to be on Spain."

Morrison took another sip of coffee. "That's right, as far as it goes. He's got a protected website – on the dark web – that we haven't been able to crack as yet so we have a limited idea of what he's saying directly. Therefore, most of what we know comes from secondary sources. Like retweets, I suppose you'd say. But his reach seems quite extensive. It's reminding some people of Al-Qaeda in the early days: an intelligent, radical voice calling the faithful to a new challenge. The idea this time is that instead of Afghanistan or Pakistan, the Prophet's propaganda is aimed at a strike at the heart of Europe. And it claims historical legitimacy because Spain was a Muslim country. The Prophet doesn't seem to really care that he's rejected as an apostate; he's willing to go outside orthodox Islam to gain a radical following and a strike that he thinks will have the most impact. They call it 'the soft underbelly of Europe'. Stuart has been involved in terms of our liaison with European partners but the truth is we don't really know what to do except in terms of general vigilance. The Prophet doesn't seem to really exist in physical space. Well, I suppose he eats and drinks somewhere but there's no physical local impact. No rallies like there were with Abu Hamza, for example. No marches, no protests, no leafletting. His only apparent point of contact with the world is the website. And maybe emails to individuals but we've yet to intercept any.

"We can see the front page of the site even though it's on the dark web but we can't get beyond that. So we know he makes a weekly broadcast and he communicates with individual cells but what he says we can't intercept as yet. And we've had GCHQ and the NSA on the job. Nothing. Everything is heavily encrypted and any wrong password results in a long wait to try again so we can't just bombard the site with random combinations until we get the right one. Actually, the password takes the form of a question so you have to know the right answer to get beyond the splash screen. There seem to be a limited number of questions but they cycle so while you're researching one, it expires and a different one pops up. Very frustrating, and clearly devised for those in the know. I actually admire it in a way. Pretty clever. And the funny thing is, there was absolutely no indication that he was this bright when he was out and about. We've spoken to people from the mosque. He was thought of as a loudmouth and a joker – nothing more. An irritation, not a serious threat. But now the tables have turned. He seems very clever and is becoming very influential. Stuart tells me you've had some success in this sort of thing in the past and you have a background in Spain. So, all hands to the pump as far as we're concerned. We're under quite a lot of pressure to see some progress so all bright ideas are welcome."

David held up his hands to disavow any such thing. Gillian was already giving him a warning stare. "No bright ideas whatsoever – honestly. And I have no particular talent for it, whatever you've heard. Bits of luck and access to a very bright house-trained hacker who so far has been able to penetrate anything we've thrown at him. Though I doubt that he'd hit the target if GCHQ and the NSA have failed to score. But if Ali's kids are connected with the Prophet and are in Spain – which they might be given that they both had material relating to the Great Mosque of Córdoba, a site with huge symbolic value for the Prophet and his followers – in that case, I'd be happy to throw my oar in."

At this point Gillian sat forward and cleared her throat.

"Eh, since we are in the business of clarifying terms of reference, there's one I'd like to clarify," she said and put her coffee cup down. She spoke directly to DI Morrison in no uncertain terms.

"David – and to some extent I – have found ourselves inadvertently caught up in a number of messy situations. We didn't choose to get involved; things just happened that we needed to react to. It eventually worked out ok. But twice now – twice! – David has taken a bullet when he got too close. That is not going to happen again. Helping decipher a website is one thing; taking on Islamic – or Islamist, or former Islamic, or whatever – terrorists is *not* on the agenda. And I speak for both of us though David might not put it that way. Just to be clear."

Morrison nodded, McIntosh cleared his throat, and David studied his footwear.

"Absolutely. We're not in the business of putting private citizens in the firing line," Morrison agreed. "My backside would be on the line as well. So that's completely understood."

"Stuart?" Gillian asked, to complete the circle.

"Of course."

"And David? Just to be clear," Gillian smiled very sweetly but there was no doubting she meant business.

"In my own defence the bullets weren't part of the plan… but, of course, no crossing the yellow police tape this time. Promise."

"Glad that's agreed." Gillian sat back, apparently satisfied, at least for the time being.

"So, what do you think you could offer, if that's not going too far? I've heard impressive stories about your tame hacker. What's he called – Digger?"

"Close," Gillian replied, now more relaxed. "Spade. It amounts to the same thing, I suppose."

"I have no idea if I – or we – could offer anything," David said. "But I did spend thirty years in Spain and worked all around the south, the province of Andalucía. Córdoba had some of my most important clients so I was there quite a lot. Maybe a bit of genuine local knowledge could make a contribution."

"We're willing to try anything. How do you think we could proceed?"

"I could contact Spade and ask if he's willing to play again – I think you'd need to pay him this time – then we could have a look at the page and see where we stand."

"Just another point of clarification here," Gillian put in. "Who exactly is 'we'?"

Morrison fielded the question again. "Well, me, certainly. I can get clearance to follow this up and I think I can get a modest budget. You – one or both, whichever you prefer – can be involved or not just as far as you want. I would take the line that you are community *leaders* – together. Stuart, do you want to be in?"

"Actually, yes, if you don't mind. If this is really heading for Spain then I'm probably going to have some liaison role at least. I might as well know what's going on. And I've dealt with Spade before. He was actually very impressive. Knocked the pants off our own IT guys, I'm sorry to say."

"And what about you, Gillian?" David turned the tables. "How do you feel about it? Just to be clear…"

"I think I'd rather have a discussion about this afterwards, if you don't mind. But no objections right now."

"Well, if nobody else minds I'd much prefer if you were involved," David said. "I know I'm biased but you're the most creative thinker I know – seriously. I'd really want you on board. If you're willing."

"Well, let's see."

The party broke up late, but not so late that Gillian didn't have the energy to initiate her promised "discussion".

"Sorry to butt in there, David, but all this talk is making me nervous – again. So I'm really not too happy about the way things are going. Feels like we've been here before, don't you think? Or am I getting it out of proportion? Of course we can always justify it and there are good reasons, but it just feels so much like how things have started before. Little beginnings that seem very innocuous then before you know it you're dodging bullets, literally. So I'm really not ready to take on *any* sort of terrorists. You crack the website and you become a target. Have you thought of that?"

David was carrying plates and glasses through to the kitchen. He set them down on a clear patch of worktop and drew breath.

"No defence," he said, holding his hands up. "I'm not going to argue about this. If you say 'no' then no it is. Or if you say 'yes, this far', then that's as far as it goes. Full stop. I'm concerned for Ali who must feel like his family has just exploded. Enver's getting good treatment I suppose and Samira's a grown-up so they both make their own choices. If we can make Edinburgh and Spain that bit safer, then I feel I have a responsibility as a human being, not just as a pastor. But I completely see where you're coming from and I'm not going to try to negotiate. As soon as you want to stop we stop. How does that sound?"

"Lovely," she said, putting her arms around his neck. "Maybe I should feel differently but I have to admit I'm more concerned about the one than the many in this case. I thought you were going to fight me there. Thanks. I love you."

She started with a tiny peck then it seemed to get out of control.

"Let's leave the dishes for tonight," she whispered. "They'll wait. I'm not sure I can."

Karim found his new status as an unbeliever – at least from Rasheed's point of view – a bit bewildering but also somehow liberating. Hanging his hat on the Prophet's teaching hadn't really been his idea. Rasheed had bullied, cajoled, shamed, and argued him into it – as he usually did with whatever scheme he had in mind – as he had been doing for at least fifteen years now. But this was unknown territory. Now Karim had finally said no and was still getting used to the sensation. It was disorientating but good. They still shared a room but didn't speak. They ate breakfast at separate tables. Rasheed went to his academy in the centre of town, and Karim wandered around or did his homework and met with Bea to practise. During one session she asked if he'd like a bit of work in exchange for free accommodation and a few Euros. They could do with an extra pair of hands. He jumped at the chance and so found himself not only eating breakfast the next morning but gathering up all the plates, including Rasheed's, taking them through to the kitchen, and then commencing to wash up. He cleaned bedrooms, took out the rubbish, collected laundry from the woman across the street, and even, with a bit of coaxing, ran a few errands with his shopping list clearly written down. And little by little he found he was able to use the phrases, expressions, and verbs that Bea was teaching him in real situations. It was great. Without going into details of why, he even asked if he could change rooms so that one afternoon Rasheed got back from his class to find Karim in the process of shifting his few possessions to the single room across the way. He didn't offer an explanation and Rasheed was too proud to ask for one, but for Karim it was like a declaration of independence and it felt very, very good indeed.

As regards just exactly what he was now if not a follower of the Prophet and, because of the Prophet, no longer an orthodox Muslim, he wasn't sure. Could you get chucked out of Islam, then just come back in again as if nothing had happened? Did you need an imam or somebody official to grant you a change of status? He had no idea. All he knew was that some people converted to Islam and were welcomed, some Muslims tried to change their faith and were in trouble, and most people were either more or less religious but didn't think about it too much. So he was in doubly unknown territory.

But just as removing a single brick from the wall weakens the whole thing, he soon found himself standing at the sink washing pots surrounded by a barrage of Spanish he didn't understand and wondering what being Muslim actually involved. Nobody he knew had ever chosen it; it was something that just came with your surname and DNA. Probably the same for most religions. He had certainly heard of people who converted from one to another, though it often seemed to bring more problems than it solved. Still, they were entitled. Then it struck him that if someone was Hindu and decided to become Christian, and someone who was Christian could decide to become Muslim, why couldn't someone who was Muslim decide to become something else? Like Samira, for example: she was going out with a Christian boy, or at least had been. What if she decided to become Christian herself? What should his attitude be? Rasheed's attitude was completely clear and it would probably be the attitude of most people he knew. He wasn't sure what his parents' feelings would be. Personally, he wouldn't have a problem, if the boy treated her well; lots of Muslim husbands didn't. But maybe that was wrong. Maybe he should be outraged. But you can't be outraged just because you feel you ought to be, he reasoned. He wasn't and that was it.

Then another worrying thought struck him. What if he got more than friendly with Bea? He assumed she was a Christian, though it didn't seem to particularly show. He certainly knew she wasn't Muslim. If he was an infidel and outcast already, would that make any difference? Or would Rasheed decide he didn't deserve to live and press the button on his app that would blow his arm off to make a point? Too many questions and not many answers. He realized he had probably been washing the same pot for ten minutes and fished it out to put on the draining board, making sure to keep the wristband out of the water. Then he went to check the time on his watch and remembered he wasn't wearing one – as happened a dozen times a day – so he glanced up at the kitchen clock. Time for his Spanish class. Theological thoughts were left behind as he felt a wave of much more pleasant thoughts popping up. *Venga*, he said to himself. Let's get going!

Meanwhile Rasheed was livid but couldn't show it. That no good excuse for a brother of his should never have been favoured with a ground-floor entry to the Prophet's new order. He had clearly opted out of the whole project now, which would make things doubly difficult for Rasheed himself. And he was fraternizing with a non-Muslim girl – Rasheed blamed himself for ever having allowed it. He was even financially independent, it seemed. He couldn't in all conscience justify using the device he'd felt so clever for clamping on to Little Brother's arm, but he was sorely tempted and the time might certainly come. If Karim had only guessed the one weakness of the scheme was battery life on the band: no battery, no bang. The solar cells he'd covered the thing with seemed to still be holding up. At least there was no shortage of sun in Córdoba. If Little Brother had been bright enough to figure it out, he could just have kept his left arm in the dark for two days or wrapped a bandage around it and been in the clear inside forty-eight hours; however, he had even failed his basic physics so there didn't seem to be anything to worry about there.

But that still left the problem of what to do now his collaborator had suddenly switched sides. He still expected that he'd need to coerce some help in the great act of liberation that they had come for, so he had to keep the threat in reserve. The really annoying thing was that Karim seemed to be completely happy and carefree, not cowed and fearful as he should be. He overheard bits of Spanish as he came and went and it was obvious that Karim's grasp of the language was going forward in leaps and bounds compared to his own painful progress. That made him furious as well. In fact, almost everything made him furious. He was coming to hate Córdoba, Spain, and particularly Pensión El Moro but, number one, he had his orders and, number two, if he moved elsewhere he would lose control of Karim entirely. This trip was not working out at all the way he had expected. Nevertheless he turned on his laptop as usual that night, put his ear bud speakers in, navigated to the Prophet's website, easily typed in the answer to this week's question (which anyone involved in the struggle should know but outsiders would not), and submitted his report while he waited for the broadcast to begin. He did not mention that things were not going according to plan.

Chapter 10

The Bridge

The two detectives and their hosts reconvened the following evening after Gillian had finished work and David had made arrangements. Spade's flat was a revelation. Tina, the new girlfriend, opened the door and welcomed them in. Signs of the presence of someone who cared whether the hall floor was covered with empty pizza boxes and old beer bottles were immediately obvious. Even Spade himself seemed to have lost a few pounds and gained an ironing board, if his current T-shirt and jeans were anything to go by.

"Well, well," Gillian muttered as they filed into the hall.

"Hi David. More internet intrigue?" Spade asked.

"Looks like it. Stuart you know. Can I introduce Gary Morrison – DI in counterterrorism?"

"Hi. Welcome to my world."

"I've heard a lot about your work, Spade. Thanks for agreeing to see us."

"No problem. This way to the Bridge…"

The hacker led them from the hall into his computer room. This, at least, was exactly as in previous meetings. Meticulous and well organized, buzzing with towers, screens, keyboards, mice, and shelves full of carefully and clearly labelled lever arch files. Gillian lingered in the hall.

"Tina! What a transformation," she whispered. "Well done!"

Spade's goth girlfriend blushed slightly and smiled.

"Thanks. The Bridge showed it was possible. I just extended his order field to take in the chaos zone as well. He didn't struggle too much."

"So how long have you been here, if you don't mind my asking?"

"Well, your party – after that carry-on with the priest – that was our first official outing. Then things seemed to go pretty well. I actually only moved in a fortnight ago. There's been some serious cleaning since then but we're getting on top of it. I think he actually likes the new reality, though he won't admit it of course. For the first time in his life I think he can find a bottle opener as easily as one of his websites." She giggled a bit. "How about you and David?"

"Well, we've only been home from honeymoon a couple of weeks so I suppose we've been under the same roof about as long as you guys. We agreed to live in my flat, at least to start with, so it's not been much of a change for me. David seems to be coping ok so far. He's reasonably well house-trained." That made them both laugh. "Anyway, good luck. Hope you keep it up!" Gillian encouraged her.

"The worst is over, I think…" Tina smiled.

The sounds of a keyboard clicking and bits of technobabble from the room Spade called "the Bridge" after its namesake on the Starship Enterprise suggested the reason for their visit was underway.

"Better see what's going on," Gillian whispered and squeezed into the computer room.

David and Stuart McIntosh were seated on either side of Spade, who was at the keyboard while Gary Morrison was standing behind them. Morrison had his laptop but Spade treated it with disdain.

"No problem. I can do it from here," he was saying as Gillian edged in.

"Just what exactly are we going to be doing?" David asked. "I don't think I understood anything I just heard."

"Well, Gary was telling me how to access the Prophet's website but I did a bit of homework after you called me so I've got a link saved already. It's all in the dark web of course so you need to have TOR installed before you can even begin looking. Fortunately – or otherwise – this is where I go to work on a daily basis, so it wasn't a problem."

"Well, that's a reasonable start already," Gary Morrison put in. "It took our guys two weeks to find it even when we knew what we were looking for."

Spade ignored the compliment and went on clicking and tapping. Soon the screen cleared to an image of a huge iron doorway. Enormous double doors covered in geometric designs were set in what looked like sandstone pillars that transformed into a flared arch surrounded by a lighter stone setting, meeting in a point above the doors. The lighter stone area was filled with delicate tracery of flower petals, spirals, geometric patterns, and Arabic calligraphy. The outline of a shield was set in the space where the arch began to curve in on either side, though the detail was worn and indecipherable. Enormous iron ring handles hung from the doors. It was hard to be sure of scale but assuming the handles were at shoulder height that would make the entire doorway something around three metres tall. Where the doors met there was a line of light showing greenery beyond. The sound of running water played in the background.

"Nice front door," Spade commented. "This it?"

Morrison nodded. "Impressions, David?"

"Well, certainly very *mudejar* – meaning Moorish in its style. Could be any of the major cities in southern Spain. I'm not saying it couldn't be somewhere else of course. Maybe Damascus or Baghdad – I can only speak for Spain. There are a lot of Moorish buildings left throughout Andalucía. Seville, Granada, Córdoba, and Cádiz are the best examples. This could be in any of them."

"Double click on either of the door knockers," Morrison said.

Spade did. English text in a mock Arabic font materialized on the ironwork.

"You have knocked on the door of the Prophet," David read aloud. "Entrance is only for those who value the past and yearn for a new future."

Spade grunted dismissively. "Sounds like a second-rate Legend of Zelda game," he said.

"Click again," Morrison told him.

The gateway cleared to a huge square tower with more rich decoration all the way up. Arches, pillars, and finely traced geometric patterns were inlaid into the sandy-coloured stone.

"This one I know," David said. "It's the Giralda – the bell tower of Seville Cathedral but originally it was the tower for the call to prayer next to the mosque. Another Islamic icon, I suppose. Like the centre of the Mezquita in Córdoba, the mosque was flattened to build the cathedral and the only thing left standing was the tower, which I suppose the Christians thought they could use."

"Click again, Spade," Morrison asked.

More text in the same style appeared. "Only those who are willing to ascend to the heights and bring our enemies to the depths can enter," David read.

Spade rolled his eyes. "What piffle," he muttered.

Morrison asked for one more click.

Now the tower vanished to show a richly decorated horseshoe arch in an interior wall surrounding a niche or alcove. Yet again the stonework was exquisite, this time in shades of red, blue, and gold.

"This one too," David remarked immediately. "That's the mihrab prayer niche at the Mezquita in Córdoba."

"And what's a mihrab when it's at home, then?" McIntosh asked.

"It's the space used by the imam who was leading prayers. The alcove amplified his voice but it was also built into the wall facing Mecca so it gave an orientation to the entire prayer hall."

"Beautiful," Gillian whispered.

"Have you been there then?" Morrison asked.

"Sure," David replied. "I used to work for a fine food and drink import–export business. We had lots of customers all over Andalucía. I was taken to a lot of the sites by clients when I was new in the area and then I would take other people who came to visit us in Spain if they wanted a tour and had a few days to spare. The whole interior of the Mezquita – that's just Spanish for 'mosque', by the way – is just breathtaking but the mihrab is the focal point. You can still see the signs of wear in the flagstones where worshippers knelt a thousand years ago."

"And its significance for modern Islam?" Morrison asked.

"Well, that's a matter of opinion I suppose. It's hugely significant in the whole history of Islam's interaction with Europe but the idea of regaining Spain for Islam – if that's what you're asking – has been a bit of a minority interest up to now. So I believe that Bin Laden did encourage Muslims to 'reconquer' Spain. I think he called it 'the lost Al-Andalus', which is just stating a fact. However, he had other more important fish to fry so it hasn't really amounted to much in terms of practical action. There was a case in 2010 I think where a group of Muslim tourists all came into the mosque, unrolled their prayer mats, and started to pray. The Spanish government has always banned that. So security was called and a punch-up ensued. It got to court but they were all acquitted on lack of evidence."

"What were they accused of?" Gillian asked. "Just praying?"

"No. Violence against the security staff, but of course the prayer was the catalyst. But the ban's still in place I believe. It's just too sensitive on all sides."

"Ok, so the first screen is an iron doorway," Morrison picked up the story. "Maybe Córdoba, maybe somewhere else in Spain, maybe elsewhere – does it really matter? The next one is Seville and this screen is definitely Córdoba – maybe the most significant location in all of Andalucía for Muslims. Which I suppose would make it the most significant site anywhere outside the Middle East. Agreed?"

"Absolutely," David confirmed.

"Ok. Click on the centre of the mihrab."

An input box appeared.

"Who wishes to enter the soul of Al-Andalus?" David read.

"You have to enter a name here," Morrison explained. "But it has to be an Arabic name in Arabic characters. We tried Tom, Dick, and Harry for ages before we figured that one out."

"Any preferences then?" Spade asked.

"If you go to this address…" Morrison put a notebook on the desk and pointed to a handwritten entry, "… this is a page from our team's database. These are the names we've found that work so far. We have no idea if you get something different depending on what name you put in but we do know that if the name doesn't follow the rules, then you just get bumped off and can't come in from the same computer for an hour. Very frustrating."

"Ok, so I can cut and paste any of these into the box?" Spade asked.

"Yes. Go ahead."

He did.

The screen cleared again, this time to a courtyard with a fountain at the centre that appeared to be resting on the backs of a circle of stone lions.

"I know this as well," David offered. "This is the Court of the Lions in the Alhambra Palace in Granada."

"Before I got started on this I thought the Alhambra was just a Glasgow theatre where Stanley Baxter performed," Morrison commented dryly.

"Well, in that case it's the *other* Alhambra," Stuart McIntosh suggested.

The message on the screen now read "Welcome" followed by a string of Arabic characters.

"Is that the name we just put in?" Gillian asked.

"Yes. That's all pretty standard stuff," Spade confirmed.

"Now this is the tricky bit," Morrison went on. "Press any key and you get the question of the week. We think that only by getting this right can you go any further – we assume, at any rate. If you get it wrong you go back to jail, do not collect £200, etc. The questions change every week or sometimes more frequently and if you get it wrong there's another long delay and you have to go through the whole process again. I think we've paid police officers and IT specialists years of salary just to sit in front of a screen waiting for another go. Drives you daft. Anyway, go ahead. The worst that can happen is we get nowhere again."

Spade tapped the space bar. The Court of the Lions faded into a blurred background image and a line of text appeared with a long white entry box underneath it.

"Jewel of the desert, delight of her lover, city of the Prophet, gift to his favourite, envy of nations, terror of the infidels, hidden for centuries, destined for glory, the missing one," read Morrison from behind Spade's right shoulder.

"Hmm. Looks like we've been here before," Gillian remarked without enthusiasm. "You're on your own this time, fellas. I'm going to keep Tina company." She left to find Tina in the kitchen stirring something that smelled very good.

"Hi," she said as Gillian knocked and came in. "Any breakthroughs?"

"Unlikely, I think. It's a bit of déjà vu for me I'm afraid. Why does everything mysterious have to be on computers these days? What happened to a good old-fashioned treasure map? Anyway, I thought I could sit with a group of increasingly grumpy men or come and speak to an intelligent woman."

"Well, I'm afraid there's just me," Tina smiled. "But I can make you a coffee if that's an alternative."

"Great. Thanks." Gillian nodded in the direction of the pot Tina was stirring. "I take it we're now living on something more than just Tunnock's Caramel Wafers."

"Yes, thankfully. He gets one with coffee in the afternoon, if he's been a good boy. And I keep the supply deliberately low in case of cravings."

"What's cooking?"

"Lamb stew. To have with couscous. But I'm not expecting to eat for a bit yet. Danny loses all sense of time when he's on the computer."

"Ah, sorry. I forgot his real name is Danny," Gillian said. "We just call him Spade. That's his online identity, isn't it?"

"Yes, but I insist on calling him Danny. I think one of us has to live in the real world!"

"So how did you guys get together if you don't mind me asking?"

"Not at all. We met through Warhammer."

"Which is?"

"It's a tabletop military strategy game based on little figures you paint, then have battles with against your pals. I'm secretary of the Edinburgh club and Danny started coming along. I know it sounds a bit pathetic – romance over battling regiments – but it's quite good fun. People aren't as geeky as you'd think. I'm actually more into the artwork than the battles. What about you?"

"Long story. The short version is that David was a pastor in Spain and lost his wife to a drugs war, I suppose you'd say. He grew up in Edinburgh so he came back here to recover. But he had to live somehow so he started teaching Spanish for the University extramural Spanish course. I was trying to brush up a bit for a holiday. It rolled on from there. I'll tell you the full story some other time if you like. It gets a bit complicated."

"And are you married?"

"Yes – less than a month actually. Not long back from honeymoon. Which sounds ridiculous at our age, I know."

Tiny was thoughtful for a bit, stirring the stew and sipping a craft beer.

"I've often wondered what it would be like to be married," she mused. "People my age and background tend to just bounce from one cohab to another. The idea of marriage just isn't really on the cards. But I like the idea. One person for life. And then when you have to work through the problems it binds you closer together."

"Well, it can work that way. I'm also divorced though so I've seen both sides."

"And how long have you actually lived together then?"

"Just the same. About a month."

"Really? So you didn't live together before? Wow. That's a bit unusual nowadays."

"Maybe. We decided early on we wanted to do it right – just from our point of view, I mean. We were both hurting from things in the past and neither of us was ready to jump into something or take a huge risk. So we just took things very slow and gradually grew together, I suppose. There were moments I felt like saying to David, 'Oh just stay the night and be done with it', but I'm glad we did what we did. It made the honeymoon really special."

"So you mean you didn't... I mean... not before the wedding?" Tina blushed. "Sorry, that's really none of my business."

"No, I don't mind. That's right; we didn't, which now I'm very pleased about. It's nice not to do what everyone else is doing just because it's sort of expected. Neither of us were teenagers though so I suppose the hormones had calmed down a bit."

"Double wow. I need to speak to you some other time about that." She put down the spoon and looked thoughtful. "I may look a bit crazy with the goth gear and stuff but I sometimes think I'm more old-fashioned than a lot of my friends. I like the idea of making things special. I mean, you don't stuff your face with meringue just because it's on the table. It's nice to have some starters, then the main, *then* enjoy the pudding!"

"What a nice way of putting it, Tina. Yes, it would be nice to get together some other time. Where do you work?"

"Blackwell's bookshop – you know, on South Bridge? Used to be Thins."

"I know it well. I work at the University in David Hume Tower. If you like we could meet for lunch some time."

"Sounds great. But I forgot to get your coffee. Sorry. I'll stick the kettle on."

Just at that point they were rudely interrupted by an almighty cry from the computer room. David had described to Gillian the roar that used to greet Atlético scoring against Real from his upstairs neighbours in Madrid. It must have sounded much like what they now heard through the wall. They went to investigate. Gary Morrison looked as if all his Christmases, birthdays, and Cup Finals had come at once,

Stuart was looking pleased as punch, and David was sitting quietly in the corner. Even Spade looked stunned, which didn't often happen.

"Pastor David pulls it off again," he muttered as they came in.

"Well, brainbox. Tell us your secret," Gillian said.

"Too many clues," he replied, simply shrugging. "The Prophet's a bit of a show-off. If he'd left it at one or two we'd have been completely stumped but he needed to tell everybody how clever he is. So it wasn't that impressive, honestly."

"Show me your working. Then tell us the answer."

"So the hint read 'Jewel of the desert, delight of her lover, city of the Prophet, gift to his favourite, envy of nations, terror of the infidels, hidden for centuries, destined for glory, the missing one'. That's really far too much. City of the Prophet sounded like Mecca but we're not talking about Saudi Arabia here, are we? So the other choice is Medina. And that's actually not that uncommon a place name in Spain. There are lots of 'Medina this' or 'Medina thats' about the place. Then, 'hidden for centuries' suggests someplace from the Moorish era that was forgotten or lost and has more recently been rediscovered. After that it was easy. Especially when it said 'delight of her lover' and 'gift to his favourite'. About halfway through the Moorish occupation a new dynasty came to power and needed a new capital city. It was called Medina Azahara. I've visited it a few times and taken others there too. It actually lasted less than 100 years at its peak, then it was sacked by invaders and lost until excavations in the early 1900s. There's a legend that the Caliph had the city built for his favourite wife, Azahara, who was homesick for Syria. Then it said, 'the missing one' and that seemed to clinch it. It was missing from his flashy introduction on the site. There were splash screens covering Córdoba, Granada, and Seville but not Medina, which would have been just as important at the time. So that was it. And the rest seemed to fit in ok too. Took a bit of thinking through and I wasn't sure which spelling they'd want but it doesn't seem too fussy about that. So that's it, I'm afraid. Nothing fancier than that."

"Well, I believe Sherlock Holmes was always irked by people

saying, 'Oh, that's obvious once you explain it', so I won't say that, but big pat on the head anyway. So what now?" Gillian asked.

"Now we need to take advantage of getting in," Gary Morrison summed up. "This is really a big deal, believe me. I don't know if there's a time limit you're allowed on the site and then there's the problem of getting in the next time if the question's different. So we need to do as much as we can right now."

"Hang on a bit. I've an idea," Spade said slowly. "Tina, do you think we'd be allowed a pizza break? You know I think better with an injection of mozzarella. Would it be a help if we could guarantee entry another time?"

"Hugely," Morrison answered.

"I'll have the meatfeast with extra pepperoni and double cheese and we'll see what we can do."

Morrison shrugged and they all headed out into the hall.

"I've learned to let him do things the way he wants," David whispered. "Don't ask why or how; just let him potter. I guarantee you'll think it's worth the money."

Stuart McIntosh agreed. "Worked for me," he said.

"Ok then. Pizza orders I think," Tina suggested. "We'll keep the stew for another day."

Pizza arrived about twenty minutes later and Spade emerged from his lair to shove as much as he could into his mouth in one go then padded back in. The rest sat in the kitchen swapping war stories. Time drifted on and the evening was getting late before Spade emerged again.

"Ok," he said. "I think this merits a Tunnock's Caramel Wafer."

"What have you managed?" Morrison asked.

"A new easy-entry door system. You'll still have to go through the splash screens but you won't need to play terrorist trivia any more. I've popped a couple of extra lines of code in the access section. Took a wee while to get in. It's reasonably sophisticated – not done by idiots anyway. So you can enter the same password every time and it'll bypass the security screening."

"Fantastic!" Morrison said. "I hope it's not one of these horrible twenty-four character passwords with dots and commas all over the place though."

"I tried to keep it simple," Spade reassured him. "Just think of me. It's 'dig dig dig'. Ok?"

Chapter 11

A&A MiniMart

That Saturday morning Ali Khan sat staring blankly into the ornamental log fire-effect heater in their living room.

"Aren't you going downstairs?" Ayeesha asked him. "Come on. Saturday's our best day."

"Can't be bothered," Ali mumbled. "Really, what's the point?"

"The point is to live," Ayeesha said as gently as she could. "And to give you something to do to take your mind off things. Look. It's half past nine. People expect you to be open. If you're shut they'll be annoyed and they'll go elsewhere."

"Let them," Ali said resignedly. "I'm fed up being bright, bubbly Ali. You work your butt off to give your family a future and what happens?"

Before Ayeesha could try remonstrating, repeating the same things she'd been saying all week, the door opened and Samira came in. Since the attack she'd moved home for a bit until her confidence came back. And, as it turned out, to try to jolly her dad along once he'd found out about Rasheed and Karim.

"Phone call from the hospital," she announced. "They're letting Enver out for the day. I have to go down and collect him. He'll be in a wheelchair but they seem to think he'll be fine if he doesn't try to walk. Not sure how we'll get the wheelchair on the bus though; I've never had to do that before."

"I'll go with you," Ali announced out of the blue. "We'll get an adapted taxi and bring him home for lunch. Ok, Ayeesha? Can you cook us up something vaguely Turkish?"

"Sure. I suppose so," she said in shock. "I'll have a look online. It's not as if we have a shortage of spices!"

Ali phoned for a taxi and it appeared about ten minutes later. Samira couldn't quite believe what was happening. All week she'd been getting up early to go out to her placement, then going straight to the hospital and eating in the canteen before getting home late. Her father was often in bed already and her mother seemed to be at her wits' end.

"He's *never* been like this before," Ayeesha had confided in her daughter. "We've had ups and downs with the business. It was hard when we were trying to get started. And of course when we were kicked out of Uganda. But he's *never* been like this. It's like he's just given up. Nothing I say seems to make any difference. Normally he loves to go down to the shop in the morning and get things organized. He loves his regulars and always thinks it's a bonus if he can get them to try something new. But this week... nothing. I try to tell him we don't know what the situation is. It might not be nearly as bad as he thinks, but it just washes over him. I'm not sure what to try next."

"I suppose I've not helped, have I?" Samira had asked quietly.

"Believe me, Sami, you are not the problem. It's been a shock, of course, but at least you're here. You seem to still want to be part of the family, don't you? Your situation is that you want to add someone to the family that we hadn't quite expected. Rasheed and Karim seem to have left us. That's what your father can't understand. He constantly thinks he should have spotted something sooner and blames himself that he didn't. I try to tell him that young people make up their own minds but he can't accept it. Believe it or not, you're the one bright light in the whole situation."

Now in the taxi, Ali was chatting to Samira as if they were simply on a father and daughter trip to the zoo. That worried her as much as if he'd sat there not saying a word. *I wonder if he's finally flipped*, she thought. But when they got to the hospital he was the soul of politeness to the staff – as he normally would have been – thanked everybody profusely, even though he had yet to meet Enver, and waited patiently in the hall until Samira had gone in and made sure everything was ready.

"Daddy, this is Enver," she finally said after she had called him in. "Enver, my dad."

"Very pleased to meet you," Ali announced, holding out his hand. "I am so sorry for what's happened to you and that it looks like my people have been to blame. Can I assure you we are not all like that!"

"Pleased to meet you too, sir." Enver returned the greeting not entirely sure what to make of it. "You don't need to feel this was Muslim against Christian, Mr Khan. Honestly. I've been thinking about it a lot while I've been stuck in bed. It's just some crazy people. We can't let them define a whole faith. There are crazy Christians too, you know. I've met some of them!"

With help from a nurse and porter Enver was gently transferred into a wheelchair. The porter insisted on doing the pushing till they got to the door, then Ali took over. The taxi driver came out and put the ramp in place and the chair was strapped securely in.

"So, Enver. Tell me a bit about yourself. Looks like we're going to have to get to know you," Ali started off as they were swinging out of the car park.

"Well, not sure where to start, Mr Khan," Enver began.

"Please. Call me Ali. Once you're married you can say Dad but till then…"

"Oh. Ok, erm, Ali." This was not what Enver had expected – Samira even less so – however he tried to maintain some momentum. "I'm Turkish. I come from Istanbul. My father was a lorry driver and my mum worked in a bakery. I got a scholarship when I was fifteen and went to a school with a good reputation for maths and science. I'd already decided to be an engineer. I applied to Edinburgh University and got in. Did my degree here. Liked the city – and Scotland – and decided to stay. Samira and I met at a charity ball. Ow!"

The taxi took a speed bump a bit too quickly and Enver's face screwed up in pain.

"Ok?" Ali asked sympathetically. "I'm sorry. You must be

140

uncomfortable from the pain – not to mention your future father-in-law cross-examining you! Let's take it easy."

Samira shot a furtive smile across the passenger compartment of the taxi. Enver's teeth were gritted but he tried to return it. Ali gazed out of the window, apparently contented and at peace with the world. Samira wondered what was going on.

If the taxi had been tricky, getting Enver up the stairs to the flat was clearly impossible, so they decided to eat in the little back room of the shop. Ali cleared a space and Ayeesha brought the food down on trays after a hurried introduction. Then, just as they were about to start, the shop door gave a noisy rattle followed by knocking. Ali groaned then went to look, returning a few seconds later all smiles with David and Gillian.

"Hi everyone – sorry to invade your lunchtime," David began. "We can hide in a corner or come back later."

"Not at all," Ayeesha said. "I made plenty. Have you eaten yet?"

"Well, yes, but only sort of," David replied with a look at Gillian.

"He's doing the 5:2 diet and today is supposed to be a fasting day so minimum calories."

"So lunch was a banana."

"That's nothing!" Ali remonstrated. "How can you possibly live on a banana?"

"That's what I ask myself."

"In that case I'll take it the answer is that you can't, so you can share with us. There's plenty naans to bulk it out if need be." Ayeesha slid everyone around a bit and managed to get a place for Gillian, though David ended up perched on a stool in the corner.

"So, just a social call?" Ali asked once food had been shared out.

"No. I've been speaking to the police. We think we have some information that may help locate the boys."

Ali paused with a fork halfway to his mouth. He tried to reply a couple of times but nothing came out.

"Excuse me," he said. "This is more than I expected." He pulled out a large tartan handkerchief and blew his nose loudly.

"There's plenty of time though. Please – let's finish Ayeesha's delicious cooking first," Gillian interrupted, taking the focus off Ali. "What's it called?"

"I can tell you that," Enver said, smiling. "This is *karniyarik* – aubergines with minced meat, onion, tomato, garlic, and parsley. These are *köfte* – meatballs with yoghurt. And the bread is called *lahmacun*. Mrs Khan, this is the best Turkish food I've had since I left home. Thank you very much."

"Well, glad you like it, Enver. And please, call me Ayeesha. I feel too young to be Mrs Khan yet. I've tried to do baklava for after but I'm not sure it's going to be a success; we'll have to see."

David seemed delighted to get a day off his diet and Ali was the gracious host par excellence. Samira wasn't sure what was happening around her. Suddenly, from being in terror of what her parents might think, and traumatized by what some of her fellow countrymen had done, she now found herself back in the bosom of the family again – with Enver, with a happy Mum and Dad, and with some allies she was just getting to know but already liked very much. She delicately took another meatball and a piece of the flatbread and tried to enjoy the moment and not think too far ahead. The baklava when it appeared was pronounced the crowning glory by Enver, who probably ate more than was good for him with that amount of painkillers in his system and a body weakened by the stresses of recovery, but he couldn't resist. Ali and Ayeesha somehow seemed determined to give him the best welcome they could to the Khan family and he was enjoying it. He managed to find Samira's ankle under the table and made contact. She looked up and gave him a broad smile, followed by a wink. Maybe things would work out after all, she thought. Enver had told her he'd been praying. She'd been praying too. It seemed too weird that they were praying to different gods who maybe had to have a Skype call to work out what to do. It made more sense to her that it was one God – maybe with different names. She knew almost all Muslims and probably most Christians would be horrified by the thought, so maybe it wasn't just as simple as that, but right now it was enough that somebody seemed to be listening.

Eventually Turkish coffee appeared – what else? – and everyone sat back. Finally, Ali could restrain himself no more.

"So, David, my friend, do you have good news for us?"

David took off his glasses and cleaned them for thinking time.

"Well, I'm not sure how good it is but it's something, and I suppose not knowing anything is the problem right now."

"So where are they? How are they?" Ali demanded.

"We don't know all of that for sure just yet," David explained, aiming to lower expectations. "I'll start at the beginning. The 'Prophet'," he did the mid-air inverted commas thing, "has a website. The police have been aware of it for some time but they hadn't been able to get access. However, they think this is how he communicates with his followers rather than anything in writing or even emails. I had a meeting with one of the detectives involved and with some help from another expert we managed to get in. It has a full record of all of his previous broadcasts so we can see exactly what he's aiming at. And there are what they call 'testimonies' of specific followers, basically talking about how the Prophet is the greatest and will lead them all to victory. I'm sure you can imagine. Anyway, that meeting was earlier in the week. I haven't been in touch with you sooner because we managed to find a way to get easy regular access and the police team have been working through the material looking for hints of the Prophet's whereabouts. In the course of this they picked up a video clip in what I would call the 'recent recruits' section, supposedly aimed at recruiting more of the same. Somebody had a listen and recognized Scottish accents. Late last night I got a call from DI Morrison, who's in charge. He gave me a police laptop, which is completely secure – they say – and is tied down to only access the Prophet's website. That's all it does. As soon as you open the lid it just goes direct to the site. He asked me if I could let you watch the video and see what you think. It might be your boys."

Ali began to rock slowly back and forth, holding his face in his hands. Ayeesha took out a tissue. For all his apparent Scottishness and disdain for "bloody foreigners" there was a vein in his nature that went much deeper than his adopted country. He began to wail softly, still rocking. Ayeesha put her arm around him and took his head onto her chest.

"Ssshhh," she said quietly and mouthed "I'm sorry" to Gillian.

Enver tried to look away and Samira held her mother's hand.

Eventually it passed.

"Show me," Ali mumbled.

"You're sure?" David asked.

"Yes. Show me. I need to know."

David pulled a laptop out of his briefcase while Ayeesha hurriedly cleared a space on the table. He pulled it open and pressed the power button. The fan began to whir. After about thirty seconds of blank screen an image of grey iron gates appeared. David clicked past that, then past a huge square stone tower, a mihrab prayer niche, and finally an enormous fountain resting on eight stone lions. Finally a line of text and a long white text-entry box appeared. David typed something too quickly for anyone to follow. Then the screen faded to black. The mournful sounds of an Arabic call to prayer started up, then it too faded. Suddenly another image filled the screen. It was a figure swathed head to toe in loose-fitting black garments standing in front of a map of Spain brightly lit from either side. Nothing could be seen of his face and without reference it wasn't even possible to guess his build or height. Then, much more prosaically, a list of menu options gradually appeared at the top of the screen and a mouse pointer appeared.

"So here we are," David announced. "These are the options: *History, Mission, Contribute, Join, Listen, Speak*."

"Doesn't look that different to any charity site once you're past all the flashy stuff," Samira remarked.

"That's what Spade – our IT helper – said," Gillian put in.

"So where are my boys?" Ali demanded hoarsely.

144

"Well, we don't know if it's your boys or not, Ali. It's just a chance. But the video stuff is here."

David slid a finger over the trackpad and clicked on *Listen*. The submenu had *Our Generals*, *Our Warriors*, *Our Supporters*, and *Our Recruits*. He clicked on *Our Recruits*. The screen cleared to a gallery of boxes, each with an Arabic name. David selected one that said *Abdul and Omar*. He clicked. A video window popped up, showing what looked like two young men sitting in front of an open window. The light from behind completely obscured their faces although they also had head scarves with the cloth wound down low on the forehead and high on the nose, allowing only the merest slit of the eyes.

"Play it," Ali demanded again. "Play it."

David clicked *play*. There wasn't another sound in the room as they listened. The first voice from the taller of the two had hardly begun before Ali put his head in his hands again and began to shake.

"Rasheed," he wailed. "My little boy. Little Rasheed. Ahh…"

They listened. It was the tone of a true believer – without doubts, without reservations, without qualms, and without regrets. He spoke of his disgust with the West, with nominal Islam, and with the tolerance many Muslims showed for all of this, including his family. Ayeesha's face was pale. At the mention of family Ali wailed again and began to tremble.

"Can you move it on?" Ayeesha asked quietly.

David dragged the play bar to a point where the shorter, stockier of the two began to speak. He lacked the outrage and fury of the first speaker but followed generally the same line. However he did add that he loved his family and wanted them to be proud of him. Then it was over.

"I'm very sorry I had to show you that," David said quietly, his hand on Ali's shoulder.

"We had to see it," Ayeesha said. "You did the right thing to bring it to us. Would you mind if Ali and I just had a few minutes?"

"Of course," Gillian said immediately. "Do you feel up to a push around the Links, Enver? Samira, is that ok? Great. Right, let's get you going."

Out on Bruntsfield Links it was a beautiful, sunny summer's day. Some Japanese tourists were out putting with deep concentration till a stray dog grabbed a ball and ran off with it, followed by what they guessed was probably very colourful Japanese invective. They had to smile and that eased the tension.

"What do you think, Samira?" Gillian asked.

"It's them," she said. "No doubt. Dad knew it and so did I. All that stuff about his family accommodating themselves to the Great Satan. I don't know how he can possibly speak like that. It must be breaking Dad's heart. Karim was always such a relaxed, happy boy. I just can't relate that garbage to my little brother. I think they must have been brainwashed!"

They walked around in silence for some minutes, absorbing the information.

"What else is on the site?" Samira asked at length.

"Propaganda of all sorts," David answered. "Roughly equally about the evils of the West and failings of traditional Islam. The general message seems to be that instead of pulling each other apart on the Middle East, all the Muslim nations ought to be working together to degrade the West and re-establish Muslim rule. The Prophet seems to reckon we are just about on the verge of collapse and need one sudden push. Then there's talking up all the resources they have – people, cash, plans, military capability; believe that if you like – and telling us they just need a few more willing people who care about Islam and humanity to get things past the tipping point. Then it's goodnight Vienna for the rest of us. And there's a load of stuff about the legitimacy of Islam in Andalucía – how it was a Muslim Caliphate stolen by the West and needs to be restored."

"And Rasheed and Karim fell for it," Samira concluded.

"I suppose so. Still, as far as we know there haven't been any atrocities in southern Spain in the weeks since they disappeared so maybe there's still time to get in contact with them and stop anything happening."

"But would they still be guilty of anything just by being there and by being part of the Prophet's organization?" Enver asked.

"I think that's a moot point," David answered. "As far as I know the organization isn't actually proscribed by name as yet so it may not be an offence to belong to it. Police Scotland are trying to find out if there is a realistic terrorist threat or if it's all hot air. There certainly seems to be incitement to hatred, which is an offence. And it also depends if they have a specific plan and possession of any illegal material."

"Like guns and explosives, for example?"

"Exactly."

"So, even if we do find them and stop them, they may have gone too far already?" Samira asked.

"I'm afraid so. Naturally I didn't want to get into that with your dad. I think he's had enough bad news for now."

They did a couple more circuits occupied with their thoughts before Gillian looked at her watch.

"Do you think we should be getting back in now? It's maybe getting a bit breezy for Enver."

By the time they came back and knocked again on the shop door, which remained locked to customers, Ali had managed to pull himself together. Ayeesha had produced a pot of hot, sweet, spiced tea and the table had been cleared.

"How are you feeling now, Enver?" she asked brightly, opening the door.

"Fine thanks, Mrs... I mean, Ayeesha. A bit drugged up to be honest but some authentic Turkish food was good medicine too."

"How is he?" whispered Gillian.

"Better. It's been a hard few weeks for us."

"I know. I'm sorry."

"Hi, you guys!" Ali shouted from inside. "Come through. I'm not dead yet!"

Cups of tea were poured as they sat down again.

"So what now?" Ali asked. "Do I make a statement to the police or what?"

"I suppose so," David answered slowly. "Do you mind if I tell my contact that you've confirmed their identities?"

"No. It has to be done. But I mean, what's the next step in terms of getting them back and putting a stop to all of this nonsense?"

"Well, I think there are two issues here," David began. "One is getting your boys back, and I think the police will be wanting to speak to you then liaise with Spanish police over that. Maybe not much we can do from this end. But the second thing is to try to find out a bit more about the Prophet himself. If we know what kind of man we're dealing with then we might have an idea of what could be coming next. Even what he might be planning that your boys have got caught up in."

"And how are we supposed to do that?" Samira asked. "We have no idea where he is."

"That's true, but we do know where he's been. He was a preacher in the Edinburgh Mosque for a while before things moved up a gear. How would you feel about a meeting at the mosque to try to get some more information, Ali? At least it might help you feel that you're doing something. You never know, we might come across something that could make a difference to other possible recruits and other families."

Ayeesha looked inquiringly at Gillian. "I thought you didn't want to get involved in any more crime-fighting," she said.

"That's true," Gillian agreed. "But David and I have talked it over. We think it's not a serious risk. We're willing to contribute if you think it would be useful. You have the contacts."

Ali thought for a few seconds. "If there's one thing worse than not knowing, it's sitting here on your arse not being able to do anything," he said. "If it can possibly make a difference to anybody – even if not to us – then it has to be worthwhile. I'll do it. I know the young man that handles all the classes and looks after the administration

of the mosque. I'll call him and see if we could meet. He's called
Mohammed bin Islam but most people know him as Trevor."

Chapter 12

Potterrow

Surprisingly enough – at least to David – the man they had unconsciously started calling "Missionary Mike" turned up at church the following morning, so Gillian did the decent thing and invited him back for lunch.

"Well, thank you, ma'am," he said. "That would be mighty neighbourly." Gillian felt she was being sucked back in time into an episode of *The Waltons*.

They walked back across the Meadows as usual after church and Mike, still carless, walked with them. He spent the entire journey extolling the virtues of Edinburgh, Scotland, and the great Calvinist saints in more or less equal measure. Gillian was getting ready to strangle him by the time they hit Marchmont but bit her tongue.

"It's roast pork today," David said. "We're having a glass of cider. You're most welcome – but if you prefer a soft drink…"

"Oh, I'll just have a soft drink if you don't mind, Pastor David. You go on right ahead though; don't mind me." It was the sort of comment guaranteed to make you feel you *shouldn't* go right ahead and that the speaker certainly *would* mind, whether or not he showed it. David opened a bottle of apple juice, accidentally catching Gillian's eye. She wasn't looking enthralled with Missionary Mike. However, they managed to get as far as sitting down to eat without further collateral damage. Gillian was determined not to ask Mike what he thought of church – or anything else to be honest. This didn't leave many topics of conversation.

"So, Mike, what do you like to do when you aren't... erm... working?" she managed.

"Golf," he said without hesitation. No one was surprised. "And guess where the great game was invented? I suppose you good folks know all about that. I haven't been able to get to the Mecca of golf yet at the Royal and Ancient Club at St Andrew's, but I'm planning a trip this week."

"Oh." She so wanted to sound interested but just couldn't manage it.

Although he tried not to discuss serious church business on Sunday, having just spoken at church, David felt it was more or less a given that the issue of funding and premises should come up so he dived right in.

"So, Mike... Wondering if you'd thought any more about what we spoke about the other week and what the next steps might be, if we were thinking about applying for some support from your group? Just for the sake of argument."

"Well, Pastor David" – *Will you stop calling me that!* David thought with some irritation but managed to keep a smile on his face – "... I really hope you don't mind but I took our conversation as an expression of interest. Nothing more of course but at least that. So I've been in touch with my board already and they are just as excited as I am. I gave them a full report on your church, at least in terms of what I could pick up in such a short time. You know – the worship, the leadership, the theology, and so on – and they are unanimous that if you wanted to partner with us, we'd consider it a privilege. I know this is totally premature so I hope you'll forgive me but I took the liberty of pushing them a bit on figures. They've suggested we might start with something in the region of $300,000 – that would be about 240,000 of your British pounds I reckon – then we could go from there. You know, maybe make it a three-year project or something like that. Help you folks out over an extended time. How does that sound?"

David sat back midway through chewing on a tender piece of pork, lost for words.

"Well, erm, that sounds, what can I say, very supportive indeed, Mike. I suppose there must be a more formal application process though? You'd have to cover due diligence at least and get some kind of idea of our current finances."

"I don't believe so, Pastor David. The board have given me quite wide latitude to make judgments on their behalf. So, forgive me for the expression, but if I say I like it then everybody gives a cheer. Know what I mean?"

"I think I get the drift."

The remainder of the afternoon was something of an anticlimax. David made it abundantly clear that this was a matter for corporate decision-making but he would certainly take the matter to their next LT. Gillian produced a lemon cheesecake with raspberry topping that Mike went on about even more than hitting a ball with a club into eighteen holes. Finally it was over and Mike insisted on shaking hands with both David and Gillian, giving them his home address in the States – *if ever you're there* – and telling them once again what a huge privilege it had been. Gillian finally closed the door behind him and breathed a heartfelt sigh of relief.

"That may be the creepiest man I've ever met," she said.

"Oh, surely not that bad," David remarked, opening a cheap bottle of Valdepeñas from Lidl with relief.

"Oh yes – that bad," she insisted. "You're the pastor – as Mike kept reminding us – and I'm not even on the LT but I guarantee that you'll live to regret it if you touch a penny of that man's money. Honestly. He gives me the heebie-jeebies!"

"Well, I don't think I can just make an executive decision on it. We do need new premises; I've told the LT that we need to talk about it. We don't have anything like enough money to afford to rent somewhere bigger, far less buy. Not to mention all the costs of conversion. It makes my eyes water just to think of it and I suppose Mrs MacInnes's even more so."

"Well – *Pastor* David – don't say I didn't warn you. There's something about that man as genuine as a nine-bob note, as my dad used to say. I'll leave it at that. And for goodness' sake pour me a glass of that. I'm gasping!"

Ali and David met the following morning in the comfortable and leafy surroundings of the Potterrow Student Centre dome near the Edinburgh Mosque to get straight what they wanted to find out.

"So much better than when I was here," David commented. "Then it was all rough concrete blocks. About as welcoming as Ally McCoist in a Celtic bar. Now all nice wood, potted palms, and comfortable seating. What an improvement."

"I had such high hopes for my boys, you know," Ali remarked. "Rasheed seemed such a high flier. We were always bragging about him. Karim wasn't so academic but he was always so affectionate. Rasheed could be a bit distant, you know, but with Karim you always knew what he was thinking. And it was usually some joke or a treat for Ayeesha. He never forgot her birthday or Mother's Day or anything like that. I just can't believe what's happened to them. I keep asking Ayeesha where we went wrong and she just says not to blame myself but I really can't help it."

"Tell me, Ali," David asked after a pause. "Would you blame yourself if they went skiing and were caught in an avalanche? Or rock climbing and fell? Or got married and it didn't work? I'm not trying to say they aren't responsible for their choices – and this was clearly a very bad one – but there are things you just can't see coming. You can't see the future and there's a limited amount we can do to protect our loved ones. I'm speaking from experience here. You know what happened to Rocío. I blamed myself for a long time for that but I finally realized that we were both adults, we both made choices, and I've had to live with the consequences. Knowing only what I knew then – not what I know now – there is no way I could have predicted what ultimately happened. Gillian has helped me see that. So blaming yourself is not only not a good thing for your own peace of mind; it's also completely unrealistic, bearing in mind that Rasheed and Karim fell under the influence of something you didn't

153

even know existed at the time. So how can you protect against that? It's like a virus that you can't inoculate against because it hasn't been isolated yet, even though some people have fallen ill. Can you see what I'm getting at?"

Ali toyed with his coffee.

"Of course. You're right. I can't argue. But emotions aren't always logical. I'm naturally an emotional man, David, as you may have noticed. It's hard not to think there must have been something I could have done or said when it was still possible."

"Well, I won't labour the point," David responded. "But think about it – and listen to your wife. It took me a while for Gillian to get through but I had to admit she was right and let it go. Anyway, what are we going to ask over at the mosque?"

They talked about that for another half an hour or so then left the dome, crossed the road, and made it to the Mosque Kitchen restaurant in good time to meet the administrator for lunch. They gave their names then took a seat and waited. A tall, willowy man maybe in his late twenties with straw-coloured hair, a wispy beard, and a friendly, welcoming expression appeared after a minute or two.

"Mr Khan?" he said, approaching the table and offering a hand before sitting down.

"Yes. Thanks very much for giving the time to meet us. I'm afraid I haven't been at the mosque much for a while. Things have been very busy. And please, just call me Ali."

"Don't worry. We're here for the whole Muslim community, however practising or not. Although we do try to encourage active involvement – you get out what you get in and all that."

"Thanks," Ali said with what sounded like some relief. "Can I introduce my friend David? I mentioned him to your secretary."

"Pleased to meet you. I believe you are a Christian pastor in the town. Is that right?"

"Yes, but here mainly as a family friend." David thought it perhaps not politic to go into the details of Samira and Enver just at that point.

"Well, I am Mohammed bin Islam, the centre administrator, which includes the mosque, the restaurant, and the teaching programme – though maybe Ali told you I'm often known as Trevor. I don't mind which you want to use."

"Forgive me asking," David said, "and I'm sure you're totally fed up with it, but if I don't ask I'll not be able to concentrate. How does a man called Trevor become Mohammed bin Islam – or vice versa?"

"No problem," the administrator replied, not looking overly bothered. "I'm used to it. It's actually not that complicated. I'm originally from Cardiff but I came to New College to study theology. I'm from a Methodist background but I was desperate to get away from home and Edinburgh seemed far enough away. I'm afraid studying theology here wasn't a great boost to my Christian faith so I ended up not really believing anything much. But I always felt there should still be a spiritual dimension to life so I just kept on looking through the various religions. And when I got to Islam I stopped. It seemed to add up so I converted."

"And Mohammed bin Islam?"

"Well, it's quite common for converts to change their name to reflect a new identity. I suppose Muhammad Ali is the best-known example. Unfortunately, everyone at the mosque already knew me as Trevor so it's hard to get them to change. I don't bother now. Some use one, some the other. It doesn't really matter. Anyway, how can I help you? I gather it's about our fraudulent 'Prophet'."

"That's right," Ali confirmed. "I don't know if you know my boys, Rasheed and Karim?"

"Sorry, I've not been in the job that long so can't say I do."

"We think they might have fallen under his influence online. They both packed in their jobs about three weeks ago and nobody knows where they are now. We think they might be in Spain planning something horrible. You know that the Prophet has this crazy idea to reclaim the south of Spain for Islam?"

"Yes, I do. But I'm afraid we don't have any up-to-date information beyond what we gave the police. Are you in contact with them?"

"Yes, we are," David replied, "and we've managed to get into his website but we're just trying to add whatever we can to the process."

"Well, of course we want to help – we've got quite an extensive anti-extremism education programme at the mosque – but I don't know what else we can help you with."

"Can I ask you, Trevor, did you know the Prophet?" David asked. "Were you familiar with his style? Did you listen to him?"

Trevor gave a rueful smile.

"Yes, I did, I'm sorry to say. At first it seemed a bit extreme but maybe just about bearable. He was very popular with a lot of the youth. He was only occasionally allowed to actually preach but he used to hold informal sessions with the young people. I was quite new myself to Islam then and I went along. It was very rousing stuff – all about injustices suffered for generations and the need to reclaim our historical rights. He wasn't actually advocating violence at that time. It seemed to be more about general consciousness raising, getting people on board. Then, I suppose, when there was enough support the plan would have been to try to influence public opinion – here and abroad – and go from there. The police have told us it's all about Spain now but that wasn't really his line when he was here. He seemed to mainly focus on the UK itself; he used to talk about 'mobilizing the Muslim millions' as if everybody was to be part of some unified new movement that would roll like a steamroller over local councils, community groups, then right on up to Parliament. It soon became clear it was a total fantasy and once he started talking about taking Britain by force, our senior people decided enough was enough. And he had started calling himself a new Prophet, which is completely forbidden in Islam. So he was warned, restricted, and eventually chucked out. And we've never heard about him – officially at least – since then. We know that some of our young people are still listening online, even though we've done everything we can to discourage it."

"So you know what he sounds like then, personally?" David insisted.

"Do you mean his style of speaking?"

"Yes. But also just his voice. The actual sound of his voice."

Trevor looked about, confused, but nodded.

"Yeah, sure. He was Pakistani but he'd been in Britain about fifteen years I think. So he had good English but a strong accent. And he spent around ten years near Leicester, so his English was quite northern, not like a Scottish accent. Is that what you're asking?"

"Is there somewhere a bit quieter we could go?" David asked. "There's something we'd like you to listen to."

Trevor shrugged, not really following where this was going.

"By all means. I share an office but I think it'll be free right now. We can go there."

In the administration office David took a laptop out of his messenger bag and laid it on a desk.

"This is a laptop the police have given us," he explained. "It does nothing else but connect to the Prophet's website. Sorry for using that title but that's how everybody is referring to him. Do you mind?"

"Go ahead."

David opened the clamshell case and switched it on. "The thing is," he explained, "the police wanted to get Ali and Ayeesha to listen to a video clip that they thought might be of their boys. Turns out it very probably is."

"Definitely," Ali confirmed grimly. "Unfortunately."

"But in the course of that we also listened to a couple of his weekly broadcasts – 'calls to the faithful' he calls them. Ali, do you want to pick it up?"

"Yes. I was surprised. I'd been told the Prophet was a man in his late fifties, but to me it sounded much younger. And it sounded more Scottish than northern English. I only heard him speak once but what we heard on the video didn't seem to match what I expected. So we were wondering if you could listen to a bit and see what you think."

"Hmm. Intriguing. Go ahead."

David clicked through a couple of menu options till he got to a dated list of talks. They had titles like "The Coming Armageddon", "Reclaiming the Caliphate from Christendom", and "Duties of the Devoted".

"Depressing stuff," Trevor commented while David highlighted one of the titles and clicked. The video window popped up and began to play. It only took Trevor a few sentences to say, "That's not him. No question. Completely wrong. You're right, Ali. The voice is much too young and much more Scottish in the sound of it. It's a good attempt at the general fervour and tone but it's not the same speaker; I'd swear to it."

David looked at his friend.

"Strike one to the good guys, I think," Ali said. He was smiling for once.

Chapter 13

Casa Maria

Karim was humming the tune of "The Girl from Ipanema", working away in soapy water. Some days he felt he got out of bed with a smile on his face and floated through the day. He was picking up more and more of what Bea's dad was saying to him and was even being sent out to take orders in the dining room. Lots of the guests didn't speak Spanish, and English was the lingua franca, but he then had to explain to Bea's mum, who was cooking, what they wanted in Spanish. It was great practice and he felt he was making progress. The highlight of every day was still his *intercambio* (Bea told him that *intercambiar* was the verb "to exchange" and an *intercambio* was "an exchange" – often used to mean a language exchange – so two native speakers of different languages could help each other for free). She told him *intercambios* with native speakers of English were like gold dust at the Official School of Languages and she'd even been offered money to share him with other students but always refused. "You're my private property," she told him. "I don't share you with nobody."

Now it was almost *intercambio* time and Karim was just finishing up some pots, humming softly to himself and doing an improvised salsa shuffle at the sink. Bea came up silently behind him, slipped her arms around his waist under his T-shirt, and whispered in his ear.

"You're doing it all wrong," she said. "It's like this," and began to move behind him, gently guiding his body with her hips.

"Mmm. Much better. Da da da da ta ta tah ta ta…"

Karim thought he could make a career out of washing dishes if this was part of the process.

"You're a bad girl," he whispered back.

"No! You're a very bad boy. You rather to wash dishes than do your *intercambio* with me. Time to go, dish boy!" She stood back, smacked his backside hard, and said, "See you outside. And put yourself a dry T-shirt on!"

They had abandoned El Rincón when Karim had mentioned he wanted to see more of the city.

"I take you places the tourist people don't know," she had said conspiratorially and so it transpired.

Today they went down a narrow street that led through a square into an even narrower street. Then Bea stopped and made a gesture like unveiling a priceless portrait.

"This is the patio of my – how would you say? – my Aunt Mary," she said, leading him through a gateway into a courtyard of pillars and ornate walls that seemed like a room of the house except it was open to the sky. It was full of tubs of flowers and climbing clematis.

"This is fantastic!" Karim said.

"So you have to say, '*Buenos días, tía Maria!*'"

"Tía Maria? You're joking!" he replied, laughing.

"No. It's true. And her husband is my Uncle Peter. That's 'tío Pepe'!"

Karim thought that was hilarious and explained why.

"I know," she laughed. "That's why I bring you here!"

Bea called into the open door, introduced Karim, and Tía Maria duly produced not a coffee liqueur but tiny glasses of ultra dry sherry. *Well*, Karim thought, *I'm an infidel anyway now. What's to lose?* However, the sherry brought an expression to his face that made both aunt and niece laugh.

"Sorry," Bea said. "I told her to give you the drain cleaner for a joke. Now she'll bring out the good stuff."

Karim couldn't even begin to follow the conversation but they seemed to be laughing a lot and he thought maybe at his expense. He tried a few phrases, which seemed not to quite hit the spot, then after a while Tía Maria said something to Bea, who nodded and looked at him a bit shamefaced.

"Are you planning to spend a long time in Córdoba, Karim?" Tía Maria asked in flawless English.

Karim did his goldfish impression for a few seconds. "I'm… well… I'm… eh… not sure… you speak English?"

"Yes," she laughed. "I'm sorry. You can blame Beatriz here. She's a devil! I worked in the Spanish diplomatic service for thirty-seven years. London and Edinburgh but also Budapest and Beijing. Bea told me she had a boyfriend from Edinburgh and we couldn't resist. I do apologize!"

It was all too much to take in. Not just Maria's flawless English – a better accent than his, he thought – but the *boyfriend* bit. He looked at Bea, who was smiling, slightly inquiringly at times. He cleared his throat.

"Em… well… I thought I would learn more quickly if I had a Spanish girlfriend, that's all," he managed to get out. Bea dug him in the ribs.

"So what has Bea been teaching you?" Maria asked mischievously.

"Lots of stuff," Karim admitted candidly. "Like never trust an *andaluza*!"

"True, true," Maria laughed again. "We have both been very bad to you. Now. It's almost lunchtime. Will you stay and eat with us? Pepe will be home soon."

Karim looked for his watch again, then, wrong-footed, looked at Bea.

"I think I need to be back at the Pensión," he said.

"No problem," Bea smiled again, thoroughly pleased with herself. "I spoke to my dad this morning. You get the afternoon off, if you want, of course…"

Karim felt outgunned, outmanoeuvred, and squarely sorted. He shrugged. "You're in charge," he said more or less to both of them. It was no more than the truth.

Pepe was an elegant man in his mid-sixties. He appeared about ten minutes later in an immaculate dark blue suit, crisp white shirt, maroon tie, and what looked like very expensive shoes.

"*Buenos días*," he said, putting out a hand with a smile. "You are Karim, I believe. *Encantado*."

Karim jumped to his feet.

"Em... yes," he managed. "Karim Khan." He just stopped himself from saying "at your service". "*Encantado, Señor*."

Bea smiled approvingly.

"How are you, *guapa*?" Pepe leaned over and gave her two kisses.

"Very well, Uncle," she replied, also in English. "We're staying for lunch."

"Perfect," he said. "I heard about the plot. You women...!"

Karim felt he should say something and not give the impression that he was totally stupid. "So you speak English too?" was all that came to mind.

Pepe smiled good-naturedly and took the glass of sherry Maria had brought out for him. "I was in banking and followed my lovebird all around the world. Now I'm in politics. I was hoping for a more leisurely life but somehow I became a councillor in the town hall. What with corruption, the crisis, and now the implications of Brexit it's busier than ever. So forgive the formal attire. It was an important meeting this morning. We had a report from our chief of police on terrorist threats in Spain."

Karim almost choked on his sherry; however, just then Maria came to his rescue by appearing from inside the house.

"No shop talk!" she said. "Do you want to eat in or out? Karim? What would you prefer?"

"Em... out... if that's ok," he said, deeply grateful for the change of subject.

Pepe gave him a close look but nodded to his wife.

"Ok then. Can you organize things, Pepe?" she asked.

"I'll do it," Bea immediately offered and jumped up.

The lunch was delicious. They had a starter of the tiniest, tastiest fish in batter doused in lemon juice before what Bea told him was *arroz caldoso con bogavante* – soupy rice with lobster. Karim was pretty sure lobster was *haram* – forbidden – not *halal* – permitted – but after everything else he hardly thought it worth complaining about. He ate till he was stuffed then had to make way for dessert, which was perfect *leche frita* – squares of a sort of custard consistency deep-fried and dusted with cinnamon. *Is this heaven?* he wondered, not for the last time.

It was all fantastic. Pepe and Maria were perfect hosts; Bea was so pleased with herself that she just sat and beamed through the entire affair. However, something was wrong and Karim was painfully aware of it. Here he was, being welcomed, accepted, wined and dined, admitted into the heart of an Andalusian family – exactly what Rasheed would have given *his* right hand for – but at the same time Karim was sitting with an explosive device on his left arm and in Córdoba really only for one purpose. He was loving the meal, the company, and the surroundings but underneath it all there was a lie and he knew it. Day after day he had tried to think his way out of it but every time drew a blank. There was no way he could think of to get out of this without either criminal charges or a risk to life and particularly limb. And there was no one he thought he could ask for help. Once or twice he thought about that guy who lived upstairs from the shop in Edinburgh, David somebody. His parents were always talking about the amazing things he kept getting involved in with apparently amazing results, but he had no way to contact him. No number and not even a phone. And calling his parents was the last thing on earth he wanted to do. All he wanted was to turn the clock back six months before all this rubbish had started. Or find someone he could trust that he'd be able to talk to, to tell them the whole story, to ask their advice. But it would have to be someone with the right connections, somebody who wasn't police but maybe was in contact with them. Somebody who would be sympathetic to the awful dilemma. Someone who could be like a father figure without it actually being his dad.

"So, how long do you plan to be in Córdoba, Karim?" Pepe asked, breaking into his thoughts.

He muttered something that wasn't even a very good lie and tried to fill his mouth with another piece of *leche frita.* Then an idea began to form. After everything edible had disappeared, the coffee had come and gone, and it was beginning to be clear that the siesta hour had arrived, Bea got up, thanked her uncle and aunt, kissed them both, took Karim's hand, and started on her goodbyes. Karim hesitated a moment then knew a better time wouldn't come.

"Pepe," he began quietly. "I wonder... would you mind... there's something I'd like to ask you. I'm sorry to take more of your time. Could I just speak to you for a few minutes?"

"Yes, of course. What is it?"

"Em... could I speak to you in private?"

Pepe's face showed some surprise but not displeasure. "Ok with you ladies?" he asked. Bea was looking a bit unsure but shrugged.

"I suppose so," she said.

"I have an office inside," Pepe said. "It'll be cooler there."

Karim had no idea if this was the best or worst idea of his life but he knew he had to do something – and this was certainly something.

Bea looked at her Aunt Maria, who shrugged as if to say, "Don't ask me; I have no idea." They refilled the coffee and sat quietly waiting. After half an hour Maria had already dozed off and Bea was getting impatient. What on earth was going on? Was he asking for her hand in marriage already? A bit premature, and the wrong person. Etiquette for dating Spanish girls? She would have told him that: do as you're told and never disagree with the parents.

The mystery deepened when Pepe and Karim came back out almost an hour later. Pepe was looking grim and this time took Bea in with him instead. Maria was still dozing, snoring softly, so Karim just took a seat and tried in vain to relax. Finally, after another half an hour, Pepe and Bea reappeared. Bea was damp around the eyes and Pepe looked very serious. Maria roused herself at the noise and went inside to make more coffee.

"Why didn't you trust me?" Bea asked Karim as she sat down.

"I'm sorry," he said quietly. "We'd just got to know one another. I didn't know what to do."

"So are there any more lies?" she asked bluntly.

"I never lied to you, Bea," he said. "I didn't tell you the whole truth but I never lied to you."

"I asked you if there are any more lies?"

"No," he said quietly. "That's it. I told your uncle the whole story."

"I think we have to show some sympathy for Karim," said Pepe slowly. "It's to his credit that he's told us what's going on at all when you consider what's at stake. I'm afraid your brother seems to be both resourceful and determined, Karim. And we already know he puts the cause way before his family. So we could have been having this conversation in casualty – or worse. Anyway, I'll leave you together for a minute while I explain to Maria." He went inside to where his wife was heating the milk.

"My Uncle Pepe is a very clever man," Bea said at length. "If he can't help you, then nobody can. He's got lots of connections and he knows all the important people. Do you know he was invited to the prime minister's birthday party but he made an excuse and didn't go? Aunt Maria tells me he could have gone higher in the bank but he wouldn't tolerate some of the things that were going on. How are you feeling?"

"Nervous," Karim admitted. "Actually, to be honest, I'm absolutely terrified. Rasheed is clever too and he's really determined. And I suppose he's got a lot to lose. I reckon I'll go to jail but maybe not for as long as him."

Pepe came back out with Maria, who was carrying yet another tray of coffee.

"This is how I see things," Pepe began. "Karim – you interrupt any time you disagree, ok?"

"Ok." Karim was tempted to call him "sir".

"Right. Someone who started calling himself the Prophet was

preaching radical Islam in Edimburgo – sorry – Edinburgh. This is contrary to your faith so he was expelled from the mosque and took up residence online and got a lot more extreme. Correct? A number of people – we don't know how many but it seems a lot – have become his followers. Unlike other jihadist preachers, though, he doesn't seem very interested in terror attacks in Pakistan or Afghanistan or even London or New York. Instead he wants to re-establish the Moorish Caliphate of Al-Andalus. Your brother Rasheed was one of those influenced by his message to the extent that he volunteered to be in the first attack wave right here in Córdoba. But he needed help. Someone who would do what he needed and whom he could control. You, Karim. Yes? So he proceeded to bully or brainwash you to come with him. You agreed though you were never as committed. Maybe as a token of his devotion or fanaticism, when Rasheed heard that your sister, Samira, was going out with a Christian boy, he decided – or he was told – to instigate an attack against the boy. So we know that he still has strong connections in Edinburgh and I think we can guess that the Prophet does too. If the Prophet isn't still physically based there, at least he still has eyes and ears in the city.

"At that point – when you heard that your sister and her boyfriend had been targeted – that was when you decided enough was enough and you wanted out. You and Rasheed had a fight, and in the aftermath, seeing that you were slipping away from him, he managed to trick you into accepting what he told you was an explosive band on your wrist. He has threatened you that any step out of line and – boom! He also took control of your mobile and you think Rashid, being an IT specialist, probably keeps an eye on your email account. So he knows where you go, probably what you do – or at least some of it – and you are not free to contact people back home. In any case, up to now you didn't know who to contact. You don't want to contact the police for fear of Rasheed finding out, and in any case the police would probably only arrest you as a terrorist suspect anyway – which, to be fair, might be an understandable conclusion. Any thought that you were near a police station and yet again – boom! You don't want to contact your family because – let's speak honestly – you are not feeling very proud of what's happened so far and ideally you would like the whole thing to be resolved without your parents knowing your part in it. And finally, as a stranger in town and with limited Spanish, you would have difficulty in explaining yourself. You've been getting friendly, shall we say, with Beatriz here, we met about two hours ago, and you decided to trust me and tell me the full story. Is that a fair summary?"

Karim had been nodding at various points through Pepe's account and did so again. "Yes. That's it," he said quietly.

"So what should we do with you, Karim?" Pepe now asked, at which point Bea gave him a sharp glance.

"Should we simply hand you over to the police, tell them we've apprehended a terrorist, and let things take their course?'

This was not what Karim had hoped to hear and he didn't know what to say.

"Or should I believe you that you have been largely coerced into this, that you hadn't perhaps realized exactly where it was all going to end, and now you are willing to make a full statement even though this might have extremely serious consequences for yourself and more so for your brother? Which?"

"You should believe him, Tío!" Bea exclaimed. "He's told you everything, hasn't he?"

Pepe ignored Bea and looked hard at Karim.

"Should I?" he said. "A young man who has come here to be part of a plot to destroy and destabilize my city. Are you a suitable companion for our niece, whom we think very highly of and naturally want to protect? What do you have to say for yourself, Karim?"

This was all going horribly wrong, Karim thought desperately. Pepe had seemed like his last hope. On the spur of the moment he had decided to trust him and now this. It felt like the Spanish Inquisition – and actually in Spain!

"I don't know," he managed. "I've told you everything I know. I never wanted to hurt anyone but Rasheed insisted it was our duty. I wanted to do what was right. Now I can see that I was wrong but at the time I thought I had to. I've been wearing this band for over a week now and want to get rid of it. I want to be free. And I want to do what's right for Bea's sake too. Rasheed made me promise that even if the Prophet told us to be suicide bombers we would do it. We had to love the cause more than our own lives, he said. I don't want to die. I want to live. I want to live with Bea. And with my family."

By the end Karim was howling, holding his face in his hands, barely comprehensible. Bea put her arm around his shoulders and looked daggers at her uncle. Maria was looking at him also in some surprise.

"Ok, Karim," Pepe said at length, more gently. "Can I apologize for putting some pressure on you? I had to be sure. I think your reaction is genuine, not just some other plot that needed you to connect with a Spanish family. It was a possibility. But we do care about Bea deeply and I will not tolerate her being put at risk. Is that clear?"

"Yes, sir," Karim managed to whisper.

"Now we've got that clear, dry your eyes. I will do everything I can to help you – for Bea and for you. And for my city. But it's not going to be easy or simple. Starting on this road, we don't know where it's going to lead us but you chose to trust me and I'll do my best to not let you down. Is that ok? Am I forgiven?"

Now Karim managed a smile in spite of a runny nose and puffy eyes. "Yes."

"So I don't see any way forward with this without involving the police. Will you trust me in that?

"Yes," he repeated in a whisper.

"The first priority is to get a hold of Rasheed and get his mobile off him, then get that thing off your wrist. The Prophet will have to wait, though he's on my list as well. So this is what I'd like you to do…"

Karim and Bea walked home hand in hand.

"I think what you did was very brave, Karim," she said.

"You're not still mad at me then?"

"I was madder at my uncle, *de verdad*. No, I'm not mad. But I am mad at Rasheed. Anyway, you remember what we're going to do when we get home. Repeat it to me."

Karim went through the instructions that Pepe had given him. Bea listened, then repeated what she was going to do. The first thing was to get her mum and dad alone in the kitchen and explain the situation – as briefly as possible. Then deal with Rasheed. As it happened, Bea's parents were waiting for them. They spoke rapidly in Spanish. Karim caught Rasheed's name but nothing more. Bea's face told a story though. Something was very wrong. As soon as she could she turned to Karim.

"Rasheed's gone," she said simply. "Packed his bags and disappeared about an hour ago. No message for you, no hint of where he was going."

"Just when we were talking with Pepe!" Karim said, shaking his head. "Now what do we do?"

Chapter 14

Gonzalez & Bravo: Jamón y Vino

Rasheed Khan knew that he was no fool and had trained himself to see opportunities others missed. One of his favourite aphorisms was "opportunity favours the prepared mind", and he did what he could to prepare his mind and not miss any openings. That's why, when the fitness band project came up at Centaur Systems, he immediately saw the possibilities even when the client couldn't raise enough on Kickstarter and canned the whole thing. So he kept working on it. First in company time, then, when Justin formally told him to cease and desist, he would work into the evenings and even at home. He had to beg some favours from the engineers to get the physical build right but essentially it was a software problem, which he eventually solved. Clearly a fitness band had nowhere like the battery power to run GPS and send a mobile message whenever a certain event was triggered, so his solution was to add photoelectric cells disguised as decoration and also use whatever power there was to scan for available local Bluetooth connections connected to a network. If it found one and there was some data it wanted to send, then it simply grabbed the connection, piggy-backed onto the wireless network, and sent its data to whichever mobile had been previously set up. He was very proud of it, but for some reason he simply couldn't grasp, Centaur in general and Justin in particular completely failed to see the potential.

So it was like Xerox and the WIMP environment all over again. When Xerox's elite blue skies skunkworks at Palo Alto – known as the Palo Alto Research Company or PARC – invented

170

ethernet, the mouse, windows, multitasking, and drop-down menus, nobody at senior level had a clue what to do with it. As subsequent commentators put it, "What did a bunch of copier heads know about computers?" But Steve Jobs, allowed in for an informal visit, saw what they had, immediately recognized the potential, went on to recreate that desktop environment – first in the Lisa and then the Mac – and the rest most assuredly was history. So the lesson was: forget the hierarchy who may not have a clue what you're doing, and go it alone before somebody else – not as creative but who can see the potential – steals your idea and becomes a billionaire. Clearly, in retrospect, all the guys at PARC should have done a corporate bunk, waited a few months, then set up their own thing and licensed the WIMP environment to the highest bidder. But they didn't and ended their days in relative obscurity, while Jobs went on to be head honcho of the world's biggest company. Lesson learned.

Although the wristband project was on a much smaller scale, opportunity still favoured the prepared mind and Rasheed saw his chance. Once he understood this was going nowhere, he checked copyright and patent laws, did as much as he could out of working hours, paid the engineers out of his own pocket, and filed a patent application for what he was planning to call "WhereWare".

Then, much later, when he foresaw another potential problem, the solution was there, simply waiting to be modified and adapted. The first version of WhereWare would keep an eye on your blood pressure and alert a designated mobile if it varied beyond certain parameters and also send the coordinates of the event. That could easily link to Google Maps and pinpoint the problem. The modification was to allow a remote message to be sent back to the band to do something – like blow up – in response to the data it had just sent about itself. Of course it could also be told to self-destruct whenever required regardless of location, or blood pressure, for that matter. Once all of that was working, Rasheed couldn't resist being a bit of a smart-ass and adding audio capabilities. Hoopla! The new band also allowed for locking. Any tampering with the clasp would trigger detonation, if so desired, though this could also be deactivated remotely. Great for tagging offenders, for example, or in this case, restraining a potential offender. Getting the band onto Karim's wrist had been the weakest link of the plan; however, Rasheed felt he could rely just on bullying to make that happen. And so it had transpired. Karim stuck his arm out when instructed to and Bob's your uncle.

Ultimately, it was, of course, a second-best solution. The optimum situation was that Karim would do what he was told simply because he was told to, and at some brute level believe in the mission. But Rasheed knew his younger brother could potentially be a victim to weakness of resolve based on emotional "humanitarian" considerations, so he had to be prepared for if and when this might happen. It was unfortunate when it did happen, but all was not lost: "opportunity favours the prepared mind". The modified band in his bag had so many possible commercial applications he had almost lost count; however, needs must and the mission was more important. So, with the band on, Karim was back on the leash and Rasheed could go about his other business with less concern.

Then, one morning in class, he got a beep on his phone to say that Karim had gone walkabout. In fact, he seemed to be wandering right off the beaten track. What was he up to? Initially there wasn't a stable enough Bluetooth/wireless link to give good data, but soon the signal seemed to stop moving and quality improved. Rasheed excused himself from the introductions to the Spanish subjunctive based on uses of *ojalá* – meaning "if God wills it", derived from Arabic *inshallah*. Rasheed knew perfectly well what God willed and it did not include Karim roaming around out of control. He picked up his books and left the academy. Across the street on a park bench he tapped on the app on his phone and started listening. What he heard grew more and more alarming. Karim was speaking to people whom Rasheed couldn't identify. As he listened, he heard first a girl – he guessed that was Bea – then an older woman. Not long after an adult male. Then chit-chat in English and the sound of plates and glasses. Ok – so they were having lunch. Nothing particularly sinister in that perhaps. He waited to see what would happen. Better to be bored for an hour listening to other people eat while feeling hungry himself than miss something possibly dangerous. Then it was over. More plates and cutlery. Finally it sounded like goodbyes and Rasheed relaxed. You could never be too careful. Then disaster struck. Just as he was about to turn off his phone and get the bus back to Pensión El Moro he heard Karim speaking again to the adult male. Still the signal wasn't perfect so he couldn't be sure what was being said but it sounded serious – not just *adiós* and see you later. Then feet on wooden floors, the opening and closing of doors, and a much more indoor sort of sound. At that point reception improved a lot – maybe they had moved nearer the router. The adult male spoke first. It was perfectly clear.

"Now what do you want to talk to me about, Karim?" followed by Karim saying what Rasheed simply could not believe he was hearing.

"What I told you earlier about why I'm in Córdoba – it's not true. My brother and I came here to blow up the cathedral." Then a silence. Then the man spoke again.

"Sorry, Karim. Maybe my English is getting a bit rusty. Can you repeat please? It sounded like you said you came to Córdoba with your brother to blow up the cathedral. I'm sure I got – how do you put it – the wrong end of the stick."

"No," said Karim. "That's exactly right. That's why we came, but now I want no part of it. But there's a problem. See this thing on my wrist?"

Rasheed listened aghast as the conversation unfolded till he couldn't bear to hear any more. He closed the app. Disaster. Total and utter disaster. He had always known Karim was flaky but dropping out of the project and confessing all to someone – whoever it might be – was a different thing. He swiped left a couple of times to show a new page of icons and opened the one called Boom. He only needed to log in, enter a password, and click the confirm button and the deed would be done. Karim would certainly lose his hand, maybe his arm, maybe his life, depending on loss of blood. Whoever was with him would certainly be injured but probably not killed. But whatever state Karim was in, his confessor would still know that a young man called Rasheed, staying at the Pensión El Moro, was planning a terrorist attack. That information was bound to go straight to the police. The Mezquita and the cathedral would be put into lockdown and the chance would have gone for good. So much was certain, whatever he did to Karim. He closed the app, went to his bus stop, got off at the *pensión*, packed his bags, and left.

The bomb disposal specialist looked at Karim and the device on his wrist and scratched his head.

"*Nunca en mi vida he visto algo así*," he said.

"He's never seen anything like this before," Pepe translated.

It hadn't taken long for Pepe to get a police response after calling his friend Captain Fernandez in the Andalusian provincial command of the Policía Nacional. The problem had been how to disable the device or obstruct Rasheed from detonating it before placing him in custody. So Pepe's idea had been for Karim and Bea to go back to the *pensión*, pretend to make up with Rasheed without giving anything away, and at least try to locate the mobile. Police would arrive in plain clothes while they were in conversation. So long as the mobile wasn't physically in his hand and the app open, they thought that with the element of surprise they could probably hold him long enough for reinforcements to arrive from outside the door and cuff him. The fact that Rasheed had already left was unexpected, to say the least. Pepe and Maria arrived about ten minutes after with police in tow. After that the question of where Rasheed was, and when – and if – he might detonate the device became all there was left to think about. Fernandez made some calls and before long a couple of vehicles turned up. Bea, Pepe, and Maria were loaded into one and Karim into the back of a van – "*por si acaso*", one of the officers explained to Pepe, who translated for Karim. It meant "just in case". Further clarification wasn't really needed. Together the convoy followed a police car to an anonymous building on the outskirts of the city.

"Counterterrorism specialist teams," Pepe explained, as they were all getting out. "Bomb disposal, special ops, IT analysis, communications monitoring, firearms specialist, counterterrorism training, and general intelligence." Outside the building the only sign said, "Gonzalez & Bravo: Jamón y Vino". Karim felt his legs turning to jelly as they went in along with their police escort.

"¿Qué tal?" Bea asked. "How are you feeling?"

"I don't know," Karim shrugged. "I don't know how much trouble I'm in. And I'd like to find out how Rasheed knew we were coming for him. He's clever but he'd not a mind reader. And I hope the guys here know what they're doing or I might need to learn how to tie my laces with one hand…"

First of all Karim was fitted with a bulky black cuff. There was no explanation but it didn't take a genius to work out it was intended to absorb any explosions that might take place before they could properly deal with things. Bea and Maria were asked to wait in a small reception room and Pepe and Karim went on alone – Pepe for purposes of translation, and hand-holding, if need be.

Eventually, after a maze of twisting corridors and locked doors that needed fingerprint authentication, they emerged into sunshine, crossed a courtyard, and entered a second building.

"This is where they practise bomb and explosives disposal," Pepe explained. "They have it in another building because they sometimes work on live materials; if anything goes wrong, then they don't lose the entire headquarters."

An ambulance was waiting next to the building, which Karim thought looked somewhat ominous. The room they eventually entered was windowless and the walls were covered with thick black foam baffles Karim had seen once before in a recording studio where his former girlfriend Sunna was supposed to be making a record. Her dreams of Bollywood had lasted about six weeks. This felt significantly different. Pepe introduced him to the specialist who had drawn the short straw to try to disarm the device but no names were given. The unnamed operative started explaining some details to Pepe. Even without understanding a word of the Spanish, Karim immediately felt he was in experienced hands. There was a calm professionalism about the way the man spoke that inspired confidence. He took the cuff off and examined the device from all angles, at some points pulling out a magnifying glass and taking his time to look as closely as he could without putting any pressure on the clasp. He spoke as he worked, leaving time for translation.

"This room is impervious to mobile signals," Pepe explained, "so at least Rasheed can't set it off remotely now. The clasp is wired to a circuit. Opening the clasp breaks the circuit. What he's going to try to do is insert a loop from one point in the circuit over the clasp, so disconnecting the clasp won't break the circuit. He says it's not the sort of thing you get two chances at, however, so he asks you if you really want to go ahead."

The specialist paused, looking keenly at Karim, eyebrows raised.

Karim nodded, not trusting himself to speak.

"Ok," the agent said, got up, and ushered Karim across to an installation he hadn't noticed before. Set in one corner of the room, it looked like some kind of glass and steel modern art. There were two quarter spheres of thick, clear Plexiglas standing about a metre and a half high and facing each other, each with a chair inside. Karim guessed they must be blast shields to protect whoever was sitting on the chairs. A low steel table stood between them, its surface scarred with blackened lines. Each of the shields had two circular holes cut facing the central table about fifty centimetres apart. On one shield the holes were occupied by black rubberized sleeves like robot arms. The other shield had a plug blanking one hole, and the other was empty. Karim guessed that things had been prepared for him. The anonymous officer beckoned him to sit on the side with the open hole.

"Pliz," he said.

Karim sat.

The officer came and, taking his left arm, extended it through the hole. Turning a dial, he closed the hole till it gripped firmly around his lower forearm with a rubber seal. Then he went round to the other side and took his place, extending both arms into the black mesh sleeves. Karim looked around to see Pepe staring out through the window of a black booth on the opposite diagonal. The steel table already held a variety of tools and the technician now proceeded to take up a set of pliers in one hand and the lance of a multimeter in the other. At this point Karim decided to look away. It felt like being in surgery. If he was lucky there wouldn't be any blood and he did feel reasonable confidence in the man working like a surgeon, separated from him by two thicknesses of one-inch Plexiglas; however, that did not mean he had to enjoy it.

The minutes ticked by. Karim kept his eyes fixed on Pepe, whose eyes were also riveted on him. It was as if there was a silver line of sight between them, which, if either of them dropped, might have appalling consequences. All Karim felt physically was a momentary light tugging on his wrist. From time to time the technician would rotate his arm slightly like a hairdresser moving a head to another angle to trim the other side. Karim felt sweat dripping down his forehead and into his eyes, stinging them, but felt he couldn't risk rubbing his eyes for the sake of losing sight of Pepe.

Then suddenly it was over. He heard a click, felt a release of tension, and the band was lying loose on the table. He turned and looked and found the technician opposite with a face just as dripping with sweat as his own. He blinked, rubbed his eyes, and pulled his hand out of the hole. The seal round his forearm automatically tightened and closed the gap. Just as well, as at that moment there was a brilliant flash, a horrendous bang, and, where the band had been – smoke. Pieces of black plastic rained down throughout the room, which was now filled with acrid fumes. Karim was deafened, screamed, and jumped back, upsetting the chair and finding himself on his back on the floor. The technician was there in a second, kneeling beside him and Pepe only took two seconds more.

"¿*Cómo estás?*" the technical asked him. "You all right, Señor?"
Karim managed a nod. "What happened?" he spluttered.

The technician went into high-speed Spanish and Pepe translated.

"It appears that when the band came off the circuit bypassing the clasp held but once it touched the steel of the table it shorted. That triggered the device. Or something like that. Even I don't really understand what he said. Anyway. You're ok?"

"Yes. Shaken but ok."

The technical wiped his brow and let off another burst of Spanish.

Pepe smiled. "He says it was a pity we lost the device. He would very much have liked to take it to bits and find out how it worked!"

There might be a place in the universe for a man who took high-explosive devices to bits for fun, thought Karim, but it didn't need to be anywhere near him. He stood up, picking tiny fragments of black plastic off his T-shirt and jeans. The blast shields had matching starburst patterns of soot, and for a second Karim regretted that Rasheed still had his mobile. He would have liked a picture.

On the other side of town, Rasheed was sitting in the bar of another tourist hostel, sipping a Coke with his mobile in his hand studying the display of an app. It was dead and had been so for the past hour. That was it, he guessed – the game was up. Somehow, Karim had slipped the noose. He was on his own now and one way or another he would have to explain the circumstances to the Prophet. Losing control of Karim was a blow. Knowing that someone – perhaps someone of importance – knew there was a plot to destroy a monument in the heart of historical Córdoba with likely collateral damage was worse. These were troubling matters. But facing the Prophet and explaining – that was what really worried him.

David Hidalgo, Ali Khan, and Stuart McIntosh sat in DI Morrison's office with the laptop in front of them.

"Are you absolutely sure?" Morrison asked Ali, not for the first time.

"Definitely. You can speak to Trevor yourself if you don't believe me!"

"We will. But in the meantime, if Trevor is right then we seem to have a new range of possibilities in front of us. Either the Prophet has a collaborator or he's using a mouthpiece for some reason we can't imagine, or he's been the subject of what we might call a 'takeover bid', or maybe he doesn't even exist any more and someone else has completely hijacked the operation and is simply using his identity to further their own cause."

"You mean the Prophet might be dead and someone else is pretending to be him?" Ali asked.

"Among other possibilities."

"Does the fact that it sounds like a Scottish voice mean anything?" David asked.

"Hard to say. It may only mean that he hasn't gone to Central Casting but is using a local contact from his Edinburgh days. But bearing in mind the range of possibilities we've just gone through, I don't think we can really be very sure of anything. However, it is a piece of information we should hold on to."

"What now, then?" Ali asked. "Are my boys criminals?"

Morrison shrugged and made a point of looking non-committal. "That'll be for the fiscal to decide – or the Spanish authorities. I really don't want to give an opinion. All I'd say is that if you have any contact from them you must let us know immediately. Stuart has initiated contact with local Spanish police to pass on what we can." He looked to his colleague.

"National Police Service in Spain, Andalucía Province," McIntosh explained. "Sorry I can't do all the proper Spanish names. We've alerted them to the fact that there may be a terror plot focused on Córdoba. The descriptions and photos you gave us, Ali, have been sent. I think the point is that whether or not they are currently guilty of something we can only hope they are picked up before there isn't any room for doubt at all."

"*Inshallah*," Ali muttered.

"And in the meantime?" David asked.

"Going through the website with a fine-toothed comb," Morrison said. "Looking for any other hints of what, where, when, and how. The fact that we can now go in at will and roam around has been a major boost so we're grateful to Mr Spade again. With a bit of luck we'll pick something up that gives us a new direction. However, in the meantime I think we just need a full statement, Mr Khan. I'll get a DC to come and speak to you."

They filed out, Ali with a young woman DC to an interview room and David and Stuart McIntosh to the canteen. They gathered up two appalling excuses for coffee and a couple of sad-looking buns and made for a corner table.

"So, what do you think of Hearts for Saturday?" Stuart asked nonchalantly.

"What?"

"Hearts. Heart of Midlothian. It's a football club, David. Playing Hibs. Hibernian Football Club. It's the local derby. Any predictions? Don't tell me you're unaware of crucial local events?"

David had to smile. He envied a man who could switch so easily from terrorist plots and a family in meltdown to what really mattered in life: fitba'. He shook his head. "Hibs five one," he said, being the first thing that came into his mind.

McIntosh was dismissive. "What?" he cried. "You're joking! Snowball's chance in hell. My money's on Hearts two one. A draw is possible. But five one? Never!"

"Sorry, Stuart. That wasn't really a prediction," David admitted. "'Fraid I don't really follow the beautiful game."

"So what do you follow? More a rugby man, eh?"

"Not that either," David had to confess. "I can watch a bit of snooker from time to time maybe."

McIntosh was appalled. "Snooker's not a sport," he snorted. "They don't even break sweat. Still, I think there was a streaker at a snooker competition once. So, at least that would make it worth watching."

David suspected he was just being wound up and a mischievous twinkle confirmed it. "Almost got me there," he said. "No, I just lack the sports gene, I suppose. Like some people simply have no interest in music, which I can't understand. Horses for courses."

"And what about the religion gene?" Stuart asked, suddenly doing the verbal equivalent of a body swerve like a Scottish Premier League forward. "Are there some people with it and some without? What d'you reckon?"

David took a sip of his coffee then put it down with disgust. He really should have taken tea. There's only a limited amount of damage that can be done to boiling water and a teabag.

"Actually, an interesting question," he replied, trying to take the sudden change of subject in his stride. "I think there has to be something in that. I've known people with a deep personal faith who just can't abide the whole church experience. And I think there are more and more people who do have spiritual beliefs but are completely informal about it. They don't have any organizational connections at all."

"You mean not even Pam Rhodes on *Songs of Praise*?" Stuart asked in mock amazement.

"Not even that."

Stuart had to smile. "So how would that work if I'm meant to be judged in the afterlife on my religious performance – just like Messi coming up before the Ballon d'Or committee – and by bad luck and a poor upbringing I happen never to have really got the bug? What then?"

"We *are* getting profound." David batted the question. "To what do I owe the pleasure?"

"Just thinking," Stuart said simply. "On my own in your old flat, not much to do except go out drinking, which has its limits. And I was thinking how it had been your place during all the time we've known each other. You used to sit in the little office room writing sermons – and praying, I suppose, maybe counselling people in the other rooms. People pouring out their spiritual woes.

Maybe some people finding the light, maybe some losing it – I don't know."

"Well, all of that," David answered, "and then some. That was where I was living when I just about lost it all myself."

"Immediately after you came back from Spain?"

"Around that time. It was a process. You know I lost my wife to a gangster dealing drugs? We had worked together for years. Church, but also lots of rehab projects, though I don't separate the projects from the church. I took the view – still do – that if you're going to kick drugs you need something even more significant to put in their place. And I happen to still think that the big questions – the 'who am I', 'what am I here for', 'is there a meaning', that sort of thing – these are questions we need to confront. And when someone's getting off drugs they do ask big questions. They want to know if there's a purpose in their lives and if they can have any significance. If they matter to anyone."

"Like people whose marriages have just broken up," Stuart remarked. "They need to know if they matter to someone else as well."

"I imagine so," David replied but left the implication hanging. "Anyway, losing my wife when we had been working together in what we both felt had been a calling from God... that just about finished me off. But I think I've more or less got my act together again now."

"Well, I'm glad about that. But as far as I'm concerned, I've just never been interested in religion – I mean not personally. It's a phenomenon you can't ignore in Scottish society, and in law and order. But I've just never found it appealing. It all seems to be about respectability and 'holier-than-thou'. People who live in their little religious bubble and think they're better than anyone else. Actually, to be honest, I would say I've probably been pretty anti along the way. That was one of the things that came between Kirsty and me. She was a bit inclined and I used to pooh-pooh it and tell her she was being brainwashed. Not really a clever way to build your marriage."

"And what about the Sunday you came to us?" David asked. "Was that a religious bubble full of zombies?"

"Well, apart from the Yankee who didn't impress, the rest of it was actually quite pleasant. Pretty relaxed, a good cross-section of Edinburgh society, I would say. So there were Morningside ladies but also young families, students or student age anyway, the middle-aged like you and me, and some kids. And Samira, of course, so I suppose you can tick the multicultural box as well. No, it was ok. As regards whether any of it is true of course is another matter. I'm used to presenting evidence to the fiscal and the courts – things you can prove. So I think that presents religion with a bit of a problem, doesn't it?"

David tried the coffee again but it wasn't any better. "Maybe," he said cautiously. "But let me put it back to you: you present cases for conviction in court."

"Well, strictly speaking it's the fiscal who prosecutes but he gets his cases from us, so yes – more or less."

"And you present evidence?"

"With the same qualification, yes."

"Some of which is hard factual evidence like forensic science reports, DNA samples, and that kind of stuff."

"Indeed."

"But you also present what I would call softer evidence, like witness statements."

"We do."

"And people are convicted on the basis of the statements of witnesses. In the old days, I suppose there were people who were hung on the basis of what people said they saw or heard or experienced."

"Certainly... and your point is?"

"That it isn't normally possible to give hard physical evidence for things in the religious or spiritual sphere, in some cases because we are dealing with historical events that are beyond formal proof; in other cases it's to do with interpretations of the facts. But that doesn't mean there is *no* 'evidence'. In fact, spiritual experience is *exactly* the same type of evidence as witness statements. Some people even call the account of how they came to faith their 'testimony'. So if you're evaluating testimony, you have to look at the reliability and credibility of the witness, their record of lying and their reputation for veracity, their rationality, and even their memory and attention to detail. And their consistency and degree of certainty. I think it's far too easy to say there's no evidence because the evidence isn't just the sort you want it to be. And you as a policeman would actually know that better than me, wouldn't you?"

"Fair comment, Reverend, but when a witness in a trial says they saw someone come out of the bank with a gun carrying a sack with 'loot' written on it, these are events that, while not very common, admittedly, do happen or could happen. When you talk about a man rising from the dead, this is unique in history, isn't it? So do we not have to conclude that any other explanation is *more* likely to true?"

"Also fair comment, Officer; however, I think that most people who come to Christianity as adults don't do so after an even-handed examination of the evidence of the resurrection – though some actually do, which is interesting. What tends to happen is that people start feeling some awareness of a God around about them, maybe intervening in events – what we call Providence – or directly communicating in some way. Only when they are convinced that there is a God who is speaking to them do they start thinking about the historical facts that undergird the message. So I would start by evaluating what people say they have experienced in their own lives and ask if they are lying, deranged, or confused. Then think about the implications of that. If they are the sorts of witnesses you'd be happy to present in court, then I think that has an implication for what they say. The question of how a God might have intervened in human history before in dramatic ways comes later."

"So you're saying I need to listen to what people say and see if I find it convincing?"

"If you want to explore the issues, I think that would be a good place to start. There's also the issue of being prepared to listen to what you might be hearing and see what you think of that."

"And how would I do that, assuming I might be interested?"

"We call it prayer, though to be honest it's better just to call it speaking or thinking in a God direction. And I would read the Gospel accounts and see what impressions you get from them. Do they sound like authentic witness statements or do they sound like fiction or lies intended to deceive?"

"Interesting. I've not heard it presented like that before. Normally people just say, 'You gotta have faith', like the song, you know? My position is that if you just don't have faith then it feels like a roadblock. No way around. Which is where I would normally place myself. At any rate it's worth thinking about further. I won't promise, but do you mind if we continue this conversation at a later date?"

"Not at all. I absolutely hate hard-sell religion so you can relax as far as that's concerned."

"Deal. Another coffee until Mr Ali Khan appears?"

"I'd rather hang."

"I understand. Maybe I've drunk that much over the years I'm immune. Tea then?"

But David didn't get the chance to reply before McIntosh's mobile went off. When he saw who it was, the DI swiped to take the call and stood up to pay attention, looking intently at his empty coffee cup as he was listening. David guessed the call might have something to do with what was going on but hearing only a succession of "yeses" and "wows" and "he's right here" didn't enlighten him.

"Developments!" McIntosh said archly. "Back in a jiffy," and left the phone on the table. David was tempted to have a look and at least see who was calling but restrained himself. McIntosh reappeared not more than twenty seconds later with a rather flushed and confused-looking Ali tagging along. He picked up the phone again.

"Hi. Yes, I have him here. I'll pass the phone over and you can put him on."

The mobile was handed to Ali who clearly had no more idea than David what was going on. "Hello? Yes it is. Who's this? Who?" Then he suddenly went shaky and sat down. "My son, my son! Thank God! Where are you? And you're safe? What's been happening? And what about Rasheed? Oh! What happened?"

Ali now sat listening intently, trying to recover himself and only making an occasional comment. Stuart beckoned David aside and explained. Karim was in Córdoba. He and Rasheed had fallen out. Karim wanted to come home. It wasn't clear yet if Spanish police would allow it. He hadn't actually been charged with anything but that was also still in the balance. Rasheed was still on the loose, however, and the threat was far from over.

"So our Ali is a happier man than five minutes ago; I think we can be fairly sure of that," Stuart concluded.

"Well, that's a major step forward then."

"It certainly is. I think we might even say, strike two for the good guys!"

Chapter 15

Bruntsfield

"It's all the TLC," Staff Nurse Simpson opined at coffee break. The ward team had been commenting on the remarkable recovery of the young Turkish man who, the story went, had been beaten up in a so-called "honour" attack on account of his Muslim girlfriend, he being a Christian. So there was already considerably more interest and sympathy for Enver than the usual trauma casualty – typically a bloke called Shane who broke a leg and ribs falling down the stairs drunk at his girlfriend Kylie's twenty-first birthday party. Then, when the lovely Samira sat by his bedside all the hours she was allowed and could get away from her placement, they all gave a collective "aahhh!" and wished them well. Whether it was the extra attention from the nursing team, Samira's obvious devotion, or perhaps even the prayers of the pastor who also came in from time to time, the final outcome was a quick and trouble-free recovery. The bones were still mending but the bruising had largely subsided, the brain scans showed no lasting damage from the concussion, and they were able to gradually cut down the pain relief without him going through the roof. The decision was made that he could go home, if – and it was a big if – there was sufficient support so he could rest and recover without having to go shopping, cook, dress himself, and manage the shower and toilet unaided. The problem was that Enver was a PhD student, which meant that he had to hang around all summer working on his research while the undergraduates he shared a flat with were all either sunning themselves in Greece or else, more likely, flat out on a production line in the hope that they

187

might be able to manage their student loan a bit better in the year ahead. So he lived alone. Ayeesha, Samira's mum, who came in with her sometimes, solved the problem.

"Well, he can come home with us, of course. As soon as he's able," she said. Samira had had the same thought but hadn't dared voice it. Ali hadn't thought of it but didn't seem to object, so that was agreed. He came to collect Enver in the Jeep, not the Audi, as the seats were higher and it would be easier to get in and out of. The stairs were managed with Ali on one side and Samira on the other, Ayeesha carrying the bag of stuff Samira had gone to his flat to gather together. He was installed in Karim and Rasheed's old bedroom, a couple of drawers were cleared out, and the Koran on the bedside table was replaced with a Bible. At Ayeesha's insistence, the second bed was dismantled and stored and an armchair was brought in, as it was anticipated that Samira would be spending quite a lot of time there – safer and more respectable than snuggling up on a single bed.

So they settled into a new routine. Ali was back at the counter downstairs a happier man now that Karim had been found but still troubled and confused by Rasheed's continued elusiveness. The questions "where is he?" and "what is he doing?" went round and round in between ringing up litres of milk and packets of tortilla chips. Ayeesha let her cake and sweets business take a back seat and concentrated on cooking and getting to know her new lodger – so much so that Samira found herself getting jealous that she had to get up at 7.00 a.m. and get the bus to the Royal Bank headquarters complex and spend the day working on new (but she thought totally pointless) HR policies, while her mum helped Enver through to the living room, sat and chatted with him, and fed him nourishing Turkish or Indian food.

Still, the combination seemed to be working. Enver was charming to everyone and soon was being taken for granted as the new son-in-law; even Ali found himself blethering easily with him in the evenings about culture and history. Samira would sit and watch it all happening around her with continued amazement. If anyone had told her three weeks before that they'd be playing happy families together and she'd be fighting with her mum over which of them could pamper her Christian fiancé, she'd had told them they were mad and suggested a good therapist. But here they were. Incredible.

Stuart McIntosh, just through the wall, was aware of the situation and happy for them all but sat alone through the evenings watching soaps until he thought he would scream, then went out for a drink or two. Reeling home after three or four, he would collapse on the bed to wake up the next morning and trudge through another working day before repeating the process. Although he was well aware of how unhealthy this must be – physically as well as emotionally – for the life of him he couldn't think of an alternative. Reconciliation with Kirsty didn't seem to be on the cards. There was no one else at the moment nor any prospect, and all his "friends" were essentially workmates and he didn't fancy the prospect of spending all day and all evening in the same company. David and Gillian had generously invited him to pop round whenever he felt like it and he had gone a few times, but that felt a lot like an imposition and hence quite uncomfortable. So he sat in a gloomy flat, watching garbage TV, eating takeaways, thinking dark thoughts, and drinking whisky. When that became too much he went to the Bruntsfield Hotel bar, thought more dark thoughts, and drank more whisky, paying treble for the privilege of pretending to enjoy himself all night with a bunch of other losers.

However, this nocturnal habit took an unexpected turn one Sunday night in the small hours when he thought he would cross the road and have a wander over the Links before crossing back to the flat. Putting one foot off the kerb on his way back he was almost flattened by a white panel van coming up from Tollcross at what must have been at least sixty. Still a policeman, even if slightly drunk and thoroughly off duty, he decided on the spur of the moment to get a photo of the rear of the van with its number and pass it on to the traffic guys for sorting.

But instead of continuing its route, the van suddenly slowed just opposite the door of his flat and the MiniMart. What happened next cleared the fog in his brain faster than double espresso. The van veered across the road, slowed to walking speed, the back door burst open, a hefty figure jumped out with something in his hand, lit a flame, and hurled the now flaming object through the window of the shop. Inside it exploded. In less than a second the sleepy, tranquil Sunday night scene was transformed into the set of *The Towering Inferno*. The shop alarm went off. The flats opposite were lit in an infernal glow. Bottles inside were exploding like fireworks. The culprit was already back in the van and disappearing around the corner. Now immediately back on duty, Stuart called treble nine and calmly explained that police, fire, and ambulance were needed now – repeat now – about 150 yards up from the Bruntsfield Hotel. Probably multiple fire units and a couple of ambulances to be on the safe side. Then he trotted across the road, took his jacket off, dropped it over his head and shoulders, and rang the bell of the Khans' flat for all he was worth. Not getting an immediate response he stepped back into the road, still trying to shield his face from the flames that had now thoroughly caught, picked up a piece of loose kerbstone, and lobbed it up through their living-room window. *That should get their attention*, he thought. Just then the common close door opened and Ali and Samira emerged with Enver between them, lit from one side by the lurid glow of the flames now billowing out of what had been their shop window. Once they had got to the other side of the road, Ali made to head back across but Stuart managed a rugby tackle and put him on the ground. Better wounded pride than to end up like a deep-fried single fish. Other residents on the Khans' close now came tumbling out, likewise dressed in night clothes, soon followed by residents from the stairs on either side. Opposite, windows were going up and residents not in danger but wanting to know what was happening were hanging out, some with mobiles to record the action. Satisfied that Ali was not going back in, Stuart crossed and approached Ayeesha as probably the best informed and most level-headed around.

190

"Who are your neighbours?" he asked. "Are they all here?"

Ayeesha immediately understood what he was asking and took a second to gather her thoughts and scan around.

"Wilsons – yes there they are. Burnley – yes. Mrs Stanislavsky – yes. Mr Maxwell…" She scanned the growing crowd. "Is that him? No… I can't see him. He's in his eighties and quite deaf."

"Which flat?" Stuart asked tersely.

"Four A."

Then he quickly looked around himself and settled on a male who looked in his mid-twenties with the build of a rugby prop forward.

"My name is Stuart McIntosh," he said. "I'm a police officer. We think there may be an elderly man still on the fourth floor. Are you up for helping me get him out?"

"Absolutely. Let's go."

"Name?"

"Richard."

"Ok, Richard. Let's do it."

Stuart and Richard headed into the common stair at an oblique angle to avoid the worst of the heat and took the stairs two at a time. The younger man got there first.

"A. Maxwell?" he asked.

"That's it," McIntosh confirmed. "I don't think we'll bother with the bell. What we're going to do is this. Lift your leg, bend at the knee, and put as much force as you can on the lock. We'll do it alternately till it gives, ok?"

"Sure. Not a lot different from kicking penalties for Heriots."

It took about half a dozen blows from each of them before the door gave way. By now they could smell smoke wafting up the stairwell. They split up to find the right bedroom. Stuart got there first. He shook the old man, who was still fast asleep. At first he tried to lash out; however, Stuart held his arms while Richard handed him his hearing aid from the bedside table. With the aid in, Stuart didn't bother explaining but just said the magic words "police" and "fire" and got a remarkably quick response despite the old man's age. With the addition of a dressing gown and slippers, about two minutes later they were back out and across the street. In the distance the sound of a fire engine siren was just audible over the roar of the flames.

About an hour later the entire Khan family along with Enver were sitting in the living room of Southside Fellowship's flat. The fire services were cleaning up downstairs but still weren't letting anyone back into flats directly above the shop. Luckily the ambulances weren't needed. Police had cordoned off the shop and pavement and were taking statements.

"Ruined. Absolutely ruined!" Ali moaned with his head in his hands.

"Ali! Shut up and listen," Ayeesha said, putting both her hands firmly on his shoulders. "We are not ruined. We are insured – for the shop, the stock, loss of trade, and personal injury. Six weeks and it'll be back to normal; I guarantee it. If you give up now you're giving in to whoever did this. We will rebuild and be stronger than before. And we'll fit steel shutters next time." She leaned in closer, a steely look in her eyes. "Go to Córdoba. Find Rasheed and Karim and bring them back."

Ali said nothing.

Opposite them Enver and Samira sat, arms around each other.

Stuart was in the kitchen making tea when he suddenly remembered something. He pulled out his mobile phone and tapped photos. There it was. The white van in perfect focus with a clear image of the plate. He smiled. *We'll get you, you bastards*, he said to himself. *Whoever you are, wherever you are, I'm coming after you. This is personal now. You'd better be ready.*

Rasheed sat in the coffee bar area of his new *pensión* staring at his laptop screen with increasing horror. He had tabs open for the BBC News website Scotland page, the *Daily Record*, *The Scotsman*, and the *Evening News*. The headline on all four was of an arson attack on an Asian-owned grocer's shop in Bruntsfield, Edinburgh. Apparently at least two men had driven past the shop the previous night and lobbed a petrol bomb through the window. There were pictures of a crowd of residents standing in the street while the shop blazed and fire engines started pouring water through the shattered window. He could easily detect his dad and mum standing looking from the middle of the street. His sister Samira was next to them, her Christian boyfriend Enver's arm around her shoulders. As well as all the normal combustibles, it appeared that the shop had just had a delivery of gallon drums of cooking oil for the catering trade and a new gas bottle had just been delivered for the cooker. The heat of the blaze had burst the oil cans, turning a moderate fire into a total inferno. The gas bottle had exploded, doing structural damage to the ceiling and threatening to bring down the floor of the upstairs flat where the shopkeeper and his wife and family lived. Neighbours said that only the daughter was at home now and that the two sons of the family lived elsewhere. Someone thought her boyfriend had been staying over till he recovered from an accident. Reporters had tried to speak to the couple but they were too shocked to give a statement at this time. It seems the alarm had been raised by an off-duty policeman who had recently moved into the flat next door, was coming home late and was nearly hit by the van. However, he had managed to get the registration number and inquiries were proceeding to find the owner. Police indicated they had no idea of a motive as yet; however, so-called honour attacks seemed to be on the increase in the city and the fact that the family's son-in-law-to-be was not Muslim might be connected. Anyone with any further information was urged to contact Crimestoppers Scotland or their nearest police station.

Rasheed put his head in his hands and wondered how things had come to this. His most recent report to the Prophet had been long on how much he was learning about the city and its Muslim heritage and his progress in Spanish, and short on Karim and his change of status from collaborator to confessor. The Prophet came back within a few hours and demanded more information. Rasheed provided it again, trying to sugar the pill. When the Prophet replied to that, Rasheed saw a side of his leader that he hadn't experienced before. This was hardly a message – it was a tirade. The Prophet berated him for inattention to detail, for failure to maintain his younger brother's commitment to the cause, and overall slackness. Apparently the Prophet had never entirely trusted Rasheed and now regretted putting such an important mission in his hands. He was considering recalling him to be dealt with by the Prophetic Council. Rasheed had never heard of such a thing but it sounded serious. Even if he were to stay it was obvious even to an unbeliever – was that meant to include Rasheed now? – that the major plan could not be fulfilled as the attack on the cathedral would need at least two operatives. Plans would have to change. He would be informed. At least this seemed to suggest that he was expected to stay; he felt a moment of relief and gratitude. How things developed now would depend on Rasheed's continuing commitment to the cause.

The Prophet was willing to offer Rasheed an opportunity to redeem himself. It was a task the Prophet could easily undertake himself; however, he would give Rasheed the opportunity to play a part. All he had to do was phone a specific mobile number and say one word: "Go!" With respect to the task itself and what Rasheed was initiating, the Prophet did not elaborate. The point was that Rasheed would be demonstrating trust in the wisdom of the Prophet and would bind himself more closely to his plans and projects. Rasheed would demonstrate his faithfulness and commitment in such a way as to render return and examination by the Prophetic Council unnecessary. The choice was his. Naturally, Rasheed responded immediately, agreeing and thanking the Prophet profusely for the opportunity to play a part in the coming new order.

Now he understood. What he had done was to unwittingly, recklessly, blindly give the order for an attack on his own parents' shop, home, and livelihood. They could have died. Now, as the Prophet himself had said, he was bound more closely than ever to the new order. Up to this point Rasheed hadn't been entirely sure if he was actually a criminal as far as the laws of Spain or Britain were concerned. This put it beyond doubt. Whatever else he might be, the Prophet was not stupid. In among all the confusion, one other confusing fact niggled at the back of his mind. In his vague memories of the Prophet before he had decided to withdraw from Edinburgh Mosque, what came to mind was an elderly man of Pakistani origins with quite a strong second-language, north-of-England accent. What he was hearing nowadays from the Prophet was a much younger voice with distinctly Scottish vowels. This was something else Rasheed didn't understand – but possibly not his greatest concern – so he filed it for future consideration.

And now he was waiting. Still going to language classes, still trawling the city for places of strategic interest, but as far as the Prophet's plan for the Mezquita was concerned, just waiting. The Prophet's parting shot had been that Rasheed's carelessness with Karim would mean a complete rethink of the entire venture. This was time-consuming, a waste of energy, and totally unnecessary; however, Rasheed's negligence had forced it upon the Prophetic Council. In the meantime, the Prophet had said in kinder tones, Rasheed should put these events behind him and wait. All was not lost and he would soon be contacted in person by an envoy who would give him something. He would know what to do with it.

He didn't have to wait long. Two days later a man in plumber's overalls approached him outside the *pensión* to ask for the flat of the Cardoso family. Rasheed had no idea and in halting Spanish said so.

"*No pasa nada*," the man replied. Rasheed had learned enough to know that meant never mind, it doesn't matter. He was just about to go on into his accommodation when the man reached into the back of his van and handed him a package.

"*Para tí, del Profeta*," he said. "*Ten cuidado*." For you from the Prophet. Take care.

Rasheed froze. He couldn't decide whether to take the package or not. Even touching it seemed like committing himself to who knew what additional, unexpected actions and consequences.

"*Es para tí, hermano*," the man insisted. It's for you, brother.

What would the implications be if he refused it? Rasheed

wondered. The man knew where he lived and if he had come with a package, who was to say that he might not come back with something else? Like a petrol bomb, for example. He took the package, stuck it under his arm as if to hide it, and turned without a word.

Upstairs in his room he put the bedside kettle on, sat in a chair, dropped the package on the bed, and looked at it. With a cup of tea in his hand he continued to look. Many cups later, as the light was beginning to fail, he finally picked it up. What was it? Why had the man insisted that he take care? He picked it up and started peeling back the gaffer tape in which it was wrapped till it lay open on his lap. It was a black, woven nylon sleeveless jacket like the protective vests worn by police and security staff. But it was bulkier. In fact, it felt like the whole thing had been pulled apart, stuffed with something hard and chunky, and put back together again. The front and back were the same. Its only other distinguishing feature was a thin yellow cord with a red toggle handing down from the hem on the right side like the toggle flight attendants were always telling you not to pull until you were outside the aircraft. Immediately recognizing what it was, Rasheed felt himself go faint. It should have had a warning on that said, "Once inside the Mezquita, pull down sharply on the red toggle to blow yourself to kingdom come." It was a suicide vest.

Chapter 16

Craigmillar

"Seriously, David. Will it make any difference what I say?" Gillian asked and put her fork down on a half-finished plate of spaghetti carbonara.

"Yes," he replied. "It will. You say 'don't go' and I don't go. It's as simple as that. That's the deal. No arguments and no complaints. Full stop."

Gillian gave a heavy sigh and looked away.

"But that's putting it all back to me. If I say no, then I'm the bad one."

"I don't think so," he replied. "We simply tell Ali and Ayeesha that together we decided I couldn't help him and I put him in touch with someone from my old church, Warehouse 66 in Madrid. So someone with reasonable English picks him up at the airport, takes him to Atocha, and puts him on a train to Córdoba. Someone from the police meets him at the other end. He sees Karim and stays as long as he wants to in respect of the hunt for Rasheed. He can do it without me. I don't need to go. And it's *our* decision – not just yours."

"But unless I say no, you'll go. That's also the situation, isn't it?"

"Well, he's asked me. We have been kind of involved in things. And I'm a Spanish speaker and also a friend. It's not going to be easy for him and he wants a pal alongside. That's not unreasonable. And he'll pay all the flights and accommodation, etc. You could come too if you want to…"

"You know that's not realistic. I've got to prepare for the start of term. And I feel a certain commitment to Ayeesha and Samira. I said I'd be around for them."

"So we're both involved."

She sighed again and rubbed her temples.

"I really don't need this right now," she said at length. "There's a huge amount to do getting new courses ready and we're two staff down."

"So, I'll tell him it's just not possible. No problem."

"But it is a problem. I know what your job is. Being a pastor means helping people in trouble and not just your own congregation. Ali's in trouble, so you help him. But does that have to include terrorist plots? It'll be bullets and bombs again. I can feel it coming!"

David said nothing. The carbonara was getting cold but had somehow lost its appeal.

"You've got to go, haven't you?" Gillian said after a while.

"I think so," David replied. "But we're not going to argue about it. Sleep on it if you like. If you're not happy it just stops here."

"Define happy!" she said with the first smile of the evening. "Ok, go. With my blessing. And any other blessing you can pick up. But please stay out of the firing line this time. Widowhood after six weeks of marriage is not in the plan!"

After they had finished eating they sat on the window sofa in the dark holding hands and listening to the CD Gillian's flute group had just released. Mozart still had a way of calming the troubled soul. At length she stirred.

"Maybe you'd better clear your diary and pack," she said. "D'you know, I really shouldn't complain? This is part of the reason I married you."

"Because I keep ending up in harm's way? Or do you mean the pasta?"

"No. Because you have a ridiculous insistence on doing the right thing, regardless."

"Are you thinking you shouldn't have said 'yes' then when I popped the question?"

"David Hidalgo! Hold out your nose while I punch it. I still love you, you stupid, stubborn, ignorant, clever, hopeless man – just."

"I was hoping for more that 'just'," he said.

"Well, that's all you're getting. Can you pack in the morning?"

"Sure. The flights are in the evening. Ali said he'd do the booking but could I let him know tonight. So I better phone him. And I said I'd phone Mrs MacInnes as well."

The call to Ali was brief: "Yes – go ahead. Singles." To Mrs MacInnes he gave his apologies for the LT planned for the following evening. Yes, of course he'd be happy if they went ahead and she chaired. The only thing was the premises issue. He still wasn't altogether sure about Brother Mike MacGregor from Charleston, South Carolina. The cash just seemed too much and too easy. The only condition seemed to be that they affiliated to their One World Foundation, which didn't seem particularly onerous. Some sort of statement in principle about commitment to multifaith dialogue. And if he wasn't involved in that already he didn't know what would count.

"All done?" Gillian asked as he came back in. David nodded.

"In that case you have another duty before you leave. Come with me."

Ayeesha ran Ali and David to the airport the following evening. The sky was overcast and there was a smell of summer thunder in the air. David went to buy an evening paper to let them say their goodbyes. As he was coming back Ali looked miserable but Ayeesha gave him a final hug and sent them off to check in and security. The flight was entirely routine; however, landing at Madrid–Barajas always gave David butterflies and a shiver for some reason. Mariano, his successor at Warehouse 66, was waiting for them.

"David, *amigo*!" he said, and embraced his erstwhile pastor.

"Mariano, can I introduce Ali Khan, a former neighbour and friend? I told you we're on our way to Córdoba to collect one of Ali's boys who's got himself mixed up in something. Thanks for the offer of an overnight. Is Maria ok with that?"

"Ali. Pleased to meet you," Mariano said in perfect English with only the slightest hint of an accent. "Welcome to Spain. Maria is delighted, as ever. We've cleared out two rooms so you can be in comfort. Not the Ritz but I hope it'll be ok."

"Much better than that, I'm sure." Ali shook Mariano's outstretched hand. "Thank you very much for your help and your welcome."

The drive to Mariano's flat in Torrejón de Ardoz, about fifteen kilometres from the airport, didn't take long. David and Mariano chatted in Spanish, leaving Ali to marvel at the ease in which the van weaved through a traffic system entirely confusing to him, past lit-up signs for products and services he could only guess at.

Ali could see that this was a wonderful reunion for David, but he didn't have the energy for it. He thanked them for the late supper they had prepared then went straight to bed as soon as he'd finished. David, Mariano, and Maria talked far into the night about Warehouse 66, about drugs and inner-city violence, about the problems of "youth", about what happens when a Muslim comes to believe that Isa ibn Maryam really was the messiah, meaning that everything they'd used to believe was now upside down.

"It can be suicidal," Mariano commented. "We've had a few conversions here but not many because the price is too high. Even those who come to what we would see as the right conclusion simply can't face how their families are going to react. They are excluded, threatened, attacked, hounded, and sometimes killed. It's not pretty to watch. And the feeling that you've brought this on the individual by sharing your faith with them – well, that can be a problem too. Some even commit suicide themselves, saving their families the effort. We had a guy jump in front of the Alcalá to Madrid train two weeks ago. I knew him. He had converted about a year before." Mariano shook his head. "At least with the drug addicts the dealers don't come and attack them for trying to give up."

"But you said the family had been supportive of the girl, didn't you?" Maria asked.

"I think all things considered that's right," David agreed. "In a funny way, if the boyfriend hadn't been attacked it might have been much harder for Samira and for the family. The assault kind of forced everyone's hand. Samira had to come out and admit she was with a Christian boy. The family had to rally around her distress. And since Enver needed somewhere to go to recover, they invited him to stay with them and once they got to know him it was a different story. He's a nice, very gentle, polite guy. What's not to like?"

"But the firebombing on the shop," Mariano asked. "Do police think that's an honour attack as well? Seems a bit extreme even in terms of what we've heard here and in the UK."

"It does seem extreme, doesn't it?" David nodded. "But there doesn't seem to be any other explanation. The family are extremely well liked all around the neighbourhood. He pays his bills. There isn't an issue about a protection racket. And it fits with the attack on the boyfriend. It looks like a warning, then a follow-up since they still accepted him. You have to wonder if it's connected with the Prophet and the two boys being sucked off to Spain to start a new Caliphate. Seems too much of a coincidence that a peace-loving family should suffer so many shocks. Anyway, it's late. I should let you guys get to bed."

"And you must be tired too," Maria put in. "You know where to go. I think the train is about lunchtime, isn't it? So sleep in. See you when we see you."

Karim was tired too but couldn't sleep. It felt like he had been questioned by police for hours every day, despite having told them everything he knew as soon as they started asking. No, he did not know the location of the Prophet or his identity except that he'd been a preacher at the Edinburgh Mosque. His brother, Rasheed, had maybe heard him at the mosque once or twice – he couldn't be sure – but it was only once he had started distributing his sermons online that Rasheed got really interested. They had listened to a lot together and left comments in the forums. Other people had responded to some of Rasheed's ideas and they had gradually found themselves part of the online community clustered around the Prophet. It was exciting to feel you were in on the ground floor of a movement that was going to change the world. They were no longer just ordinary Muslims feeling that the world was against them. They were part of the new community who were going to change everything. Their friends, family, co-workers in some cases – they were all sleepwalking to oblivion. The Prophet was willing to fight back and it was exciting to be part of it. Karim immediately admitted to having been part of a plot that would have seen a terrorist attack in Córdoba. But it wasn't just as simple as that. Looking back, he could see that he had only gone along with it because Rasheed had browbeaten, bullied, cajoled, and forced him into it. He had been quite happy working for his uncle and going out with Sunna and he wished he was back there now. Pepe had hired a lawyer to represent Karim, who was present at all the interviews and who forcefully claimed a defence of coercion, the exploding wristband being the ultimate example.

Finally they seemed to be done. They asked for as detailed a description of Rasheed as Karim could give them, then at last they left him alone. He was bailed into Pepe's care though he continued to stay with Bea's family at the Pensión El Moro. Then he was finally allowed to phone his family. He was expecting his dad to be shocked and horrified; however, it turned out that he seemed to know what was going on anyway and was overjoyed to speak to him. Then, a few days later the news came about the bomb. By now he had come to see that the Prophet had no limits and would do anything but he was shocked to think that Rasheed might have had a hand in it as he had in the attack on Samira's boyfriend. That was followed by the news that his father was coming out to see him and bringing the Christian pastor who used to be their neighbour. Karim didn't care whether his father was going to bring the Dalai Lama for company – just so long as he came. But waiting at the railway station he was nervous. What would his father's attitude be? He knew that he had been stupid and couldn't claim to be blameless. He needn't have worried. When Ali saw him on the other side of the ticket barriers he almost broke into a run, and as soon as he was through just grabbed him and held on.

"My son, my son," he kept saying. "It's like you were dead and have just come back to life!"

After that they retreated to a more secluded corner. David could see earnest conversation going on, Karim mostly talking and Ali mostly listening. He could guess what the topics might be. Then Ali was nodding his head. Karim looked emotional but was managing to hold it together. Then father and son embraced again and came back across.

"My son, Karim," Ali said proudly.

"Pleased to meet you, Karim. I'm David. I don't know if you remember. I used to live next door and came into the shop sometimes. I love your mum's home-made naans!"

"Yes, everybody does. Sure I remember you. Thanks for coming."

Now David glanced around and noticed two officers in Policía Nacional uniforms. He approached them and introduced himself.

"Sí, Señor," the older one greeted him. "Capitán Gomez Hernandez. Jorge. Your colleague Stooart has been in touch with us. I am sorry for my very bad English but I'm the best in our class!"

He led them to a waiting car and then they were off, out into the Córdoba sunshine.

Gary Morrison and Stuart McIntosh sat studying the computer screen in front of them in Morrison's office. Stuart had previously sent the image he'd taken of the van and with a bit of added contrast and brightness the number was completely clear. With that it was straightforward to check DVLA records and come up with a name, which could then link into criminal records.

"Abdul Masood," Morrison read. Date of birth 22 January 1975, which puts him in his mid-forties. Pakistani passport holder. UK resident since 2005. Address in Craigmillar. 'Businessman' it says

— you can guess what sort of business from the list of previous convictions: assault, breach of the peace, opening of lockfast premises, domestic violence, taking and driving, etc etc. Owns a scrapyard but also works as 'security' for a chain of saunas. Partner in a taxi firm. Did time six years ago for possession of a firearm but otherwise usually manages to get off with lack of evidence or alibi. A few fines and driving disqualification. If it was him driving that'll be another thing – although the least of his worries I imagine. So, normally I'd pass this to a DS and DC to handle but maybe this one I'll take myself. We'll get some uniforms and DCs out looking for the vehicle while I pay a personal visit. Want to come along? I think we'd be well advised to get the ok for firearms."

Abdul Masood's AM Breakers and Dealers yard was not far from his given address in the high-rise council wasteland of Craigmillar.

"Been a while since I've been here," Stuart McIntosh commented, stepping out of the unmarked car and straight into a pile of filth. "Ahhh! Hasn't changed much, I see."

"Be careful where you walk would be good advice," Morrison commented dryly. "Then be careful who you talk to and what you say. In fact – just be careful, full stop. It's been a problem for all the blue light services for years, and despite all the heart-of-gold, rough-diamond types that sit it out I'm afraid it doesn't seem to be changing very quickly. And I doubt if Mr Masood is raising the tone very much."

Morrison surveyed the outside of the yard behind a high wall that had maybe been whitewashed thirty years before. The top of the wall was studded with broken glass. The gate was corrugated iron and had rusted completely through at various points, leaving razor-sharp edges around red crumbling gaps. Both wall and gate were well decorated by "Chas", "Doofy", "Banzai", and "Mojo", who, along with their names, had left some rough sketches of various body parts like primitive cave art – and invitations for the police to do what was anatomically impossible.

"Charming," McIntosh muttered.

"Well, let's see if Mr Masood is in for visitors," Morrison said, pushing at an equally rusty door set into the gate. Surprisingly, it yielded. They stepped over the threshold into a scene of vehicular carnage. Wrecked, rusty, flattened hulks that might previously have been roadworthy cars were piled all around the inside of the perimeter wall. Puddles shone rainbow colours from leaking petrol. What grass and weeds there were among the cobbles were black with engine oil.

"Couple of years since any spare parts were extracted from these," Morrison remarked. They followed what seemed to be the main route around more puddles and mud towards the hut that might or might not have been an office. Suddenly a huge Alsatian came bounding across the yard, stopping only a feet away, barking furiously and baring its teeth, hackles up. Stuart found himself unconsciously feeling for a baton, forgetting that he had been out of uniform for more than ten years.

"Hitler! Shut your mouth!" shouted a figure emerging from the hut. "Shut it!" The owner of the voice and presumably of the dog looked like a darker-skinned version of the Michelin Man before his diet. Rolls of fat joined his head to his shoulders, then continued cascading down from there, pausing slightly at a belt around the waist of filthy jeans, before gathering force again for an encore above enormous thighs. His chest and stomach were of a size that forced his shoulders out and back, making his arms hang slightly behind him. He wore a baseball cap that may once have been navy blue that proclaimed the benefits of Champion Spark Plugs. The big man advanced, belly first, with a short piece of pipe in one hand.

"Couple too many butter chickens," Stuart mused.

"Morning, gentlemen. Something I can help you with?" The accent was a mixture of Pakistan English, Leicester vowels, and Scottish glottal stops.

"You can start by putting the pipe down," Morrison said calmly but clearly.

"Now why would I want to do that?" the proprietor asked innocently. "Just been cleaning it, ain't I? And who would be asking anyway?"

Morrison walked past the dog, which was still not happy but seemed willing to defer ripping them to pieces until later. He held out his ID, as did McIntosh.

"Ah, gentlemen of the constabulary. That's different. Always welcome."

"Would you be Abdul Masood, by any chance?" Morrison asked.

"That's what my mummy calls me," Masood replied, smiling. "And what can I do for you today?"

"We're investigating an incident involving a white Peugeot Boxer van, which is registered to you."

"Ah, what a pity," Masood looked genuinely heartbroken. "Sold it last week."

Morrison took out a notebook. "To whom?" he asked.

"My cousin. But he drove it down to Birmingham and I think he's now in Hyderabad – on holiday."

"Name of the cousin?"

"Mohammed, I think. But I have so many."

"Anyway, you'll have completed the proper DVLA transfer documents then?"

"Hmm." Now Masood looked troubled. "Must have slipped my mind, I'm afraid. I'll get to it first thing in the morning. Promise."

"So no idea as to its whereabouts?"

"None whatever. Sorry."

"And can I ask where you were and what you were doing last Thursday evening at around 1.30 a.m.?"

Masood paused and pondered till the solution to the riddle finally popped into his mind.

"In bed," he said brightly. "Screwing the wife. You can ask her yourself if you don't believe me."

"I will," Morrison replied.

Just then a radio issued a burst of static and called Morrison's name. The DI pulled it out of an inside pocket and adjusted his earpiece. "Right," he said. "Very helpful. Thanks." He turned to address Masood. "Well, Mr Masood, it appears that your cousin has come back from holiday unexpectedly and seems to have left the van outside the address of your known associate Omar Ashad. Surprised?"

Masood took off his baseball cap and scratched his head.

"Astonished. It's totally unaccountable. He specifically told me he was going to Birmingham then home to visit his dad. Remarkable."

"Indeed. So, given that the vehicle is so handy, why don't we have a little wander around and you can tell us what a great buy it would be."

Masood shrugged. "Fair enough," he said. "But my brother – I mean my cousin – has the keys. So we can look at the paint job and kick the tyres but that's about all."

"Well, how about I have a wee keek in the office. Maybe I can find them."

Masood didn't look overjoyed about that.

"Warrant?" he inquired as if asking for a light for his cigarette.

"I don't happen to have a warrant right now, Mr Masood. However, you can either permit access to your office on the basis of helping police with their inquiries or I'll get a warrant and tear this entire yard to bits for everything down to a pair of earrings that shouldn't be here. You choose."

Masood seemed to give the matter serious thought. "Well, we always like to help the law with their inquiries," he said gloomily.

"DI McIntosh will just keep you company here while I have a wee dekko."

"Dekko away."

Morrison walked around some puddles and jumped others, all the while closely watched by both Abdul Masood and Hitler the dog. One looked troubled, the other outright hostile. It didn't take long. Morrison came back less than a minute later with a key on a string with a dirty cardboard tag.

"Peugeot van, it says here," he announced.

"What a surprise," Masood responded without enthusiasm. "Must be a spare."

It took only a few minutes to walk round to a tower block with broken paving stones, cracked windows, and more of the artistic efforts of Chas and Co. or associates. The van was parked without any attempt at concealment up against the kerb. A mutt that may have had a bit of collie in its ancestry had its leg raised at the front offside wheel. Masood gave it the customary greeting and aimed a kick — maybe because kicking the constabulary wasn't recommended.

"The van you saw?" Morrison asked his colleague.

Stuart McIntosh checked his mobile's camera roll and pulled up the image.

"Recognize this?" he asked, pushing it under Masood's nose. "In particular, the number plate?"

"Seems he didn't go to Hyderabad after all," the big man mumbled. His shoulders were down and it looked like the fight had gone out of him.

"What say, we have a look inside? With this key I happened to find."

At that point the owner of the van concluded that discretion was the better part of valour and decided to leg it. Stuart McIntosh was not a 100 metres champion but a gentle jog was enough to keep up with the runner. A couple of uniformed bobbies appeared around the corner of the block at that minute and Masood decided that maybe his blood pressure wasn't up to it and came to a sudden halt.

"Cuff him," Stuart instructed the uniformed officers and headed back to the van.

Gary Morrison had by this time unlocked the sliding side door and pulled it open. Inside was a dirty cardboard box, which had apparently at one time held Smith's Crisps. Inside were a selection of glass lemonade bottles, rags, a red plastic petrol can, and a plastic funnel.

"The petrol can's the only thing here that's probably legal," Morrison remarked dryly. Then he pulled his nose out and walked over to where Abdul Masood was being entertained by the uniformed bobbies.

"Abdul Masood," he said. "I am arresting you on suspicion of causing criminal damage and attempted murder. You are not required to say anything…"

"Can it," Abdul said. "I know the rest!"

"Just as well he leads with his belly," Morrison remarked as he and McIntosh headed back to their car. "If he had to lead with his brains he'd be walking backwards."

"Absolutely," McIntosh agreed. "I think…"

Chapter 17

Medina Azahara

David and Ali got rooms at the Pensión El Moro, met Bea and her parents, and spent the rest of the day relaxing and regrouping. Ali and Karim had lots of catching up to do and David instinctively wanted to leave them alone but Ali insisted that he join them. Bea brought some coffee to the breakfast room and the four of them sat around a table.

Karim cleared his throat.

"I'm really sorry for dragging you all this way, Mr Hidalgo. But thanks for coming with my dad."

"No more sorries," Ali broke in. "We've been through all that. People make mistakes. Ask your mother about me. The thing is, I thought I'd lost you both; now at least I've got one son back. We just need to find Rasheed then we can all go home."

Karim grimaced. "I don't think it's going to be as easy as that," he said. "Rasheed is very determined and he believes 100 per cent in the Prophet. You'll have to kidnap him."

"But first is necessary find him," Bea said. She had been sitting quietly but now reached over and took Karim's hand. "My uncle Pepe has contact in the *policía* and lots of others but nobody know where he is."

"So he just left without any notice?" David asked.

"Notice?" Bea didn't understand.

"*Sin previo aviso*," David clarified. "*Sin antelación*."

"No," she shook her head. "Nothing. Only took his bag and go."

"And there'll be a hundred other hostels like this one in town…"

"More," she said.

"Well, we have a meeting with police later. They can put out the word. What do you think he'll do, Ali?"

Ali shook his head. "I have no idea," he said bleakly. "It feels like the boy I brought up has been replaced by someone I don't know. We always taught the boys to love Scotland, to do the right thing, and to ignore nasty comments."

"Did you get many of these?" David asked Karim, who shook his head.

"Very few," he said. "And when it did happen it was from people you didn't know. Pals at school – never."

"So where did Rasheed get this new attitude from?" David pressed him.

"I don't know," Karim admitted. "He just seems so angry about everything. Like he needed to take revenge on the whole world. Jewish people have never done him any harm, as far as I know. We don't even know any. And he hates Americans too, though they always seem friendly enough to me."

"Sometimes too friendly," David added ruefully, "but I know what you mean. The Americans I knew in Madrid were always warm and generous."

"Well, that means nothing to Rasheed," Karim carried on. "He isn't even that interested in politics. He just seemed to feel that he's a victim and wants to get even. I don't know why."

"And the target was the cathedral in the Mezquita?" David continued. Karim nodded, looking down. Bea gripped his hand a bit tighter.

"I'm not trying to be difficult, Karim." David tried to sound reassuring. "But we need to know where we should look for him if there's no chance of finding him in a hostel."

"We visited all the Moorish sites," Karim explained. "Anything with Islamic calligraphy or history. He would take photos and tell me how beautiful it all was."

"Well, they've doubled security at the Mezquita so I think we have to say that's off the agenda unless he just leaves a bomb in the street. So where else might he go?"

Karim shrugged. "I have no idea. I didn't even take much notice of all the places we went to."

"But he doesn't even have any explosives; he knows nothing about all that stuff," Ali insisted. "How can he blow anything up?"

"The Prophet said he would give us what we needed when we needed it. That's all I know." Karim sounded hopeless and resigned. "I've told the police everything, honestly."

"Well, Karim," David said thoughtfully. "Maybe you've told them everything you think you know but there might be some hint or comment Rasheed let drop that you've forgotten. Maybe a plan B, if for some reason the cathedral became impossible."

Karim shook his head again. "Not as far as I know," he said. "It was always the cathedral."

Capitán Gomez – more informally Jorge – came to speak to Ali and Karim later that afternoon. David asked for a private word.

"Was the photograph Mr Khan gave you good enough for distribution?" he asked.

"Yes. Fine. We've put it to the main tourist office and they are sending it to the hostels and tourist sites. Officers throughout the city are on alert. He'll never get into the Mezquita but we can't close down our entire tourist industry indefinitely. He may even have left the city and we wouldn't know."

"So what now?"

"Watch and wait. And any intelligence from your Edinburgh police would be helpful. I understand they have access to the Prophet's website now."

"So I believe," said David without further elaboration.

Rasheed had no idea what to do with a suicide vest. Should he hang it in the wardrobe, push it under the bed, or dump it in a rubbish container outside? He was rapidly coming to the conclusion that, one way or another, his life was over. Some internet searches quickly revealed that even planning a terrorist attack could attract a life sentence, far less carrying it out. So what would be worse: doing nothing till he was inevitably caught – he clearly didn't have the resources of a great train robber to disappear and start a new life somewhere else – or at least attempting the thing that he would be convicted of planning, die a martyr, and immediately enter paradise with all its attendant pleasures? Either way he would lose his family and friends. To some he might be a hero, but to others he would simply be a dangerous fanatic who would be much better out of circulation – jailed or dead, they wouldn't care. And what about the Prophet? He didn't seem particularly grateful for the sacrifices Rasheed had already made, including having a pivotal part in attacks on his own family that could certainly have been fatal and might well still be fatal to his parents' business. All he did was shout at him without allowing him a word of explanation and then give him another task, the results of which he was still coming to terms with. The suicide vest lay on the bed, a silent reproach. On the one hand it seemed to be speaking about his miserable lack of courage and commitment to simply strap it on, walk into the Mezquita, and pull the toggle. On the other hand, it seemed to speak just as loudly of his treachery to his own family. As far as the Prophet was concerned, they were just Western, comfortable compromisers but he knew them as a normal, loving family. What was so wrong about making a living, being at peace with your neighbours, and bringing up your kids to do the same?

Suddenly his thoughts were interrupted by a knock on the door. He grabbed the vest, being careful to fold the pull cord inside, and delicately slid it under the bed.

"Señor? Señor?" a voice called from outside.

"Yes. Come in," he managed, thinking it was a maid to change the beds and towels. Instead it was Señora Camargo, the owner. The door was pushed open and she appeared with a tray. On the tray was a plate of a thick vegetable soup, crusty bread, creamy white cheese, a couple of oranges, and a can of alcohol-free beer. She smiled at him and nodded towards the tiny table that currently held his laptop and Spanish books. He jumped up to clear a space.

"So sorry – my Enlis is very bad. But I worried for you, Señor. You not go out now three days. I think maybe is sick so I bring. You need eat. If you need doctor I phone for you. Yes?"

Rasheed felt a wave of gratitude sweep over him despite himself.

"No. No doctor," he managed to say. "But thank you very much. *Gracias. Muchísimas gracias. Tan amable.* Is that right?" The señora swept his thanks aside with a wave of her hand.

"Is nothing," she said. "I have a son like you. Is twenty-nine. If he sick I make him food. So I think, why not for the English señor? You eat, get strong again. Be happy. Ok?"

"Ok." Rasheed responded as she kissed him on both cheeks, gave him a final affectionate look, and bustled out of the room.

Rasheed sighed heavily and looked at the tray. *What have I become?* he thought. *A monster? An enemy of humanity? And for what? So my religion can again dominate all others?*

He sat down and ate, trying not to think any more. Then he slept properly for the first time in days. When he woke the new day's sun was already up. He could feel its warmth through the light gauze curtains of his room. He roused himself, pulled open the double windows, and breathed in the scent of bougainvillea, jasmine, and hibiscus. The house opposite had a white painted gable end covered in vines and creepers and dotted with terracotta pots of crimson geraniums. He absorbed the morning air, listened to the birdsong that filled the sky before it grew too hot and songbirds took shelter in the shade and grew still. Then he prayed for success, took off yesterday's clothes and dropped them in the bin, showered, shaved, patted a little aftershave around his cheeks, put on his best clothes and a new pair of soft leather shoes he had bought a few days before, and carried the tray downstairs. First he sought out Señora Camargo in her kitchen. He thanked her properly for yesterday's meal in a prepared speech in his best Spanish, laid the tray down, and kissed her on both cheeks. She blushed slightly and once again said it was nothing. Then he went through to the breakfast room, greeted the few early risers already there, and helped himself to fresh orange juice, coffee with milk, three or four magdalena buns – which he dipped in his coffee, Spanish-style – and a couple of delicious sugary pastries. After a second coffee he bounded back up the stairs, unlocked his room, and sat again at the desk. He laid his laptop to one side, picked up his mobile, and got ready to send a text. First he selected his father and mother, then added Karim and Samira. He did not have a number for the Prophet but wouldn't have included him even if he did.

It did not take long to write the message, as he had been planning what to say for some time. When it was completed, he read it through only once to check for mistakes then hit "send". He sat back, smiled, and felt a huge weight slip off his shoulders. He felt particularly glad his parents were safely far, far, away and would only get the message when there was no chance of doing anything to intervene before it was all over. He hoped they would be able to retain some good thought of him. The sun was growing intense outside, the air heavy with perfume. The city was breathtakingly beautiful. It was a perfect day to die.

Ali, David, and Karim were finishing a leisurely breakfast when Ali's phone beeped.

"Sorry – better check this," he apologized. "Might be the wife!" He pulled out his phone and had a glance at the message, taking another sip of the excellent coffee. Then he set the cup down. David noticed his expression change. His shoulders slumped and he leaned one elbow on the table, supporting his head while he held the mobile in his other hand. "Where is Medina Azahara?" he asked in a whisper.

"About five miles out of town. Why?"

"Rasheed is going there to detonate a bomb and kill himself. Read this."

David read then passed the phone to Karim.

"The Prophet must have given him a suicide vest," Karim said, incredulous.

Ali, who ten minutes before had been full of optimism, was now destroyed. He sat, paralyzed, with his head in his hands.

"I thought we just needed to find him and go home," he said in a barely audible voice. "Now this. It's impossible. Even if we got there, what could we do?"

David said nothing for a few seconds, then roused himself. "I'm so sorry," he said and put his hand on Ali's arm. "You may be right – maybe it is impossible. But we don't know that for certain yet. Let me call Jorge. At least we need to let the police know, then get there as fast as we can ourselves. Karim – do you think Bea could drive us?"

"I'll go and ask."

"Ali," David said firmly. "I need you to not give up. We'll do what we can, ok?"

Ali shook his head as if trying to shake himself awake. "Ok."

"So let's look at the message again. You know him better than I do. What does he say he's actually going to do?"

Ali picked up his phone. "He says the Prophet has supplied an explosive vest and a gun. He's going to a place called Medina Azahara. He says that used to be the Caliph's palace. Then he's going to wait till he's in the middle of as many tourists as possible, pull the toggle, and explode the vest. He says that'll mark the beginning of the fight back to restore what was lost." Ali shook his head again hopelessly. "How on earth he thinks that's going to do anything other than murder dozens of people, I can't understand."

"And who was the message sent to?"

Ali had a closer look. "Just the family."

"So he thinks you, Ayeesha, and Samira are in Scotland and Karim doesn't have his mobile. That means he thinks nobody can intervene and nobody here will even know until it happens."

"I suppose so."

"Which gives us an advantage."

"How?"

"Well, firstly we can contact police. If he says he's going to Medina Azahara then it means he's not there yet. If he's in a hostel in the city he's going to have to go by bus and that's going to take at least half an hour. If we can get police to close the site that might stop him. But even if he gets in he's not going to expect you to be there. Maybe you'll be able to say something that would stop him."

"Huh… You don't know Rasheed. Even when he was young, if I said 'don't' that just made him all the more determined."

"And how does he say he's going to explode the device?"

Ali looked at the phone again. "He says he's going to pull the toggle. But I don't see how that makes any difference. How can you stop him? Even if police shot him he could probably still do it."

"Maybe. I have an idea though. Can you phone Jorge? I think you have his number. I'm going to speak to Bea."

Bea drove like she had never been allowed to before. David took the view they simply didn't have time to wait for a police driver or escort and told her to get there as a matter of life and death. She hadn't long passed her test and her dad still insisted that he drove everywhere with her and had the very annoying habit of constantly telling her she was going too fast. Now David was sitting beside her telling her to go faster. They arrived at the entrance to the Medina Azahara complex at the same time as Jorge Gomez, who was in the lead car of three. Two ambulances and a van full of officers in riot gear pulled in as they were parking. Gomez acknowledged David only very briefly before going to the ticket kiosk. He walked past a large "closed" sign and exchanged a few words with the woman behind the desk. She shook her head. He came back to where David, Ali, Karim, and Bea were just getting out of the car.

"Looks like either he's not coming or he's inside already. They have the photo but haven't seen anyone like that. We closed the entrance immediately after you phoned. Site staff are getting people out now but there's still maybe up to 500 visitors inside. Rasheed could easily be among them and we wouldn't know."

Suddenly Gomez's radio crackled and burst into a stream of Andalusian Spanish even David had problems following.

"That's site security," Gomez said tersely. "A tall, slim, Asian-looking man has about forty tourists corralled in one of the halls. He's got a gun and is threatening anyone who comes near. It looks very much like a suicide vest he has on. He's demanding TV cameras and press. He says if he sees any police or marksmen he'll detonate the bomb."

"Rasheed – my son, my son!" Ali groaned.

"Come on, Ali," David said. "It's not over yet. Remember what I told you in the car. Do you think you can do it?"

Ali rubbed his temples and groaned again. "I've no idea. I'll try," he mumbled.

"Jorge," David turned to the police captain. "Ali and I have had an idea. See what you think."

The Medina Azahara site covers over 200 hectares, only 10 per cent of which have been excavated. The entrance and ticket office are situated at the foot of a hill that gradually slopes up towards the more important buildings. As they half-walked, half-ran, up the hill everyone else was coming down. David could hear fragments of complaints from the tourists that had made the extra effort about coming all this way and being thrown out before they'd finished. *You don't know how lucky you are*, he thought. They pressed on along paths lined with cypress and orange trees, past low walls that might once have been houses, shops, storerooms or barracks, then up a flight of steps, across a paved courtyard bordered by the remains of an impressive portico, and towards the citadel. In the distance David could already see the facade of all that remained of the most impressive Moorish relic of them all. Gomez was trotting briskly ahead with a half-dozen uniformed officers while David and Ali did their best to keep up. Suddenly Gomez stopped.

"Look," he said. "They're in the throne room. We better not go any nearer in uniform. There are snipers on the way though. You won't see them but if he makes one move to pull that toggle it'll be the last move he makes."

David and Ali advanced cautiously. The inside of the throne room consisted of pillars and arches exactly like those of the Mezquita, but instead of leading to a place of prayer they led the eye to where the throne would have been. And instead of a Moorish ruler sitting surrounded by courtiers and an armed guard, what they could now make out was a crowd of tourists herded up against the far wall and made to sit down. A tall, slim figure in a bulky waistcoat stood a few yards in front of them. He held a pistol in one hand and a loudhailer in the other. His shirt and trousers were black and a black headscarf covered his head and the lower part of his face. The only hint of colour was a red toggle hanging by a chord from the vest. Despite the covering, Ali immediately recognized his son. At about fifty yards Rasheed noticed them. He raised the megaphone to his mouth.

"Keep back," he shouted. "No one comes in till the cameras arrive."

"Rasheed!" Ali shouted back, still advancing. "It's me. It's your father!"

Rasheed seemed to freeze in mid-movement, the loudhailer halfway between his mouth and his hip. They were close enough now to see his lips moving. They kept on advancing.

"Rasheed! Put the gun down," Ali shouted again. "Let's talk. I'm here for you!"

They were near enough now to hear his voice.

"Babu?" Rasheed said in disbelief. "What... how...?"

At twenty yards David stopped and let Ali advance alone.

"I've come for you, Rasheed," he said. "It doesn't need to end this way. Put the gun down. Your mother is waiting for you. Samira and Karim, they're waiting too. We can all go home."

Rasheed looked down for a second, then slowly and deliberately raised the gun. His voice was choked and thick.

"No, Babu. You don't understand. This *is* how it has to end.

219

There's no other way. I can't come back with you now. Even if I wanted to. I can't turn the clock back, Babu. I'm not your son any more."

Ali kept advancing, looking past the gun straight into Rasheed's eyes. He was close enough now not to have to shout.

"Who told you that?" he asked. "The Prophet? The Prophet is an imposter. He's a liar. You are who you always were. And I'm who I've always been. We are father and son. Let it go. Come home."

Ali could see the barrel of the gun shaking, but Rasheed still kept it pointed at him. He was silent for some seconds.

"I'm sorry, Babu," he said eventually. "I'm sorry for Samira. And the shop. I didn't know. I swear. He made me do it. I would never hurt you."

"And what about all these people behind you, Rasheed? Will you hurt them? What will that achieve? They have nothing to do with whatever harm you feel has been done to us. Let them go."

Rasheed glanced over his shoulder, while still keeping the gun facing forward. Tourists of maybe a dozen different nationalities were sitting silent, cowed and terrified.

He shook his head.

"No, Babu. I'm sorry but this is the only way. The world has to wake up. Nobody pays attention if you write a book or go on a march. This is all they listen to. The Caliphate must come again and this is the way to start the war. Then they'll know who we are."

Ali was still coming closer, no more than ten yards now. The terrified tourists behind would normally have demanded his attention but today he only had eyes for his own flesh and blood. He felt the sweat running down his back and smarting in his eyes. He couldn't look away, blink, or wipe the sweat. He daren't break the link.

"And who are we, Rasheed?" he asked quietly. "What are we? I came as a beggar and they made me a guest. I had nothing and they made me a citizen. And you, then Samira, then Karim, were accepted too. Who is it that has hurt you so much? Who are you so angry at?"

Rasheed studied a pattern on the stone floor just in front of him. Behind him there was a muted echo of sobs and moans.

"You wouldn't understand," he said quietly. "You haven't listened to the Prophet. He explains it so clearly. We have to do this – to reclaim our history, our heritage. Then we won't be either beggars or guests. We'll be in charge. Like it used to be. Like it should be."

"So you won't come home with me, Rasheed? Your mother misses you. Let her see you again."

Rasheed shook his head.

"I can't," he whispered.

"Then let me go with you, Rasheed. My life is over if I lose my eldest son. We'll go together. Let these people go."

"Would you do that, Babu?" Rasheed asked, amazed.

"Yes," Ali repeated. "Let them go."

"They can't go, Babu. If we don't make an impact nobody'll listen. Let's go together. We'll be remembered forever."

Ali edged forward, delicately fingering something in his pocket. Rasheed gradually lowered the gun as he approached.

"Babu," he whispered and embraced him.

"Rasheed," Ali whispered into his ear. "My son."

Then he took half a step back, still holding Rasheed's arms and looked at him from head to toe. He touched the red toggle.

"Is this how it works?" he whispered.

Rasheed nodded.

"Then let me do it. The last act of a father for his son."

Ali could see the tears running down Rasheed's cheeks.

"Yes, Babu. Do it."

"Ok, my son. Close your eyes. Lift your hands to Allah. Soon we will be with him."

Rasheed closed his eyes and let his head fall back towards the heavens. He felt a momentary tug on the cord. Then – nothing.

Ali took a step back.

"That's it," he said, in a voice quivering with exhaustion.

Rasheed opened his eyes.

"What? What have you done?" he asked, confused.

Ali stepped further back again and held out his hands. In one hand was a pair of sharp kitchen scissors. In the other hand a three-inch length of yellow cord and a red plastic toggle. Rasheed stared down at the vest. Where the toggle had been there was nothing. The severed end of the cord had slipped back inside. Nothing was left to hold onto or pull.

"You tricked me!" Rasheed screamed. "You tricked me! What have you done? You cheat! You liar! I hate you!"

All he had worked and planned for was a statement. A powerful statement, An explosive statement. Something that would shake the world and announce that things would never be the same again. Now that was gone. All he was left with was the gun in his hand. And what good would that do? Shoot a couple of meaningless, pointless tourists before the police shot him? A trivial event that could have happened anywhere: in the street or when they were queuing for ice cream. The significance of Medina Azahara would be lost. It was all lost now.

The gun, now useless, fell from his hand.

Ali felt the remaining strength seeping out of his limbs. He slumped down to a half-sitting, half-kneeling position with his head in his hands.

"I can live with that," he muttered.

Chapter 18

Madrid

Ali looked like a man who hadn't slept for a fortnight when he finally made it down to breakfast the next morning. He was unshaven, his hair in a mess, his shirt only half-buttoned, and his eyes bloodshot. In short, the total opposite of the chirpy, dapper man hundreds of customers knew across the counter in Bruntsfield. David and Karim were sitting having a second slow coffee. Jorge Gomez had just arrived and Bea was in the kitchen making him a fresh cup.

"Good morning, Ali," David tried to say as brightly as possible as he appeared in the doorway.

"Is it?" Ali asked, slowly pulling out a chair.

"You were fantastic, Dad," Karim enthused. "You're a hero. You saved all these tourists and Rasheed. It's in all the papers. Bea showed me."

Ali sat down, sighed heavily, and said nothing. Bea put his usual black tea in front of him along with a plate of pastries.

"Everyone is very proud of you," she said quietly. "My parents think you have done a miracle."

Ali shook his head.

"No," he said. "I have just condemned my son to twenty years in jail. For Rasheed that will be a living hell – worse than dying. It wasn't a miracle, just the least bad alternative. And it wasn't even my idea."

Jorge sipped his coffee and helped himself to a bun.

"My colleagues are asking me how you came up with that plan, Señor Hidalgo?"

David shrugged.

"You can thank my wife for that," he said simply. "She's a sailor. We were out on her boat recently and even though it was just in a river she insisted I put a life jacket on. I asked her what happens if you lose the toggle or break it or the chord snaps. She said without the cord nothing would work. So when Rasheed was talking about pulling the toggle to set off the jacket I just found myself remembering the life jacket. Then the idea just came. Ali's the man who made it work. I imagine you have some very grateful tourists this morning."

Jorge nodded.

"Indeed. There have been rumours of something in support of the Caliphate for years but this is the first time we've had an actual attempt. And we've also been pretty successful in keeping radical elements out of Spain. Of course, whatever you blew up wouldn't have the slightest effect in actually restoring Muslim rule – that's ridiculous – but on the other hand something symbolic might encourage other attempts. And it would affect tourism and the economy. Which would probably make the whole city more security conscious, which restricts reasonable people because of a few fanatics. I'm sorry to refer to your son like that Mr Khan, but that's how it seems."

"You're right," Ali agreed without enthusiasm. He had finally managed to pick up the tea Bea had brought him but didn't seem to have the energy to actually put it to his lips. "He has turned into someone I don't even know. I just don't understand how it could have happened. We always thought we were a fairly normal family. Now this. Maybe I've been fooling myself. I was blind to what was happening right in my own household."

"No, Babu," Karim insisted, putting his hand on his father's arm. "It's not like that. You've been great parents. It's not your fault. We were exploited by others. Other people took advantage of us and filled our heads with rubbish. You mustn't blame yourself."

"Can I speak to him?" Ali asked the policeman.

"Of course – you can try. But he's not speaking to anyone so far and has said he doesn't want to see you."

This seemed to hit Ali like a physical blow. He winced and closed his eyes.

"What can I tell Ayeesha?" he asked no one in particular.

"You can tell her you're bringing Karim home," David said gently. "And that Rasheed is still alive and may be able to change in the future. You've given him that chance. And that you've saved lives and helped the reputation of peace-loving Muslims throughout the world. Do you know this is on the national news in twenty countries? The fact is not lost that this was a Muslim man of peace who put his life in danger to save non-Muslims from a suicide bomber. The fact that he was your son makes it all the more dramatic. You're sending a message all over the world that your people are *not* automatically terrorists – that the vast majority are peace-loving people who want to see the violence stop. You shouldn't underestimate that."

"Exactly," Jorge agreed. "It's like Córdoba used to be. Different races and religions working together."

"You made it possible, David," Ali said. "I would never have thought of that or been able to do it but for you."

"Accessory before, during, and after but you're the man they want to interview."

Ali groaned.

"Oh no. Can I refuse?"

"Of course," Jorge confirmed. "You'll have police protection as long as you need it. We'll need to do some more detailed interviews at the police station but after that you're free to stay or go as you please. Have you thought about when you'll want to go home?"

"Not much. I suppose it depends what happens to Rasheed now…"

"He'll go to court. I'm afraid there'll be a long list of charges."

"Meaning what?"

"If he's found guilty, a long time in jail. I'm sorry."

"In Spain?"

"Not necessarily. He could be extradited and serve his sentence in Scotland. But it's really too early to say."

Ali nodded slowly.

"And the Prophet?"

"A very wanted man," Jorge confirmed, adding another spoonful of sugar to his cup. "Incitement to hate crime and terrorism can happen from cyberspace just as much as from the street. But I think your Scottish police are at work on that too."

"Will you come home with me, Karim?" Ali asked.

"Of course, Babu, if they let me. I want to see Mum. But I think I might want to come back to Spain," he turned to Bea. "I'm only halfway through my Spanish course."

"Or I might want to go to Scotland," she countered. "I need to improve my English too, you know."

"We all need to go back," David agreed. "Gillian has seen it all on the news as well and doesn't quite believe I'm still in one piece. And Ayeesha needs to see you too, Ali."

Ali finally managed a mouthful of tea and a bite of a biscuit.

"I know. I have about twenty messages to reply to. So, if I could give a statement today could we leave tomorrow?"

"Fine by us," Jorge confirmed.

"I've been checking flights," David replied. "Nothing tomorrow but the next day might be possible. But we'll need to get up to Madrid. We could leave tomorrow if the police are happy, have a night in the capital, then fly the next day. How does that sound?'

"Actually, the chairman of the Córdoba Tourist Authority wants to meet you if possible as well," Jorge added. "Just to say thank you – and pay for any travel and accommodation. Sky's the limit – do you say that?" Jorge asked.

"Yes, we do," David agreed. "Sounds generous. Personally I've always fancied the Ritz."

"And what's wrong with the Pensión El Moro?' Bea inquired, dipping another *churro* into her cup of thick hot chocolate.

They had a final police debriefing and told the entire story yet again. No, Ali had no idea how his sons had come into contact with the Prophet and been radicalized, and no, he had no idea of the Prophet's whereabouts or plans. The Tourist Authority was a nicer meeting. A very lavish reception was laid on at short notice and all the VIPs were present – those directly involved and the usual hangers-on and the "anything for a free lunch" brigade. Strictly speaking, Bea and her parents and Karim might have fallen into the second category but they were unrepentant and managed to find a corner of the splendid Moorish-era room they were using with plenty of food and drink and no cameras. Tío Pepe and Tía Maria joined them.

"This is so weird," Karim whispered to Bea. "This is exactly what Rasheed wanted – to see behind the scenes and appreciate the wonders of the Caliphate that tourists don't normally get access to – and where is he now? He's in jail and I'm here." She smiled and squeezed his arm.

David was not a natural public reception animal but had been through enough of them not to be too troubled. He smiled, pressed the flesh, and kept calm. Ali didn't. A busy gathering in a foreign language and culture with him as their centre of attention thanking him for something he wished he hadn't had to do… David had to stick to him like glue, whispering instructions and translating key phrases of the speeches, repeatedly reassuring him it wouldn't be long, to stop him dumping his paper plate of tapas and bolting for the door. The cameras got what they wanted, but not without a fight, and a flock of photographers eventually left grumbling about whether they'd be able to Photoshop a smile onto the father's face.

Finally it was over and they were allowed back to the Pensión El Moro to pack. This time there was nothing David could do to make Ali more sociable and he immediately disappeared. David was tired too but Bea's parents insisted on a few glasses of something kept for special occasions. Pepe and Maria had also come back and Pepe produced a very nice bottle of oak-aged Jerez.

"Have a taste of this, Señor Hidalgo," he said, taking David aside. "And I defy you to call it *sherry*!"

"No problem," David laughed with some relief. "I actually used to buy and sell the stuff so I think I can get the name right."

"So you're the man that worked out how to disarm the bomb?" Pepe continued. "Quite a trick."

"Just a lucky – sorry – a fortunate circumstance," David replied, thinking about Juan back home in Edinburgh and his absolute allergy to the work *luck*. "And I believe you're the man who persuaded Karim to trust him, which opened up the whole situation."

Pepe shrugged.

"I almost didn't," he said. "I was a bit concerned about who Bea was getting herself involved with. It was a toss-up – is that the expression? – a toss-up between taking him under my wing and throwing him to the wolves."

"Well, I'm glad the wolves lost out. I think he realizes how stupid he's been. But he was never the fanatic Rasheed has become. I think it's right they should be treated differently."

Pepe inclined his head, as if tending to agree but not yet fully convinced.

"Remains to be seen," he said. "They're letting him go back to Scotland in the meantime but he'll have to have his day in court as well. We'll get him a good lawyer and hope for the best. But I'm interested in your part in all of this. I think 'just a family friend' isn't really the whole story, is it?"

David took another sip of the excellent Jerez and thought for a moment.

"Yes and no," he admitted. "Yes, I am a family friend and I'm here to support Ali. But probably no as well, in the sense that I've been through a few things most people don't have to go through. It gives you a certain presence of mind to think things out."

Pepe gave David a closer look, as if considering the claim.

"Well, according to my sources it's more than just a few things. You know a man called Mariano from Madrid? From Warehouse 66 in Torrejón? He's my wife's cousin – and your successor, I think. He'd been telling me some stories. You know you can't fool all the people all the time – *Pastor*."

David gave a wry smile as if caught trying to race a traffic warden to his car and just missing out.

"I see not much gets past your watchful gaze. I didn't know."

"Well, I try to keep my eyes and ears open and I don't advertise all my connections. So an evangelical pastor in Madrid, enemy of drug dealers, freer of trafficked girls, nemesis of paedophile priests, and now rescuer of startled tourists about to be blown to kingdom come. Quite a record. Still just here as a family friend?"

David held his hands up in protest.

"What can I say?" he mumbled. "It's not my first choice of career, I assure you. These things just seem to come my way."

"But the difference is that you let them stop at your door, whereas other people just let them pass. I find that quite interesting. Let me say I'm not a religious man – I abandoned the 'faith of our fathers' when I was seventeen and I haven't seen anything yet that would persuade me that I made a mistake. But when a man is willing to take the sort of risks you take, ostensibly for his faith – then it makes me pay attention. You understand?"

"I do. I'm afraid I've always been a kind of 'all or nothing' guy. It's a weakness. And I was very much influenced by a man who had been through great hardships for his faith. That impressed me. I've never thought it's about winning the argument but about looking for change. The world is full of self-help books and gurus. Real sustained personal change is, in my experience, actually quite rare. So when you do see it you have to pay attention. My late wife, Rocío, changed dramatically when she found faith. It made me think."

"And what did you think?"

"I thought it was worth thinking about."

Pepe let out a laugh.

"Touché, Pastor David. Well said. We'll speak more. Now I think we're neglecting the party. If you make sure Karim treats Bea well,

I'll try to find him a good defence team. Rasheed can go to the wolves as far as I'm concerned, which doesn't mean I'm not sorry for his parents. But everyone has to choose for themselves and bear the consequences.

"Now," he said in a louder voice, "who would like some of this excellent Jerez?"

It was a very different train journey back north from the one they had taken less than a week before. The scrubby landscape of hard-baked earth and olive groves and the dazzling light were the same but everything else had changed. Ali remained despondent despite everything encouraging David and Karim tried to say. He sat in the carriage staring out of the window like a man half-asleep and not having good dreams. Rasheed was being kept under observation in police custody pending an appearance at court – belt and shoelaces removed. He had indeed refused to speak to his father or even see him. According to Jorge he had consistently refused to say anything even to the lawyer the state had provided. His only request was to be given food that was halal – which was granted – and to have his mobile and laptop back, which was of course denied. Ali had asked several times to see his son and got as far as the cell but Rasheed made it plain he did not want to communicate and the police had to honour that request. It had been Ali's last hope, and now the hope was dashed, he totally collapsed. He hardly ate or drank on the train and could not be coaxed into conversation.

Bea had decided to make the journey with them as far as the airport and she and Karim were like kids on a day out, chattering, giggling, and pointing at things. Karim, in the aisle seat, was keen to indicate points of interest that involved leaning half across Bea to indicate something out of the window. She tended to notice things out of the opposite window that equally needed drawing attention to. David sat quietly wrapped in his own musings. *How ironic*, he thought, in terms of the usual Christian/Muslim narrative. Instead of being at each other's throats as extremists on both sides would like, they had in fact collaborated to stop another atrocity. He was under no illusions that it would effect much change to the general sabre-rattling – one side going on about immigration, birthrate, and radical politics; the other about Western interference and threats to traditional values – however, in the meantime, people from both backgrounds with or without any particular religious habits continued to live side by side. Day by day they continued to dig snow from each other's paths, loan a set of jump leads when the car wouldn't start, or just greet each other in the street and complain about the weather. But as well as that nice, neighbourly "getting along", there were still times that needed a certain "getting up on your hind legs" – as his mother would have put it. So even though they were going back to Scotland with some sense of accomplishment, there were still outstanding issues to be dealt with, starting with the problems closest to hand. David was now quite concerned about Ali. When a bout of anxiety from unexpected stress turns into a "condition" he wasn't qualified to say, but by now Ali had hardly spoken a word for almost three days and looked terrible. Maybe some professional help would be needed. He'd need to have a conversation with Ayeesha.

Then there was the Prophet. Who was he, what was he, and where was he? The deeper question of "why was he?" would have to wait for a more detailed analysis. They knew he had originated in Pakistan, lived in Leicester, moved to Edinburgh, been chucked out of the Edinburgh Mosque, then reappeared in cyberspace. But to stop his influence on others he would have to be physically found and put where the internet didn't reach. Besides that, beyond the fact that the voice online did not seem to match the poor English and confused ranting of the man himself, almost nothing was known. Gillian had made it perfectly clear that the expedition to Spain should not involve physical risk and he had managed to just about keep within the letter of the law on that one. Still, now it would be a police matter and really nothing to do with him. That would be a relief. Going back to his home city felt like going back to what was familiar and safe. Maybe an illusion, but one he was willing to entertain.

The train pulled into Atocha Station at around 2.00 p.m. For Karim it was like a travel theme park with everything exotic and exciting. Bea insisted on taking them around the old redundant grand hall that had been turned into a huge arboretum complete with palm trees, giant ferns, and a terrapin pool. David brought up the rear with Ali, who still didn't seem to be registering anything. To minimize the hassle, David had acceded to the tourist chief's suggestion and rooms were waiting for them at the Ritz. He suggested a taxi, which took them quickly and easily to the front door. They checked in, found their rooms, Bea and Karim firmly in separate singles – Ali had at least roused himself enough to insist on that – and David and Ali sharing a twin. The formalities took only a few minutes in flawless English, then they were ushered upstairs by the porter with their bags. It was sumptuous and David immediately wished Gillian had been there to enjoy it too.

Karim and Bea came waltzing into David and Ali's room full of themselves.

"Half the stuff in the bathroom I don't even know what it's for," Karim declared.

"Now I know what's wrong with the Pensión El Moro," Bea joked.

They decided to eat out, and after showers, freshening up, changing – or in Ali's case simply staring out of the window – they ended up wandering first along the Paseo del Prado then on to the adjoining Paseo de Recoletos, both broad tree-lined avenues flanked by monumental buildings. They passed museums and galleries, the Spanish Stock Exchange, the Cibeles fountain, and some huge buildings that looked as if they had been carved out of icing sugar. David had El Espejo – The Mirror – in mind for eating and it lived up to his memory. He had once been brought here by the Spanish Minister for Justice, who looked after sacred and secular relations and was at that time on a charm offensive with evangelicals. That turned out to be short-lived but at least it served its purpose in getting him a very nice dinner with very pleasant wine in very comfortable surroundings. Karim and

Bea were still like kids in a sweet shop. Karim had been to plenty of Indian restaurants back home but was now experiencing a degree of posh he'd only ever seen in a Bond movie. Bea knew the language and thought she understood the culture but it turned out that the global culture of luxury was a different thing again.

They were ushered to a table and sat in the middle of highly polished dark wood, gleaming glass, beautiful ceramic decoration, and very well-heeled urbane company, and started leafing through the menu. Ali mumbled responses, but despite every effort David just couldn't seem to shake his lethargy. It was as if someone had left the taps on and his entire reservoir of personality had ebbed away. David tried to imagine what he was feeling and what his new reality might be. He imagined the next time Ali was stopped in the street and asked how the family were. *"Oh yes,"* he might have to say. *"They're all well. Samira's engaged to a Christian boy, Karim lives in Spain with his Catholic girlfriend, and Rasheed is a terrorist serving twenty years. We have to be thankful for small mercies."*

"What would you like, Ali?" David tried to break in on the gloom.

"I don't know. Whatever."

"No curry I'm afraid but very nice fish or seafood."

"I'm not very hungry actually. You just go ahead."

This made everybody gloomy and what could have been a treat turned into an ordeal. David ordered for Ali and Bea ordered for Karim. The youngsters finished first and decided to go wandering, with an agreement to meet at the entrance next to the jazz quartet in forty minutes. This left David and Ali alone. David was by now getting a bit fed up with trying to jolly things along.

"Ali, you haven't touched that *arroz con leche*. Do you mind if I...?"

"No. Go ahead. I told you I didn't want it."

"Ali – you are going to have to eat."

"Why?"

David put down his spoon and looked him in the eye.

"Because you still have a life to live. Rasheed's fate is beyond

233

your control now and you still have another son and a daughter and a wife and a business and friends. All of these things need an Ali Khan who is awake and functioning."

"Really?" Ali commented dryly. "Well, you may be right but there's only one thing I want to do."

"And what's that?" David asked, hoping there was something positive coming.

"Find the man they call the Prophet and kill him."

"And what does Ayeesha think of this idea?" David asked, keeping his voice as neutral as possible.

Ali shrugged.

"I have no idea. I haven't managed to call her yet."

"What? You're joking. You mean you haven't called her at all? Not since before Medina?"

Ali wiped his mouth with his napkin, though he'd eaten almost nothing, then dumped it on the table.

"There didn't seem much point. I didn't know what to say."

David stared out of the window for a second then seemed to arrive at a decision.

"Well, Ali," he said, "I'm your friend but I'm Ayeesha's friend too. She has a right to know what's going on. They're her children too."

In fact, David knew that Gillian and Ayeesha had been spending a lot of time together and everything he and Gillian had talked about would have been shared; still, this seemed his best bet for getting Ali to move. He pulled out his mobile and tapped the screen a few times.

"Sorry, Ali, but that's not on." He listened for a few seconds then, getting up, he passed the phone across the table.

"I think your wife wants a word with you," he said and headed for the bar to pay the bill.

The Madrid night was balmy and fragrant – now the heat of the day had dissipated – as David emerged onto the pavement outside. Couples, families, two older men – maybe brothers by the look of it – tourists from every nation on earth, were all wandering peacefully by as if an extra-slow pedestrian speed limit had been applied. The jazz quartet just inside the door was playing "Autumn Leaves" – a bit out of time with the seasons but the melody fitted the evening atmosphere exactly. All was perfect – except – except – he didn't have anyone to wander with. Karim and Bea approached hand in hand and he realized how much he was missing another warm hand and a voice of comfort and reason.

"How's Dad?" Karim asked.

"Speaking to your mum."

"Thank goodness for that. I've never seen him like this. If anyone can calm him down it'll be Mum."

"Well, let's hope so. And what do you think of Madrid?" David asked, changing the subject. "I suppose you know the place quite well, Bea?"

"No, not really," she answered. "I studied in Granada. We only came to Madrid when we had to. My parents always found it too big and too noisy."

"And what about you, Karim – what do you think?"

Karim shook his head as if having difficulty finding the words.

"It's amazing," he said. "Pretty different to Glasgow. Though maybe a bit like Edinburgh in some ways."

"How?' Bea asked.

"Just that they're both beautiful and international, I suppose. You have to come and see for yourself sometime."

"I intend to," she said, smiling.

At that point Ali emerged. He finally looked at least partially human. His eyes were red and his cheeks wet.

"You spoke to her?" David asked unnecessarily.

Ali nodded, pulled out a handkerchief, and sniffed.

"How is she?"

"Well. Wants to kill me but that's nothing new."

He managed a ghost of a smile. "I need to get home," he said.

"We all do," David agreed. "There's still some unfinished business."

Chapter 19

Silver Sands

It was a late flight, and although Gillian, Ayeesha, Samira, and Enver were waiting for them, Gary Morrison had taken pity and told David just to get Ali to Police Scotland headquarters by mid-morning the following day. Ayeesha was red-eyed but had a steely glint and immediately took Ali aside and could be seen giving him a few choice words. Gillian kissed David, wrapped her arms around him, and whispered nice things. Karim overhead the word champagne and felt like an odd man out; however, Samira gave him a hug as well and Enver shook his hand – a bit stiffly but he did his best.

After a night of rest and some bracing Edinburgh air, David, Gillian, Ali, Ayeesha, and Karim appeared at the appointed hour and were shown into a conference room with DI Morrison for counterterrorism, DI McIntosh for European Liaison, and a clutch of other officers in plain clothes who remained un-introduced. Morrison welcomed the attendees, particularly the Khan family, and started proceedings.

"I think we're all aware of recent events," he began, "at least from the media if not professionally. However, just to recap, Rasheed Khan is facing a boatload of charges in relation to a planned terror attack – which only failed to be a real attack by some remarkable presence of mind around this table. Karim Khan, I'm afraid it's likely that you're going to face charges and have to go back to court in Spain; however, in the meantime we are taking the view that you are helping police with their inquiries. Accepted all round?"

He paused and scanned around the room. A few nods and no objections.

"Ok then. Mr and Mrs Khan are here because of their family involvement and in the hope that they might be able to remember or think of something – along with Karim of course – that might shed some light on the Prophet, which is the main focus of this investigation now. David Hidalgo is present as a witness and family friend, not as a pastor or an investigator. All clear on that?"

Gillian gave David a brief glance as if to say, *and don't you forget it*, while David cleared his throat self-consciously.

"And DI McIntosh is here in case we're looking at a location outside the UK given the focus on Spain so far. So let me bring everyone up to speed on where we are." Morrison opened a file in front of him and turned over a few sheets. "The individual we know as 'the Prophet' – real name Saddiq Mustapha Bukhari – was expelled from the Edinburgh Mosque about eighteen months ago. The mosque authorities have been very co-operative with us in terms of information about him up to that time; thereafter there has been no sign of him physically but he has been making his presence known very strongly online and building quite a following."

David felt himself drifting from a mixture of exhaustion and since the facts about Rasheed and Karim were by now well known. Then the next bit of news suddenly snapped him back.

"We are certain that the voice on the web broadcasts is not the same man as was expelled from the mosque," Morrison continued. "In fact, we now have some independent verification of that in the form of a witness statement from a Mr..." he glanced down and consulted his notes, "Mr Callum Henderson."

He glanced around. Gillian was sitting up, one eyebrow raised, concentrating on what might be coming next.

"Mr Henderson is half-Jordanian on his mother's side and is a drama student at Queen Margaret University. According to his statement..." Morrison glanced down again and began to read, "'I am a third-year drama student at Queen Margaret's University.

In February this year I answered an advert on the internal student notice board for a fluent Arabic speaker to do voiceovers for a drama/documentary. I was contacted by a man who claimed to be the producer of the series. I was asked to send a demo video reading a script supplied by email and dressed in a costume sent by post against a blank white background with no other identifying objects in the frame. The drama department have a couple of small studios and a member of staff helped me set up the scene as described. The resulting movie clip was about four minutes long and was sent to the email address I got the script from in a digital format. About a week later I was contacted again and told that the test was satisfactory. I was told that if I was willing to do the work I would be paid £500 for every two-hour slot, which would happen either once a week or once a fortnight. A contract was included that I was required to sign, which included a confidentiality agreement. I was told a further sum of £5,000 would be forwarded to me one year after the conclusion of the work on condition only that confidentiality had been maintained. I was told that I would be paid monthly by bank transfer. I was told that the producer was based in Los Angeles and would not be able to meet me but would send further instructions using the same email address.'"

Morrison paused, took a sip of water, and continued.

"'I was further told that the material I would be speaking would be in Arabic and English and was excluded from any hate-crime legislation since it was a drama documentary and hence fictional. I accepted this explanation. The rate of pay I was offered was far in excess of anything normally available to drama students so I did not inquire any further into the details and did not tell any of my friends or tutors about the work. I have completed in total thirty-seven scripts each in the region of twenty minutes long. I accept that the content was highly inflammatory and amounted to incitement to hate crime and terrorism; however, I believed at the time that this was to be presented in drama/documentary form to expose the type of material being disseminated online as part of a campaign aimed at countering such material. I have not seen or been aware of the context in which my work has been used. I was told that the production would not be released for another eighteen months or so and that I would be sent a final copy. On seeing a report on television news about a planned attack in Córdoba, Spain, and hearing a clip of my own voice used to justify such an attack, I came forward at once to make a statement to police in the hope of apprehending the individual or individuals responsible. I have made this statement… etc, etc.'

"So, Callum Henderson – despite the name, and being a British citizen – turns out to be the best link we have so far to the Prophet. Comments and questions?"

"Wow," Gillian said after a few seconds' pause. "Incredible. And has he been able to say anything that tells us more about where the Prophet might be?"

"Some," Morrison commented. "The emails he received came from Scotland but we can only trace them back to an internet café not an actual customer so that's of limited help. We've checked the café's records and got a name for that machine at that time but it's clearly false – unless 'Ben Dover' is really a terrorist agitator, which I doubt."

Muffled guffaws from the plain-clothes end of the table were quickly silenced by a glare from Morrison.

"So, forgive me for being a bit slow on the uptake," David interrupted. "Callum Henderson is the voice of the Prophet?"

"He is indeed. We've played him some of his own material on the website and there isn't any doubt. He's held his hands up. In the circumstances it seems unlikely that there'd be charges."

"But he never saw who was employing him, never spoke to them – nothing?" David pressed on.

"No. Nothing. Nada. Zilch – hard as it is to believe. I think the sound of falling £500 notes drowned out his sense of what's too good to be true. However, better late than never. I think we now know that things are at least still connected with Scotland. The internet café's in Lothian Road and that's where all the emails came from. Apparently the owners couldn't put any name or appearance to the time slots, which were usually in the middle of the night; however, they have said they'd look at any likeness we come up with. So it's not much but it is something."

Morrison closed the file and scanned around the table again.

"Mr and Mrs Khan, I'm sorry we haven't heard from you yet. Anything you can add or anything you'd like to ask?"

Ali sat with his eyes down as he had throughout the meeting so far but Ayeesha spoke up slowly but clearly.

"So what you're saying is that the voice of the Prophet is just an actor? So who actually is the Prophet then? Is the whole thing a fiction? Maybe the Prophet isn't Muslim and isn't even a real person at all?" She sounded somewhere between disbelieving and furious. "People all over the world think this is yet another Muslim terror plot when it could all be that there's nobody who's even orthodox Muslim involved at all!"

"I'm sorry, Mrs Khan, but that may well be the case. Whatever the Prophet's agenda is, it's definitely outside of mainstream Islam. We really have no idea what's going on at this particular point but it's certainly not the usual kind of thing. There's a lot more to this than meets the eye."

Ayeesha shook her head in disbelief and groaned.

"As if it wasn't hard enough among our own," she muttered.

"So what happens next?" David asked. "I think you know everything Ali, Karim, and I can tell you."

"We do. This is an information briefing; I thought you were entitled to it. It's 100 per cent a police matter now. We'll just keep chipping away. Anything of consequence that affects the Khan family or you we'll be in touch. And thanks for coming in."

"Isn't this just perfect?" Gillian sighed happily the next Saturday and lifted a wicker picnic basket out of the boot of her silver MX5. "I don't think I've been to Silver Sands since I was twelve. You know Dad wasn't very keen on anything churchy but my friends were going on the Sunday school trip and I absolutely begged him till he gave in."

"Did it live up to expectations?" David asked, swinging a picnic rucksack onto his back and lifting out a couple of plastic deckchairs.

"Absolutely. It was one of these moments – you know – when you think, right now, I am absolutely happy. Mum was away on a bender so things were more relaxed at home. Dad was doing some redecorating and I remember him halfway up a stepladder whistling along to the radio when my friend's mum came for me. He was happy and so was I. Ros was away at Guide Camp and it was just us. He climbed down and gave me a kiss on the top of my head and said 'don't get converted now' then stuck five pounds in my pocket. I'd honestly never had so much money and I was thrilled. It was perfect. We all bought streamers from the paper shop and hung them out of the bus windows, stuffed ourselves with sweets, and sang 'The Front of the Bus They Cannae Sing' for thirty miles. It must have driven the adults mad but nobody complained."

They had gathered up all the picnic stuff and had both hands full. Gillian managed to lock the car with the remote and they set off down towards the beach where a bus had already disgorged most of Southside Fellowship along with various friends, guests, hangers-on looking for a cheap lunch, and a posse of spouses, kids, grandparents, neighbours, and workmates.

"Looks like it might be a record this year," David observed as they headed down the hill from the car park. "What did you enjoy so much?"

"Just the freedom to be normal I suppose. On a Sunday School trip I wasn't the child of an alcoholic parent any more. I was just me along with my friends. We could do the races, eat the sausage rolls, and sing the songs, and nobody thought I was any different from them. This old guy we all called Uncle Andrew – I suppose you'd have to be pretty suspicious nowadays but it was different then – anyway, I remember he told us a story about a man in the desert who had a camel. In the middle of a sandstorm the camel asked if he could just put his nose inside the tent. So the man let him. Then the camel said it was so very stormy he'd like to put his head in so the man let him. Then it was his neck, his front legs, his hump, his tummy, his back legs, and his tail. Finally the camel was all inside the tent and the man was all outside."

"And the moral?"

"I can remember it like it was yesterday," Gillian laughed. "Beware the camel's nose! You weren't supposed to do any tiny thing wrong because it would lead to worse things. So don't shoplift a sherbet fountain because it'll lead to robbing banks. Don't take a sip of your mum's sherry because you'll end up an alcoholic."

"And did it work?" David asked, pausing to swap hands on the heavier load.

"Actually, it did, strangely enough. I was holier-than-thou for years. I never bunked off school, stole anything, told lies, or drank alcohol till I was twenty-one. It's incredible how powerful a kids' talk can be."

"And was it for the better, do you think, or just brainwashing the vulnerable?"

"Completely for the better. I had friends who were pregnant under sixteen, those who got expelled from school, those who started smoking then wished they hadn't. All the usual stuff that I had said no to."

"Miss goody two shoes then?"

"You can mock. It saved me from stuff that wouldn't have done me any good. That trip still stands out in my memory as the single happiest moment from my entire childhood. Can you believe that? Did you do trips?"

"I'm afraid not," David confessed. "My dad thought the whole thing was a plot to corrupt the young and banned it outright. My mum wouldn't have minded but I wasn't bothered so I never pushed it. I'd rather be off smoking and drinking and inviting the camel back for tea."

Gillian laughed.

"You were terrible."

"I know. How did I turn out so charming, do you suppose?"

"Divine intervention – it's the only explanation."

"You may have a point there. Anyway, pick your spot, as they say – it's going to get busy."

As pastor and pastor's wife they were expected not only to be at the annual church outing – the term "Sunday School Trip" being now thought a bit passé – but to arrive on time, officiate in general, give thanks for the grub (pastor), present prizes for the races (pastor's wife), and finally do a kids' talk (either of them). Aberdour Silver Sands had been popular Sunday School trip territory for generations and although the outing name had changed, the basic format was more or less the same: as many members and friends as could be got into a fleet of buses and cars and driven to some seaside beauty spot or park, then a few hours of very amateur athletics followed by a picnic, culminating in cream buns and juice for the kids and cups of tea for the adults. Afterwards, a pause to digest it all then there was football for the males (largely) and shopping for the women (largely) though the proportions doing the opposite seemed to be growing year by year.

They found a sheltered spot just down from the dunes – but near enough the makeshift camp kitchen – and spread out a tartan rug, deckchairs, picnic baskets, and windbreak (this being the Fife coast) and sat down. They didn't have to wait long. Ali and Ayeesha arrived first, Ayeesha bearing a dozen cardboard cake boxes full of various delicacies. Karim had said he wouldn't come but then did in the hope of a decent game of football. Then Gillian's colleagues Stephen Baranski and Fran McGoldrick, who were now very officially "an item" and had moved into Stephen's very posh New Town flat in Dublin Street, appeared.

"Ok – but I'm coming for a picnic, not a sermon," Stephen had said when Gillian invited them. Fran dug him in the ribs.

"Don't be such a klutz," she said. "Just enjoy it and forget about being an atheist for a minute!"

Tati and Elvira – two girls David had had a hand in getting out of a people-trafficking scam – arrived looking fresh, youthful, and ready for anything despite having spent the morning meeting their latest batch of Eastern European temps and getting them sorted with accommodation prior to a briefing meeting on Monday. Elvira's previous boyfriend, Michael, hadn't proved lively enough for her so had been consigned to history. Tati remained married to the business. Kisses were exchanged all round as more deck chairs and rugs were set up and picnic baskets opened.

"Looks promising," Gillian commented as Fran opened something that looked like a giant Christmas hamper from Fortnum and Mason.

"Stephen gets twitchy if he's more than ten minutes from chilled Albariño so we have to bring the kitchen sink to keep it all cool. I'm happy with a can of Irn Bru but I suppose it takes all kinds."

Mrs MacInnes was in her element as usual and had roped Juan and some of the other supposedly more mature adults into blowing whistles, holding finishing lines, measuring courses, and tying scarves for the two-legged races. Eggs and spoons, sacks, balloons, beanbags, and all the rest of the regular paraphernalia were dished out, age groups sorted, and races run.

"Thank goodness that woman didn't work for the Third Reich or we'd all be under the heel of fascism," Stephen commented from a rather superior deckchair, sipping his chilled white wine.

"It's the likes of Mrs MacInnes that kept the home fires burning," David responded. "She'd have taken on Rommel single-handed if required."

"And sent him home with a flea in his ear," Gillian added, taking a bite of an egg sandwich. "I actually really admire her. There's a heart of gold under that brisk and businesslike exterior, without a doubt. How come we never hear about Mr MacInnes, though I imagine there was one at some time?"

"Unexpected heart attack, I believe," David said, "when their only child, Alison, was a teenager. After that she just soldiered on.

I think she ran the entire furniture department at Jenners before she retired. As well as several generations of ministers."

Ayeesha got up to pass around a cake box full of marzipan delights.

"These are fantastic," Fran enthused. "You should start a business."

"I have," Ayeesha smiled. "Eastern Promise: Cakes and Catering. Weddings, bar mitzvahs, church outings – all the usual."

"University staff club balls?" Fran inquired.

"Certainly. Up to a hundred people. After that it stops being fun."

"I'll bear it in mind. I'm on the committee this year. And how's business with you, Tati?" she continued. "David told me you've got your first big contract."

Tati beamed.

"We have. Standard Life. Twelve-month contract for all secretarial and admin temps. They have to do a specialist course for two weeks before they start but they pay us for that too. Then the terms and conditions are very good. The girls love it. They get temporary membership of a sports club and good introductory rates for financial products. I'm so proud of them."

"You should be proud of yourselves," Gillian put in. "You've made it happen."

"She's a miracle worker," Elvira commented, smiling at her colleague.

No one made reference to what they had both been through. It was understood and, like Mr MacInnes, consigned to history.

The afternoon wore on with races, beach volleyball – an innovation this year mainly for the youth – tea from a massive urn, buns delivered by a local baker, more sports, football, and lots of mingling. The atmosphere fitted David's philosophy of pastoral care perfectly. *Forget the holy moly*, he often thought. *Football, decorating, cleaning, cooking – that's when you find out what's really going on and where people need help.* And a dose of sunshine on a trip day didn't hurt at all.

"Fancy a bit of a wander then, David?" Stephen asked in a moment of calm when most of the athletics were over and the tea had just slipped down.

"By all means. Good for the digestion." Gillian gave him a push out of his deckchair and they set off along the beach.

"Good day," Stephen commented. "Nice to see the righteous at play."

"Well, it keeps us from brainwashing the masses I suppose," David replied wryly.

"But seriously, I am impressed," Stephen continued, picking his way round other islands of picnickers. "Here you are, just back from another derring-do mission and three days later you're back on duty building the kingdom of God."

David gave a pained expression.

"Well, I don't know what you've heard but there was very little daring and almost no doing. Ali did what was required. And as for the kingdom of God, you do have a tendency of seeing reds under the bed. It's just a bunch of friends out on a picnic. For me it's just safe, routine, normal life – what I try to focus on when other things don't keep getting in the way. Honestly – it's nothing subversive."

"Ah, David, you might fool the Khan family but you don't fool me. Surely this is all in aid of pulling in the fringes without making it too obviously religious. So it's 'just a picnic on the beach', but lo and behold we have a Muslim family, a young Turkish convert, I think I spy some Chinese over there…"

"South Koreans actually."

"Whatever. So Southside Fellowship out for the day is enjoying itself with the subtle unspoken message that church is fun, there's no pressure, it's all how God intended things to be, and you can cosy up without anything scary happening. And since you're a man who never does anything without a good reason, I further take it that it's a deliberate strategy. Am I close?"

"You never let up, do you?" David said, but with a laugh, not crossly. "You're right of course. It's all a plot to hook in passing atheists and convert them through the medium of fresh cream buns and football."

"The fact that you joke about it makes me think I am right. Or are you going to maintain it's all just innocent tradition?"

By now they had cleared most of the picnickers and wandered down to the damp, firmer sand between the tidelines. David bent down, picked up a thin pebble, and sent it skimming into the surf.

"Well," he began, "if you're going to be ruthlessly sociological about it, yes, I do believe that the church picnic has a point. For me the kingdom of God includes everything that Christians do: picnics on the beach, preaching and worship, making babies – everything. I hope people like it and see that there might be something deeper behind it. But really it's not as Machiavellian as you think."

Stephen picked up a worn piece of driftwood and examined it.

"Did I ever tell you I was brought up by monks and nuns?" he asked.

"No," David replied. "I'm amazed. I thought you were third-generation non-believer."

"Well, my dad was a philosophy professor whose philosophy did not include children. My mum was a New York socialite who could drink us both under the table then go on to the next party. So if you want to know what happens when an irresistible force meets an immovable object – I'm that result. I was their attempt to hold things together between the latest movement in philosophy and the latest lover half her age. I really was an encumbrance to both of them so I was packed off to a Catholic boarding school at seven and came back when I was seventeen. Harvard was *my* salvation."

"That must have been horrific."

"It was. But the experience of separation was nothing compared to the experience of religious discipline. I won't even begin to describe it. It's a too nice a day."

"So," David continued, sending another stone bouncing into the waves, "I can understand your hostility to religion."

"No – don't get me wrong, David; I think it's all poppycock for sound objective reasons as well. That's why I'm intrigued by what you're trying to do here. It's all very relaxed and fun but I can see the serious purpose and I approve – I honestly do. As far as I'm concerned you can take all the theology you like and dump it in the river if people can't actually behave like decent human beings. And that's what I see here. Fran gives me a blow-by-blow account of everything when Gillian takes her to church and to be honest it all sounds ok – apart from being based on myths and legends, of course. In terms of the practice it actually sounds quite attractive."

"Well. I stand amazed. You are indeed what we call *una caja de sorpresas.*"

"A box of surprises?"

"Indeed."

"And the truth is, there are times I'd like to suspend my critical faculties but I can't. Like swimming the butterfly or tight rope walking. Tried and failed."

They had reached a stream flowing down into the sea that would require either an Olympic leap or a long detour so by mutual agreement they turned and headed back. Squeals of excitement and triumph came drifting along the sand.

"What on earth are they up to now?" Stephen asked.

"I think it's pie fighting," David replied.

"Pie fighting?"

"Yes. Gillian introduced it last year. You have a marked-out arena called the Pie-R-Square, and contestants try to hit each other with plates of shaving foam. They each have an assistant called the Second Helping who gets the ammo ready. You get points for full on the face and less for glancing blows. I must confess I haven't actually tried it yet."

Stephen let out a guffaw.

"And you lot are also a box of surprises. I like it that you don't take yourselves too seriously."

By the time they had meandered back there was a definite change in the air. The sun was lower, the temperature falling, and there was an unspoken feeling that it was time to pack up and go. David sat and took the glass of fizzy apple juice Gillian offered him.

"Interesting talk?" she asked.

"Fascinating; I'll tell you later."

Gillian glanced around, taking in the women packing up their camp kitchen, the guys boxing up all the sports gear, and families shaking out their rugs and cramming everything into huge canvas-style shopping bags.

"Well, well. Look who's here," she remarked.

David twisted around to see a figure in his characteristic polo shirt and chinos striding down over the dunes.

"Finally found you," he puffed. "I have been on every beach between Seton Sands and Timbuktu. You are indeed the underground church!"

"Mike – sorry you had such trouble." David stood up and held out a hand. "I didn't realize you were planning to join us or we could have come in convoy."

"No problem, sir." Mike waved away the apology. "I'm here."

"But I'm afraid you've missed the fun," Gillian explained. "We're just packing things up."

"Not a problem. Actually I just needed a word with this gentleman." He was still gripping David's hand. "Bit of admin that needs attended to. Anyway, I suppose you didn't have American Football anyway."

"No, not this year. So what can I help you with?"

Mike sat down in the chair Gillian had rapidly unfolded again and took a can of Coke.

"Actually, it's a bit embarrassing. Remember I told you there wasn't any paperwork for the grant application? Well, the funding committee are now saying they want a brief summary of the plan, what the money would be used for, and the signature of the pastor."

"But we haven't agreed to ask for any money yet, Mike," Gillian put in, frowning slightly.

"Oh, I understand. But it just makes things a whole lot easier if we know for sure whether you'd be eligible. This isn't applying –

it's just clearing the ground. Then an application can go through on the nod if you do decide to go ahead."

"And can't it wait until Monday?" David asked, also sounding a bit wrong-footed.

"That's the thing, Pastor David," Mike said, looking genuinely troubled. "The committee have their meeting on Monday, then nothing till next spring. So it's kind of now or never. Actually I've drafted the text, all it needs is you to glance over it and add your autograph. Nothing binding – just clearing the way."

David sighed quite loudly. He'd been hoping for a quiet drive somewhere other than Edinburgh and a nice dinner in a country pub, not signing documents for something they still hadn't decided they wanted or needed.

"Ok," he said at length. "What do we need to do?"

"Well, if your lovely lady wife doesn't mind, my hire car is just up here. We can swing by my place, look over the documents, add a signature, then I'll fax it off and that'll be hunky-dory. If the lady doesn't mind."

Gillian very clearly did mind but didn't feel in a position to put a total embargo on it.

"You know I don't trust that man further than I could throw him," she whispered as the last of the uneaten sandwiches and a bag of rubbish went back into the picnic hamper. "Be careful. He's up to something."

"Don't worry," David said, smiling and giving her a peck. "I'm on my own turf now. I think I can take care of myself."

Chapter 20

Craigmillar

Ayeesha had suggested coffee to Gillian since she was going home alone but she finally declined. It had been a busy day and the sun, fresh air, and sea breezes – not to mention the over-forties ladies race and supervising the pie fights between the teenagers – had all taken their toll. She felt the call of a soft bed in a darkened room. But first things first – she put the kettle on, made a cup of Ceylon Broken Orange Pekoe, took it through to the living room, and put "The Four Seasons" on very low. When she woke the house was in darkness. She slowly came to, feeling disorientated, and looked at her watch. Past ten thirty. She must have been exhausted. Still feeling groggy, she got up slowly, drew the living-room curtains, turned on a standard lamp and a couple of table lamps, and went looking for David. He must have come in very quietly and left her sleeping. That was kind. First she wandered along the hall into the kitchen, still feeling a bit floaty and dreamy. Everything was as she'd left it. *Hmm. Maybe he went for a sleep as well.* But the bedroom was equally empty. Nobody in the bath, nobody in the office or the spare room.

"David!" she called out. "Are you there?"

Silence.

That *was* unusual. She knew his routines by now and Saturday night was not for late-night escapades. He dutifully – you could even say *religiously* – went over his sermon notes and without fail took at least half an hour of silent prayer organizing his thoughts while making sure it wasn't *just* the thoughts of Chairman Dave.

251

Something pretty important and unexpected must have come up. She went hunting for her mobile and rang his number. It rang out then switched to voicemail. She started to feel a little nervous. It was now nearly eleven. "Calm yourself, Gillian," she said to herself aloud. What could have happened? She tried to think logically. Could he have dropped in on the Khans to talk things through? That sounded quite likely. She gave them a ring despite the lateness of the night. First the line was engaged so she waited through a very slow ten minutes then tried again. Karim answered. No, David wasn't there. He asked his dad if they'd seen him. No, nothing since they'd seen him go off with the American after the picnic.

Unfortunately, she didn't have either a landline or mobile for Missionary Mike. Nor, come to that, an email – which was odd in itself. He just seemed to turn up from nowhere and disappear back to nowhere without any way of initiating contact. Come to think of it, he had been for lunch but never invited them back or talked about where he lived or anything. Nervous was now becoming anxious. *Stuart McIntosh*, she thought. David might have stopped off there on the way back. Or, if he hadn't, then Stuart would know what to do. She phoned the very well-remembered number that used to be David's when he was living in the Bruntsfield flat. Stuart was a night owl and picked up immediately. No, David hadn't been there. They hadn't seen each other since the case briefing three days before. Then she could almost hear him clicking over from pal to professional. Where and when had she seen him last? Doing what? Going where? With whom? "Ok," he said. "I'll be round in ten minutes. Walking, I'm afraid – couple of drams in a nightcap."

She made more tea while she was waiting and walking up and down the floor in front of the living-room window despite herself. *This is Edinburgh*, she told herself, *not Beirut*. People didn't disappear just like that. In a couple of minutes he'd walk in, apologize for not letting her know about some congregational crisis that had come up, explain as much as she needed to know, then offer some oatcakes and cheese before they turned in. She'd be a bit cross that he hadn't let her know but also relieved that it had been nothing. He'd apologize again and they'd make up in bed. But that hopeful scenario still hadn't happened by the time Stuart rang the doorbell and came up.

"Mike MacGregor? From Charleston? Yes, I think David did mention something about him but it was just by the way. He didn't sound particularly concerned. What's his organization?"

"It's called the One World Foundation. But now I think about it, we only have his word to go on that it even exists. He asked David to go over and sign some papers for a meeting of their board that was supposed to be happening on Monday."

"Well, if you're worried, why don't we have a look for it and at least see that it's legit? Then that's one less thing to worry about."

Gillian got her laptop out, flipped it open, and Googled the name. It came up readily enough and did indeed seem to exist – at least in cyberspace. They clicked through a series of menus and options including the Google Maps link to a location in downtown Charlestown.

"Seems ok," Stuart opined. "Do you feel any better for that?"

"No – actually I don't," Gillian admitted, taking another sip of her tea. "For some reason or other I've never taken to Mike or his mission. Do you think it would be too late to phone Spade and get him to have a look?"

Stuart grunted.

"I very much doubt it. I think he operates on Tunnock's Time – probably five hours after the rest of us. I've got his mobile here."

Spade did indeed answer very readily. McIntosh explained briefly that they were checking out what might be a dodgy website connected to a dodgy guy and would he mind very much despite the lateness of the hour?

"That's fine. He'll have a look and call us back."

Gillian glanced at the wall clock. Twenty past eleven.

"Do you think he could have had an accident? Mike was driving him, then I suppose the plan would have been to drop him off here. David doesn't use a car in town."

"It's possible. I'll give our incident room a ring and see if there's anything that might connect."

Gillian left him and went to boil the kettle again – not for any other purpose than for something to do. She gathered up a few plates and put them in the dishwasher and put a few jars back in the cupboard while listening to Stuart speak at the other end of the hall. On the way back to the living room she felt an almost overwhelming urge to put on her coat and outdoor shoes and go walking, as if David might be loitering outside the delicatessen downstairs or even lying in a heap behind the bins across the road.

"Nothing matching David's description noted," Stuart said as she came back in. "Of course, these things take time. If there had been a traffic accident or something it could take up to an hour to get the details on the system."

Gillian nodded dumbly, then got up and began pacing again. McIntosh knew better than to give false reassurance. He was also starting to feel uneasy.

His mobile rang, making them both jump. He answered and she heard him thank Spade for calling back so quickly. Then he covered the mouthpiece and asked her for a pencil and paper. She rummaged around, found something, and put it on the table in front of him. He asked Spade to repeat what he had just said and started scribbling. Gillian made herself wait and not try to read over his shoulder.

"That's great, Spade. Very helpful. Thanks. Bye."

"What?" she asked.

"The website exists of course – we visited it. But it's not hosted in Charleston, South Carolina. Or any other Charleston, for that matter."

"Where then?"

"Qatar in the Persian Gulf. Downtown Doha, to be precise."

"I told him not to trust that man," she groaned. She sank to a chair and put her hands to her temples. "I bet this has something to do with the Prophet. It was just too much of a coincidence that Mike turned up just as we got involved. Do you think David's safe?"

Mike MacGregor was his usual charming, over-polite, ingratiating self on the run back into Edinburgh. *If he apologizes one more time*, David thought, *I'll open the door and jump the barriers into the Forth*. Eventually the subject did change, however, and they spoke about Charleston in comparison with Edinburgh. David had never visited the southern city but had known some friends who came from there. He was a bit surprised to find that he seemed to know more about the city than Mike did. "Well, we lived a bit out," was the vague reply. "We only really went into town for shopping." *Strange*. Then they talked about Spain. Now the reverse appeared to be true. David had worked and travelled extensively through the peninsula but he couldn't name anywhere south of Madrid that Mike didn't seem to know about. Cuenca, Chinchón, Aranjuez, Toledo, as well as all the bigger Andalusian cities – it seemed Mike had visited them all. "When I was a student," he said. "Doing the grand tour."

"You never told me where you're living," David remarked as they came along Queensferry Road, the back way into the city from Fife.

"Oh, just got a little place. Could have organized a house in the suburbs but this was handier – and within the budget." It must have been a pretty low budget, David thought as they left behind the city centre and headed out towards Craigmillar.

"Not such a great neighbourhood," Mike acknowledged as they drew up outside a modern monstrosity tower block next door to a scrapyard with a rusty corrugated fence around it. "However – 'where sin abounds there grace abounds more so' – that's what it says, doesn't it?" The light was dying as they got out and picked their way past chip papers, pizza boxes, and miscellaneous filth to arrive at the main entrance. Mike unlocked the steel door and ushered David in. He pressed the lift call button and they waited together. David was far from unused to blocks like this, but it wasn't normal territory for an international jet-setter like Mike must be, he thought. It's either a deliberate decision to live among the poor or else the One World Foundation doesn't have as much cash as they claim. He pushed his doubts down and got into the lift after Mike.

They stopped at the fourth floor, turned right, and stopped outside a plain wooden door painted a dirty rose pink. Mike fumbled for his keys again and pushed the door open.

"My humble abode, sir. You are welcome," he said, as if ushering guests into Trump Tower instead of a dingy council flat in a rundown neighbourhood. David walked in and heard the door slam behind him.

By 1 a.m. Gillian had gone through three more cups of tea and several glasses of something stronger. Together she and Stuart had checked the road traffic unit, all city hospitals and several in Fife, all of David's friends and contacts that might conceivably had seen him, and finally Mrs MacInnes herself. Once roused she immediately offered to come round but Gillian didn't think she could trust herself to be civil in the face of well-meaning fussing and put her off. Mrs MacInnes nevertheless insisted on putting something on her ladies' prayer chain WhatsApp group on the new iPad her niece had got her for her birthday.

Eventually, Gillian got to the point of accepting that there was nothing more they could do meantime and urged Stuart to go home. This he did reluctantly – there was work in the morning – however, he had already planned to abandon that day's scheduled activity and replace it by moving heaven and earth to find David Hidalgo. Gillian got into bed and turned the lights out but did not immediately sleep. *If you have harmed one hair of his head, Mike MacGregor, or whoever you are...* was the last thought in her mind before consciousness faded.

"So, can we get this paperwork dealt with, Mike?" David said, trying not to show too obviously his feelings about having his evening hijacked. But Mike MacGregor seemed to have disappeared. The man standing in front of him was silent, the constant irritating smile and the expression of cheerful optimism unaccountably vanished.

"Do you mind if we get on with this, Mike?" David repeated, uncertain but trying to keep things on track.

"I'm sorry to disappoint you, Señor David, but I'm afraid plans have changed," said a voice but it wasn't the voice of Missionary Mike. The southern accent had been replaced by something that sounded Eastern European – maybe Hungarian or Balkan. A gun came out of his pocket and was held loosely pointed at David's chest.

David paused, frozen.

"Who are you?" he asked eventually.

"Not who you think."

"That seems obvious."

"My name is Martinas Kovač. I thought Mike was close enough. The MacGregor was just a nod to the Scots – I thought it would go down well."

"You want to tell me what's going on?"

Mike, who had suddenly become Martinas, gestured with the gun, pushing David further down the hall and into a sparsely decorated tiny living room.

"Sit down," he said. "We've a lot of catching up to do." David dropped into a torn black vinyl armchair as Martinas perched on a dirty radiator and ran a hand through his hair. "First, you can tell me what your interest is in the Prophet, and why you went to Spain."

"How about you tell me what your interest is?" David countered. Kovač sighed.

"This is not a game," he said irritably. "And, anyway, I think I have the upper hand. What and why?"

"I have absolutely no interest in the Prophet other than a general distaste for hatred. I went to Spain to support a friend."

Kovač stared up out of the window as if trying to control his impatience.

"That doesn't even begin to sound credible," he said. "A peace-loving pastor with a cosy congregation doesn't get involved in matters out of his depth without a reason. What's your reason?"

"I've told you – I'm allergic to hate. A member of my congregation

257

was beaten up for the simple reason of loving the wrong person. When I spoke to the girl's family it turned out their two sons had left their jobs to follow some kind of radical preacher. I chose to help a friend try to find them."

"Yes – Rasheed and Karim. I know all about them. But the idea that you do all this simply to hold the hand of a casual acquaintance isn't credible. Who do you work for?"

"I'm a Christian pastor – who do you think I work for?"

"Very funny. Well, we'll find out in due course. So the next question: I know you're in touch with the police. What have you discussed with them? What do you know about the Prophet?"

David said nothing. Instead of looking at the gun as would have been natural, he glanced around at his surroundings. The wall coverings were dirty woodchip painted off-white. The black armchair he was seated in had a mate on the other side of the room – also ripped. A chipped coffee table with cigarette burns lay between them. The carpet had maybe once been a rusty orange colour but was now covered in what looked like oily footprints, crumpled-up scraps of paper, and all manner of domestic detritus. The only decoration on the walls was a Leicester team poster from four years previously. The glass of the windows was so dirty it was barely transparent and was framed by scraps of net curtain. Dirty tins of dog food were piled on a sideboard.

"Can't say I'm impressed by your interior designer," he commented.

"He's a slob. But a useful slob," Kovač said with a shrug. "Now, I'm not known to be the most patient in my family. We were talking about your conversations with the police."

"I don't think we were," David countered. "You were asking about it and I was asking what *your* interest in the Prophet might be."

"You'll find that out soon enough, don't worry. Now the police…" The gun came a little higher and Kovač's grip seemed to tighten. "The conversation."

"The Khan family are friends of mine. Their sons were missing. The Prophet's preaching was implicated. I simply sat in on some conversations about what the motivation was and its connection to Spain, given my history there."

Kovač smiled.

"Very good," he said. "Now we're getting somewhere. And the website?"

"Curiosity. The police were trying to get access. I suggested an approach that got them in."

"Yes – Medina Azahara, if I'm not mistaken." The gun was lowered as if Kovač seemed to be feeling he was getting his way. "We were intrigued by the increased traffic from Edinburgh IP addresses. It looked like a whole new batch of converts for a bit. A pity it was just your great constabulary."

David shifted in his seat, trying to find a position not marred by foam that had lost its spring last century.

"And just who exactly is 'we'?" he asked calmly. "We know the speaker online isn't the same man that was thrown out of the Edinburgh Mosque. Have you taken his place?"

"Well done, Pastor David. You could say that."

"Why?"

"Because he was an underused resource. He was like a gold mine somebody was working with a teaspoon. You're from the capitalist West – you should understand that. I simply helped him achieve what he really wanted to achieve but didn't have the capacity for."

"You mean blowing things up?"

Kovač grunted and wiped his forehead.

"A means to an end but no – the aim is far greater than that. Anyway, enough questions for now. We have a few days before your little trip. We'll have time to talk."

"My trip?" David asked, eyebrows raised, not feeling quite so calm now.

"Yes. You're going on holidays. To somewhere warmer – without the interference of Scottish police."

"Am I permitted to know where and why?"

Kovač shrugged.

"I don't see why not. It's all signed and sealed – it just needs to be delivered and that'll happen very soon. You'll have the pleasure of a private jet flight. Edinburgh to Doha – that's Qatar, if you don't know."

"I know. And why?"

"My – how can I put it – colleagues have an interest in a high-profile international guest who might be useful in hostage exchange. Or something else. You are just going to be money in the bank. Insurance. And it'll have the secondary – also useful – purpose of keeping you out of my hair with all of these little conversations you just happen to sit in on."

"So your taskmasters are in the Gulf?"

"Not taskmasters, just paymasters."

"And I suppose that's where the 'One World Foundation' has its little office?"

"Well, it's a total figment of course. But in a manner of speaking, yes."

"But why would you be offering money to Christian churches if you are pursuing a radical Muslim agenda? And why Southside? Why me?"

Kovač sighed.

"Last question," he said wearily. "Being a missionary in Scotland has been perfect for identity purposes. A Christian missionary is not a Muslim terrorist or anything like it and vice versa. But I also have an interest in influencing opinion in the longer term. Anti-Muslim sentiment in society in general and of course the church is a great place to start. You're all so earnest and serious and activist, aren't you? And there's already a mood from the far right. I just want to make it more mainstream.

"But how to work the identity and gain acceptance? Well – money of course. You bit as 99 out of 100 would. As regards why you, I was doing the rounds. I happened to contact your congregation like many others. You happened to be on holiday and Juan took the chance to ask me to preach. It seemed perfect. Then the church fitted the profile perfectly as well. Small congregation but growing. Ambitious plans but clearly no money. The fact that you blundered your way into my alternative identity was just a bit of bad luck; however, we're now about to turn that around and make it a bit of good luck. But enough of that. On your feet, Pastor David. There's someone I'd like you to meet."

Kovač levelled the gun again and David stood up. Kovač edged around to the side and gestured David towards the door, into the hall, and towards another door.

"Open it."

David pushed the door open. The room was the size of a small bedroom. Inside were two dishevelled mattresses, one pushed into each corner. An off-white radiator was on the wall between them and a window above that. There was no other furniture of any sort. On one of the mattresses an old man in a dirty white robe was lying, handcuffed to the radiator.

"Meet the Prophet," Kovač said.

The old man looked up expectantly and smiled.

"Welcome, my brother," he said happily. "Do you have a cigarette?"

Gillian woke up groggily from a restless night. The entry phone was buzzing.

"Hello?"

"Stuart here – are you up and about yet?"

"Almost. Thanks for coming."

She went back to the bedroom and grabbed a dressing gown. Stuart got to the door just as she was putting the kettle on.

"Come in. Good of you to come. On your way to work?"

He came in, closed the door, and followed her through to the kitchen.

"This *is* work," he said. "I've been on to Gary Morrison and some other of the 'high heid yins'. If this is an abduction then every resource we've got will be thrown at it. And I'm leading the team."

Gillian managed a weak smile as she made two coffees.

"And is that what you think? Not an accident or something else we haven't thought of?"

McIntosh took his coffee and added three generous spoonfuls of sugar.

"Looks that way," he said. "Nothing from the hospitals, no road traffic reports, nobody jumped off the Forth Bridge."

Gillian looked pained and sat down.

"Sorry," McIntosh apologized. "I know it's no laughing matter. Too many years in the polis."

Gillian supported her forehead on the heel of one hand, her elbow resting on the table.

"Don't worry," she muttered. "It's not a problem. I don't think David is the jumping-off type. Not now anyway."

She took a sip of her coffee. "So what's next?"

"Well, firstly, twelve hours isn't that long yet. I know it feels that way to you, but it's very early days. Abductions almost always have some sort of follow-up fairly soon: a ransom, a threat, a demand for transport, and so on. So we may get something like that in the course of the day. But, from our side, we've got a team on it. I've got some of Morrison's DSs and DCs plus all the uniform resources. I've called a briefing for eleven o'clock. You're welcome to attend but you don't have to."

"No, I'll come," she said heavily. "I won't be in a fit state to say much but I'll show up. I certainly won't be fit for work and I don't know what else I'd be doing."

"So, you'll need some time now to get sorted. Is it ok if I just sit in the living room and make some calls in the meantime?"

"Sure. I'll not be long."

Stuart and Gillian arrived at Police Scotland headquarters at 10.45. Stuart led the way and took them straight to a conference room with a large central table, a data projector on the table, a screen at one end, and a trolley with two large urns, a jug of milk, sugar bowl, and a tray of shortbread biscuits at the other.

"Can I get you something?" McIntosh asked.

"Yes – more caffeine won't go amiss. Just milk."

DI Gary Morrison came in just as two cups were being put on the table.

"Gillian," he said briskly but not unfeelingly. "I am so sorry. I just heard this morning. You can rest assured no stone with be left unturned. Absolutely none. Stuart is leading the team and we've got some good people on it. I'm hopeful."

"Thanks," she managed. "I appreciate that."

"I'll come in for as much of the briefing as I can manage. You're in good hands with this man here." He nodded in Stuart's direction.

By a few minutes past eleven the room was full. *Well*, Gillian thought, *at least they're pulling out all the stops*.

"Morning, everyone," Stuart began. "Most of you know each other. We have a few guests – Andy and Yvonne, welcome. Can I also introduce Dr Gillian Lockhart, Reverend David Hidalgo's wife? She's here as a witness, an interested party, but also a very keen mind – which I plan to make full use of. Everybody happy? Ok, Gillian, can I turn to you first? David was last seen leaving the beach at Aberdour with the man calling himself Mike MacGregor. Can you elaborate?"

Gillian did. Including her suspicions – apparently unfounded at that time – about "Mike the Missionary". She described their first meeting at Southside, his impressive offers of cash, and the fact that he had come for lunch but never reciprocated and that nobody knew where he lived.

"Did David have his phone on him when he left?" a power-dressed woman in an expensive tailored suit asked.

"Yes. As far as I know. I'm sure he did."

"So that might mean that either he was immediately incapacitated, or the drive didn't lead to anywhere suspicious; otherwise he might have managed a quick call."

"Thanks, Yvonne," Stuart said. "Any comments on that?"

A considerably older – and considerably less well-dressed – male colleague spoke up.

"I can see where Yvonne's coming from," he said. "The question is, how far did they drive? But I don't think we can infer anything either way from the lack of a call. They could have picked up some extra muscle on the way, in which case David would have had no chance to call, then they drove a hundred miles or they could be just around the corner. There's really no way of knowing."

"Ok, folks. Let's leave that one," Stuart replied, making a note on the pad in front of him.

"I think we want to talk about 'who' first rather than 'where'. And the one might inform the other. David Hidalgo had only recently come back from Córdoba in southern Spain in connection with the Khan boys – we all saw the TV coverage. That was all tied into the man we're calling 'the Prophet' and a terrorist bomb plot. The two boys, Rasheed and Karim, will be facing charges in Spain. Rasheed is in Spanish custody and Karim is home on bail, having done all he could to get out of it, and has now provided some useful information. So do we take the view that David's disappearance is connected? Gillian – any other explanation you can think of?"

"None," she said emphatically. "We've been involved in a few things we'd rather not have over the past few years but I can't see how it could be a throwback to any of that. The Prophet was trying to bomb and kill in Córdoba. David had a hand in stopping it. I think it's natural to see a connection."

"Ok then – working hypothesis," Stuart agreed and scribbled something else down. "And where does Mike MacGregor feature in relation to the prophet? Andy?"

Another fresh face at the end of the table looked up and answered in a distinctly non-Scottish accent. *MI6?* Gillian wondered. *GCHQ? Not Police Scotland, I suppose...*

"Well, he's not Mike MacGregor and he's not a missionary," Andy began to nods around the table.

"Hmm. Not the least bit surprised," Gillian muttered.

"Indeed. So the website is a total fabrication and the One World Foundation doesn't exist. That's to say, there are various entities *called* the One World Foundation…" He looked at his notes. "A health food shop in Seattle, a refugee support centre in Islington, and a free-trade lobby group in Brussels, among others. But nothing connected to Christian/Muslim relations and evangelical church support, which is what 'Mike' seemed to mainly be pushing."

"So who is he then?" Gillian asked, impatiently.

"We're not 100 per cent sure but we think he may be Martinas Kovač – Bosnian by birth, linked to various terrorist groups as well as mainstream crime. He's generally been a freelancer but recent reports have linked him to a shadowy breakaway group in Qatar – ostensibly Muslim in identity but in reality secularists who use a Muslim cloak to raise funds for what they claim is jihad but in reality is whatever they might want to do. There have been bombings, kidnappings, hostage-taking, drug dealing, internet fraud, and…" he glanced down then briefly in Gillian's direction, "… well, a bunch of other stuff. I'm sure you can imagine. Actually he trained as an actor then worked as a TV journalist and current affairs producer before abruptly dropping off the radar. Wanted in seventeen countries – if it is the same man. We've been in touch with your… eh… Mrs MacInnes… and got some photos taken at the church trip before he left with Mr Hidalgo and compared them with Europol records – it seems a good match."

"Clever," Gillian remarked. "You don't hang about."

"I told you we were pulling out all the stops," Stuart McIntosh said in her direction. "So, next question – what's he up to? Yvonne, can you take this one?"

The power dresser shuffled a bit to add an inch or two to her sitting height and began.

"The organization Kovač is currently linked to is based in Doha, Qatar, as Andy has said. As far as we can tell they've kept themselves out of the Shia/Sunni feuding except for mainstream criminal activity exploiting destabilized states – much like criminality in Northern

Ireland actually. So it's been hard to figure out what the endgame is. However, this attempted attack in Spain has actually been very enlightening. The 'Prophet' – the guy they basically hijacked after he was kicked out of the mosque – we think provided both a legitimate identity they could make use of and an idea. For all the Prophet's general raving, when he was still active in public, there was one consistent theme. The mosque – I think the guy's name is Trevor – has been very helpful in giving us recordings of some of his preaching. He didn't go much for Israel and Palestine or American interference in Middle Eastern states. Or even alliance forces out of Afghanistan. He seemed to be obsessed with the reinstatement of previous Islamic grandeur in Europe itself – and that means mainly Turkey and Spain. We reckon that he maybe thought Erdoğan seemed to be doing a good enough job of re-Islamizing Turkey so he turned his attention to Spain. In fact, we've found out that he had a few trips to the province of Andalucía around 2015/16 and that might have started him thinking in that direction. The background is that the Spanish authorities have been very alert to this kind of thing so Muslim prayer in the Mezquita in Córdoba is prohibited. There is freedom of speech online but it's monitored very closely, and unwelcome elements are quietly shipped back to where they came from – mainly Morocco and Egypt.

"So, whether or not it stands any chance of success – ETA fought for years for Basque independence and it came to nothing and Catalunya is still working in that direction – the fact is that there are very visible symbols of an Islamic past in Spain and it's the only place in Western Europe where that's true. So it works well as a symbolic struggle. And any religious/political struggle like that also provides a lot of scope for general criminality, threats, extortion, violence, and so on."

"So you don't think they are seriously pursuing a modern Islamic state in Spain – it's just a criminal enterprise using a cover? Is that what you're saying?" Stuart asked.

Yvonne nodded. "Exactly."

David Hidalgo sat on the dirty mattress provided for him, handcuffed to the radiator, leaning against the wall, and ate some kind of nameless pie, the contents of which he didn't want to speculate on. Kovač sat on a kitchen chair at the door. The "Prophet" had slumped back onto his bed after his brief greeting and seemed to be already asleep, snoring softly. The sounds of a man Kovač had introduced as Abdul roaming around in the kitchen or living room could be heard in the background. David guessed he was the "slob" who owned the premises. Initially, David had taken the view that if he was to be smuggled out of Scotland then he was more valuable alive than dead and would not be treated too badly. So he'd refused to put on the handcuffs Kovač had tossed to him after taking him into the bedroom at gunpoint.

"Put these on. The other side to the radiator pipe," Kovač had said, a gun trained on him, held in both hands.

"Don't think I will," David had replied, testing out the boundaries.

"Please, let's not make things more unpleasant than they already are," Kovač replied regretfully. "You can do it or Abdul can. Of course he might break your arm in the process. Abdul!"

Abdul Masood of the AM scrapyard appeared, huge in the doorway, munching a quarter of a pizza.

"The great David Hidalgo!" he announced. "Nice to meet you at last. What a prize pain in the arse you are!"

David thought it might be better to keep both arms functioning and picked up the handcuffs.

"Abdul is out on police bail, if you're interested. You might have heard he was involved in a little retribution. It's wonderful what an expensive lawyer and £100,000 of bail can achieve. There will be insufficient evidence, believe me."

"You beat Enver?" David asked heavily.

"And torched the shop," Masood agreed happily. "Much more fun than watching *Strictly*."

David looked away in disgust.

"Abdul has a – what is it you say – a *short fuse*. Shorter than mine, which is saying something. And he likes the sound of bones breaking, I'm not sure why. So it is best to cooperate." Kovač offered his advice in just the same tone as if suggesting it might rain so better take your umbrella.

"So are you planning to tell me what this is all about?" David asked. "What's the point?"

Kovač adjusted his position on the chair and waved Masood away.

"Well, it's almost always about money," he began, "but money usually comes through control. So I guess it's about control."

"Of what? How?"

"Well, of people obviously. And as to that, you should understand more than most. What's the most powerful force known to mankind? More than Mongol hordes, more than celebrity, more than Wall Street?"

David didn't reply.

"Come on. It's not that hard… religion, of course. If you can persuade the people that God is on their side and that even if they die they go directly to paradise, there's absolutely nothing you can't achieve. Nothing. You should know that. It's beautiful!"

David listened in spite of himself as Kovač warmed to his theme.

"And when you have differing religious viewpoints at war with each other – *both* believing they're going to go to heaven – well, double the fun. And enormous scope for the making of money and running the show. I learned that very early in my career and it's been confirmed by everything I've learned since."

David shifted on the mattress to try to find a softer spot.

"What was your early career before you turned to kidnapping?"

"Entertainment."

"Can't say I see you as a song and dance man."

"But that's indeed what I was. TV newshound. Entertainment, if ever there was. I had a posting to Northern Ireland. It was a revelation. Then I got into production and saw the big picture. 'When religion is rife there's sure to be strife.' My motto. Hope you like it."

"Well, if you've studied it so much you'll know that I'm actually not religious."

"I know, I know. 'Relationship' – isn't that what you call it? But it's all religion to me. By any other name. I grant you your congregation aren't terrorists – yet. But threaten their security and freedom of belief and we'll see how long it takes."

In a way David could just about imagine Mrs MacInnes swapping her teapot for a hand grenade, but only to defend, never to attack. He shook his head.

"You've got it wrong," he said. "Entirely wrong. And the people of Spain won't permit you to destabilize their country. You'll never win."

Kovač stood.

"But you don't understand," he said, almost offended. "Winning is merely a supplementary goal. Nobody seriously expects the Caliphate to be restored. At least no one in their right mind. Even destabilization isn't the final goal. Hatred and fear are all we need. Marches for this and against that. Low-level bombs and bullets. Just enough to make people hate and distrust one another. Then they turn to strong men to protect them. Look at America or Turkey. Let's see what happens once a peace-loving Scottish pastor goes on the Prophet's website about to get his brains blown out by some wide-eyed crusader for the Caliphate, then we'll see how public opinion changes."

David felt something turn hard and heavy inside of him. He couldn't think of anything to say.

"Anyway, I hope you enjoy our hospitality. Even though it's just a short break. We'll soon be flying to Doha."

Chapter 21

Edinburgh

Gillian drove home slowly after the conference. Stuart McIntosh had offered her a support officer but she'd turned down the suggestion. Likewise she thanked Irene MacInnes for her call but declined a home visit. Finally the car ended up driving, as if of its own accord, to Bruntsfield and stopping outside the remains of the A&A MiniMart. The windows were still boarded up and the wood around them charred, but the door had been replaced and there was a sign on it saying "Business as Usual" and what she guessed was the equivalent in Urdu below. She parked and came into the shop not entirely sure why or with any plan of what to do or say. The inside was not at all as she'd expected, though, compared with the outside. The walls and ceiling were black of course and all the normal paraphernalia of a grocer's shop had gone but, despite that, everything else suggested quiet industry, and indeed – business almost as usual. A refrigerated display unit hummed quietly in one corner and makeshift shelving had been arranged around the walls. Sacks of basmati rice, red lentils, various different sizes of beans, and different flours were open next to them. Boxes of fruit and vegetables took up the gaps and another stand held assorted tins. The centre of the floor space was taken up by a table piled with cakes, sweets, and pastries. Samira was standing behind a cut-off length of kitchen worktop balanced on two columns of lemonade crates. In place of the till there was only a calculator and large ledger notebook. She immediately brightened on seeing Gillian come in.

"Hi," she said as soon as she recognized her. "How are you? Oh – sorry – I shouldn't ask. Stuart McIntosh told us." The greeting petered out.

"Hi," Gillian replied with an attempt at a smile.

"I'm so sorry about what's happened," Samira continued. "And that it happened because of us."

"Well, we don't know that for sure," Gillian said quietly, although that conclusion was inescapable. "Mum in?"

"Yes. I think so. Do you want me to call her? Or you can just go straight up."

"I'll just go up if that's ok."

Ayeesha was in the kitchen pouring a bowlful of coconut flakes into a massive mixer. At first she didn't hear Gillian knocking over the rhythmic beating sound.

"Hi, anyone home?"

Ayeesha gave a jump and turned.

"Gillian. Come in. Sorry, I didn't hear you. You gave me a fright."

"Thanks. I think we're all a bit on edge."

Ayeesha put down the bowl, turned the mixer off, came round to the other side of the table, and gathered Gillian in her arms. The dam that had been held in check throughout the night, through the police briefing, and on the road broke. Ayeesha held on and said nothing. Eventually the moment passed and Gillian pulled herself away. She groped in a pocket for a tissue but Ayeesha got there first with a box.

"I'm sorry," Gillian managed.

"For what?" Ayeesha asked. "For being human? I'm the one that should be sorry. If our boys hadn't got mixed up in something they didn't understand, none of this would have happened. Sit down. I'll put the kettle on."

"Is Ali about?" Gillian asked.

"No. He and Enver have gone shopping. All the stock was lost of course so we've had to replace everything. The cash and carry have been very good giving us extended terms till the insurance comes through but actually we're selling more than we've ever done so they're having

271

to go back every two to three days. The whole community seems to have gathered around. We get people in saying, 'I'll take all the naan bread you've got and give me ten kilos of rice.' It's been amazing."

Gillian laughed and broke the tension.

"So something good's come out of it."

Ayeesha blew out a long breath.

"I don't recommend being firebombed," she said, "but whenever you're in trouble it does show you who your real friends are – like you and David, for example."

Gillian gave a grim smile. She wanted to say "it's nothing" or "don't mention it" but couldn't.

"How's Ali?" she asked instead.

"Better," Ayeesha said with a smile. It's taken a few days but he's better. Actually Enver's been very good for him. Almost like the missing son in a way. Karim is back at work in Glasgow but Enver's been living here while he recovers so he's been helping Ali with things. He's full of ideas and very keen to help. Ali's been getting over things by just being practical with Enver – collecting stuff, reorganizing the shop. It takes his mind of Rasheed."

"That's very good," Gillian said approvingly. "He's a nice young man. And plans for the future... he and Samira?"

"Well, they want to get married. But beyond that we haven't spoken much. They'll both have their careers so I'm not sure that's going to involve the shop or the baking business. She hasn't said anything more about converting for a while though. I think she'll need more time to decide who she really is now. It's her decision. Anyway, we'll see. At least I think Ali is reconciled to having a Christian son-in-law and that's a big step forward. You know, it's funny how it's people who claim to be Muslim that have done all the damage, and the people we're supposed to be fighting that have helped. Of course, we've had a lot of support from the mosque and our Muslim friends. I just mean people who help you aren't based on any particular religion or set of beliefs at all. They're just people who care, whatever the label."

"I know," Gillian agreed. "Ironic, isn't it? And what about Karim and Bea?"

"Oh, he's mad to get back to Spain. As soon as he can save up again. That last escapade cost him every penny. I think they Skype every day. It's nice. And she's a nice girl."

"Does the fact she's Catholic bother you?"

"Well, no more than anything else. I'm afraid through all this the labels are meaning less and less. She's a nice girl. Beyond that – who really cares?"

They sat in silence for a time and drank tea and ate some of the sweets Ayeesha had finished earlier.

"What happens next?" Ayeesha asked at length. "With David."

Gillian shook her head.

"Who knows," she said quietly. "There's supposed to be a police briefing every morning. I can go any time but I don't have to. I haven't decided. To be honest it's a blank. I can't think about anything. I try not to imagine where he is or how he is but you can't avoid it. I have no idea how you would go about trying to find someone in a city when someone else wants to keep them secret. I suppose if this were Sherlock Holmes, the Baker Street Irregulars would be out in force, then you'd have a hundred little urchins scouring every corner. That's what we need – a hundred or a thousand volunteers looking for a missionary who isn't and a pastor who usually doesn't want to be. I suppose it'll be on the news and there'll be posters or something. I'm determined not to do the tearful wife thing at a press conference though."

David spent a wretched night listening to the Prophet mumbling in his sleep. The old man had clearly lost his wits, though whether from mistreatment, malnutrition, or simply as the result of an unhealthy obsession, he couldn't say. He was beginning to think of him as the Mad Mufti. Masood came in next morning with two greasy mutton pies and a can of cheap Lidl cola each. The Prophet wolfed his, apparently before noticing David. His waking conversation seemed to be limited to finding out whether David was his long lost brother and begging for cigarettes. David couldn't help with either. After breakfast they were both taken for supervised toilet breaks, then shackled up again. David had at least been allowed to keep his watch, though his phone had gone. Shortly after Kovač had first shackled him to the radiator he had taken the phone out of his pocket, laid it on the floor, and smashed it with a hammer. What was left was gathered up and dumped on a bucket.

"Let's see if 'Find my Phone' works after that," he remarked.

Now he appeared a few hours after what passed for breakfast, planted a kitchen chair in the doorway of the bedroom again, sat astride it with his arms crossed on the back, and inquired if David had slept well.

"I've had better nights," David managed to reply.

"I do apologize for your roommate," Kovač said with elaborate courtesy. "He may have been mad before but he's certainly mad now."

"He really needs medical care," David said, glancing across at the dozing form. "Unless you plan to add manslaughter to the catalogue."

"He's not needed now." Kovač dismissed the idea. "All he does is eat, crap, and ask for cigarettes. He's served his purpose."

"To give you an identity."

"Of course. You know I actually trained at drama school in Belgrade before going into news. I think it's come in handy. Which do you prefer: Prophet, Missionary, or international agitator?"

"I can't say any of them would win Oscars."

"But Missionary Mike was good; you've got to admit."

"I take it you have some experience of the type or did you get it all from the televangelists?"

Kovač scratched his chin reflectively.

"Well, they are all actors too, of course – that's obvious. Good enough at what they do, I suppose – bringing in money – but as actors... hams, every one of them. Over-actors and hams. But the audience is so enthralled they never notice. As I was saying last night, with God on our side everything else is a blur."

"So where did you pick up your identity then?" David thought playing on Kovač's obvious arrogance might yield some useful information, if he ever got out of here to apply it.

"South Carolina, like I said," Kovač had slipped into a soft southern drawl. "Yes, sir. First Baptist Church. Mike MacGregor – car park attendant, then steward, then on the Youth Committee, then Feed the Homeless co-coordinator. Assistant pastor was my next goal," he reverted to his normal voice, "but I didn't quite make it."

"Why not?"

"Because I saw through the whole confidence trick and packed it in. You may not believe this, Pastor David, but I actually went to the United States for a new start. I genuinely wanted to leave the past behind – the chaos of the war in the Balkans and all the rival warlords. So America – 'Land of the Free', top nation, defender of democracy, and so on. And I was sick of the violence that used religion as its excuse and just produced chaos – no tangible benefit for anyone. So I thought, I'll go to where religion is peaceful and try to make a new start."

"What happened?" David asked, interested in spite of himself.

"I saw it for what it is. It took some time but I saw through it. Actors, all of them – pastors, preachers, personalities. They're all pretenders. When push comes to shove – that's right isn't it? – they're all just as much empire builders as Karadžić and the rest. So I decided that if genuine religion didn't exist I would use the power of false religion for my own benefit."

David thought for a moment.

"Something happened, didn't it?"

"Well, the church decided they didn't want my services any more but I had already made up my mind by then. If ignorance and fanaticism were the name of the game, then maybe it could be turned to a more constructive purpose. My purpose. I set up a few example projects, then contacted some sources I knew through the Balkan wars. They were receptive to my ideas."

David shifted on the mattress to try to get some relief for the pain in his back.

"And do you consider me a fanatic as well then?"

"Well, in the nicest possible way – yes I do. I've heard what happened to your wife in Madrid. Anyone who would take risks like that with their loved ones has to have a streak of fanaticism about them, don't you think?"

"I call it commitment," David said. "Men and women throughout history have changed the world for the better by being committed and willing to take risks."

"And what about the effect on them? How about Jesus – did his risk pay off? Or Paul. He was a fanatic before his conversion and a fanatic after, just in a different cause. I think it's better to take the power that's latent in religion and at least turn it to someone else's benefit – not just the preachers that rake in millions."

"They're not perfect; there's no debate about that," David admitted. "But you helped with the homeless programme, you said. The youth programme. Surely you must have seen that these things did good. We worked with addicts in Madrid. We saw lives transformed. Guys injecting their eyeballs because every vein had collapsed got straightened out, were able to work again, married, started businesses, had kids, contributed to society. They found faith and that brought life. They tapped into a power greater than themselves that utterly changed them. I'm sorry you didn't see something that changed your mind. Or maybe didn't want to see it."

Kovač didn't reply. He stood up, lifted the chair with one hand, then returned it to its place in the hall.

"Have a good day," he said, closing the door.

Gillian *did* attend the morning briefing; she had nothing better to do and had been granted leave of absence from work. Stuart McIntosh met her at reception and took her first to the canteen. Over a coffee he told her they'd postponed the briefing by twenty minutes to allow some late arrivals to get there.

"Are we pulling in James Bond on this one then?" she asked as they sat down.

"Virtually," he replied. "I shouldn't really say, but we've got some help from what you might call 'central services'. It's obviously a bigger deal than we're used to dealing with in Police Scotland."

"Anything involving the letter M?" she asked innocently.

"You might think that; I couldn't possibly comment," he replied with what passes for a twinkle in the eye of an aged cop.

"And what exactly does that contribute?"

"Lots of things. Communications experts, political analysts, intelligence officers – almost anything you can think of."

"And is that going to be enough?" she asked, then immediately added, "Sorry; that's not a fair question. Forget I said it."

"No, it's fair enough," he replied wearily. "Nobody can say. But nobody's invincible. If he's still anywhere in Scotland I think we stand a good chance." He glanced at his watch. "Ok. It's time. We should head along."

Stuart chaired again although this time there were a number of new faces around the table Gillian thought hadn't been there the day before – un-introduced as usual. Gary Morrison also appeared, gave her a grim smile, and sat down. The opening update followed on and confirmed much of what had been said the previous day. It looked like the identity of Martinas Kovač had been confirmed. They had CCTV from Edinburgh Airport three months previously, and although he had come in on a false passport, the image matched very closely what they already had on snaps from the church trip. Links to a quasi-Muslim group in Qatar were also confirmed. As far as local links were concerned, the two key connections were Abdul Masood and Callum Henderson. Masood was almost certainly somewhere in the mix; however, so far, while his involvement in the firebombing was virtually certain – a jury would decide – and Enver's beating highly likely – evidence there was more circumstantial – there didn't seem any obvious connection to the Prophet. Against the petition of the fiscal he was now on the loose, thanks to some heavy financial backing from who knew where. On the other hand, Masood didn't even possess a computer and showed absolutely no interest in radical religious politics. Maybe he was just muscle for hire, which might make it hard to trace back the transaction.

Regarding Callum Henderson, the drama student, the trail seemed even colder. He'd had transfers into his bank from an account in Bermuda that took security very seriously and had only had instructions by email from an AOL account that no longer existed. The one telephone conversation he recalled had been with a man who spoke in a flawless American accent, which made – at least in his mind – his identity as the producer of an as yet unnamed drama all the more likely. Meanwhile, the Prophet's website was functioning as usual, but it held no clues as to the identity of any of the players. Its physical hosting had been traced back to the Persian Gulf; however, governments there either didn't have the mechanisms or the will to provide any more information than that. Technical staff had crawled all over the archives, changing the IP address of their computer every time to try to avoid attracting attention and being thrown out. So they still had access, though for how long nobody could be sure. In any case, it was all much of a muchness – ravings of the "Prophet", otherwise known as an Anglo–Jordanian actor from Queen Margaret University's drama department. The vehicle Kovač had been driving when he and David had left the beach had been described but without a registration number. So traffic and beat cops had been alerted but it would be a needle in a haystack or a major stroke of luck to find it.

Gillian's spirits sank lower and lower during the meeting. *Lots of irrelevant information*, she thought. *Not much that takes us further forward.* Then she corrected herself. *No, that's not fair. It's all relevant, just not answering the key question: where is my husband?* It felt like they had done a good job of working out who owned the farm and what kind of tractors they had but were absolutely no closer to knowing which haystack to look in. And there seemed to be nothing she could add. Stuart's team now knew more than she did about David's movements in Spain and since he had come back. They had followed up and reported on anything she had thought of relevance and much that she didn't. So much then for McIntosh including her for her "very keen mind". She guessed it must have been a sop to those who didn't want outsiders involved and he was trying to keep her in the loop. Previous times there had been a problem to solve, at least she and David had been in it together and could bounce ideas off one another.

She thought back again to the Baker Street Irregulars and something tugged at her mind. Suddenly something she hadn't considered before became very important. Just as they were allocating tasks and getting ready to shuffle off back to their desks she spoke up.

"Would anyone mind if I met Callum Henderson?" she asked. "I know there's nothing he knows you haven't been through. It's just that he's the only person we know who's definitely been in touch with Kovač. I'd just like to meet him."

Stuart cast an eye around the table. Nobody objected.

"Fine. By all means," he said. "I'll get you his contact details."

In a filthy bedroom in a shabby flat in a crumbling block in a run-down council housing scheme, David Hidalgo tried to sleep – unsuccessfully. The old man next to him – who on closer examination turned out to be not so old after all, just emaciated and filthy – had no difficulty. He slept all night, only varying between gentle snoring and the sound of the midnight mail train. Through the dirty window, which had been painted out, he could hear the night-time sounds of an inner-city wasteland. Cars – whether owned or stolen – racing around the streets at double or treble the speed limits. The idea seemed to be to accelerate as hard as possible, brake as hard as possible, keep as many people awake as possible, and use as much fuel as possible. As virtue is said to be its own reward, so joyriding. The howl of the exhaust, the screeching of tyres, and the squealing of brakes were the soundtrack to Craigmillar nights – that, along with breaking bottles, shouting in the street, which might have been in another language for all David could make of it, the more focused and businesslike sounds of actual fighting, and something like the sound of running feet and others running after them. Meanwhile the mattress stank, the flat reeked of curry, and the pipes banged. At least it wasn't cold, but David wondered if the late summer heat encouraged fleas as he began to feel distinctly itchy.

"*A few days,*" Kovač had said. What was it now? The church picnic had been on Saturday. He had been here three days. So Tuesday night, Wednesday morning. Not long to think of a way out. Although necessity might be the mother of invention, that doesn't mean its offspring arrive on cue. When the house had gone quiet he had tried shouting, only to have Masood come through and batter him on the mouth. Clearly there was no sure way of knowing who was around when. He guessed one or other of them would always be on duty. He'd tried hiding a knife from the meagre meals he was served but another bang on the face that made his head spin proved that not a good idea either. He had tried spitting on his wrist to try to work the handcuff off but had only ended up with red and bleeding skin. Radiator pipes clearly couldn't be sawn through – if he'd had a saw. There seemed less chance of escape than in *The Shawshank Redemption*. And once on a plane out of the UK he'd be basically beyond recovery except by hostage negotiation. He didn't hold out much hope for that.

Then his thoughts turned inevitably to warning signs he'd ignored. Gillian had had a pretty poor opinion of Missionary Mike and been suspicious from the start. If he were honest he'd have to admit that he'd pooh-poohed her fears as coming from someone who still might have some residual prejudice against the wackier fringes of evangelical faith. *It was one thing to allow for the lunatic fringe*, he thought bitterly, *quite another to ignore an obviously fake personality*. Looking back he realized she'd been spot on. Mike was too good to be true – and hence not true. The famous nine-bob note – false currency passing itself off as real. Had he been too ready to believe him because of the lure of free cash and his plans to extend Southside? Was it all ultimately down to pastor's pride? A bigger, more successful, more modern, more everything ministry than yours – a common failing that went with the territory but he'd thought he'd been safely resistant to. Maybe he'd been deceived precisely because Mike held the promise of a shortcut to greater things. He might have called it helping more people but it certainly wouldn't have hurt his reputation. Well – just desserts maybe.

The night noises continued outside and in as he managed finally to drift off into a restless sleep. His final thoughts were of Gillian. Where was she? What was she going through? What steps were being taken? What brilliant ideas might she have had that were already taking shape and only needed time to be put into effect and get him out of this mess? The Prophet was snoring more gently and muttering in his sleep – something about his granddad and a football. It made no sense but that meant it fitted perfectly. Nothing here made any sense.

As David was thinking of her, Gillian was lying awake thinking of him. Or, more precisely, trying to get the building blocks in place of what might be called the beginnings of a plan. That "something" that had been tugging at her brain in the case conference had grown arms and legs. It would need all shapes and sizes of ducks to line up precisely. It would need everyone to play their part to perfection. It would also depend on a huge slice of luck, or whatever word Juan considered acceptable – good fortune, providence, whatever. It would mean things working when she had no right to expect them to. It would mean sending out a message without any control over who might hear it and what if anything they might do. Reasonably, it was beyond all reasonable probability. But on the other hand incredibly unlikely things happened every day. *Imagine a snowflake*, she thought. At 30,000 feet the chances of that particular snowflake falling all the way, buffeted by the wind, swirling around housetops, and coming to rest just on the tip of your tongue would be so remote as to be negligible. But still it happened. She felt her idea was no more substantial than a snowflake falling. *Oh God, may it fall where it needs to*, she thought, then put it into the more formal language of prayer. Somehow having even the slenderest of hopes brought some peace of mind that no hope couldn't. She rolled over just as David was rolling over. Miles apart they slept together.

Next morning early she called Stuart.

"Can we meet before the briefing?" she asked. "I've got something I'd like to run by you."

She arrived at his office at 9.15 prompt. He was going to take her to the canteen but she admitted she probably couldn't stand another of those plastic cups of something that may once have been attached to a coffee plant but no longer bore any chemical resemblance. Instead she took him to a little Italian café about a mile away.

"So spill the beans," he said. "You've got something on your mind."

"Yes," she agreed. "I don't suppose there's any reasonable hope of it working but it's better than feeling there's absolutely nothing I can do. I know you're all doing everything you can – and it's all very impressive – but I just need to do something, even if it's a total waste of time."

"I can understand that," he said. "I'm sure I'd have the very same impulse. What do you have in mind?"

It didn't take long to explain. Stuart let out a low whistle.

"Well, that's certainly a very different approach," he said. "I certainly won't tell you not to. And we'll help in any way we can. What do you need?"

"Well, I'll need to speak to Callum Henderson urgently. It might help if I had the long arm of the law with me."

"No problem."

"Next I'll need Spade again. I have no idea if he'll be able to do what I want but if he can't then I don't suppose anyone can."

"Agreed. I can pay for his time."

"Then I'll need a dedicated line with a trained person to take calls. In fact, a rota to cover twenty-four hours a day. They'll have to be very well briefed and very convincing. I think we'll only get one shot at this and it's got to be absolutely perfect."

"I can see that. I can think of a couple of British Asian officers who would certainly sound convincing. I'll get them pulled off other duties. We can speak to them together. Anything else?"

Gillian rubbed her temples and pulled a loose strand of hair back behind one ear.

"I don't think so," she said slowly. "Oh – a reward. Would that be possible? And photos. I'll let you know if anything else occurs."

McIntosh allocated Gillian a detective from his team and got him to phone Callum Henderson. Whatever he was doing he should stop it immediately and be prepared to be interviewed again. No, they couldn't explain about what. He would be bringing a civilian expert with him who would explain further.

They found him waiting in the foyer of the drama department building looking distinctly worried. Gillian suggested they go the cafeteria and on the way reassured him that he wasn't in trouble and there wasn't anything further they wanted to ask about what had happened. What they needed now was his cooperation in something that might undo a lot of the damage his earlier broadcasts had done. She explained about David's kidnapping and what they now needed from him. He immediately agreed, just relieved not to find himself charged with anything and destined for the front page of *The Sun*. Gillian gave him some papers to read and they waited while he took his time.

"Perfect," he said. "I can do this. I'll go and book some time. Would this afternoon work for you?"

After they left Callum they headed over to Duff Street in Gorgie. Spade was expecting them.

"Yes, in theory," he said. "I've seen it done but that was on an open web address – not something in the dark web. I'll have to have a think. When would we have the material?"

"Hopefully by the close of play today," Gillian replied. "Ideally I'd like the whole thing to be working by midnight."

"Phew – not much room for movement then. And tonight's usually Warhammer. I suppose I can skip it for a week," he added with mock reluctance but with a grin. Gillian thought she knew him well enough by now to guess what that really meant. It was like Scotty telling Kirk they'll have warp drive back in three hours and Kirk saying make it two. Scotty would scratch his head and say, "I'll see what I can do, Captain" – all the while simply looking for the opportunity to show off. Spade's grin said, stand back, watch, and be amazed.

Then it was back out to Musselburgh to the Queen Margaret University campus. Callum had booked space in the same studio he'd used before and was waiting for them.

"I think I've got it off," he said. "Sounds very authentic. You've done a good job."

They had allowed an hour but in the event it only took forty minutes. Then everything onto a memory stick and back into town to Spade's place. By this time Jamie, the DC loaned to Gillian, thought a taxi driver would have done just as well but kept his thoughts to himself and happily broke all the speed limits, his blue light flashing at every opportunity.

Spade stuck the memory stick into the main computer tower in his Bridge computer room and together they looked at the contents.

"Seems fine," he concluded. "Not too big. I've got something worked up that might pass muster. It's not going to stand a lot of close examination but the front page will be ok. We can dummy some of the menu options and put others to 'site under construction' pages and hope for the best."

"Sounds good," Gillian replied. "Get it working and you get a year's supply of Tunnock's Caramel Wafers."

"I've been banned," he replied sadly. "Tina. First she made me cut down, now it's birthdays and Christmas. I try to be good…"

Gillian and Jamie repaired to the kitchen while Spade worked away. Tina was out at World of Warcraft and the Tunnock's Caramel Wafer tin was indeed empty – Gillian couldn't resist looking. But at least there was decent coffee and a couple of Kit Kats so they roughed it. Just after 10.30 Spade came through and took them into the Bridge.

"This is it," he said, "and this is how you find it. How does that look?"

Gillian smiled and gave him a peck to his great surprise.

"Perfect," she said. "Exactly what I had in mind. Send the bill to Police Scotland."

"This one's on the house," he said. "Hope it works."

"When does it start?" she asked.

"When I press this button," Spade replied, eyebrows raised.

She nodded and he pressed.

"Bingo! Here we go…"

Chapter 22

Airport

Ajeet Singh buttered another slice of toast and started munching as he opened his laptop on the kitchen table. He glanced at his watch. Just past 4 a.m. His shift at the airport started at 6.00 but he liked to be prompt. And he liked a routine. Since his beloved Nimmi had passed away last year he depended on it more than ever. Whichever shift he was on, he liked to start the day with buttered toast, black tea, and something interesting from the internet. His latest interest was the regular broadcast from a man who called himself "the Prophet". This was interesting not because Ajeet was Muslim – in fact he was a Sikh – but because he was a keen student of rhetoric and enjoyed good speechifying from whatever quarter. A colleague from work who was Muslim had recommended it, knowing his tastes, and he did indeed find it intriguing. In the world of inspirational speaking, Churchill was of course his favourite, then came Martin Luther King, then Kennedy, then FDR, then the also-rans. There were many of these, including ancient Greeks, Native Americans, philosophers, generals (like William Wallace), abolitionists, and religious leaders. The Prophet was an also-ran – not in the major league but entertaining nevertheless. And of course not persuasive in terms of his content – unlike Churchill and King – but it was all quite skilfully put together to make patent nonsense sound great and noble. Like Hitler's Nuremberg addresses, for example.

The Prophet also brought a lot of passion to the party, which certainly helped. Nobody could be interested in a speech that couldn't even inspire the speaker. So he got excited, he raged and threatened, and then he would just as suddenly drop his voice and speak confidentially – just to you – telling you that your hopes, fears, worries, and aspirations had not been overlooked. On the contrary, they had been heard and would be acted upon. The time had now come to add *your* effort to the struggle, to put *your* shoulder to the wheel. With your vital help the juggernaut would roll again and crush its opposition. Àjeet chuckled at the ridiculous nonsense it all was but still enjoyed the delivery. Not everyone had realized at the time how famous the words of Churchill and King would one day become, so it was important not only to study the great words of the past but also to be alert to new contenders. Maybe one of the Prophet's speeches would go down in history, perhaps for a terrible reason, but down in history nevertheless.

He buttered another slice and clicked the button to connect. His friend had shown him how to avoid that tedious question screen. Like a private party, you could be invited by a friend who would vouch for you and get you in the secret back door. The usual screen appeared with the face of the Prophet swathed in black. He waited a few seconds for the video to buffer, took a slurp of tea, and settled back to be entertained. But this morning the words of the Prophet carried an unusual message. Rather than broad generalizations and wholesale appeals to a sense of grievance or wounded pride, he seemed to be speaking in sadness. He told a tale about a true believer who had given much to the movement but had lost the faith. Apparently he had been seduced away by the twin evils of greed and pride. A once worthy warrior had fallen at the final fence and his betrayal now jeopardized years of planning and many lives more steadfast and faithful than his own. True believers were now called to find this apostate and bring him to justice. Anywhere he was seen, in whatever circumstance, despite whatever protestations of innocence. The guilty one should be found and brought to swift and merciless retribution. And to be sure, here was his face, here was his name, and here was a confidential number you could phone free from anywhere in the world. Act now, the Prophet urged, and not only will you be saving the revolution but you would also earn the Prophet's undying gratitude – and a substantial reward. *Well, well*, thought Ajeet Singh. *Trouble at mill*. He popped the last morsel of toast in his mouth, gulped the last mouthful of tea, wrapped a scarf around his neck – even in summer Edinburgh could be cold at 4.30 a.m. – and headed downstairs to his scooter.

"Good morning, Pastor David," said Martinas Kovač, switching on the single bare bulb that hung from the ceiling of the bedroom cell. "Rise and shine. It's five thirty and it's a holiday. Today we're flying to the sun."

The Prophet muttered something incoherent in his sleep and rolled over. David felt like he might have been asleep for half an hour and struggled to come to.

"Come on now, David. Wake up. Alas, I can't offer you breakfast as we have to administer some medication and they say it's better on an empty stomach. But I thought you should at least wake up a last time in Scotland before we go off to pastures new."

Abdul Masood squeezed past Kovač, unlocked the cuff around the radiator pipe, and lifted David by the elbow as if he were a stuffed toy. He was half-carried, half-dragged through to the filthy toilet and left with the door only half shut.

"Hurry up, David," Kovač shouted. "Time and tide – you know."

Still bleary-eyed and stiff from a bad night, David stumbled back out only to have Masood instantly grab him from behind with one arm like an iron bar around his chest and the other holding a chemical-laden rag over his mouth and nose.

"Anything?" Gillian asked, rubbing her eyes and sitting up beside DC Tariq Hassem, the assigned officer in the ops room they had set up specially for possible phone calls. He shook his head.

"It's not 6 a.m. yet. It's only been up since midnight, hasn't it?"

Gillian nodded sleepily. She had come directly from Spade's flat to the room McIntosh had hastily set up with a telephone line watched over by a rota of officers from a British Asian background, a couple of laptops, and a pile of briefing papers. Stuart had managed to fit a lounger into the corner of the room and a blanket but it hadn't been a good night. Gillian thought it felt like one of those moments when you need an urgent reply to an email and find yourself checking every five minutes despite the rational unlikelihood of anything having changed. She managed to rouse herself, brush her hair, and make it to the canteen – police coffee or no police coffee – for a makeshift breakfast. All that seemed to be left was a variety pack of coco pops and raspberry Pop Tarts. She opted for toast and marmalade. Later on, back in the ops room, McIntosh popped his nose around the door at 8.30. He raised his eyebrows and she shook her head.

Ajeet parked his scooter in staff parking next to the Citroens, Audis, and trendy Minis and went into the airport concourse. He swiped his pass at the security point, keyed in the passcode, and held his index finger against the reader. Security seemed to be getting tighter and tighter every week. *Next they'll be asking for my mum to come and identify me*, he thought. The office of the Special Assistance Team held a couple of desks, a large arrivals and departures display suspended from the ceiling, a single filing cabinet, a shelf of health and safety and procedures reference manuals, a large whiteboard with names, flight numbers, times, and details, and a low table with a coffee maker and a tin of biscuits. The first thing Ajeet did on arrival for every shift was to greet his fellow workers and turn the kettle on. This morning only Marie and Alex were in.

"Where's the boss?" he asked, spooning some instant coffee into his Taj Mahal mug.

"Gone walkabout," Marie answered. "Checking on wheelchairs."

Ajeet grunted, filled his cup, helped himself to a Bourbon biscuit, and stood back to survey the whiteboard.

"Busy day," he commented to no one in particular.

"Tricky one at 3.15," Jamie remarked, barely looking up from his *Daily Record* sports pages.

289

"What's that then?"

"Private plane taking a patient for treatment. Two further passengers. Patient comes on a stretcher apparently. They say he's some wealthy Arab going home for treatment of a skin condition."

"Hmm. Normally it's the other way, isn't it?" Ajeet commented.

"Ours is not to reason why," Marie offered, dropping her current copy of *Chat* onto the table and picking up another. "Want to toss for it?"

"No," Ajeet shook his head. "I don't mind. Maybe more interesting than a kid in a plaster cast or an elderly countess who can walk perfectly well but prefers not to. And there might be a tip."

"You know the regulations have changed," Jamie informed him. "We're not supposed to take tips now."

"Ah, Britain. What a wonderful country," Ajeet sighed sadly. "They do everything they can to stifle private enterprise."

Just because David Hidalgo wasn't allowed breakfast was no impediment to Abdul Masood indulging. *No telling when I'll get another feed*, he thought to himself as he fired up the gas cooker, hauled out an enormous frying pan, waited for the fat to melt, then dumped in two slices of square sausage, two slices of black pudding, two eggs, and two tomatoes.

"How can you stomach that muck? And isn't it forbidden anyway?" Kovač asked, making a cup of tea and a sandwich.

"Each to his own," Masood answered, happily fishing out the tomato sauce and a tin of beans. "Have you thought how we get the body down the stairs? That contraption is never going to fit in the lift."

"Yes," Kovač answered pointedly. "The contraption goes upright in the lift and you carry the body."

Masood's shoulders dropped.

"Might have guessed," he muttered. "And if I meet anyone while carrying a stiff wrapped in bandages?"

"You will cover him in something else first, of course – like a carpet, for example. Or a tarpaulin. I'll trust to your native wit if someone stops you."

"Anyway, what's the hurry? You said the flight wasn't till mid-afternoon?"

"Have you heard of eventualities?" Kovač asked, as if asking an infant if they've heard of sums. "Things can take longer, get delayed, or go wrong. I want to be at the airport in plenty of time and allow plenty of time to get through security. They won't be used to travellers flat on their back. I've booked Special Assistance but that may take more time too. So just finish that heart attack on a plate and get him down to the van."

Masood finished frying, loaded up his plate with the results plus two slices of white toast, and carried it along with an enormous mug of tea into the living room. The form of a human body dressed in an Arab robe similar to the one worn by the Prophet (though actually clean) lay on the floor. Hands, neck, and face were wrapped in bandages.

The day wore on in the ops room. McIntosh appeared from time to time with sandwiches and coffee. *This might be a total waste of time*, Gillian thought repeatedly but since she didn't know what else to do, she just hunched up in the corner with her laptop and tried to work on a book she was hoping to publish to be called *The Sound System of Scots: 1745–1950*.

Around 10.30 the phone rang and almost made Gillian drop her coffee all over the laptop.

"God is great," said Tariq as he picked up a pen and pulled his notepad closer. Gillian listened intently though it was hard to make anything of it. The conversation seemed to mainly consist of the officer being asked again and again how much the reward was and how it would be paid. Finally he brought things to a conclusion, thanked the caller, and put the phone down.

"Caller from Kuala Lumpur thinks it's his brother-in-law," he said. "A man of eighty-three with only one arm. Sounds like some bad family blood."

Gillian breathed out and tried to gather her thoughts again. There were two more calls that morning, but nothing that even nearly matched what they knew they were looking for. Gillian tried hard to focus but again and again found her thoughts dragged back to wondering where David might be, what he might be thinking, and what he might do if the positions were reversed. Once they had been and she knew what he had done, but that was different; he had been told where to go. He knew the risks and he'd gone anyway. She would have gone in an instant if she had only known where to go.

About noon Stuart again popped his head around the door.

"Masood was due in court this morning," he said. "Didn't show up. I'm going round with a couple of uniforms. Keep you posted."

She nodded and wondered what that might mean.

Martinas Kovač was dressed in a smart beige linen suit and had an expensive leather carry-on case in the shade they call cognac. Masood wore dishdash, Arab headdress, and black shoes. The body was manhandled down the stairs past a mum and toddler and another in a rickety pushchair waiting for the lift who knew better than to ask. Masood's own van had been impounded so they had acquired another. He had also been making sure not to be seen out as it seemed certain he'd be required to help further in police inquiries. So now he had to venture out, the disguise was welcome. The doors were pulled open and a rolled-up carpet bumped in.

"Careful!" Kovač warned. "The package needs to be in good condition."

Masood shrugged as if bumps and bruises still counted as good condition as far as he was concerned, locked the doors, and went round to the driver's side.

Ajeet Singh knocked off for lunch. It had been a normal, uneventful morning. He made a point of always trying to engage the passengers he was helping in conversation and this morning had spoken to a Panamanian diplomat with a broken leg, a Romanian basketball player who had been on tour and twisted his ankle, and a tall, blond South African engineer who suffered from chronic back pain and couldn't walk more than twenty metres. They had a good talk about the changing price of gold. He went to Costa for a takeaway chai tea and took it back to the team room to drink with his cheese and tomato sandwiches. The stretcher case would be his first in the afternoon.

Stuart McIntosh rang the doorbell of Abdul Masood's given home address after finding the breakers yard empty apart from the ferocious, fascist dog. Uniforms they'd sent round over previous days had been far less thorough than they should have been so McIntosh was now doing beat bobby work in person and had brought a team.

"Call the RSPCA, will you?" he said over his shoulder as they tied the yard door shut after having forced it open. "That animal sounds like it hasn't been fed for a fortnight."

The address they had was now occupied by what looked like the cast of *Trainspotting* – hence the null result from previous attempts – however, even modest effort checking with a neighbour yielded better information.

"He's just roun' the corner. He telt me if he won the lottery this was whar tae send them."

McIntosh rolled his eyes at the standard of young recruits these days and set off with a scrap of paper in his hand. The alternative was indeed just around the corner but the lift had stopped working so they trudged up four flights and eventually found the door. As expected, knocking had no effect. McIntosh peered through the letter box and thought he maybe heard some sound that might be human from inside.

"Ok, Johnson," he said. "You've got the biggest feet. See what you can do with that."

The door didn't seem made to withstand a strong breeze, never mind police size twelves, and gave way on the third kick. McIntosh immediately retched at the smell. The hall was empty and together they cleared the flat room by room. The kitchen showed signs of recent occupation. A litre of fresh milk was lying on a worktop and wasn't yet sour and a few slices of still reasonably fresh bread were next to it. The living room only held the cheapest and most worn-out furniture but several rolls of bandages lay on one of the armchairs. The first bedroom they looked into was empty, the bed unmade and clothes scattered on the floor. Then, just as they were pushing open the door to the second bedroom, they heard a distinct human groan from inside.

McIntosh let out a fairly modest expletive and the next officer in, something much more colourful. Two mattresses lay on the floor, the leftmost one occupied by a pitiful figure. It was now clear where the sickening smell was coming from. The old man was both wet and soiled and lying in his own filth. His cheeks were hollow and skin a waxy yellow. He turned his head slightly as McIntosh crouched beside the mattress.

"Welcome, my brother," he whispered. "Do you have a cigarette?"

Masood parked the van in short stay, got out, and opened the back doors. He pulled out the wheeled stretcher then unwrapped the bundle next to it. Together he and Kovač lifted the inert form onto a stretcher and tightened three straps around it. Kovač checked in his pocket for the passports and the doctor's letter that he'd received in the post from Doha the week before. All seemed well. He also had all the details of the private flight to show at check-in, security, and at the gate. This was all going very nicely. Soon they'd be out of the appalling Scottish weather – this excuse for a summer – and he'd be in receipt of the half million dollars agreed for the transfer. Córdoba had been a real shame, with so much time, effort, and planning gone into it. He had had very high hopes for young Rasheed and Karim but then it had fallen apart piece by piece. First the "meddling minister" had got involved over Samira and Enver. (He enjoyed "meddling minister" almost as much as "Missionary Mike".) It had been very bad luck that she had decided on a dalliance with a member of the Hidalgo congregation, bringing the family into contact with a man who just didn't seem to know when to quit. That had alerted the family to Rasheed and Karim's disappearance. Then Karim had got in tow with that Spanish girl – Bea, was it? – and decided he preferred a conventional life to a glorious death. That in turn had shone a light on Rasheed and brought Daddy running from Scotland accompanied by the meddling minister again.

Then somehow the moment it was all leading up to turned out to be the dampest squib of all. No matter that it hadn't been in the Mezquita – that would have been perfect – but Medina Azahara was a perfectly acceptable substitute. Plenty of tourists in both. But then something had gone fatally wrong in the sense that when Rasheed tried to pull the toggle, setting the device off, it proved not to be fatal at all. According to the news the cord had been cut, leaving nothing to pull. Apparently also David Hidalgo's doing. He regretted not letting Masood give the body a good kick as he dumped it down in the back of the van. However, all was not a total loss, as sometimes a high-level hostage – and anyone from the West would be high-profile since apparently Western lives are worth so much more than Arab ones – could attract just as much publicity and over a much longer period. That would encourage more knee-jerk restrictions from populist politicians and generally stoke the fires. Once the hostage negotiation had been drawn out as long as possible with hopes raised and dashed, then the body would finally be dumped on waste ground somewhere significant – maybe the hill country of South Yemen, for example – and calls for punitive strikes would intensify. That would naturally inflame passions on the other side, and so the roundabout went round. Lots of potential there for easy pickings in the mayhem.

Between them they pushed the stretcher into the airport complex and up to the special flights desk. The girl at reception was expecting them, smiled sweetly, and asked them to wait for Special Assistance.

McIntosh told one of the uniforms with him to phone for an ambulance while he went for a glass of water for the old man. Trying to control his retch response and with the help of the other officer, they got the old man half sitting and put the water to his lips. He sipped the water weakly.

"Going on holiday," he whispered. "Somewhere warm. Bloody Scottish summer."

Stuart gave him another drink.

"Who's going on holiday?" he asked.

"The fat man and the thin man and my brother. He didn't have any cigarettes."

The officer who had been phoning had also raked around in the kitchen and now came through with a bottle of Lucozade. McIntosh took it and held it to the old man's lips. It was tempting to dismiss what he had whispered as random rubbish, but they were looking for a fat man and a thin man and one other.

"Who are they? Where are they going?" he asked.

"On holiday. Somewhere warm. Airport," he muttered. "The fat man was carrying my brother. Perhaps he wasn't well. Do you have a cigarette?"

This was beginning to sound like two and two that just might make four.

"See if you can find something to get this off," he told one officer, pointing to the handcuff. He eased the old man back onto his mattress and walked through to the living room. Again he noticed the bandages. He pulled out a radio. A fat man, a thin man, someone else who was sick. Bandaged. Somewhere hot. A flight. It was beginning to add up.

"Gary Morrison," he said pointedly into the radio. "I don't care if he's meeting the Queen – get him out of it. And get an alert to Edinburgh Airport. Abdul Masood, Martinas Kovač, and a third party that may be in a wheelchair or a stretcher and may be bandaged. Gary? Stuart. I think we've got something."

Chapter 23

Departures

"Doctor Hassan?" Ajeet Singh inquired politely. "Good afternoon, sir. My name is Ajeet. I am here to help you."

The thin man smiled and shook his hand.

"Very pleased to meet you," he said. "Unfortunate circumstance but thank heavens for the British health service. My patient came on holiday and suffered a completely unexpected flare-up of his skin condition. I'm afraid it is so painful that thick cream and sedation are the only way to manage it. Still, he'll soon be in the best medical facility in the world." He looked at his watch. "Flight in about two hours, I believe."

Ajeet Singh consulted the list on his clipboard.

"Yes, sir. 15.55. We'll get you through security in no time. May I just see your passports and boarding cards? Very good. Thank you. Now if you'd be kind enough to come this way."

Ajeet led the way but not directly to security. He needed time to think. When he'd worked in Left Luggage at Paddington when they'd first arrived in London almost twenty years ago, he'd developed a habit of trying to memorize faces and link them to the item they'd left to keep the boredom at bay. Then he'd hold up his hand – before the customer had time to hand over their ticket or announce their name – and scurry back into the vaults, only to return with the right case and hand it over with the right name to the amazement of the party concerned. It had been a useful facility for saving time and he enjoyed the attention from the customer – and sometime a tip – but he'd never thought of it as more than a parlour trick. Nevertheless, once learned, never forgotten. Now he was walking leading the man whose face had appeared on the Prophet's website that morning. He was sure of it. But what to do next? He paused by the trolley park and pulled out his mobile.

"Very sorry, sir," he smiled at the two men. "Just had a buzz. It'll only take a second. Plenty time."

He walked a few yards away and spoke as clearly as he could into the handset.

"Yes, sir. Of course sir. Right away, sir. No, it's no problem."

He came back to the men, who were where he had left them.

"Terribly sorry, sir. Bit of a mix-up. It looks like the gate for your flight may have been changed. Have to phone to check. Just be a moment."

Ajeet Singh had absolutely no personal interest in the Prophet's agenda, except to see it for what it was – nonsense, and dangerous nonsense at that – but the chance to take an active part in events behind the rhetoric was too powerful to resist. Taking half a smile and raised eyebrows for reluctant assent he walked a few paces away again and dialled a number he had also memorized. It answered on the second ring.

Gillian had almost dropped off to sleep on the lounger. The sound system of Scots was clearly insufficient to keep her awake in a stuffy room with nothing going on after a terrible night's sleep. Suddenly the phone rang. Tariq answered. She listened to one half of the conversation and saw the officer unconsciously sit more upright in his chair, pull the pad nearer again, and start scribbling furiously. At length he replied.

"Very good, my brother. You have done very well. Remain where you are. Our brothers will come to you. You will be well rewarded."

"What?" Gillian said, urgently staring at the officer.

"We may have hit the jackpot."

A special operations team is always on standby for possible incidents at all major UK airports. They are armed and trained for anything from a hoax to a major incident. Gary Morrison took Stuart McIntosh's call from Masood's flat with a degree of irritation, having been called out of an important briefing. That evaporated in two or three seconds as he listened to the story. His response was brief and to the point.

"Understood," he said. "I'll get onto the airport squad."

At that moment Gillian Lockhart and the officer who had taken the other call came bursting into his room.

"We've had a caller," she said. "A worker at Edinburgh Airport. He's identified Kovač and Masood. He says they have a third figure on a stretcher. They're supposed to be flying to Doha in forty minutes."

Morrison instantly grasped the implications.

"Ok," he said. "Stuart is on his way to the airport. The armed airport police detail need to be alerted. And I'll go myself. Want to come?"

"Try and stop me," she said.

Martinas Kovač wasn't yet worried but he was beginning to feel slightly twitchy. Over the years he'd grown to recognize and trust that feeling and, if necessary, act on it. Now the funny little man in the turban's explanations and apologies were tugging at his twitchy nerve.

"What seems to be the problem?" he asked politely.

"Oh... nothing, sir. Nothing at all. Perfectly normal," Ajeet Singh replied with a smile. "They just tell me that the gate hasn't been decided yet so we have to wait."

"But I thought the plane got in more than an hour ago? How can they not know where it is?"

"Refuelling, sir," Ajeet replied without batting an eyelid. "Sometimes they have to go to another place for refuelling then they come back to a gate for boarding. And there are a limited number of gates that can accommodate your patient, sir. Maybe somebody made a cock-up, sir. So we just have to wait. Not be long now I'm very sure."

He made to wheel the stretcher over to a seating area but Kovač stopped him.

"But presumably there's no reason why we can't at least go through security," he said.

"Oh, no reason. No reason at all, sir," Ajeet agreed, wondering how long it would take for the Prophet or his minions to show up. "I thought you might be more comfortable here."

"I don't think so," Kovač said firmly. "We would be more comfortable through security."

"Whatever you like, sir, whatever you like," Ajeet agreed, hoping his brow wasn't showing the beads of sweat he imagined must be there. "In that case, we go over to the lift."

To Kovač, the lift seemed to take an eternity to arrive but at least they were going in the right direction now. The Gulfstream G650 should have been waiting for them refuelled and ready well before the time they arrived at the airport. With a range of almost 13,000 kilometres and top speed of over 900 knots they should be safely in the air in less than an hour and home and dry in less than seven. If they could just get this little man to get things organized. There might have been time for a whisky and soda in the bar, but he'd rather forgo that and have it on the plane.

Ajeet wheeled them out of the lift and along the wide walkway towards security. As they approached he asked for their passports and papers again. Kovač produced them and Ajeet handed them to security. Everything was in order and they were wished a good flight. Ajeet wheeled the stretcher through the priority route with Kovač and Masood right behind. Before pushing on through the labyrinth of perfumes, overpriced spirits, packets of 1,000 cigarettes, and enormous novelty chocolate bars, he decided to risk another stoppage.

"Ah, one moment, sir," he apologized. "My phone is buzzing again. Maybe more news." Again, he walked a few paces away and with his back turned tapped *redial last number*.

"We are through security now, sir. Yes, sir. Just waiting for the gate. Do you have any more updates for us?" he spoke loudly enough for the others to hear.

"Ah, thank you very much, sir. That will be much appreciated."

He turned to the increasingly impatient Kovač.

"Almost sorted, sir. Just a few minutes more, I think."

Kovač stared out of the window in annoyance. At a very minimum a complaint that might jeopardize the little man's job would definitely be appropriate once he got onto safe territory and near a computer. Then he noticed something.

"Look," he said. "Isn't that our plane there?"

A white Gulfstream in the livery of the One World Foundation was indeed sitting on the tarmac just a few gates down from where they were.

"What's going on?" Kovač demanded. "Why aren't we boarding? Abdul!"

Masood grabbed Ajeet and held him firmly with one arm around his chest as Kovač took his phone off him and pressed redial. The voice at the other end said, "Hello, my brother. God is great. Thank you for calling the Prophet."

Gary Morrison and Gillian Lockhart made it to the airport in twenty minutes, which Gary later thought might be a record. An armed police squad was waiting in the foyer. McIntosh and his officers arrived seconds afterwards. Morrison assumed command and briefed the team.

"The last message was that they were through security," he said, not wasting time on small talk. "Then they got a caller from the same mobile that hung up. Might mean they're alert to what's going on."

At that moment a siren started blaring throughout the airport. One of the airport police pressed his earpiece in slightly more firmly and listened.

"Shooter situation in the gate area," he said.

Immediately on hearing the response from the number Ajeet had been dialling, Kovač realized something was very wrong without knowing exactly what. He reached under the stretcher into a lead-lined box welded to its underside. He pressed a release clip and took out a handgun. Then he pulled Ajeet from Masood's grip, held him by the shoulder, and pointed the gun to the middle of his forehead just under where the turban stopped.

"Ok, little man," he said. "We are boarding that plane and you are coming with us. Is that clear?"

Ajeet tried to nod.

"Yes, sir. Perfectly, sir," he managed. "This way, sir."

The gate area was cleared of the public in less than a minute. This was the sort of situation airport staff regularly trained for. All flights except those already rolling were put on hold. Armed officers were through security in seconds and approached the little group with the stretcher from both sides.

"Stay back!" Kovač shouted. "Guns down!"

With Kovač and Masood crouching behind the stretcher and Ajeet looking like a frightened actor who had just forgotten his lines, standing with his hands up between them, a clear shot was impossible. The entire group backed towards an unattended gate.

"Open the gate!" Kovač shouted. "Or you know what happens!"

"Sir?" one of the response team looked to DI Morrison.

"Anybody clear for a shot?" he asked.

The officer glanced around. He shook his head.

"So I don't think we have much choice."

Gillian seemed to have been forgotten in the melee and stood just behind Morrison's shoulder.

"You're not letting them get away?" she said, aghast.

"No, we're not," Morrison answered tersely. "But we can't stop them at this point. The hostage and David are both in the line of fire."

One of the armed team spoke into his radio, then nodded to Morrison.

"It's open."

"The gate's open!" he shouted. "What do you want?"

Kovač ignored the question and backed towards the gate, pulling the stretcher and keeping Ajeet upright between him and the line of fire. Masood was a big man and had difficulty squatting behind their scant cover but found remarkable reserves of suppleness and strength when his life depended on it.

Kovač pushed the door open and pulled the stretcher through. He stood up behind the glass with Ajeet held firmly in front of him and the point of his pistol jammed into his hostage's neck just under the jawbone.

"Get the body down the stairs," he commanded.

Masood interpreted this liberally and unstrapped the still inert body of David Hidalgo, slung it unceremoniously over his shoulder, and took the stairs two at a time. Kovač backed down behind him, still holding Ajeet in front of him.

"What now?" the officer standing next to Morrison asked.

"Can you get armed officers onto the tarmac?"

"Sure."

"Do it then."

From the foot of the stairs Kovač, Masood with David over his shoulder, and Ajeet, wondering why he had recklessly felt the need to get involved in the Prophet's business, which was none of his business, backed towards the Gulfstream, which now had its boarding steps deployed. It was barely fifty yards but seemed to take an interminable time as Kovač backed up step by step. Officers were now emerging on both sides of him from the main terminal building at ground level and deploying behind luggage bogies and transfer buses. Masood carried David in such way as to shield his entire body. Ajeet was pulled backwards by Kovač behind him. The foot of the boarding ladder was growing nearer and nearer. Finally they made it. Abdul backed up the steps, then Kovač behind him with Ajeet. Watching from the gates level above, Gillian felt herself growing faint. Why didn't they shoot? Surely once they got onto a plane with two hostages it was all over.

Masood finally backed into the cabin, turned, and dumped David's body onto a seat. A slight groan could be heard through the bandages that still wrapped his face. Kovač came behind him holding the now terrified Sikh man.

"Shut the door!" he shouted. There was a click and the stairs glided silently up behind them. As they hissed shut there was a palpable sense of relief. Kovač shoved Ajeet down into a seat. Two hostages for the price of one would be all the more brutal and hence all the more valuable to the "One World Foundation".

"Don't move a muscle," he said, "if you ever want to see the Punjab again."

"I live in Corstorphine," Ajeet squeaked.

Meanwhile Masood had reclined a seat and manoeuvred David's body into a more normal sitting position. Groaning sounds were now coming louder and more frequently from the body. Masood unwrapped the bandages from around David's head and strapped him in. Kovač walked forward and pulled open the flight deck door. The pilot and co-pilot were where they should apparently be, ready for takeoff. Surely only minutes at the most would separate them now from blue skies all the way to the Persian Gulf.

"Ready to go?" he demanded brusquely.

"Ready to go, sir," the pilot confirmed. "We're clear from the tower. Just need to secure the cabin. There's a summer electrical storm south of Edinburgh. It's going to be bumpy."

The weather outside looked perfectly clear; Kovač shrugged, walked back into the cabin, and sat down in one of the sumptuous ivory leather seats. It was nice when you worked for someone for whom money was truly no object. He glanced around. Everything seemed good. Ajeet was sitting ahead of him – facing the tail of the plane – on the opposite side of the aisle. The still inert body of David Hidalgo was slumped facing Ajeet, and Masood was behind him opposite Kovač. All were safely gathered in. The engines were running, the fasten safety belt signs clicked on, and the pilot was taking one last look around the cabin. Kovač felt sufficiently relaxed to lay his gun on the coffee table in front of him and gather up both ends of his seatbelt.

"Better make everything extra tight, sir," the pilot repeated, coming back into the cabin. His freshly ironed short-sleeved white shirt, shoulder tabs, crisp black trousers, and headset were all very reassuring. He went around the cabin systematically, taking his time to make sure everybody was secure. He took a close look at David but passed on without commenting. Masood couldn't even find both ends of his belt around his enormous belly and the captain reached across him without a murmur, however unpleasant it must have been, dug down, got the end, yanked it up, adjusted it for length, clipped it in, then pulled extra tight.

"Sorry, sir," he muttered. "Got to keep the passengers safe!"

Next he attended to Ajeet, seemed satisfied, then lastly moved to Kovač. Again he pulled the belt slightly tighter than was fully comfortable. Kovač didn't really mind; they were home and dry after a sticky half hour. He'd have to quiz the little Indian on what exactly had been going on. From nothing the airport was suddenly crawling with armed police and maybe detectives. He had even caught a glimpse of the pale face of what might have been Gillian Lockhart. She was a very pleasant lady and would certainly have made a more congenial hostage than the funny little Indian. However, it was what it was and he was content.

"Better stow this somewhere, I suppose," he joked with the captain. "Not sure guns are safe against turbulence."

Given the tight restraint of the belt he had to stretch to its limit to reach for where he'd laid the gun. In the instant it took to stretch out the pilot had already picked it up. But instead of handing it back to Kovač, he took a step back, made sure he was well out of Masood's reach, gripped the handle, and turned the barrel towards Martinas Kovač.

"The tower has cleared us for takeoff," he said, "but Police Scotland haven't."

Gillian's first instinct when she arrived at the departure gates floor and saw what she assumed was David prone on a stretcher was to run towards him, but she knew that would be madness. She immediately recognized the man they had been calling Missionary Mike holding a member of airport staff hostage. The little Indian man – complete with Sikh turban – was looking like a rabbit caught in the headlights, the barrel of a gun jammed into his neck just under one ear. Another figure she didn't recognize was taking cover behind the stretcher. She could only see the top of his head fifty yards away and a bulky torso half-kneeling, half-crouching, and using her husband as a human shield. DIs McIntosh and Morrison were cool and detached. She was not. She felt the blood draining from her face, her mouth going dry, and her palms moist. Her knees felt weak and she sank to a sitting position, her back against one wall. She probably shouldn't have been here at all but nobody said no so she had just run with the pack. Now she was wondering if it had been a good idea. She was only putting herself at risk while contributing nothing.

The quartet across the hall were backing towards a gate. There was some shouting back and forth then the gate opened – presumably there must have been some remote locking and unlocking mechanism. Part of her wanted them to shoot, and for the other part that was the last thing she wanted. It was like being stuck halfway up a cliff and trying to think whether up or down would be less dangerous. She was paralyzed and could only watch while the group slowly worked their way through the gate then disappeared from sight down the stairs beyond.

Just at that moment Stuart McIntosh took a call. He nodded, then whispered something in Gary Morrison's ear. Morrison also nodded; however, his expression didn't change. She couldn't tell if McIntosh's information – whatever it had been – made things better or worse. Right now she felt only like useless baggage and guessed the best thing to do was to keep quiet, out of sight, and leave things to the experts. But David... what was he doing prone on a stretcher? From the briefest of glances she had got she thought she'd seen bandages around his head but couldn't be sure. Was he injured, bleeding, dying?

Then the police team seemed to be on the move again. McIntosh and Morrison had been speaking in hushed, urgent tones to the commanding officer of the armed team. They suddenly split into two groups and headed in different directions. No one paid any attention to her and she wasn't even sure if her legs would support her so she stayed still. All at once she was alone. Then she felt she couldn't just sit there waiting. She managed to get onto all fours and crawled over to the large plate glass window. Below was a waiting executive jet, with Kovač and the group edging backwards toward it. *Why don't the police do something?* she thought. *They're completely in the open. They could easily take shots at both of them without any risk to the hostages.* It was maddening. She knew she couldn't see the full picture, but it seemed obvious. *Shoot! Shoot for the love of God!*

Then they were at the steps and moving up towards the body of the plane. Another few steps and they'd be safe. It would be impossible to hit them without damaging the plane. Then they were in. It was unbelievable. They were in without the slightest response from the police. The steps swung up and the outline of the door faded into the fuselage of the plane. Her heart turned to stone. That was it then? Surely it was over. The next thing she'd see was the aircraft taxiing across the tarmac, onto a runway; then it would be away. With David Hidalgo on board.

She waited for something without knowing what. Then the last thing in the world she expected happened. McIntosh, Morrison, and three of the armed, uniformed squad appeared out of wherever they had been hiding and walked perfectly calmly – in the open – towards the plane. As they approached, the door became visible again and the steps swung slowly down. No gunshots, no noise, and no fuss. Next an ambulance sped across the tarmac and came to a halt at the foot of the steps. The police team climbed up the aircraft steps and disappeared inside. Barely thirty seconds later first "MacGregor" then the fat Asian man appeared at the door, each handcuffed and escorted by an armed officer. Next the little Indian man came down with a policeman and climbed into the back of the ambulance. Then two ambulance staff climbed up and into the plane. She had seen enough. Shaky knees or not she made it to the gate, pulled the door open, and ran down the stairs.

Chapter 24

Aftermath

David Hidalgo threw up several times before he was able to hold down first a glass of water, then a cold Coke, then a milky coffee. He had a furious headache, felt like his insides had been on the high-speed spin cycle, and his eyes wouldn't focus. His ears were ringing, his eyes watering, his throat dry, and his nose running. And for some reason he also felt surprised. Maybe he was surprised he wasn't dead. A very attractive woman had a hold of his arm and didn't seem to want to let go. She looked blurry but familiar. A man in a dark suit that the woman kept speaking to and calling Stuart was trying to explain something to him but none of it made any sense. The woman did seem remarkably happy about something though so probably it was all good. A second man in a dark suit and tie kept flitting in and out of his limited range of vision and even more limited range of attention, but he couldn't work out who he was or what it was all about. He did remember his friends Ali and Ayeesha but couldn't see them anywhere, so whatever was going on it couldn't be anything to do with them. Or that man – what was it he called himself? – the Preacher or the Poacher or something.

While it was all hopelessly confusing, on the other hand he was lying on a fairly comfortable couch in a warm room, not on that mattress with the constant smell of human filth in the air, so that was fine. He looked around but couldn't see any sign of the old man who kept calling him a brother and asking for cigarettes. *Pity. Maybe somebody here might have a cigarette to give him.* Now someone in a doctor's white coat was bending over him, shining a light in his eyes, and speaking in a calm, friendly tone. He had to follow a moving finger just with his eyes. If they wanted him to look at a finger, why couldn't they just keep it still? It hurt to move his eyes. And it hurt to look at the lights. Did it have to be so bright? Someone came in and the door clicked shut behind them. It sounded like a collision. Then – *oh no, not again* – he felt he was going to be sick one more time and retched into the bucket the woman held up for him. It felt like his insides were making every effort to get outside. He lay back and let a wave of nausea sweep over him, bringing out a drench of sweat. Even the loose-fitting gown he had on seemed oppressively hot. Come to think of it, where were his clothes? Then he closed his eyes and at last he was in the blessed dark and quiet.

Gillian looked at the airport doctor with raised eyebrows.

"What do you think?" she asked nervously.

"He's been pumped full of drugs and been bounced about quite a lot to judge by the bruising. It'll take at least six to twelve hours to fully work out of his system – maybe more. But after that I don't think there are going to be any lasting ill effects. I'd like him overnight in hospital just to keep an eye on things, but I'm not anticipating problems."

Stuart McIntosh was sitting on the opposite side of the treatment couch.

"I think he's probably going to have a rough week – psychologically maybe more than physically. We have a PTSD support team. If you think either of you might need it just ask."

Gillian nodded.

"Thanks."

Two days later, after an uneventful stay in hospital, Gillian brought him home. Two days after that he felt up to receiving visitors. It was mid-afternoon and the sun was out, slanting in the bedroom window. Lunch was scrambled eggs and Lucozade. As part of the recovery, Gillian felt he needed to be able to ask all his questions to those who knew and not just hear her version of events, so she had arranged for Stuart McIntosh to visit and give the full story. Gary Morrison claimed paperwork and that suited her. One voice would be enough.

She perched on the bed next to David while Stuart sat on a kitchen chair.

"How much do you remember from the point where you left the church trip with Martinas Kovač?" he asked.

David pulled himself a bit further up the bed, took a sip of water, and thought.

"I think I remember most of it. There may be gaps – one day kind of merged into the next and the nights went on forever – but I think I can remember most of it."

"You might find it helpful to write it all down while it's still fresh, then add new bits as you remember them," Stuart suggested. "I'm afraid you'll very probably be called as a witness."

David nodded.

"Hadn't thought of that," he said.

"Well, Kovač and Masood are charged with false imprisonment, assault, a bunch of immigration offences, publishing hate materials online, and conspiracy to cause explosions – and that's just page one."

David smiled.

"So they never made it to Doha then?" he asked.

McIntosh gave something midway between a grunt and a laugh.

"They will be going on holiday, for sure, but not to Doha."

"So Gillian has given me her version, but if you don't mind can we just run through it one more time?" David asked. "Indulge me."

"I think the story goes like this," McIntosh began. "Martinas Kovač is a Bosnian 'Christian' – if we can call him that. At least he's not a Muslim."

"I'll take that in the spirit it's offered," David smiled.

"And he was an actor, then a young TV news reporter," Stuart continued. "He did some reports from Northern Ireland after the Good Friday agreements then covered the NATO bombing of

Kosovo. It appears that the experience was highly traumatizing and we know he spent time in a psychiatric hospital. Seems that once he was back on his feet again he decided to leave Europe altogether and try his luck in America."

"He told me some of that," David said. "Except about the breakdown."

"In the US he does actually seem to have tried to make a new start. He got a job in local radio news and wrote about the Balkans for some national dailies."

"And he joined a church, didn't he?" Gillian put in.

"Yes. We've been in touch with First Baptist of Charleston. For a time he was well liked and got highly involved. Seems to have bought into the whole thing – forgive me for putting it like that. He ran some church programmes and was completely trusted."

"Then, I'm guessing something went wrong," David suggested.

"Indeed it did. He was accused of raping a thirteen-year-old in the youth programme. He was charged but jumped bail. Then people started looking a bit more closely and found irregularities in the cash accounts he was responsible for. Before they could close things down he had used a church credit card to buy a car and take out $10,000 in cash."

"A bit more than just the petty cash tin, then," David commented.

"Indeed. And it was while he was on the run we think he made contact with some former Balkan crooks he'd previously reported on, looking for an opening. Claimed he was disillusioned with the West and wanted to see it taken down a peg or two – while failing to mention the offences that got him kicked into touch. These contacts were Muslim, at least in name – though basically criminals by any reasonable assessment. They in turn had connections in the Gulf, which put him in touch with his eventual backers. Seems the One World Foundation and his cover as Mike MacGregor were his idea to try to get into the UK, though at this stage we don't know whether he was already aware of the Prophet and had decided on a takeover bid or if that came later."

"Do you know how long he'd been holding the old man for?" Gillian asked.

"Months," Stuart replied. "We don't have a date since the Prophet lived alone and once he was out of the mosque he seems to have become a bit of a recluse."

"No wonder he was like a living skeleton then," she added, shaking her head.

"How is the old guy anyway?" David put in. "I got quite attached to him in spite of the smell. He seemed to have lost his mind but he was always cheerful."

"He's in hospital, of course. They reckon the confusion was at least partly an effect of toxaemia – he may pick up a bit once he's put some weight on and gets fit. Or it may remain as a permanent consequence of prolonged neglect. Apparently it's wait and see."

"Maybe he'll forget having been a prophet of hate then and become an all-round nicer bloke?" David suggested. "That would be at least one good outcome of this whole affair."

Stuart inclined his head in a maybe yes, maybe no gesture.

"It's incredible that Kovač was prepared to leave the country and just let him starve to death there in the flat," Gillian said with feeling. "There was absolutely no reason for that. They could at least have taken him in the van and dumped him somewhere on the way where he'd be found and get some treatment."

"Well anyway," Stuart continued, "once Kovač got his hands on the Prophet he had a ready-made vehicle for stirring up any amount of hate and grievance in the Muslim community and, by consequence of that, in the non-Muslim West. The plan to blow up the cathedral in the Mezquita would have been equally welcomed and abhorred by both sides. Rasheed and Karim were simply pawns in the process. Karim came to his senses just in time; however, Rasheed seems to have been immune to reason. The word from Spain is that he refuses to accept that the Prophet is simply a cover for criminality."

"So a *false* prophet in fact," David put in.

"Fair comment," Stuart agreed. "The beating of Enver Durak,

which first got you involved, and the firebombing of the shop served two purposes: to underline the Prophet's radical credentials and to bind Rasheed closer in. He was now implicated in two hate crimes simply by virtue of giving the word 'go' over the phone. Whether or not that would make him guilty of a crime he didn't ever know the nature of remains to be seen; however, he thought it did, so from his point of view, he was now in it up to his neck with no easy way out."

"Poor, foolish, boy," Gillian said. "I'm not excusing him really, but he just seems to lack the power to discriminate between the genuine and counterfeit."

"It's Ali and Ayeesha I feel sorry for," David remarked. "Rasheed did some things he didn't understand but he was also ready to do something he fully understood and was willing to kill to make a point. How is Ali by the way? He was in a pretty poor place the last time I saw him."

"Recovering, I think," Gillian replied. "Ayeesha keeps him busy and he and Enver are getting on like a house on fire. Sorry – that's maybe not a very good analogy. Samira tells me she's jealous of the amount of time they spend together!"

"So the plot to blow up anything in Spain – be it the Mezquita or Medina Azahara – is foiled," David concluded.

"Yes. Thanks to you," Stuart put in.

"Well – really thanks to Gillian and her safety drill for survival at sea."

"Got to keep the crew safe for more scrubbing of decks," she interrupted, giving him a poke.

"Anyway, nothing in Spain gets blown up, so what then?"

Stuart took a sip of coffee and began again.

"So then Kovač was looking around for a plan B. Remember the aim was simply to sow as much discord as possible, try to create uncertainty and civil unrest and a breakdown in law and order, then move in and take advantage – like what he saw in Northern Ireland with basic criminality once the Troubles were officially over. And he still had control of the Prophet's website, thanks to another, perhaps less than brilliant unwitting accomplice – Callum Henderson from Queen Margaret University's drama department. So, maybe inspired by the hostage beheadings broadcast online by IS, the idea must have occurred to kill two birds with the one stone."

"Almost literally," Gillian said quietly.

"So David was going to be shipped out to the Gulf, appear on the Prophet's website for a while, with who knows what final result?"

"I think I can guess," David remarked, shuffling a bit in the bed.

"Then we had two lucky breaks and one stroke of brilliance. Abdul Masood had already been tracked down thanks to the fact that we had the van's number the night of the firebombing."

"Was that the stroke of luck or the stroke of brilliance?" Gillian asked innocently.

Stuart tried unsuccessfully to look modest.

"Once a cop..." he admitted, "even off duty. Anyway, we wanted to talk to him about the Prophet but he managed to evade the uniforms we sent out. Then, when he failed to turn up at court, getting our hands on him became even more of a priority since he seemed to be our only link to the Prophet – because we now knew that the Prophet had ordered the firebombing. And your kidnapping had to be somehow connected with the Prophet too. So I took a couple of uniforms out to look for him; luckily a neighbour gave us another address and we got the right premises. Unfortunately the birds had flown by then but in an odd moment of lucidity the old guy mentioned the airport."

"So, despite all the confusion he must have been taking things in at some level," Gillian said.

"I suppose so," Stuart agreed.

"This is getting a bit complicated," Gillian added. "Do we need more caffeine?"

She went to the kitchen and David and Stuart sat in companionable silence for a few minutes: in Stuart's case trying to hold all the threads in his mind to tell the story as clearly as possible, and in David's case trying to make sense of it. He still found himself tiring quickly and it was a lot to take in. Gillian came back with a tray of coffees and plate of Tunnock's Caramel Wafers.

"I got them in honour of Spade," she confessed. "Not as many calories as you'd think!"

"So the other stroke of brilliance?" David asked, looking at Gillian out of the corner of his eye.

"We should let the lady explain," Stuart said with a grin.

Gillian took a sip of her coffee and peeled a Tunnock's Caramel Wafer.

"Aikido and Sherlock Holmes," she said simply.

"No, no, you don't get away with that," Stuart said firmly. "We want the working as well as the answer."

"Ok. So I was thinking how difficult it was to look for a single person in a city. Holmes's solution was to recruit those with their ear to the ground anyway – the Baker Street Irregulars. A hundred or so street kids who knew everything and saw everything. He used to send them out with the offer of a shilling for whoever got the information he needed. Then, in the middle of all of this, I had to miss my aikido class."

"Aikido?" Stuart asked, pretending total ignorance.

"A martial art that uses the opponent's size, weight, and movement against them. It's much more circular and flowing than karate. Have a look at Steven Seagal's early films – before he got ridiculous. So I just thought about who might have their ear to the ground in terms of what the Prophet was saying – his audience – and how we could maybe use his own people against him. Kovač hijacked the Prophet so I thought we might hijack him back. Callum Henderson was willing to do the broadcast and Spade was able to catch all the traffic that would normally go to the Prophet's website and redirect it to a dummy site he set up – don't ask me how."

"And Ajeet Singh was a fan – and worked at Edinburgh Airport," McIntosh put in, completing the circle. "He watched the broadcast and although he's Sikh, not Muslim, he couldn't resist the drama when he saw the man Gillian had featured on the site – Kovač. He phoned it in and that confirmed what the original Prophet had said about the airport."

"Ohhh, this is making my head hurt," David groaned.

"Still, you've got to admire the mastermind behind it all," Stuart said, pointedly looking at Gillian, who was concentrating on her biscuit but did seem quietly pleased with herself.

"I do, I do," David agreed very readily. "And at the airport?"

"Well, that's when things went a bit wrong," Stuart explained. He picked up a biscuit in compensation.

"Ajeet was doing his best to stall things. He'd been told that the Prophet was going to send some of his followers, though of course he didn't know who or when. Kovač smelled a rat, phoned Ajeet's last number, which of course was the call-in number, realized something was amiss, and took Ajeet hostage too. By then they were beyond concealment and just made for the plane. The final stroke of luck was that with the delay in boarding, we were able to get an officer in as a substitute for the pilot."

"And it was Tariq – the officer who'd been working the phones – who volunteered, I heard," Gillian added.

"He did indeed. Seemed to feel some personal interest and wanted to set things straight."

"So what happens now?" David asked.

"Lots of paperwork. Preparing the case for the fiscal and trying to link Kovač to his backers in the Gulf in the hope we can roll up the whole lot. I'm guessing the authorities in Qatar are no happier with the One World Foundation than we are."

David leaned back on his pillows.

"I've never been to Doha," he said.

"Let's keep it that way," Gillian replied.

Finally, they were alone again. David slept for a couple of hours while Gillian pottered about then cooked something simple. After all the talk she was enjoying the stillness. It was as if the complicated explanations were needed to still the waters, but now all was quiet and there was just a sense of peace and contentment over everything. She didn't put any music on for fear of waking David but just wandered around the flat humming Van Morrison's "Someone Like You". Around five o'clock she brought him through a cup of tea.

"How're you feeling, honey?" she asked as he slowly opened his eyes.

"Peaceful. And very impressed."

Instinctively she tried to play it down.

"You did as much in Spain. Funny how some little piece of information from the past just slots into place sometimes as if it were made to fit that hole."

"Maybe it was."

"Meaning…"

He was silent for a moment, thinking it through and still not fully awake.

"Well, in Spain," he said at length, "with our young folk, we used to tell them there's no point in asking God to help you in your exams if you haven't studied. But you *can* ask him to bring back to your mind the information you have when you need it. I don't know how many times some verse of Scripture has come to mind and just seems to fit the moment. Maybe we both got a bit of that."

"Are you suggesting then that we don't get all the credit?" she asked in mock seriousness.

"Exactly," he said. "We call it 'grace to help in time of need' and I think we have both been in times of need."

"Hmm. Interesting… and comforting in a way. That kind of suggests that, though things seemed utterly out of control from our point of view, there was some control at another level."

"That's the whole basis of what we believe, isn't it? If that's not true then it's not just Kovač who's a fraud."

They sat in companionable silence for some moments, David half up in bed leaning on his pillows and Gillian next to him, her legs stretched out in front of her. The sounds of normal life – buses, taxis, kids shouting in the street, vacuuming from the flat upstairs – were going on all around them. It was comforting in its normality.

"Did you hear the one about the Christian, the Muslim, and the Sikh who walked into a bar?" David asked abruptly.

"I think I was in it," Gillian laughed.

He stretched round and kissed her on the shoulder.

"I thought I'd really lost you this time," she said at length.

"I know," he replied, "but really not my fault for once."

"I told you I didn't trust that man further than I could throw him," she added with just a hint of reproach.

"But I don't think either of us thought it wasn't safe even to visit him. Anyway – thank you for your intervention in the case Inspector Hound."

She smiled.

"Just like always," she said. "You rescue me, I rescue you."

"The way it should be in every love story."

"I guess so. And I think we do qualify as a love story."

He turned his head in her direction. She leaned down and kissed him lightly then snuggled down beside him.

"You rescue me, I rescue you," he said dreamily.

"But please – not too many times more," she whispered in his ear before they both fell asleep.

Sound asleep, they didn't hear the letterbox softly open and close. A roughly printed leaflet fluttered to the floor. *Vote for me*, it said. *Stop the migrant flow. Let's make Britain Great again.*